HOST WRITER

Book 1: The Archivist

W. F. Kuehn

First Edition, April 2015

ISBN 978-0-9961652-0-4
eBook ISBN 978-0-9961652-1-1

www.wfkuehn.com

This book is dedicated to Mike:
Alongside you, creating an eternity of archives will seem but a
moment.

What is there more kindly than the feeling between host and guest?
-Aeschylus

Chapter 1
VESTIGES

Prestbury, England

John examined the grave markers that surrounded him, each capped silvery in the moon's light. He found a granite marker wide enough to conceal his broad shoulders. He knelt in the damp grass behind the stone and waited for his assignment. His assignment was Zoe Edevane, a free spirited Oxford student who studied English and completely lacked the survival skills needed for the world she was about to be thrust into.

He had not relished the purpose of tonight's mission. Zoe's mother, Kathryn, had trained him and taught him about their world. Unfortunately, Kathryn had died before telling her daughter anything about the responsibilities of their family. It was now up to him.

He glanced at a nearby grave marker, the one he knew she came to find—no sign of her yet. Zoe and her captivating sea-blue eyes, framed by dark hair. The tresses cascaded in soft waves down her back to her small waist. She usually dressed in a sweater or a pullover, wearing her trousers tucked into expensive leather boots or simple wellies. She stood tall and slender giving the impression of delicacy.

But the past month of monitoring her had dispelled that perception. A month had passed since Kathryn's death and his assignment had changed from observing the mother and daughter, to only watching Zoe. He had shadowed her around the globe while she did activities at every stop she travelled. He discovered her to be extremely athletic, not delicate in the least. It had been difficult to keep up with her and at the same time not be discovered by her. She had run along the Great Wall of China, hiked through the Himalayas, rock-climbed, and raced rally cars at astonishing speeds throughout Europe—mainly solitary activities that tested her skill and endurance to its limits and kept her mind off the death of her mother.

And, to top that, she didn't believe in the afterlife—imperative in the line of work he was to introduce her into. He didn't know why Kathryn had kept her in the dark. Because Zoe wasn't prepared, he ended up at the cemetery with a mission that would turn her life upside down.

The corners of his mouth turned up in a grin. She had found the grave. It was a start.

I'd been to cemeteries before, but never after midnight, never alone, and never to fulfill someone's dying wish. I'd seen both my parents buried. My dad died ten years ago when I was eleven, and last month my mum. But here I sat like a crazy person in the front seat of Mum's old Bentley, adjacent to a sinister looking graveyard near Prestbury. Why had I decided to do this? I felt a combination of stupidity and mortification that I had actually come here, and I considered forgetting about it and driving home. I could be home in less than fifteen minutes and be sipping tea in less than thirty.

I rolled down my window to receive some air and stared into the night at the rows of granite headstones that looked like uneven dominoes scattered in the grass. Rows of ivy-covered reminders of the endless numbers of people we'd never see again. The English countryside, green and beautiful—and laden with cemeteries and churchyards that filled me with dread. My family grave plot lay on a hill by my home, which I had visited twice—once for my father's burial and once for my mother's. I didn't see a reason to visit and despair over buried bodies. Photos of Mum and Dad were spread over walls and tables throughout my home—weren't those enough reminders that they were gone?

The light from the moon's orb peered through the trees to depict a leaf shadow dance on the front of my car. The sheer size of the forty-year-old car created a protective feeling; it enveloped me inside its black body that seemed to meld into the vacant car park. The smell of autumn's rotting leaves blew through the window and mixed with the faint scent of my mother's perfume that lingered in the orifices of the car.

The clock on the dashboard read half past one in the morning. My heart fluttered. I had thirty minutes to find the mysterious gravesite and needed to control my uneasiness and actually step out of the car. The longer I sat there the more my imagination ticked off scenes from recent horror movies I'd watched—scenes of masked villains holding butcher knives to the throats of lone females foolish enough to go to a cemetery in the dead of night.

I glanced at my manicured nails. They were chipped from yesterday's rock-climbing adventure and smeared with black dust that had rubbed off the charcoal piece I held in my hand. I placed the charcoal on the dash, wiped my hands on my black trousers, and glanced outside. The wind blew leaves off the trees and created a swirling leaf-twister that arose from the ground with a rustling noise, twirled along the pavement, and disappeared behind a pine tree where the blustery sound dissipated. I removed a band from off my wrist and used it to put my hair in a ponytail that hung in a wavy mass to my waist. In a tree next to me an owl hooted from a branch and caused me to jump. I grabbed the handle and rolled up my window the rest of the way. With my task filling my mind, it had not occurred to me that I'd become this jittery.

Mum's lovely and kind face appeared in my thoughts. Her white-toothed smile, her wavy, dark hair and long-lashed eyes—picturing her face calmed me, somewhat, because I still felt anger towards her. Ignoring my anger and determined to discover the purpose behind her bidding, I grabbed my denim bag. It had a long strap interwoven from patches and strips of material dyed the neon shades of a sunset. Inside I carried my life—and a letter I found in Mum's desk drawer during the last few minutes of her life. She had been very weak—too weak to talk.

I pulled a torch out of my bag. The weight of the metal shaft gave me assurance on my strange errand. With the torch lit, I grabbed her letter. Even during the weakness of her final day my mother hadn't rested until she pointed her trembling hand towards her desk drawer where I found an envelope. Written across the front of the envelope in her lovely script handwriting was "my sweet Zoe." I had cried when I saw it, as I thought she had written a personal note for me. I picked it up and turned back to her bedside to thank her, but her arm hung over the edge of her bed and the intensity in her eyes had disappeared. Instead they stared at nothing. I ran to her and touched her cheek. I climbed in bed beside her and wrapped my arms around her and cried, her warmth still radiating from her body, her precious letter crumpling in my hand. When I at last sat up, I tore open the envelope and cried more. Instead of reading an affectionate and memorable note of goodbye, I discovered it to be an absurd letter instructing me to make a grave rubbing. The letter was only a senseless dying wish, complete with the details of when and where along with the name on the gravestone, John Link. Enraged, and with my heart broken, I decided not to return to Oxford. I took a leave from university and moved back home. I kept myself busy with activities my mother disliked me doing, while I counted down the days to the next full moon.

I gazed out of the car's window. I didn't know what was more daft, her dying wish or my putting my life on hold in an attempt to fulfill it. I didn't even know this John Link and with him being dead I wouldn't know him now. I wondered at the need behind her wish. She had never mentioned him until I read his name written in the letter. Of course that could have been my fault, because for several years we had rarely spoken. I had seldom listened to her suggestions when she had been alive and it seemed a little late to be paying attention now. Besides, the entire letter appeared odd with its detail of not seeing John Link's grave until the next full moon. This John Link was a complete mystery to me, but he had meant something to my mother and it had become my goal to find out why.

With renewed determination to find out the reason John Link had been so important to her, I took one more look at the blowing shadows, stuck the letter back in my bag, and opened the door of the old car, which didn't squeak until I shut it. After glancing around to make sure the owl and the shadows hadn't noticed the sound, I made a mental note to speak with Benny about the car's maintenance.

I looped my bag over my head and under my arm before realizing the charcoal remained on the dash. I opened the door, grabbed the charcoal with a tissue, shoved it in my bag, and carefully shut the door—no squeaks. Relieved, I held my torch in front of me like a sword and took a step. As I stepped forwards a hedgehog scurried out from under the warmth of the car's engine and brushed my shoe with its tiny spines. I jumped as it snorted and ran away.

A bit rattled, I headed to the pebble path where a border of ancient, gnarled trees framed both sides. The trees were large with uneven burls on their trunks and branches that appeared to reach out to me. The orange and amber leaves glistened with moisture in the light of the moon and the cool breeze. My torch saturated the narrow pathway with light while I tried not to think about the years of dead residents lining the path, their markers revealing their short life spans.

Mum had instructions written down in her letter that said to park in the northernmost section of the cemetery. From there I was to count twenty trees along the right side of the path. In between the trees the headstones caught my light and cast shadows over the locations of bodies buried through the ages. I had to remind myself that there was nothing here to be afraid of. At tree number fourteen my reliable torch flickered and went dark. I froze in place and tapped the metal shaft with my palm—nothing. I listened to the silence and waited for my eyes to adjust to the moon's light before I rummaged in my bag to find my phone. But it sat back in the car all cozy on the passenger seat. An owl hooted, a breeze rustled the leaves, and then absolute stillness—as it should be for this place. I shrugged at the craziness of it all and took a deep breath.

When the silhouette of the tree trunks became visible again, I counted off six more burl crusted trees and turned right, which meant venturing off the path. Determined, I stepped onto the grass and into the zone of death to search for the row of headstones that would have fig leaves carved into the sides of the stone. The only thing written about the carved fig leaves was to find them and count. So far Mum's instructions had been clear, but finding the carvings would be difficult with only the moon as my light source.

I worried about the time. The letter had been very specific about getting the rubbing at two o'clock. I shook my head at myself. I considered myself mental following every step of her instructions right down to the preposterous time.

Another owl hooted, maybe it was the same owl following me. I turned towards the sound and noticed a fig leaf larger than my hand, carved at eye level into the side of the marble headstone next to me. Smart owl. I calculated the direction the headstone faced and counted along the line of sixteen headstones with the carved fig leaves. The sixteenth was short; I found it when my knee slammed into the stone. Hobbling around the grave in pain I debated whether or not to curse. Best not to defile the *hallowed* ground with my cursing. Better to grab the charcoal and paper from my bag, and get the rubbing.

The moon hid behind a cloud and without my torch I couldn't verify that the inscription read John Link. A glance at my illuminated watch said I had a couple of minutes. The cloud drifted by until the moon's light shone on the marker and lit up the inscription—John Link—with no dates or other clues to give more information. Other than his name the marble stone was smooth. I felt my anger rekindle.

Before leaving for the cemetery I had searched John Link on the Internet, both alive and dead. My search came up with a hedge fund manager in Iowa, a photographer in South Africa, an offer for a subscription to an ancestor-search site, and a billion-and-a-half other hits for John and Link. No luck there. No clues here. He had probably been Mum's lover and the reason she had often left me, with no explanation, in the middle of the night. Anger and curiosity had outweighed common sense and here I wandered, alone.

After removing the charcoal and a piece of parchment paper from my bag, and at precisely two in the morning, I crouched down and pressed the parchment against the cold stone bearing John Link's name. I looked skywards and said, "Here's for you, Mother."

I held the charcoal and made one stroke across the paper when a deep shout broke the calm night air. The suddenness of the sound caused my arm to jerk sideways. Losing my balance, I toppled and fell onto the dewy grass. The shout had been close, a man's voice with an accent—maybe Russian. Another cry pierced the air and I clamored behind John Link's small headstone and curled myself into as little a ball as possible to keep myself from being seen. Unable to see anyone around me I feared the whites of my eyes might spotlight my location. A fearful moan wavered in my throat and I covered my mouth to stop my trembling from turning verbal.

I ventured a peek between the headstones and saw the soft light of a lantern held by a man. The light illuminated an ivy-covered gazebo with a distance of fifteen to twenty meters away from me. At least two men stood next to the gazebo. Between the grave markers, I could barely see them walking about. I remained still, grateful my torch light had gone out and afraid of calling attention to myself if I moved.

A male voice with an English clip to his words yelled, "I've tried everything."

I didn't understand the response, but it came from a different person.

"It will not work," said a man, who sounded Russian or Northern European. His voice was gritty and harsh. "No," he said, followed by a slap to someone's face, and then two more strikes, along with weak pleas and whimpering that came from the person being struck.

If I moved away from my position by the marker I'd put myself in danger. I could sit there and listen to the horror by the gazebo, or if I stayed low and knelt down I might at least complete Mum's wish so I never had to come back again. This obsessive compulsion to get this rubbing just might get me killed. I peered between the lines of markers to where the men stood. Their backs were turned towards me and they looked extremely busy punching their victim. I took advantage of that and moved into a kneeling position, held up the charcoal and paper to the stone, and then caught sight of something that stopped me. Intense fear migrated through me. I shivered, not daring to move.

A light flickered next to John Link's grave—so fleeting I didn't know for sure what I saw. The light lifted from the ground and grew in intensity. It was not a torch. A torch doesn't wear shimmering garments. The translucent fabric swirled and brushed the tops of the grass. A jolt of panic froze me in place with charcoal and paper held in mid-air. My panic prevented me from looking up to see what or who the swirling material covered. In the moment I blinked—it vanished. My mouth formed into a scream. "Zoe. No." My scream caught in my chest as someone grabbed the shoulder strap of my purse, crossed it over my mouth to stifle my scream, and rolled me behind a tall grave marker. Before I could give a muffled yell, a masculine voice whispered in my ear, "Quiet, or it'll be the end of us both."

I wriggled to get free, trying to look beyond the blackness around me.

"Zoe, stop struggling. You know me, we've had several English Lit classes together."

I continued to try and remove my hands, which were caught by his.

"My name's John," he whispered. "I'm not going to hurt you."

My first thought: that's what all the criminals say. I kicked my feet, aiming for his shin. I kicked something that felt like muscle and bone, probably a knee.

"Ugh," he said.

I must have hurt him. Through clenched teeth, he whispered, "If the men by the pavilion hear us, they'll kill us both."

I held still.

He said, "Please…look at me. You'll recognize me."

My captor's face was inches from my own, too close to see his face clear enough to recognize him. Did he say he went to university with me? He had the same dark hair and lean muscular build of a student I had noticed in class last term. But I wasn't sure and had never heard his name. He could be here with those beating the man by the pavilion. There was a slight loosening of his hold on my hands. As soon as I noticed I pulled my right arm free, but he was too quick and gripped my arm.

"Do you want to die?"

I stopped squirming and shook my head, my mind in a turbulent whirlwind of trying to digest the events happening around me. The men by the pavilion, a being that wore shimmering fabric, and this guy—busy cemetery. John seemed to be the safest alternative if I indeed knew him.

A nice-looking bloke, who blended into the night with his black hair, black-leather jacket and navy denims, scooted in front of me. The fingers on his left hand gripped my purse strap that held me fast. I thought about trying to escape right then, but his smile grew visible in the waning moonlight and made me pause.

"Don't you recognize me?"

My purse strap still covered my mouth, catching my drool, but I nodded and voiced a soft moan. I recognized him from Oxford. He was the bonnie lad that a classmate had tried to find out about. She had tried to talk to him once. She said he had rounded the corner in front of her and disappeared. Now he appears out of nowhere? Mysterious.

Near the pavilion, a man continued to plead for his life.

John whispered in my ear, "When I uncover your mouth, stay quiet. If those blokes hear us we're dead."

I nodded. He was definitely the safest alternative to the men doing the torturing by the gazebo. John shook my purse strap—with a tug it unwound—releasing me as his hostage. Able to move again, I glanced around to see if any signs of that strange light remained. I saw nothing but granite markers and gnarled trees. Disappointed, I grabbed the saliva-soaked strap and put it over my shoulder. John set a finger to his mouth, signaling me to be quiet and tipped his head towards the car park.

Holding up the charcoal and parchment, with desperation I whispered, "I need to finish this rubbing. It's for my mum." He shook his head, took my arm and pulled me off the ground and towards the path. I saw he had a noticeable limp.

"But…" I pulled back from him. His hand gripped my arm tighter. Disheartened, I put the charcoal and paper back in my bag and sauntered along beside him, his hand still gripping my arm.

When we arrived at my car, he grabbed the keys from my hand and began to climb into the driver's seat. I grasped his arm in protest and asked, "What about your car?" At the same time several gunshots barked through the trees. I jumped in alarm. He raised his eyebrows at me. Sufficiently motivated, I put the thoughts of the apparition and the rubbing into the back of my mind, ran to the passenger-side door, and scrambled inside.

Without giving him any directions, he weaved the car through the narrow country lanes to Brightly Manor, the home I grew up in and now stayed. The car purred while we waited for the heavy iron gate to swing open and allow entrance to the property. I hadn't said a word since hearing the gunshots. My mouth was dry and my body trembled.

"How do you know where I live?" My voice sounded weak. I felt safe enough, with one scream the staff would come running. A cook, several housekeepers, a gardener, and their families all lived on site.

His eyes turned my way and in a reassuring voice he said, "We'll get inside and make you something to calm your nerves. I think you're in a bit of shock."

I nodded. The glowing fabric, the man being beaten, the gunshots and this guy coming out of nowhere—of course I was in shock. "What's your last name?"

"Link. John Link."

"The grave said John Link." Confused, I asked, "Can you show me your ID?"

He put the car in park and pulled a burgundy coloured passport out of his jacket pocket. "That's convenient," I said.

He smiled. "I figured you'd ask."

Sure enough, the British passport had his photo and name. "How can you also be a John Link?"

"A distant relative."

This sounded reasonable, but didn't explain everything. "But you knew him? You can tell me about him?" He remained quiet and studied my face. Irritated, I said, "It can't be a coincidence that your name is the same as the one on that grave."

He paused, and then said again, "Let's get you inside."

The shock and the frustration made me feel faint. What had my mum got me involved in? I didn't want to pass out next to this strange guy and decided to delay my questioning until we were safe inside my home.

He put the car back in gear, entered the gateway, and followed the stone driveway past the helipad, past the pond, circled around the pool house, and chose a covered parking spot closest to the back kitchen door. He pulled the car in and turned off the engine. Fifteen minutes later we sat in the lounge where I sipped a cup of tea, which tasted like John had added something extra. The liquid burned my throat, but calmed my shaking hands and legs.

I studied the guy pacing the room. He looked to be late twenties in age with an agile physique. His perceptive, green eyes were lined with dark lashes. He had a straight nose and an air of aristocracy. He picked up a photo of my parents—the last one taken before my father died. Expressions of sadness, pain, and anger crossed John's face while he held the photo. He placed the photo back on the table, almost reverently. The picture next to it held my mum and a group of friends she had known most of her life, which she affectionately referred to as the "Blue Bloods." But only one of them had attended her funeral—a beautiful and lanky, black woman whom I called Aunt Phoebe.

John pointed to the photo, "Did any of them come to your mother's funeral?"

I stared at him in surprise. "Just Aunt Phoebe."

His head turned, rather quick, to look at me. I too had been amazed by the lack of respect Mum's friends had shown by their no-show.

I watched him. His speech and mannerisms implied he came from money. I tried to make sense of Mum's dying wish in relation to his presence at the graveyard, but my mind was too foggy to connect anything. "How do you know my mum?"

John walked to the sofa and sat next to me. His chest rose, taking a deep breath. "She left me with a heavy charge, a family obligation customary for parents to reveal." His eyebrows creased together and he wrung his hands.

"What…?" I asked. "Financial obligations? They would be better discussed with my brother—maybe at a more reasonable hour."

"Finances? No, this isn't about finances." He paused before he continued. "And your brother, Shaw, this can't ever be discussed with him.”

“Shaw? Why?” I grew agitated.

“He can’t know.”

“Maybe he already knows.”

“I looked into that already and he can never know.” Annoyance marred his face.

I stood up and glared down at him. “No knowledge of what? You need to speak less cryptic, because without knowing what this is about I won’t agree to not tell my brother. He’s all the family I have left.”

He stood up. The frustration left his face and he smiled. “Before I’m able to speak less cryptic to you, you need to give me your word, make a covenant with me. I need to know you’ll never tell anyone, including Shaw, the information I tell you.” His eyes pleaded with mine.

“Covenant?” I asked, thinking, what was this, 1000 BC? “Other than a bloke who saved my life and was in my English class, I don’t know who you are or why you were at the cemetery, and what you have to do with my mother.”

John took my cup and put it down on the side table. He then took both my hands in his. His hands were calloused and icy cold. His smile vanished and the seriousness in his eyes connected with mine like a steel hook. “All you need to know is that I was a friend of your mum’s and sent by her to keep you safe, and for Shaw’s safety and your own, you must promise you’ll never tell him, or anyone else, anything I’m about to tell you.”

The night had been long. From a man getting shot, to the mysterious and shimmering fabric, to this dark-haired stranger telling me to trust him about an ominous secret I couldn’t tell anyone, including my brother, all culminating with the inability to fulfill Mum’s wish—I had had enough. I pulled my hands away and stepped back.

"No. If it's not safe for Shaw to know, it's not safe for me to know. All I wanted was to find out about the man in that grave and why Mum's last message to me involved getting that rubbing. But if my dead parents were involved in something crazy like a cult, I don't want to know about it." I pointed to the door. "You had better leave."

He opened his mouth to say something, but instead he looked at the floor. I almost felt bad for him.

"John, thanks for saving me from a mugging at the graveyard, but you need to leave." I turned around and picked up my mobile phone from the table. "I'm going to ring the police and report the shooting."

"Don't do that," he said, rather loudly.

"Why not?" Surprised by his reaction I held my phone ready to dial.

"No one need know you were there. It's dangerous."

"But I'm a witness."

He breathed in deeply. "I'll handle it. No one should ever know you were there tonight. No one."

Maybe it was his green eyes and handsome face that caused me to not question his behavior. Or maybe I was too tired to think clearly, but I found myself agreeing with him. "Fine," I said, "I won't say anything." Though I'd probably regret it tomorrow.

He smiled again, softening the intensity in his eyes. He walked towards the door and grabbed his black leather jacket on the way. At the door he stopped to slip his arms into the jacket. "Will you be back at university this term?" he asked.

"No," I said. "I withdrew and took a leave. I need to stay here until Shaw comes to help with the estate and that could be weeks away." As an afterthought, I added, "But I won't say anything to him."

He nodded, "I'll give you some time to think about the fact that your mum *wanted* me to talk to you."

"I'll think about it and maybe I'll be back at that grave next month. But don't get your hopes up."

"My hopes are already up. Cheerio." He smiled and walked outside.

I closed the door behind him and leaned against it for a second before I threw the door back open and stepped outside. How was he going to get wherever he needed to go? The Bentley remained where he parked it. I glanced around the moonlit courtyard—empty. I listened to the silence of the night and realized I had no way of contacting this mysterious John Link with his cold hands and sudden appearances and disappearances.

I pulled the door shut and noticed a smudge of charcoal residue on the back of my hand. My finger wiped at the blackness as I thought about John's appearance after the rubbing and after the bright light. Had he appeared because of the rubbing? Was he a spirit? A dismissive, high-pitched laugh sprang from my throat. What about the shimmering fabric that floated above the ground? The laugh stopped and I shook my head to try and clear my thoughts—I didn't believe in that rubbish. I believed death was final, the end, bon voyage, the time your body was waylaid by earth, buried as a reminder for the living to live more meaningful lives. I pictured the windy hilltop near my home with a granite marker that announced my parents were gone forever and I was alone. Moisture bubbled in my eyes and rolled down my cheeks. I did have Shaw, my elder brother by a decade, who lived in South Africa and rarely came home, even for a holiday. So, basically, I was alone—alone with my internal ghosts. I wiped the tears from my face. My body needed sleep. It had just gone half past four in the morning and my thoughts sounded a bit hysterical as they bounced around inside my skull. I turned around and wandered to my room. I determined that if John wasn't a "spirit" he'd have a long walk to his destination.

Chapter 2
BRIGHTLY MANOR

When Kathryn had become too sick to continue training John, and with only one week left to complete his mission, Zoe had arrived home. She had been everywhere he needed to be, hovering alongside her mother's deathbed, pacing through the halls, wandering about on the grounds. Why she didn't take a drive in one of their fancy Bentleys and get off the property long enough for him to complete his task had perturbed him. Zoe was the one person who could destroy their years of work.

Because of his stint at Oxford to keep an eye on her, John's assignment would have come to a halt with a simple eye-to-eye glance between them at her home. Seeing him in class and then at home she would have recognized him and thought he was some sort of stalker. Her arrival had certainly complicated his mission. By the time Zoe had arrived, her mother was no longer in any condition to talk to her.

With her mother dead and buried and Zoe not returning to university, it had rendered him unable to investigate and search their property freely. Zoe had created an impossible situation for him to find what he needed in order to complete his assignment. When his superiors had reevaluated his mission they decided for him not only to observe Zoe, but also to get to know her enough to regain full access to Brightly Manor. He had chosen the time to introduce her to the basics behind her legacy when she went to find John Link's grave. He thought he had chosen the most suitable place to teach her. That had been a bit dodgy; they could have both been killed. To further complicate matters his gut told him she thought *he* was a spirit. Blimey. He didn't know if that idea would further delay his mission or do the opposite. Either way, he had one month left to convince her.

The morning after rescuing her he woke up late. He felt like a certified stalker sleeping in the woods outside her home, but it was necessary to keep her safe. He had slept in a comfortable grassy spot he found situated next to a gurgling spring. The spring ran through the wilderness area outside the perimeter of the tended gardens near her house. Angry with himself for waking up late, he brushed the leaves out of his hair and rushed to get into position on the grounds closer to her home, hoping she hadn't left the property yet.

The country house was positioned near the center of the family land that spread over sloping knolls, golden wheat fields, and tree-covered wilderness that still included more than 500 hectares. The Edevane family and their descendants had lived here since 1175. The residence had started as a gatehouse and a hall built from wood, with a keep to observe the surrounding lands. After a fire destroyed the hall, they rebuilt using only stone from the surrounding countryside and added ramparts and battlements to create a formidable fortress with a keep tall enough to watch over the vast distances. The original crenels and merlons of the battlements still adorned the roofline across the manor and the cloistered section in front of the main doorway.

Their wealth grew, and so did the house to include additional cloisters and floor to ceiling paned windows with views of the ponds and manicured shrubs and gardens. In the gardens assorted plants and flowers grew. They included red and yellow roses, yellow honeysuckle and bright dahlias, fresh herbs and vibrant green and blue evergreens. In the last 250 years they added a three-tiered decorative fountain on each corner of the court at the rear of the manor with statues of knights and horses along the walkways. The walkways were extended across the acreage and led to various bridges that crossed the river and its tributary springs that meandered through the property. Sheep had grazed on the hills for centuries. In recent decades they turned the stables into a garage and filled it with various aged Bentleys, a silver 1964 Aston Martin, and a green 1951 Rolls Royce, all kept in original condition. In case driving wasn't an option a helipad was situated in an open field adjacent to the house.

John crested a hill where he had a panoramic view of Brightly Manor, the battlements still and peaceful in the crisp morning air. He gazed over the courtyards and gardens. He paused when he spotted a figure dressed warmly in a cream-coloured wool coat and wellies. Even from that distance he knew the figure was Zoe. The woolly scarf she wore around her neck and hair couldn't contain the tresses that blew around her shoulders and above her waist in the slight breeze. He hid himself behind a gnarled tree and watched. She skirted the area by the back fountains and took the flagstone trail along the trimmed hedges. The hedges continued without a break on either side of the trail. His line of sight showed her silhouette walking between the centuries old yew and oak trees that grew along the trail near the hedge. The trail angled alongside the river. When she reached a crossroad she turned right, passing between two statues of knights that beckoned her through a trellis covered with wisteria, and over a stone bridge. She then headed up the hill neighboring the one he stood on. He realized she was walking towards the family grave plot.

The moment he realized her destination he began to run through the trees and down the backside of the hill, slipping and sliding in his rush to get closer to the graveyard and find a place to hide before she arrived. He wondered if the things they discussed the previous night were on her mind. If so, he may have found the right time and place to tell Zoe about her family and about herself, and convince her that her parents had not been involved in a cult. He knelt behind an evergreen tree with branches so heavily laden they brushed the tops of the thyme growing in the soil below. After being disturbed, the scent of the thyme wafted through the air around him. He had come prepared to spend time outdoors and wore a coat over his pullover for added warmth, but his non-waterproof trousers soaked up the dew.

Zoe's determined steps followed the path next to the fieldstone fence that outlined the family gravesite. She paused near the entrance and observed the surrounding markers draped in ivy and green moss, along with the older limestone markers pocked with age. Those shorter than knee high were fragile with barely legible inscriptions. A crypt was positioned on each corner of the cemetery and a Celtic cross reached into the sky. The Celtic cross marked the center of the plot with several of the first knights in the family buried in crypts nearby. A newer section had a rectangular, white granite tomb, the sides and top stained a deep green where the moss had recently been removed. The names engraved were James Charles Edevane and Kathryn Tate Edevane. When her eyes found this, she stared for a moment, shook her head, and almost falling she sat on the frost-covered fence with her back to the cemetery.

Her face pointed away from him and she barely moved or took a breath. Another minute passed and her shoulders shuddered. Her hands flew up to cover her face as her shoulders continued to shake. The sound of a low sob pierced his ears and heart with guilt. Her delicate fingers wiped at her eyes and across her trousers, doing this several times between deep, rasping breaths. Sensing her anguish, he took a slow and quiet breath, but remained still, his jaw set and his eyes half closed, allowing her this private moment. This would not be the time to divulge the family secrets. Surprised by the depth of his own feelings, he wiped at his eyes and tried to gain control over his emotions and the weight he carried of her heartbreak and loss.

Chapter 3
FAMILY OBLIGATIONS

John peered through the bushes as the old Bentley entered the graveyard a second time, the same graveyard where they had met a month earlier. "Persistent little devil," he said aloud, but he appreciated her persistence, it made the accomplishment of his mission easier. At least during the past month she had remained near home and her choice of activities seemed to indicate her preparation for a return visit. He stepped into the shadows and towards John Link's grave and hoped that for this second visit she had brought an open mind. He no longer had the luxury of presenting things to her in a delicate way. The allotted time his superiors had given him to convince her had passed. Tonight he would turn her life upside down.

A month had passed and with it came a more prepared me as I again drove the Bentley into the cemetery car park. There were no other cars, which didn't necessarily mean John from Oxford hadn't shown up. But I felt a little let down anyway. To feel safer, during the last month I had learned to shoot a revolver. I had discovered the revolver in the car and decided it had to be Mum's. I had seen my dad kill a fox with a shotgun when it had attacked our sheep, but I had never seen a pistol or revolver at our home. After my initial shock I decided it might come in handy. To make it official I joined a target-shooting club and obtained a firearm certificate. Since I had the shooting rights over my land no one questioned me. I carried the loaded revolver tucked at my waist and hidden under my coat. If my friends saw me they would think of me as a Brit-gone-crazy-American from the Wild West. Of course, I held no thoughts of using the thing. But it helped me make a confident trek along the moonlit path of the cemetery. With my charcoal and paper tucked into my jacket pocket, I again counted the trees along the path and then the fig leaves carved on the grave monuments.

I knew the gunshots John and I had heard at the cemetery had killed a man. I had read about it in the paper. A small caption headed a story about the body of a gunshot victim located in the cemetery, but they had no leads. Chances were nil that men with guns waited in the cemetery again, but I took the revolver just in case.

No owls hooted on my second walk to John Link's grave. The silence was more eerie than their hoot calls. As I approached the grave, my skin prickled and my heart raced. In my head I heard the distant gunshots and my last trip to this graveyard played through my mind. My replay stopped at the thought of John's handsome face as I wondered if his was the face of a ghost. I laughed and shook my head before the recollection played to the end: the man beaten, the gunshots, the mysterious dead man's body twisted on the grass. Nervous perspiration beaded on my forehead. I took a couple breaths to calm myself down and pushed the story aside like one of my own short stories that I could control. Determined to think rationally, even while doing something as irrational as returning to this grave, I stopped thinking and went to work. I had to stop thinking, because why I returned made no sense to me. Curiosity was not a good reason and I had this pull, this internally combusting desire that required me to return to this grave. I glanced again at the marker, knelt next to it, and unrolled my paper. I shook my head at the lack of reasoning for doing this and grabbed the charcoal from my pocket. I scooted closer to the marker and held up the paper.

"It won't work," said a voice behind me.

I spun so fast the charcoal flew out of my hand like a shot-putt. "What the…?"

As I spoke, John stepped out of the shadows and smiled. He held out his hand. He had caught my "shot-putt."

I didn't smile back. "What?" I stammered. A swarm of emotions went through me—anger, relief, and joy. I also experienced a bit of wonder as he had again appeared from nowhere—maybe he was a stalker. I doubted a ghost could have caught the charcoal. "What?" I stammered again, feeling and sounding foolish.

He stood there looking intolerably handsome and at ease. Again he blended into the night with sleek, black trousers and his leather jacket. This time he looked tan and his hair was longer and wavy. I didn't remember his hair being wavy. I had not stopped thinking of him since he had disappeared into the dark. My thoughts were a mixture of curiosity about what I hadn't allowed him to tell me, along with rage at being followed by him. After our last encounter I rang my former classmate to discuss the mysterious, dark-haired student—leaving out the parts that sounded crazy, which included most of our meeting, as well as my family possibly being members of a cult. She knew nothing about him.

"I told you I'd give you some time and figured that tonight you would return." He pointed to the full moon.

He must know about the timing specified in Mum's letter. I held my hand out for the charcoal.

"You're shaking," he said.

I put my hand in my pocket and felt the gun under my jacket. Oh yeah. I forgot I carried it. With my reaction time I'd be mugged or dead if anyone but John had surprised me. Mum's dying wish was taking its toll on me.

"Hand me my charcoal," I said, with as much irritation as possible in my surprised and shaking state.

"And a good evening to you too," he said.

"Cut the crap, John. Why are you here?"

"How charming of you," he said.

I held my hand out again for the charcoal.

"Did you ask yourself why it was so important to your mother for you to get this rubbing? Or why it's so important to you to follow her unbelievable wishes of coming here at two in the morning on the night of the full moon?"

I had thought about that, but didn't tell him. I probably showed up here at this hour because I felt guilt—guilt at not being a better and more loving daughter, one that my mother would have spent more time with—and it was none of his business anyway. "The charcoal," I said, my face feeling hot as I glowered at him.

He ignored me and went on, "It's instinctive for you. It's that simple—instinct."

As bizarre as it sounded it did feel a bit compulsory to do the rubbing. "Maybe. Or maybe it's simply Mum's dying wish."

This time he went silent. His head leaned towards me and I saw his attempt to not roll his eyes. The wording he used the last time we were together had been the term "family obligation." During the past month I'd searched my family home, tossing drawers, browsing through books and photos, but nothing had seemed out of the ordinary and nothing alluded to some strange family obligation. I had even tried to ring Shaw, but had no response.

"Okay John, you win. Explain to me my 'family's obligation.'" I put my fingers up symbolizing quotation marks around the words. I decided that by giving in maybe he'd leave me alone if I listened to his craziness. Afterwards, if he continued to stalk me I'd ring the Bobbies.

He smiled and led me to a granite bench, garnished with ivy. We sat down on its hard coldness. He turned to me.

"This won't be easy to believe," he said, enclosing my hands with his.

I recalled the coldness of his hands last time we met. "I'm known to be a skeptic."

"Maybe, but you're also known for your intriguing stories."

"What? Well now you're just flattering me." But I couldn't help feeling the sense of satisfaction that he had read some of my work.

"This will sound like a story, a fantasy. But it's real and I'll prove it to you."

His tone went serious and my attention focused on him. I nodded and touched his arm for him to go ahead, but also to make sure his arm was tangible and he wasn't a ghost.

"I am human." He smiled and my face grew hot with embarrassment. "I'm also a writer. I write biographies and histories. All my writings are complete truth."

I didn't recall having read anything written by John Link. I probably hadn't—I enjoyed stepping away from reality, fantasy, science fiction, anything magical captivated me.

"I interview the source and write word for word from what the 'Host' tells me." He emphasized the word host like he wanted me to question it.

"The host? You mean the person?" I dutifully asked.

"Not quite." He paused and then said, "Your father was a writer."

I laughed. I knew that wasn't true. "My father hated writing."

"Yes, but he wrote more than any biographer I've ever heard of, or known."

"That's not true. I would know if it were. There are no books in my home written by my father. And what does this have to do with the obligation of my family?"

A few seconds passed before he said, "Your father was a Writer and your mum the Host."

I opened my eyes wide, gave him an incredulous look, and in my most cheeky voice I said, "How mysterious—they kept a family journal."

"No, but similar. Your mum was a Host for others."

The chap was mad—he didn't even catch my cheekiness. I raised my eyebrows and waited.

"I told you I'd prove it to you."

"What? Prove that my father did something he hated with such contempt it actually ignited my desire to become an English Lit major in order to prove that I could do it? And, my mum acted as his host?" I shook my head at the ridiculousness of it all.

With a gentle grip he took my hands. "She was a Host, with a capital H," he said.

"And what is a *Host*?" I asked.

"A Host is what it sounds like, a person who volunteers their body to be inhabited by a spirit for a brief period while they're interviewed by a writer." He paused. "We acquire truthful and accurate history this way."

That was it. I pulled my hands away and stood up. "Nonsense. I recently read that book and one about the body snatchers." I held out my hand. "Now give me my charcoal." He seemed proud of his explanation, but the bloke was crackers—the most crazy, bonnie lad I'd ever seen—too bad. But it was time for me to finish Mum's dying wish and exit the loony bin.

"You think I'm daft," he said quietly.

"Of course I do." Without the charcoal I couldn't finish my task and I became irritated. With the present company hanging about in the cemetery I might have to wait several months before I could return to get the rubbing. I turned around to leave.

John said, "This is the reason it's crucial the parents explain this to their offspring."

I turned back around to face him. "Sorry, John, how very convenient to have both parents dead when trying to convince someone of this craziness. I'm leaving."

He stood up and studied my face. "Can't you see that your mum tried to tell you, but she was too sick, and your father never had a chance before he was killed?"

"Killed? Are you serious? The lengths you will go." I took a step away and he grabbed my hand. Surprised, my heart skipped a couple beats. I wondered if I should fear for my life. I also wondered if I was capable of shooting him to protect myself.

"Zoe, I'm serious."

I studied his face. I wasn't one of those people who could tell if someone was lying. I still had faith in people and generally regarded what they said as truth, but saying my father had been killed was preposterous.

"I thought you knew," he said, in a very quiet and gentle voice.

My head began to ache. A distant memory in my brain wanted to surface. I rethought what he said about Dad being murdered and I wobbled sideways. John steadied me and helped me sit back down on the bench. I shivered. Why would he lie to me? He could be a stalker, but something in what he said and the way he said it hit a chord within me.

"He was shot." He paused and shook his head before he softly continued, "Your mum, she was killed too—poisoned."

I began to shake, "No…." His arms went around me and I felt his strength, a non-crazy type of strength. A torrent of memories flowed—Dad's cautious behavior before he died, men with guns at his funeral, Mum's gun in the car, and some of her last words. Her weak and shaking voice made them almost unintelligible. As garbled as the words had been they now made sense. I thought I'd heard, "Dad. No car…Shaw…me…boy…son." I thought she was thinking about Dad and that Shaw didn't have a car, or she didn't want him to have a car. Neither made sense. But she had to have said, "Dad, no car, shot. Me, poison." And that made sense.

Tears slid down my cheeks and I sat there thinking for several minutes before, with a hardened desire to understand my family and what my mum meant with her dying wish, I decided to give John another go. I wiped the tears away and looked into John's eyes. I blinked and a remaining tear drifted down one cheek. He reached a finger up and wiped it away. His finger felt warm and gentle.

"Tell me everything, John. I can't say I'll believe it, but I'll at least listen.

Chapter 4
THE CAPTAIN

Things were progressing well. Zoe had calmed down and some trust in him had developed. All good if she made it through the next test. Most people did, but John had heard of a few who went completely mad and needed medication to function in society again. When Kathryn helped him his first time, he had almost gone unconscious. Zoe seemed to deal well enough with the discovery of the fate of her parents. He hoped she wouldn't be one of those few too weak of mind for the burden of what remained for him to show her. He had to continue with his submissive act too, so he wouldn't frighten her—an act that gave him an unpleasant feeling because it was so foreign to him.

I listened to John and forgot about the coldness of the bench while I attempted to understand what he told me—a story that, before he told me anything, I had to covenant with him and take an oath to not reveal to anyone, which already had me rolling my eyes. And, after hearing the story, I didn't believe any of it. Yet, he said he could prove it.

"So you're telling me that my father was a writer of biographies or some sort of an archivist, and my mum rubbed the graves, or began a rubbing, at which time she became the ghost host." At this point I started to giggle, but took a deep breath and rhythmically continued. "My father then interviewed, wrote down—verbatim, what the ghost through the host or Mum's body said." I couldn't help it, I laughed out loud and didn't stop. Poor John. He looked uncomfortable from his serious expression to the nervous wringing of his hands. He must have thought I'd believe him. "John, really, I never saw my father with a pen or pencil in hand. He had nothing to do with computers or typewriters. He liked to travel and oftentimes took us with him, but we never visited cemeteries or churchyards. Mum wouldn't even let me near gravesites—not even when Dad was buried. They never said anything about ghosts and spirits. Even when Dad read, other than the newspaper and the Bible, he read everything except non-fiction. I doubt my parents were even murdered. Kidnapped for ransom would have been more plausible, but murdered? There's no point in that—you're wrong."

John continued to wring his hands. He looked uncomfortable, but nothing compared to my own discomfort—I didn't know him. I had to be ready in case he didn't just sound mad, but really was crazy. I wasn't going to be taken in by this mysterious, bonnie bloke.

"You're asking me to believe that ghosts entered Mum's body so my dad could shoot the breeze with them. And, they archived and kept all these records in some kind of hidden shrine. Where are all the records that Dad supposedly wrote as the 'Archivist who wrote the most?' Now would be a good time for that proof, since I really want to go home." I didn't think I should trust anything he said.

I glanced at my watch. It had just gone half past two. John caught my glance and said, "The two o'clock thing is just a good time to catch the cemeteries and churchyards empty."

I smiled. "Of course. How about the full moon?"

"Provides light. We can do this almost any time."

"Almost?" I asked.

"Those details will come later. Come." He went to take my hand in his, but I pulled my hand back and reached down and grabbed the charcoal he had placed on the bench. I followed behind him as he walked back to John Link's grave.

"The charcoal won't work. You need this." He showed me a black-painted tin box he retrieved from his pocket.

Drugs? "No. I don't think I need anything like that." But that would explain plenty right now.

He looked confused, then shook his head and smiled. "Oh, this isn't what you think. Take a look."

He removed the lid. Inside was a small mound of something soft and pliable. It looked like biscuit dough. He gave some of it to me. The stuff felt pliable as a wet sponge, but sturdy as a rubber eraser. "We call it mana."

"Manna? Like what the Israelites ate?" I was the one laughing now, remembering the stories Dad used to tell me when I was young. I brought the spongy substance up to my nose; it had a smell like aged bread.

"No, it's spelled M-A-N-A. Our mana, or grave wax, has been around longer than theirs."

"Yeah, I'm sure it has." I gave him a cheeky scoff.

"Allow me to prove everything to you before you become a complete skeptic."

"By all means!"

"Place the parchment over John Link's name and roll the mana over the inscription."

I paused. If I touched the grave that could mean I'd become the Host—that is if I believed all this rubbish. I decided I'd have to decline being possessed by some ghost—just in case. I told him no.

"You're going to decline?" He didn't have to sound so incredulous.

"Yes. How about I be the biographer? After all, I write for a living," I said.

John's laugh rang out. "You have a trust fund for your living."

I couldn't deny that so I gave him my best smile and said, "Fine. I write for spending money."

I shoved the parchment and the sponge-like mana into his chest until he grabbed them. I patted his back and moved a couple steps back.

"Biographer Zoe, if I didn't know any better I'd think you were a believer," he said, imitating an American Southern accent.

"Just because I stepped away doesn't make me a believer." If he convinced me that life continued after death that would indeed be something.

He pressed the paper against the name John Link and held up the mana like he was toasting me. "Are you ready?"

He continued smiling, dimples showing in both cheeks. Hmm, maybe it didn't matter what he did as long as I could watch him smile; he was entertaining. I nodded, and in case John Link turned into his "relative" I moved one more step back. I never thought for a minute he'd really become his ancestor. I thought he'd put on a good show of pretending to be a ghost of John Link's past and then ask me to invest money in some crazy scheme. He used his dimples to get suckers like me to give him money. He was a smart crook. He'd spent plenty of time investigating my past from which he concocted a terrific story, even had me crying about my parents, which I had already attributed to a late night.

He parted some ivy growing over the inscribed name and knelt down. He held the parchment over the inscription and then made quite a display of rolling the mana around before he stood up. I thought, "Here it goes, he'll start yelling like a banshee and wave his arms in the air while I pretend to be hysterical before falling over in a laughing fit."

Instead nothing occurred—except a hooting owl, that I thought I recognized. John didn't do any of the yelling banshee stuff, nor did he spit or foam at the mouth. Considering the quietness of the night and the fact that he stood there in silence, I decided I should say something. I put my hands on my hips. "Next time we'll rub the grave at two o'clock."

I expected laughter, but John didn't move. Instead a deep voice laughed from behind me. I don't care what people say about the hair that prickles on the back of their necks, I didn't wait long enough for my hairs to prickle. I bounced forwards, leaping into John's arms, glad of his sure footing and quick reflexes. Only after his muscled arms surrounded me did I turn my head to see what or who owned the voice. At that point, with my one glance towards the sound of the voice, John became the tree and I became the feral cat clawing for the top branch.

A man with dark hair, like John's, but with streaks of grey, stood before us. His body and clothing had an aura lit by light and beauty. He smiled to reveal dimples and kindness; the dimples must be a family trademark. Although tall and well muscled, he stood shorter than John and spoke with a thick Irish accent. Amazed, I realized he had not possessed John's body.

As I dealt with the knowledge that I had to believe in the afterlife, John continued to support my shaking body while he chitchatted with the see-through man who wore dark baggy trousers, a black tricorn hat trimmed in gold, and a translucent white shirt with a matching bow at his collar. I also realized those were the same trousers I thought I'd seen floating above my head during my last visit here. I had considered plenty about that wispy fabric and decided it had been a torch, or the moonlight and a bit of fog. Indeed the afterlife existed—either that or I had gone crackers.

So many thoughts went through my mind. Most centered on my dead parents and how I never thought I'd see them again. I had become an orphan both in a physical and mental sense. Mum and Dad had ceased to exist—thoughts of them replaced by a black void. I stared at this spirit in front of me so full of light and life that warmth entered my soul, the warmth of an expanding ray of hope that replaced my dark abyss. John's hands loosened their grip on me as I calmed down enough for him to introduce us.

"Captain John Link, meet Zoe Beryl Edevane, daughter of Kathryn."

I whispered in John's ear, "Do I shake his hand?"

He gave me an odd look and said, "He's a spirit, what do you think?"

I didn't know John had a cheeky side. I said, "Nice to make your acquaintance, Captain Link." And then I curtsied to show my elegant side, but my knee buckled. John caught me and we were back to him suppressing laughter.

I ignored him and asked an obvious question. "You were a Captain?"

"I have been many things, but Captain suits me best."

Not the answer I had hoped for, but maybe the spirits were quiet about their pasts and saved their stories for the interviewer. I went on to another question, this one for John. "Why isn't Captain Link possessing your body?"

"Let's just say in times past people believed as soon as they saw the possessed Host, but in more recent times we had skeptics who thought the Host was faking—acting."

"Really?" I asked, raising my eyebrows with as much surprise as possible.

"Archivists came up with a way to show new Archivists proof," said Captain Link.

"Captain Link volunteered to be one of the Convincers who offer proof," John said.

"One?" I asked, wondering about the size of this dynasty.

"There are Convincers all over the world," said John.

Hands at my sides to try and look like I did this sort of thing everyday, I tried to comprehend what I saw and heard—the vastness and the numbers of people involved through the ages, including my parents. How had they kept this a secret for so long? But of course, there was that covenant I had taken.

"How long have you been an Archivist?" I asked John.

"When I began working with your mother," he said.

"Not very long to know so much," I said.

"No. But my nana has helped to fill in my family history and your mother trained me."

"If you weren't one until you began to work with my mum, why did you come to work with her?"

"A long story. But basically Nana sent me to be trained by her," he said. "And we discovered that it worked for me to write while Kathryn hosted, and Nana told me that it would work for me to write with you since you're her daughter."

Captain Link had watched us while we talked and added, "Yes, that's the way it has always been."

I asked, "You mean it wouldn't work if you wrote for any other Host?"

"No," said Captain Link. "It would be impossible for him to hear or understand the Host."

"We can try it tonight if you'd like?" John asked.

"No, I'm okay for now." I shivered. "I believe you."

Captain Link laughed. "It is fine, child."

John looked me over and said, "I'm really shocked at how well you're handling this. Are you sure your okay?"

I nodded. Although it was too soon for me to attempt the Hosting business, I was more curious than scared by the things they had said. "With this being my family obligation, why didn't my mother ever tell me?"

Captain Link answered me. "After your father was killed, she feared for your life, and because Shaw never became an Archivist, keeping your abilities hidden from him would have been more difficult."

John and I sat on the nearby bench under the spotted red and orange foliage with the moon casting a glow on the lazy fog that billowed around our legs. We listened to Captain Link convey the incredible tale of how the Hosts and Writers obtained and documented human history by interviewing the dead. Unbelievable maybe, but the one who schooled me had been dead for over two hundred years.

"Where are these biographies kept?" I asked, picturing mounds of books stacked on shelves and in vaults for selected individuals to pour through and file. I smiled and continued, "In the United States Library of Congress?"

Both of their faces became serious, their mouths set, their eyes focused on mine. I stopped smiling and wondered what I had said.

"No," said John. He retrieved my left hand in a grip, not painful, but intense. He then told me, "In the beginning the Archivists realized that all the records needed to be sealed up somewhere secret and safe. In addition, for the past fifteen hundred years no person in any political field has been a Host or a Writer. No exceptions."

Captain Link broke in. "It became apparent, years ago, that men could not remain unbiased when they had power, or were in positions of power, and had access to these records. They could not obtain the information we secretly collect without subjecting their own intentions for the use of the records and the Archivists."

"I can see that," I said. "But think about it. The information may also free people from injustices, be used to locate medicines, and instruct us so we don't make similar mistakes already made in history. Knowledge is power and a great gift."

"Yes. Exactly," John said. "And we have ways to funnel only needed information to the world, thus getting it into the right hands."

I decided to put that argument off until a time I wasn't so tired. "So where are the records kept?" I barely got the question out before Captain Link raised his hand into a stop position. He pointed behind us before he disappeared, leaving a swirling fog where he had stood. John took my hand and chose a grave maker large enough to duck behind and low enough that the fog hid us up to our chests.

I didn't hear or see anything unusual. John whispered in my ear to follow him. He kept my hand in his. Bent at the waist, we crept through the growing mist that moved in, making it difficult to see the way ahead. We tried to keep from stepping on a crispy, fallen leaf or tripping on a stone, grave, or other obstacle. We hadn't gone far when John bumped into a barbed wire fence—face first. He sprang back, grabbing his cheek. One glance around us, we realized we were trapped. The fence cornered us on two sides, voices were heard from behind, and thick woods intertwined with cords of ivy confining us from escaping on the fourth side. If we concealed ourselves quickly the wooded wall would hide us from whoever had joined us.

Because of the rustling leaves and snapping limbs, John elbowed his way through just the front layer of tree branches and tangled ivy. We ducked behind a tree with a big enough circumference to hide us both and remained still, afraid we may have already given ourselves away. By the time we moved into our concealed position, my coat and trousers had mopped the limbs and bushes until I was saturated and shivering with cold. John shivered beside me, his breath warming my ear and neck. We hunkered down with him behind me. He encircled his arms around me to use our combined body heat for warmth.

The voices continued to move closer and a slight exhale of breath escaped me when I saw several dark shadows slithering from gravestone to gravestone. Their dark, masculine outlines revealed weapons. At least four carried knives as an extension of their arms, three others held guns, ominous silhouettes against the light of the moon.

They stopped near us. The closest figure stopped about four or five meters away. A couple of them fanned out until each found a large enough grave marker to crouch behind. Once they were in a crouched position they disappeared in the swirling mist.

I didn't dare make a sound but my inner thoughts screamed, "Now what!" This was one active cemetery. How did any of those buried here get any rest?

One of the men spoke in a rough and gritty voice with a foreign accent. I recognized the gritty voice as the Northern European who killed that man the last time we were here. "Pierre, you have until daybreak. If no one shows…we assume you're crazy…and then I end your life…for wasting four months of mine." Even though I knew he had killed a man, the gritty roughness in his voice alone made me cower. Add to that he coughed or spit after every four to six words—not a very clandestine bad guy. Poor Pierre had spent four months with this man?

"No, Jaak." Jaak was pronounced like Yauk and sounded odd coming from the Frenchman. "I promise I am not wrong. I have seen these spirits. The people, they come on a full moon, and always these ghost spirits, they come too. My information, it is good."

Another spew of saliva hit the grass before the killer, Jaak, responded. "Unless your story is proven, your life ends at sunrise." A couple men snickered before all went quiet.

I felt very nauseous and faint. Unless John and I did something, Pierre would die at sunrise. We could save him—we could prove his story and he would live. I waited a few seconds for John to acknowledge this but he didn't. Why did John not say anything? I swallowed the bile at the back of my throat and felt my stomach lurch. To stop from heaving and giving away our location, I took a quiet and deep breath. I'd feel better if we found Captain Link and had him appear to these men, convince them to save Pierre's life. How could I live with myself if I didn't?

I turned my head until my lips were near John's ear. "We can get Captain Link and save his life."

His head turned slightly back and forth. "Not possible. They will kill us."

"I brought a gun and I know you have at least one."

He shook his head again.

I opened my mouth again and his hand covered it before I said anything. With his mouth almost in my ear he said, "They have over a dozen men. They have no intention of allowing anyone who enters this cemetery to live, including Pierre. I think you know that Jaak is the same man we saw before."

John grew quiet as some of the men moved about from grave marker to grave marker. A few of them spoke in low voices. I hadn't seen the number of men that John mentioned. "How did you count that many?"

"They're positioned around a broader perimeter. I saw at least one with night-vision goggles. Be quiet and don't move."

My jacket and pants had been wet before we huddled in the grass, now my hair and feet felt moist and cold. While the men with weapons continued to situate themselves, John and I made cautious movements until we sat as comfortable as possible behind the tree, with him leaning against the tree and me in front of him, my gun pressed against his leg. After a sigh, he removed it. He probably thought I might leap from my hiding spot and make an attempt to save Pierre; I had certainly thought about it.

Two hours passed by—owls hooted, moisture from fog soaked everything, John's arms kept me somewhat warm. I tried to keep my mind on anything besides the remaining time that Pierre had with the saliva-spewing man and his gang. I listened to what Jaak and Pierre discussed. It had to do with this hosting and writing stuff that John and the Captain told me about. My parents had been murdered because of it and possibly this second man here tonight. If he didn't survive that would be four people—four that I knew of. No wonder John had me covenant to not say anything to Shaw—or anyone— about these Archivists. This was a lethal business. Too lethal. Even after meeting Captain Link I would be daft to get involved. So I made a decision, and if Pierre died it would catapult that decision into action.

I must have dozed off because my eyes flew open when I heard John whisper in my ear, "They're leaving." My ear buzzed with warmth while my mind sorted out where I was and what had happened. The pieces of sky that peeked through the ivy canopy were the grey of early morning. John hadn't started to move yet and I remained still and listened. Near us the sound of heavy footsteps tromped through the grass, followed by three gunshots that pierced the air. John and I jumped at the first round and then the muscles in his arms went taut.

"Move out men," said the gritty voice.

No sound came from the Frenchman.

We remained like statues for five minutes and after we stood John did his best to remove any signs of our hiding overnight in the woods while I remained in a shocked haze. When we emerged from the woods it was easy for me to see whether or not the spitting man really shot Pierre. A black mound lay next to an RIP message. After John confirmed the Frenchman was dead, I felt myself slip into hysterics. I fell on the grass and sobbed. Several minutes must have passed. John tried to console me. My fists were muddy and sore with grass clutched in my fingers. I pounded on his chest and said, "I suppose you're going to tell me not to say anything about Pierre's death to the authorities?"

He nodded.

"Then you will never get me involved in this Archivist stuff. I want nothing, nothing at all to do with it!"

He stood up and held his hand out to help me. I ignored him and stood up by myself.

We walked through the cemetery alongside the fence to a road that ran next to the cemetery. I walked, staring at the fence-line, not wanting to talk. I didn't register the noise from the car motor that came from behind us. It pulled beside us and stopped. The boot opened and John pulled out a red wool blanket.

I gave John an incredulous look. "You had people nearby? We could have at least tried to save Pierre."

He ignored my comment and told me to get inside the back seat. Too tired and cold to say no, I slumped into the seat and allowed him to wrap me in the blanket's warmth. I didn't mention anything more about Pierre, nor did I ask about my car, which I had left in the car park. I got the feeling that John was well connected, but only when it suited him.

Chapter 5
THE ALTHING

John watched the house and the gardens from the vantage point near the stream where he had constructed a makeshift shelter from pine branches and leaves after her first scare at the cemetery. He had the cook and staff convinced he sneaked in and out of the estate to protect the bashful Zoe and her secret relationship with him. It had been an easy lie. They had seen him talk with Kathryn many times and then they saw him that first night with Zoe. And when a maid walked in on him, as he secretly shaved in the guest wing bathroom, he held his index finger up to his mouth in the quiet sign and the entire staff kept his secret. He continued to sleep outside and sneak in during the wee hours to shave and clean up. He saw from his vantage point that whenever the maids passed Zoe, or if she sat in a room where they worked, they giggled and whispered as they performed their duties.

He kept a vigilant watch on Zoe and snooped around the estate unquestioned—the perfect cover. With such a large estate, Zoe never saw him. He began to enjoy himself, which was good because even though he had convinced Zoe about their secret society, his task was not complete. He wasn't about to tell his superiors that she didn't want to fulfill her destiny and become an Archivist. He had lied to them, telling them a story about her not developing the gift yet. He hoped that time would soften the images of the horrific events she'd endured, and that he could convince her to trust him.

During the next three days I poured through the local gazette and listened to the telly, but nothing mentioned Pierre, the dead Frenchman in the cemetery. To my relief John didn't telephone me or stop by. Instead he surprised me with a visit the day my brother was due to arrive at Brightly Manor.

That day I raced around the manor to get the details done before Shaw returned, which basically consisted of nagging the cooks with food ideas and pointing at dust balls or lurking spider webs for the housekeepers. I had cornered one of the help under a blowing cobweb in the foyer when John walked into the house carrying a bouquet of daisies and roses. He arranged them in a vase on the foyer table. How did he know I loved daisies and roses? But I couldn't help myself and gave him a whispered snippet of the anger I held. "I know of a fresh gravesite where we can put those."

I had mixed feelings upon seeing him. During the past few days, I had thought through several scenarios that may have saved Pierre's life. John could have sent a message to his contacts, the same contacts that drove the car that showed up in a timely fashion when we left the cemetery. In my other scenarios both John and I ended up shot or knifed, but maybe we would have lived—and Pierre too.

"John, I thought I'd been clear about my decision."

He didn't say anything.

I watched him sort the arrangement and had to consciously keep my mouth from hanging open. I hadn't seen a man snip stem bottoms and pluck imperfect leaves before. The whites and yellows of the daisies alongside the maroon red roses were striking. It was the first time I had been speechless all morning and several of the staff greeted him with a pat on the back. They then smiled at me, knowingly, like they didn't want me in on their joke. I was really starting to become irritated at them.

John's wavy hair had been trimmed short enough that the wave had disappeared. When I walked up to admire his flower arrangement, random hairs stuck on the shoulders of his pale blue shirt. Several cut hairs had drifted to the foyer table where they scattered about the vase. A maid carrying a feather duster caught my glance to the table. On her way by she smiled and whisked the black hairs away before I said anything.

John finished with the flowers and surprised me with a kiss on my cheek, which made me wonder what he was up to. "When does your brother arrive?" John asked.

I could think of other topics I'd rather he talk about, but not with the staff around. Topics such as how we spent our most recent time together having a long talk with the spirit, Captain John Link, or our overnight camp in the woods by the cemetery and witnessing another murder. Obviously the staff had the wrong idea of how we spent our time. Snickers came from the nearby music room and caused a blush in my cheeks that gave validity to their snickers. "He should arrive by dinnertime."

"That gives us the day for a drive."

I began to protest as I looked down at the dust on my black trousers and my forest-green sweater. He put his arm around my waist, grabbed a jacket one of the staff held out to him, and escorted me out the door. Was that applause I heard echo through the doorway? Maybe I owed the staff a night out on me; I had been hard on them while I dealt with the mysteries of this new reality.

I stopped resisting John when I saw the waiting car—a car

worthy of a country drive, a two-door, four-seat convertible Bentley with over six hundred horsepower. The crystal blue paint accentuated the sleek lines. The open roof revealed the plush and inviting linen-coloured leather interior.

"Are we going to a cemetery?" I asked.

"No. Not even close."

For a moment I considered the promise I had made to myself. But—with the sunshine and the six hundred horsepower—I gave in.

"May I drive?" I pleaded.

"No. I know where we're going." John opened the passenger door.

Before I sat down on the leather seat, I made another attempt. "You can navigate. I'm an excellent rallycross driver," I said, giving him my biggest smile.

"No."

He pushed my shoulders down and I slumped into the leather. His lanky physique climbed in beside me. I continued to pout until he woke the six hundred horsepower engine up on a straight stretch of roadway heading North towards Cumbria.

"Where are we going?" I asked, leaning my head back to soak up the sun beaming on my face. The day was both warm and sunny, a rare day for northern Britain in late October.

"You wanted to see where the archives of books are kept. I'm taking you to one of the locations."

"Hmm, okay. But seeing one will not make me change my mind." What could it hurt to take a look at one of these giant archives? The idea of an archive captured my curiosity. I'd pictured so many configurations of how to house a human-race-sized library of books that I had built high hopes of how they accomplished such a feat.

"I haven't read any news stories about Pierre," I said.

"Who?"

"Pierre, the Frenchman at the cemetery," I said, irritated.

John's head turned towards me and then back at the stone-lined road. "It's been taken care of," he said, his voice flat.

"This job of ours must be extremely hazardous if you've seen so many murders that it's become blasé for you."

"What makes you think that?"

I rolled my eyes. "Don't be coy, John. You can tell me what's going on."

"I thought you didn't want anything to do with the Archivists."

"You're correct. I don't. But I would like to find out who killed my parents."

He let a few cottages roll by before he spoke. "It seems someone may have broken our covenant of secrecy and talked. We need to be more cautious. You need to be more cautious."

"Me? I haven't said a word."

"We know."

In surprise I turned towards John. "Who is this we?"

"Let's get to our destination first."

I opened my mouth to interject and he made a point of turning up the radio. He gave me a glance and tapped his hand on his leg as "Piano Man" rang out over the hills. His eyebrows raised, his mouth opened, and a lovely male vibrato joined Billy Joel's vocals. I looked at the time, nine o'clock, and the fact that today was Saturday. Instead of reading nine o'clock, the time was sung in unison by Billy and John. No kidding? Who was this John and how was it possible to have such impeccable timing?

Several songs later John steered the convertible down a narrow country lane, bordered by untrimmed hedges, mixed with grass and interlaced ivy. Trees of different ages peeked their oranges and reds above the hedges and created a sculptured skyline. At a pause in the hedge-line he turned right and parked the car a short distance from a helicopter pad. I didn't know anything about helicopters, but seeing it I realized our destination was not close. The rotors began to rotate. A man in a pale-blue jumpsuit and grey cap sat in the pilot's seat. He nodded our way before we bent down and ran beneath the rotors to step into the machine. We were the only passengers.

After skimming over the white-capped Irish Sea for forty minutes we landed on what I knew to be the Isle of Man. I had been there many times with my parents when I was young. I had hated those trips. My parents had left me for hours with this craggy old woman who only spoke Manx to me and pretended not to understand one word I said. She made me sit on a stool in a corner, except when she allowed me to eat. First she would have me watch her eat fish and capers, which she also fed to her obese calico Manx cat that purred in delight. After she and her calico feasted, she would hand me a couple dry crackers. When my parents arrived to pick me up, she spoke complete and perfect English saying how elated she was to have spent such a glorious time with me. She went on and on about the fun we supposedly had while I stood behind my parents and stuck my tongue out at her with my stomach rumbling from hunger. She'd smile and give me a hug as if she missed me already. After numerous times with the same routine I wised up. Once, when she wrapped her arms around me, I encircled my arms around her bulky neck and weaved my fingers around a tuft of her grey hair and yanked. I pulled out a sizeable chunk of coarse hair. She covered her yell with laughter, a loud and hideous, "Ow ha ha."

I carried that tuft with me until we flew over the ocean where I planned to release the grey wad out the helicopter window. My parents, who had no idea what my fist held, wouldn't let me slide the window open and allow in the freezing air. This sparked a new idea. A smile stayed on my lips the rest of the way home. I kept my fist in a tight ball to hide the hair. Once home I waltzed straight to the loo. I scattered the contents from my hand into the toilet. I then did a morbid thing, something I now had a difficult time admitting even to myself. I capsized the floating, grey spots of hair with a very personal tribute. My childish vendetta served me well. The next time I saw her she had a scarf tied around her head and she didn't hug me when we left. Best of all, she included a morsel of cheese with the crackers.

Within a year after I gathered that hair tuft, my parents began to leave me at home. I thought the craggy woman snitched on me, but now I wondered if it was because I had become a teenager and asked too many questions.

The Isle had not changed much since I had been there years before. I breathed in the sea air. The scenery of rolling green fields and semi-rocky coastline, the spatter of homes and businesses clumped together—this could be the same village my parents had brought me. I wondered if the craggy, grey-haired woman still lived here. She'd be a centurion by now.

"My parents used to bring me here."

"They would have been storing their records in the Althing," said John.

I hadn't heard that term before and John wouldn't give me any hints or clues. I began to picture the archives as a place of magic—an enchanted black hole where infinite volumes of human history were stored and where one could categorically retrieve or add to the endless capacity. Or maybe this Althing was an electronic library, an e-book with unlimited storage in its existential memory.

We walked along an overlook of jagged rocks that crisscrossed down to the channeling waves. I stood on one of the large, rough boulders and took in the view. Below me the agitating waves created churning foam. Seaweed patches dried on the lower rocks, positioned above the froth. Beyond the froth spread the Irish Sea—grey and cold, frightening and stunning—birthing poetry along its shores.

After a five-minute walk, we came to the edge of town, which consisted of a spot of stores along a narrow street. The land was dotted with quaint cottages, green grasses, and sheep. We entered a pub situated between a field and the end of a narrow street. John leaned down so his head didn't hit the ancient doorway. After entering, he pulled the door shut and latched it so no one else could enter. I assumed this was routine and looked around in the dismal light. Immediately the feeling of time etched into the walls and tables gave the appearance of secret meetings held behind the latched door. The entire structure stood firm and dark except for a bright photo, placed upon the bar, of a smiling young family.

The pub was a mural done in brown. Inside were chunky-square, dark chocolate tables with scratches etched into them and their matching benches. Dark russet walls and a wood floor, blackened by concourses of inhabitant's shoes, surrounded the tables. Even the lights were auburn brown from soot. The only other colours were the bright copper eyes of the brown Manx sauntering across the bar and the canary-yellow belt the bartender had on to hold up his tan pants, the belt clearly visible beneath his barrel chest and lean abs. His massive chest looked ready to burst the brown buttons off his milk-chocolate shirt. My first thought about the brown: maybe they couldn't import blue or red hues here.

John nodded to the fair-haired bartender and walked over to him. They clasped hands and gave each other a warm hug, patting the others back before releasing their hold. John turned to me and said, "Zoe Edevane, meet my old friend Owen Beasley." Since Owen wasn't old, I gathered that they had known each other since they were lads. As I walked forwards and could see the faces in the family photo better, I recognized Owen's face as the father.

My hand disappeared in Owen's grip. "Nice to see you again," he said. His accent sounded rich with the influence of Irish, Scot, and Manx. He knew me, but I couldn't place him.

With his eyebrows raised, John asked, "You know each other?"

"It seems she doesn't remember. You used to visit the Isle and stay at old lady Wheeple's charming abode. I met you when I made my milk deliveries. You were a young thing. You became famous for the bald spot that appeared on the back of her head."

I began to giggle. My memory returned of a fair-haired boy who sneaked small bottles of milk to me when the craggy lady turned her back to find her coin purse and pay him.

"Of course I remember you. And thanks for the milk."

Owen asked me, "Whatever did you do with that lock of hair?"

"You don't want to know."

Owen's laugh rang through the pub. "That's good 'nough for me." He let go of my hand. "Decent people, your parents." He wiped down two glass pints, filled them up with frothy golden-brown liquid, and handed one to John and one to me. He grabbed a third glass, filled it until the froth ran over the top, and then held it up. "Here's to those gone before they were ready." I nodded, the glasses clanked and I took a sip while they poured theirs into their open mouths.

After several gulps and a loud sigh, Owen asked, "You think she's ready to see below?"

John interrupted my response and said, "I don't know if she's ready, but she's certainly excited."

"Stop talking about me in third person."

They laughed.

"I am excited, I feel ready, and I have the right to see what it is we do."

John gave me a long stare. "She's correct about that."

"That, she is." Owen looked past us and out a window situated high enough on the wall that I couldn't see out of it. "My lads are coming. They'll be here in a few."

I picked up the photo and Owen said, "That's my wife, Melanie, and my three boys."

"They're lovely," I said. "How old are they?"

He pointed to the photo and the smaller and shorter duplicates of himself. Each boy had fair hair and blue eyes. "That's Charles. He's eight. Next to him is six-year-old Edwin, and sitting on Melanie's lap is Peter. He's five." The proud dad smiled big. "They are a handful with their scheming and conniving, but they are sweet to their mum. They're almost here and we don't want them to see what I'm about to reveal, so we best hurry."

He turned around and pushed a sequence of buttons on a wall-panel behind a shelf of glass liquor bottles. With the sequence entered, a pocked-metal, floor to ceiling mirror opened to reveal a set of carved-from-stone stairs. Each step was worn down about a shoe's width in the center.

I laughed. "No, I don't suppose you'd want them to see this."

"Give us two hours," John said.

"Carry on," said Owen, pointing down the steps. I hesitated and John took my hand. Behind us the wall shut. I followed him to the bottom of the stairs and my mouth gaped open in shock. Beneath the brown-mural pub was a cavernous room displaying an amazing array of books in both colour and size. Books stacked in red, purple and blue bound leathers, piles of aged papyrus, along with antiquated metal plates, all sorted on shelves of varying heights and depths. Ancient runestone markers, many emblazoned in the colours of a sunset, stood at the head of every section of shelving. Each runestone had intricately carved inscriptions, which I couldn't read. Recently, someone had translated the names of the countries and wrote them on metal tags that hung by elaborate chains around the tops of each stone. I followed John along the edge of the line of runestones and read the English nameplates hanging above the runic engravings. Some of the countries had several old names listed, such as Persia, Mesopotamia, Albion, and Nalbin. Each country had a different number of shelves, less shelves for less populated countries such as Iceland, and numerous rows for countries such as Germany, France and Spain.

John turned down one of the aisles to where a set of tunnels dispersed in all directions. Some of them had lights and reminded me of the Tube. "Did this start as a mine?" I asked.

John nodded. "More than a thousand years ago, until the Archivists made it a perfect place to store 'all things.'"

"The Althing library," I said.

"This is the Tynwald Hill Althing."

I thought archive or library sounded cleverer, but Althing seemed more universal.

"How many Althings are there?" I asked.

"Numerous, all over the world, some more ancient and older than Tynwald, others modern and electronic masterpieces. All contain the history of the world in the voice of those who lived it. These underground locations have been kept secret, most Archivists only know about their local facility," John explained.

"But some know about all?" I asked.

"The Keepers, or the heads of our Order, have the knowledge of all locations."

"Who are the Keepers?"

"Only a few know. It's safer that way."

"Do you know?"

"No."

The Althing had every scrap of space used for shelving. I turned to study a set of six shelves carved into the rock wall. Next to this carved rock shelf stood a shelf built of wood. The red runestone between them was labeled "Germany." Both shelves were roughly the same size, just over a meter wide and one shelf taller than John. Both the bottom shelves were spaced higher than the shelves above and held the larger leather-bound books.

I glanced at John for confirmation before I reached up to an eye-level shelf to grab one of the leather bound books. I removed a book with a cover wrapped in burgundy leather. The leather felt soft and smooth. After opening the pamphlet-sized book, I read the name "August Gottfried, son of Wilhelm Gottfried. Born first of May, Sixteen-hundred-ninety-eight, in Leipzig, Germany."

I looked from the book to John's face. "I've never heard of him."

"We don't just have the histories of famous people; most names of those whose histories we write you won't recognize."

"But that's billions of people," I said.

"Yes, but remember this: Individuals Who Have Ever Lived Matter." He paused and smiled before continuing, "Or the acronym IWHELM."

"IWHELM? You just made that up," I said.

He laughed and shrugged his shoulders. "It's better than overwhelm."

"Unless you have an app for recording people's lives that's just not possible. There have been billions and billions of people on the earth."

John took the book from my hands, closed the cover and placed it back on the shelf. "It's a full-time job."

"How many Hosts and Writers are there?" I asked.

"Maybe a couple hundred or so. Too few to not be

overwhelmed."

I took a deep breath, breathing in the warmth of the leather smells surrounding me. Shaking my head, I said, "IWHELM?" I laughed and followed him to the next corridor.

Chapter 6
THE BREAK-IN

Prestbury, England

Their adventure to the Isle had gone well. John had convinced his superiors of the necessity to bring her there. But on the way he had developed some concern. Two Ducati motorcycles had followed the convertible to the turn-off for the helicopter before continuing on their way. He didn't know if it was a coincidence, or if the cyclists had been assigned by his team to tail them. Then, while on the Isle, he saw another Ducati on the street down from the pub. Both times the riders were dressed in similar padded racing leathers. He figured they worked for the same people as himself. He couldn't be sure until he checked in. Glancing at his watch, he realized that wouldn't be for another ninety minutes. The not knowing made him restless and he couldn't shake his concern, but he couldn't call his superiors with Zoe listening. As soon as they got back to Zoe's home, he'd make the call. He just hoped it wouldn't be too late to warn Owen if he found out the riders weren't from his team.

John had been quiet on our return back to my home. After traipsing through endless corridors of shelves containing the records of human past, I had to admit my interest in him and the Archivists had grown. Although I didn't want to be a part of the Archivists, I did want to see what it was like to Host a spirit and to interview one. To become someone else intrigued me. To be the one questioned or be the one to interview, then to read their story and journey to the Althing to make the deposit for them—the deposit of their life—would be fascinating. I wanted to ask John about the rules for interviewing recently dead people, but didn't want to lead him to believe I was ready to become an Archivist. I was interested in speaking with my parents. I couldn't wait to talk to Mum and Dad. I wanted to discuss the life they kept hidden and ask them about their deaths. Maybe they knew who had murdered them. Writing my parent's histories would come later. The satisfaction that came from knowing I could see and talk to them was beyond my words to describe. I felt less alone, less abandoned, and full of renewed hope.

"We're here," John said, as my mind surfaced from my thoughts.

The convertible rolled up the drive to my home and I let out a yelp. A tall, broad shouldered figure stood with his hands in his trouser pockets and wandered about the front drive. His sandy hair was neatly trimmed. I leapt out of the still moving car, left the door open, and ran to hug my brother. "Shaw!"

His arms opened for an embrace. He released me and his blue eyes searched my face. "Zoe, you look so bonnie."

I laughed at him.

Shaw asked, "Who belongs to that Bentley?"

I turned around, keeping my arm hooked through Shaw's. John approached us in a stiff British manner. The British equivalent to the machismo bravado or the American testosterone swagger of male strangers meeting male strangers—uniformly universal, especially with a female present.

"John, meet my brother, Shaw."

I waited for the quintessential nod. Instead their hands clasped with bulging muscles filled with confrontation and challenge. More like arm-wrestling than strangers meeting.

"John," said Shaw, with no emotion.

"Shaw," returned John in the same manner, still clasping Shaw's hand.

I gave what I'm sure was a quizzical glance and asked, "Have you two met?"

A simultaneous "No" resounded. It felt awkward as they continued their grip. Then Shaw threw a smile at John and I relaxed. I'm sure only an infinite two seconds passed. Hoping to control the situation, I unhooked my arm looped through Shaw's and took John's left hand. He let go of Shaw and shot me a puzzled gaze. I gave John's hand a quick squeeze and let go. The situation controlled, I turned around and noticed two suitcases next to the door. Why hadn't Benny taken them upstairs?

"Did you just arrive?" I asked Shaw.

"A bit ago. I rang the bell, but no one came. The door's bolted."

Strange. I had at least three staff members assisting us with dinner. I turned the door handle and pulled. Locked. I received a raised-eyebrow look from Shaw.

"You don't believe me." Shaw laughed.

I rang the bell, pushing the silver button several times. The chimes empty response echoed inside.

"We left this morning thinking we'd be back by dinner and before you arrived," I said.

"Zoe?" I hadn't noticed John step around the bushes to the windows. He peered into a corner of one window. He drew a pistol, or maybe it was a revolver, that had been hidden under his sports jacket in a shoulder holster.

"What do you see?" I asked.

Shaw's eyebrows pinched together and he stepped between John and me. "What's the gun for, John?"

I thought it sweet that Shaw had this protective side, but I was more interested in what John saw inside. I took a step in his direction.

"Stay there," John said.

Shaw grabbed my arm and held me at his side. "How long have you known this bloke?"

Not wanting to answer that question, I said, "Shaw, he's fine."

Using the house as cover, John bent down, went to the next window, and looked inside. I ignored John's suggestion to stay and moved away from Shaw's hold on my arm. Shaw let go and I walked around the bushes to the first window that John had peered into. On my tiptoes I gazed inside. Chairs were tossed to the side and turned over, lamps broken, and couch cushions lay on the floor. Someone had destroyed all the preparations and cleaning the staff had done all week.

Shaw came next to me. In a voice loud enough for John to hear, he said, "Looks like we've been burgled. Why did he take you away for the day?"

"I'm sure he had nothing to do with this."

Around the corner from where we stood a motor started up and revved. In unison, John and Shaw began to run. They jumped a bush and then a row of hedges, racing across the fresh cut grass. I wasn't sure what they wanted more, to outrun each other or to catch the man dressed in black leather riding a Ducati over our lawn. The motorcycle rode across a cobble path, onto the roadway, and then disappeared around a bend down the lane. Fast and maneuverable, the bike was out of earshot in seconds.

Shaw and John returned, both red-faced and breathing hard.

"If he took anything, it was small," Shaw said.

The intruder had left the side kitchen entrance open and John stealthily entered. With his gun pointed straight ahead, he peeked around the doorway. He held a tense position for a second or two before his muscles relaxed and he waved for us to follow him. He appeared familiar with this type of situation, as if he'd dealt with this type before. The gun was an extension of his arm and his manner most solid and sure; something that warranted me asking him questions.

I followed behind Shaw and entered through the kitchen door. My jaw dropped open and I forgot about the questions I wanted to ask John. The window perspective had looked less destroyed than the up-close version, which was not limited to one room, but began in the kitchen. Tables and chairs had been pushed about. Our mince pie dinner lay uneatable across the floor. Our Windsor chairs lay on their sides. Pillows, papers and books had been thrown to the ground. Several glass vases were nothing but broken shards on the slate floor. Mirrors were pulled from the walls, but not broken— superstitious thief. Paintings had also been pulled from the walls. The intruder must have thought we had a safe—big disappointment for him. Family photos were also turned over on the shelves and tables.

I walked back into the kitchen, kicking chunks of veal and raisins strewn over the floor, when I heard some muffled cries coming from the pantry. Thinking the obvious, I stepped over the debris of paintings and glass to pull open the pantry door. Five pairs of eyes squinted and blinked at me. All five sat on the ground facing each other in a circle. Every mouth was covered with tape and all hands tied behind their backs, while the five pairs of legs were bent at the knees and bound together in the center of the group.

I yelled for Shaw and John to assist me. Shaw came in and helped untie old Benny who looked like a rabid dog. The tape was attached to his sagging cheeks, but not his upper or lower lips. No doubt he yelled a string of profanity until his mouth became uncovered. I didn't know what Benny's life was like before he worked for us, but he went from genteel and well-mannered to crack-pot psycho without notice. And the look on our cook's face as I released her and she launched herself away from him, seemed to indicate Benny's current mood. Benny had probably never seen the inside of this pantry. For reasons I had yet to discover, he wasn't allowed in Fiona's kitchen.

"There were two men," Benny said, between expletives.

Fiona's head of tight, grey curls leaned over her daughter, who had the tape tangled in strands of her shoulder length, black and purple hair. Between breaks at university she stayed here with her mum and cooked. She had arrived that morning.

John appeared in the doorway. "Did you say two men?"

"Yes," Benny said. "After they ransacked half the house, one received a telephone call and told the other to meet him at the rendezvous point. Then he rode off."

"I don't think this was a random theft," John said. He turned to Shaw. "Ring the authorities."

Shaw nodded.

Harold, our gardener, rubbed his thin wrists where Shaw had cut off the bands. His eyes reminded me of a pug dog; they bulged as he looked around. He stood up slow and easy, stretching his short, skinny arms and legs. He shuffled through the raisins mashed with veal and began to right the chairs into position so Fiona and her daughter had a place to sit. Once seated, Fiona continued to work on freeing her daughter's purple and black locks from the tape. Her pudgy fingers shook so bad the strands became more tangled.

I untied the last prisoner, our maid Charlotte—the youngest and smallest in the group. She shook her bleached blonde head of tiny curls and said something unclear in her Cockney accent, then threw her arms around me for a brief hug and walked off mumbling and crossing herself.

John grabbed me by the hand and took me aside. "Zoe, I need to leave for a few hours. Wait for the bobbies and stay home until I return." He paused before adding, "Be cautious what you say to them, and don't mention me or where we went today."

I didn't question him as I watched him leave. In the background I heard Shaw on the telephone describing the situation and explaining that we weren't in any current danger.

Chapter 7
THE GROTTO

With Shaw recognizing him, John couldn't be at the house when the police arrived. The surprised glance Shaw gave him when Zoe introduced them was a rare slipup—Shaw was one of the best. But his face recovered, making John wary. Although he had made preparations in case Shaw saw him, he never anticipated that the Manor would be burgled and coppers would arrive. He thought back through what he knew about Shaw. In former years, he'd worked with Shaw in South Africa and heard that Shaw had grown frustrated with his parents and their secretive lives and the way they kept their son in the dark. John had learned from his talks with Kathryn that since Shaw hadn't inherited the Archivist abilities and with his inquisitiveness, James and Kathryn chose not to include their daughter in anything referencing the Archivists. They kept her at a distance from a young age, right after she had an incident. Whatever this incident had been, Kathryn never told him. And because she hadn't told him, he had chosen to keep quiet about it as well. One of a few necessary things he kept from his superiors.

The leaders of John's organization were becoming restless. He thought that maybe they had put a rush on things and planned the break-in. He checked in with them and discovered the men on the motorcycles did not work for his team or anyone they knew. With the cyclists not being a part of the team, he worried about the Ducati outside Owen's bar. He immediately rang Owen to warn him. The phone buzzed in his ear until it went to voicemail. He wouldn't take any chances with his friend, Owen, in possible danger. He'd go with his gut instinct and get back to the Isle. He had his pilot meet him at their rendezvous point with the helicopter—his fastest way back to the Isle of Man.

The last detective, a very large man, drove away in his green Mini-Cooper. The car leaned to the right from the extra weight of its occupant. My head ached after my attempt at making careful responses to the pointed questions from the police. Although Shaw thought it was a random theft, from John's reaction I wasn't so sure. Of course Shaw had no idea about the Hosts, Writers, and our parents being murdered. I wanted to let my brother know about all of it, but one of my best attributes was keeping promises. I understood why John didn't want Shaw to know, and carried on with John's plan in order to keep Shaw safe.

I entered the library, but there was not a chair to sit on that didn't lie on its side or was layered with books pulled from the shelves or tossed aside family heirlooms. So I stood there in the middle of the room, feeling vacant and tired.

Benny carefully picked up an unbroken cup and saucer. He set them down on the oak library table that he had righted and positioned near the wall. He had arranged the table far enough from the wall to allow room for someone to stand and re-hang the painting of Dad and his pack of hunting dogs that normally hung above it.

After the bobbies had taken our statements we sent our terrified staff to their rooms to rest. Fiona and Lizzie had cleaned up and thrown away the spoiled and crushed mince pie before going to their rooms. Benny went to the dining room, picked up the chairs, organized a bit, and then began straightening the library.

I felt like I was on auto-pilot as I leaned over, closed the cover jacket of *Oliver Twist*, and stacked Plato's *Republic* on top and then *Absalom, Absalom!* I set the stack on one of the many empty, wooden shelves in the library. We could sort them later. I picked up another stack of five leather-bound books and placed them on a middle shelf. Methodically, I continued to pick the books up off the ground until I filled two shelves.

Shaw came to the doorway, stood in silence for a second before he bent down and picked up a book. He held it up to show me. "I think I'll start with this one."

I laughed and said, "*Crime and Punishment*, an appropriate title." I picked up a book and held it up for his review. "How about this one?"

"*Things Fall Apart*. Even better. You win." He loaded a stack in his arms. "I walked through several rooms of the house and haven't noticed anything missing." He continued to stack a shelf with books lying near the door entrance.

"Me neither." I picked up a heavy bookend shaped like a fleur-de-lis with a flat bottom. I slid the bookend across the wooden shelf and jammed the books into an upright position against the side. While leaning forwards, my toes balanced me by pressing down on the floor until I jammed the books to the right. The rocking motion caused my toes to lift up and touch the overhang of the bottom ledge. I felt a click.

I gasped when a crank lever sound resonated from behind the tall row of shelves. I jumped back to watch the middle stack of shelves, along with the wall behind it, rise like an elevator towards the heights of the ceiling. Shaw spun around almost dropping his armful of leather classics. Benny, reminding us he hadn't left the room, uttered a few choice expletives while he stared at the moving wall. When the stack levitated at about my height, the crank and shift noises stopped.

"Shaw?" I asked. "Did you know we had a secret room?"

I looked at my stunned brother and received my answer.

"Benny, grab some torches," Shaw said. He deposited his armful of books on the table and almost jogged across the room.

We both stared into the curious abyss. At least four rock stairs curved downwards below us and seemed to disappear into the earth beneath our home. Beyond what the ceiling lights from the library could penetrate was a void of deep blackness. I breathed in the smell of damp soil and rock permeating from below. Neither of us took a step down. I, for one, wasn't going to walk into the earth without a reliable light source. It seemed Shaw had the same notion.

"Do you think they were looking for this?" I asked Shaw.

"The thieves?"

"Of course, the thieves." I rolled my eyes.

"We didn't even know it existed. From the smell, this doorway hasn't been opened in decades." Shaw's nose wrinkled.

Benny crossed the room carrying three torches. He gave us both one and kept one for himself.

"I'll go first," said Shaw. He turned on his light and took a step forwards.

"Zoe?" said a voice behind us. We all jumped—I almost dropped my torch. John's dark figure crossed the room, his face a mixture of emotions.

"What's this? A grotto?" John asked, peering into the darkness.

"Family business," said Shaw, his lips set in a grimace.

I hit my brother in the arm with my fist. Shaw nodded his head towards the opening and said, "Come along then."

"A torch?" John asked, looking around.

Shaw smiled. "Take Benny's."

Benny's eyes narrowed. His hairy knuckles on the hand that gripped his torch whitened. Since I didn't feel like listening to more of Benny's verbal assaults, I slapped my torch into John's palm and took his muscled arm before Benny offered me his. Benny's arms resembled grey shaggy rugs.

We clicked down the stone steps. Shaw, the first to enter, rounded the corner and the area instantly lit up with a fluorescent light hanging from the ceiling. When the light beamed on us, the opening, with its cranks and rotations, closed and shut us inside.

I stood gobsmacked, leaning onto John's arm. No one said anything—no one except Benny exclaiming his verbal assaults—everyone stood still, shocked. I'm sure their thoughts were the same as mine, how would we get out of this grotto?

John interrupted my silent thoughts and Benny's expletives. "The light triggered the door to shut."

"Motion sensors," said Shaw, in agreement with John.

John's use of the word "grotto" described the room well. It was cave-like. The room spread out long and narrow with uneven walls carved out of the rock. A stone fireplace was built into one end. The fireplace mantle spanned the width of the room. Featured above the mantle were framed portraits of our relatives, including my parents—front and center. In each photograph, or painting, they wore armour. Each family member held a helmet tucked under an arm and a jewel-crested sword hung at his or her side.

The armour of breastplates, shields, and helmets was displayed across one wall of the room. The wall opposite depicted a museum's worth of medieval weapons. Nearest the fireplace hung the halberds, axes and pole axes, swords and longbows. From there, a time-line of killing gadgets progressed across the wall of weapons until knives of various lengths, and rifles to automatic machine guns, hung closest to us. I pictured my parents at the round table enjoying a pint with Arthur.

Last year I had written an article about medieval weaponry. That would have been a perfect time for Mum to give me some of her knowledge. She hadn't shown the slightest hint of our family's tenacity for war. Amazing how my parents had kept so many sides of them a secret.

"This was unexpected," Shaw said. He set his torch on the mahogany table that extended down the center of the room.

John squeezed my arm, no doubt to indicate caution with what I said. The two of us knew more about the reasons behind the contents of the room than what we could explain to Shaw. I regretted Benny gaining knowledge of this room. We walked around, each of us peering closely at different objects that interested us.

Shaw said, "I don't remember Mum or Dad ever mentioning anything about being a knight or lady." Shaw pointed to the caption written under their portrait: Sir James Edevane and Lady Kathryn Edevane.

"Not even a hint," I said, maybe a bit too cheeky from the raised eyebrows John gave me.

I walked to the center of the table to admire a small stack of papers with three rolled up parchments on top. I unrolled the longest one to discover a topographical map of Denmark, Norway, and Sweden with Jamtland circled in red. The next map was of Britain and the Isle of Man. Several areas were also circled including Dingwall, Scotland and on the Isle of Man both Castletown and an area with Tynwald Hill written next to the circle.

The smallest rolled map was of Iceland. Nothing was circled in red, but written in pencil was Pingvellir's Lawrock. I recognized the significance of these marked maps, especially since John had just taken me to one of these locations. If the ransacking of our home had something to do with the Archivists, these maps could have been on the list of what the muggers had searched for—these maps displayed the underground facilities that housed some of the Althings.

I casually rolled up each map and tucked them under my arm, along with the papers I found under them, but Shaw noticed what I was doing.

Shaw asked, "What are those?" as he hung up a sword with a square emerald in its hilt.

"Old crusader maps," I lied. "Can I keep them? They'll help me with an article I'm writing."

Shaw shrugged and picked up another sword with a ruby surrounded by emeralds. He wasn't interested in anything other than the museum pieces that hung on the wall and hadn't noticed my deceit. Relieved, I held on to the maps, which I might later show to John.

John, the only guy in the room not consumed with the weapons, stood next to a bookshelf with several books in his hands. He walked to the table and set them down. He pulled out one of the mahogany chairs, noticed me coming over and pulled out a second chair. Both scraped along the stone floor. A plume of dust arose from the woven cushions as we sat down. The title of the top book read "Albert Joseph and Mary Elizabeth Tate"—my grandparents on my mother's side. Other titles included "Charles Edevane I," "Zoe Oliver," and "Charles Edevane II." These were biographies of my grandparents and some of my great-grandparents.

I turned around and let my eyes wander over the six shelves.

There appeared to be an extensive collection of biographies belonging to my family, going back hundreds of years. I could spend hours and days absorbing every detail of the fascinating stories that might contain confidential tales if my ancestors were Hosts and Writers.

John leaned his head next to mine. "Maybe these are what the intruders were after."

"My family's history?" I found that hard to believe.

"Not necessarily, more like the secrets of your family's history."

"What secrets?" Shaw asked.

We hadn't spoken quietly enough. I regretted my promise to keep these secrets from Shaw. It was his family too.

Sounding natural and without a pause, John said, "Someone may have information about the wealth of weapons with the inlaid jewels at your home."

"These are worth a fortune." Shaw held out a ruby infested handle of a dagger. Red sparkles twirled around the room. Blue dots of light joined the red as Benny toyed with a matching dagger containing inlaid sapphires. It was then that I noticed the pattern hung around the walls—an exhibit for what appeared to be the red team, the blue team, and the green team. Each group of weapons and armour had a distinct set made with rubies, sapphires, or emeralds. This room was obviously a former knights hall, not a ladies room. As far as I could tell, there were no bejeweled necklaces and rings.

Shaw sighed. "I think we're all tired. Let's see if we can get out of here and get some sleep."

Shaw's eyes searched Benny and John's pockets and hands to make sure they were empty. We turned on our torches before John found a switch for the overhead light. When he pressed the switch, the levers and cranks sounded again, raising the doorway. We walked out one by one. Shaw came last. "I wonder how to shut it," he said. His back foot entered the library and immediately the shelf-wall lowered into place with a heavy boom sound. Everyone except me began to search the shelves to see how to get the grotto door open again. Because of the confidentiality needed for the journals, I decided to keep the knowledge to myself of how to open it. Later I planned to return and explore, alone.

Chapter 8
INHABITING OWEN

John reclined in the bed enjoying the feather-down comfort, relieved to sleep indoors for the first time in weeks, but sleep failed to come and shut out the events of the night. He had failed. If he had notified Owen as soon as he spotted the Ducati and its rider outside the bar, Owen would still be alive.

He glanced at the clock on the dresser. It had just gone half past three in the morning. An hour ago he received information that his friend Owen's body had been removed from the pub and was being transported to London.

When he arrived back at the pub, he immediately knew Owen had paid the ultimate price for keeping silent. The age-old tables Owen had wiped down several times a day for years had been used to smash his body. They had started with his extremities and moved towards his chest. Owen probably passed out while internal bleeding took his life.

The cyclist's blatant actions had confused his superiors and him, and John wanted vengeance. He had been the one to inform Owen's wife. He had held her hand and listened to her cry while he watched their three young boys play catch with a hairy mutt behind their home, the last glow of the sunset lit up their laughing faces. He would make the murderers wish they had driven over a cliff. But first he needed to talk to Owen.

I walked along the path that ran beside the rose garden. The morning sun stretched the shadows of the branches over my feet. I had slept well knowing both Shaw and John slept in rooms down the hall. After exiting the grotto, Benny had told me to allow the poor bloke to have his own room and quit hushing him about. I had no idea what Benny had meant by that, but later in the evening when John returned I offered him a room. His feet dragged and his expression was as dark as the circles under his eyes and he gratefully accepted. Benny exclaimed that it was about time. Benny's jagged laughter had echoed off the stone of the entrance hall walls as he took the zombie-like John upstairs to prepare his room. I didn't press John to find out what had happened and where he had gone, he'd tell me when he felt ready.

The scent of the late blooming roses followed me along my walk back through the gardens. I climbed several steps to the courtyard outside the breakfast room and my stomach growled. I pushed open the windowed patio doors and entered the room, leaving the double doors open to allow the fresh air inside.

The table had three place settings. John sat reading the morning newspaper and Shaw walked in carrying a bowl of strawberries. He sat down across from John.

"Good morning," I said.

John lowered the paper and smiled at me—how charming. Shaw tossed a strawberry in my direction. I caught it, popped it in my mouth, and savored the juicy ripeness. John reached for a strawberry and said, "I have business that will involve most of the day. Can we meet for dinner tonight?"

I sat in the chair next to John. "Sure," I said. I turned towards Shaw. "Shaw? Can you join us?"

"No."

Bluntly put, but full of meaning.

John propped the newspaper in front of his face and said, "If you change your mind I'll be here before dark."

"I won't."

"Shaw," I said, dismayed and shocked by my brother's rude response.

"What do you really know about him, Zoe?"

"He…," I stopped myself. I couldn't very well say he saved my life—twice. That would bring up questions I couldn't answer.

"He's what?" Shaw grinned. "Thank you for proving my point." He slid another strawberry into his mouth.

I had paused too long. John seemed to be enjoying our rift. He lowered a corner of the paper and with a smirk on his face he glanced from Shaw to me. He stood up, folded the paper, and placed it on the table. "Until later then." He put his hand underneath my chin, raised my face until my surprised eyes looked into his, and he did a most uncustomary thing. His lips encircled mine and he gave me a rather possessive kiss. I felt such a conundrum of emotions that I almost missed his fingers sliding a piece of paper into my hand. His lips left mine and he walked out of the room.

Shaw's face was red with anger, but he didn't say anything. My face flushed also. I cautiously hid the folded note inside my pocket with the understanding that I shouldn't read it in front of Shaw. I then endured a couple hours of my brother interrogating me about what I had been up to recently, beginning with questions about John. I assured him that we did not have a relationship and to steer his questions away from John, I told him about my latest rock climbing escapades and my new best time at the rallycross track. Just mentioning the rock climbing put him on a thirty-minute rampage about my safety. In between his questioning we reviewed our family finances and went through some of Mum's things. When Shaw finally allowed me to take a break, I went to my room and pulled out the note. It read: *Pack an overnight bag. I'm taking you to London tonight. Bring your gear. We'll be back before lunch tomorrow. It's urgent. J.*

Sounded like another adventure—an adventure I didn't want. The adventure I wanted was to visit with Mum and Dad, which John avoided my questions about, something I guessed he didn't want to do with Shaw around. He seemed intent on showing me how to safely play this game. Being in the car alone with him might give me the chance to talk about my concerns. I guessed that his gear reference did not have to do with ropes, karabiners, and harnesses. It had to be his way of suggesting, without saying specifically, what we needed for archiving. I packed a few toiletries and a dark green sweater. For my Host gear I included wellies, my torch, a bit of mana that John had given me, and a recording device. Lastly, I added Mum's revolver, which from recent experience seemed a necessity.

John picked me up in the convertible. Due to the chilly evening he had the roof closed. Half way to London, he stopped at a chippy to eat. The smell of deep-fried cod and chips beckoned me as he opened the door. He told me what to order for him and said he'd be back in five. I watched him leave and then I approached the counter with the fifty-pound note he gave me—maybe he tipped like a Yank. Ever since this morning when Shaw posed the question of how well I knew John, I'd been thinking things over. Other than being enamored by the man and his life-saving techniques I didn't know much. The one experience I couldn't deny—I had seen Captain John Link, the spirit. And of course I couldn't explain that to Shaw as proof to trust John. My brother would carry on for hours about how I'd been fooled by an illusion of sorts. I wondered myself if I had.

After I placed my order, a grey-haired lady used her fingers to pinch the chips in the fryer. I winced for her. Years of dipping her fingertips in the hot oil had deadened her fingertips and made them numb to the heat. She pinched the chips, ensuring they were cooked just right, before she pulled them out of the oil in a metal colander and dumped them in a basket.

The smell of oil, fish, vinegar, and potatoes sent me back to a summer drive with Mum and Dad. Mum loved to drive our convertibles. The day of that summer drive she drove the one in which Dad was later killed—all I remembered was its black colour and she drove until her hat flew away in the breeze. She pulled the car over so I could jump out and run along the grassy side of the road to recapture her hat. Dad then kept his hand on top of her head, holding the hat in place, tapping his fingers to the music playing on the radio until we stopped at a local chippy to eat. That was a good memory of my parents. Memories fade, but I could have a second chance and create new memories with them if I became an Archivist. Due to the danger involved in becoming a Host, it was hard for me to envision. Certainly it would be different if Shaw was there beside me, learning and training together, and discovering the stories and tales of our family who had done it before us.

I looked across at a corner table. A watercolour of an English garden hung above it, featuring pale-green stems and yellow flowers—this was the same chippy my parents had taken me that day. I remembered pointing out the flowers in the watercolour to my dad. That summer Dad and I planted yellow lilies, similar to the watercolour, in our own garden.

The steaming plates clattered to the counter and brought me back to the here and now. I grabbed a bottle of malt vinegar, balanced the two plates on my arms, and walked across the room to sit at the pub-style table under the painted lilies. John came in and sat down. Between bites, I questioned him—hoping to discover that he would help me see my parents, even if I chose not to join the Archivist's secret society.

"When you're not Host writing, what do you do?"

He swallowed before answering. "I'm a freelance photographer."

I had seen a John Link as a photographer when I had searched his name, yet I had never seen him with a camera. "Where's your camera?"

"I have it, just not all my lenses and gadgets."

"Really? And you call yourself a photographer? I'll bet you have your own trust fund as well."

To that he responded with a glint in his eyes.

I took another bite before my next question. "Where did you grow up?"

He smiled, "I see an inquisition coming."

I smiled back, hoping my teeth were as clean as his. He ate another chip, swallowed and continued.

"I was born in Wales. I've spent most of the past ten years in South Africa. I own a flat there, but lately I've spent time at my family home in Wales."

I hadn't pictured him with a family, or married with kids. "Your family? Brothers…sisters?"

"I have a half-sister who now lives in Toronto with a family of her own. She has a daughter. I haven't seen them since my father's funeral. My only brother was killed in Afghanistan. My parents are

both dead. My grandmother still runs the family home in Wales."
He grinned. "She's a character."

"Your brother served in the war?"

"He was a young soldier and died in combat in 2006."

"I'm sorry." I paused before deciding to ask my next question. "Did your parents die in similar circumstances as mine?"

"No." The tone of his voice was different and the smile left his eyes. For his own reasons, he lied to me.

I didn't press for more information about his family, nor did I ask the question about talking with my parents that I'd been leading up to. After returning to the car I asked, "Why are we going to London?"

A pained expression covered his face, no smile or joy in his eyes. Only darkness. "Owen, from the pub yesterday?"

I nodded.

"He was killed last night." He spoke with quiet anger in his voice.

I gasped. "How? Who did it?"

"That's why we're headed to the morgue in London. We're going to interview him."

"Interview…Owen?" I asked.

He nodded and I cringed.

London, England

Staring at a sheet-covered corpse was not how I anticipated it to feel; it felt worse. My guts wrenched up my fish and chips into the metal rubbish bin next to the gurney. My spine and body shook so much I thought a spinal block might be necessary. That was all before John uncovered Owen's body down to his waist. One look at me and John threw the sheet back over him. Too late. An ice pick couldn't scratch my eyes enough to remove the image of the mangled, grey-coloured skin, and bloodied and bruised body that I had seen yesterday as the fair-haired, laughing man showing me photos of his three fair-haired boys and beautiful wife. That man was now forever absent from any more family photos.

John's arms steadied me. "Will you be alright?"

"Peachy," I said. The photograph with the faces of Owen's young boys danced in front of my eyes and beckoned clarity of mind within me. I shook my head. "I'm not alright. My parents, Owen, your parents." He started at that and I silenced him. "John, I'll help you tonight, then I'm through with this. But I have one condition." I had his attention. "You help me talk to my mum and dad. I need that. I think you owe me that."

He didn't move.

"John?"

"That's not a good idea, Zoe."

"What? Talking with my parents, or not becoming an Archivist?"

"Both."

"Well, I can't think why either would be a bad idea. That's my deal. Otherwise I ring a cab." I stared into his eyes. "Whoever took Owen from his boys will have to answer to you John—I get that—my dad was taken prematurely from me, too. And Mum would have lived a long life…she and I…she and I may have been able to fix things between us if that time hadn't been shortened by someone."

"But, Zoe. You can't ask them about their murders."

"Maybe I don't plan to ask them. Maybe I just want time with them, to see them. I never believed I'd ever see them again. I want to take advantage of this Archivist gift now—not wait until I'm dead. Isn't that why we're here with Owen? To use our gifts?" I asked.

"Yes. But with your own family it's different," he said, fidgeting.

I glanced up at him in surprise. "You haven't talked to your parents since their deaths?"

He didn't answer, nor did I have the energy to pursue the conversation. For a few moments we both stared at Owen's sheet and thought of the man it covered.

How was it possible that his ears were no longer on the sides of his head, but positioned lower and towards the back? His collarbone sunk with hills and dells; his arms listed left and right from the multiple compound fractures.

"As long as you don't ask about their murders, I'll agree to your terms," he said.

Staring at the sheet, I wondered if I really wanted to be a Host. If not for the opportunity to talk to my parents, I wouldn't do it, and he was out of his mind to think I wouldn't ask my parents who killed them. I'd let him think that for now. I glanced at John and tried to capture some of his strength before I committed myself. In a steady voice I said, "Thank you, John. Now, how do we interview Owen?"

"Did you bring the mana and some paper?"

I opened my bag, dug out my wellies, and set them on the tile floor. Ignoring John's snooty laugh, I pulled the mana out from the toe of one boot and gave it to John. Then I reached into my bag and gave him a recorder.

"What's this for?" he asked, holding up the recorder.

"Isn't it obvious?"

"The voices of spirits can't be recorded."

"Why not?"

"It's impossible—they're spirits."

"But I've heard their voices on the telly," I said.

He sighed. "Trust me, it's not possible." He dropped the recorder inside my bag and asked, "Do you have paper?"

"I'm a writer, I *always* carry paper," I said, with the hidden meaning implied.

He caught my meaning and held up his smart phone. "I have a photo app."

"Well, that must make you a professional photographer," I said, sarcastically.

He held up his phone and snapped my picture as I handed him a notebook and pen from the side pocket of my bag. He blocked the steel door with a stainless steel examination table and said, "There's no hocus-pocus. It's real simple. Take the mana, slide it over the sheet in an 'X' and then say his full name, Owen Beasley. After saying his name, repeat the words, 'I give you permission to use my body as Host.' It might take a minute and then before you know it you're done."

I drew a hand-sized doughy "X" on the sheet and said, "Owen Beasley, I give you permission to use my body as Host."

I kept my eyes on John and he nodded. Fog began to appear and dance around the gurney. "What's this stuff? It looks hocus-pocus to me."

"We don't know why the fog comes. We think it's a kind of gravitational pull—a veil between our world and the next."

I didn't feel scared, maybe a bit cold as the mist covered my legs and crept up and over the gurney to encompass the lumpy sheet.

"You'll be fine," John said.

The fog enveloped me and I shivered. Dampness penetrated my eyes and covered my face, and I licked the moisture from my lips, took a deep breath and waited.

"Zoe, you did great."

I felt the coldness of the floor below me and blinked to try and see John through the mist. The fog swirled around my face and created condensation that dripped into my mouth. John handed me a towel to dab my face.

"Did it not work?" I asked. No time had passed.

John held my closed notebook up for me to see it in the fog. "Three pages," he said.

"But I don't remember anything."

"You won't. It's similar to being put under with anesthesia for an operation. You wake up a little confused because time has passed and you don't recall anything."

"Oh." I felt dismayed. The thought of speaking for a spirit or with a spirit had seemed so incredible to me. Next time I wanted to be the one to interview them. That I would remember. I reached a hand towards him and John took it and pulled me up from the floor. I swayed a bit. His hands went on either side of my waist and he held me in front of him, our bodies touching. With the fog swirling around us it felt surreal.

"Do you feel steady enough to walk?" he asked, his face near mine.

Not anymore, I thought, and almost forgot my question. Feeling awkward, I asked, "Did you find out what happened to Owen?"

"Thanks to you, we know more."

Behind us the stainless-steel door swung open, a middle-aged man wearing a white jacket entered. John must have already unblocked the door. The man gave a curious glance at the swirling white puffs and our two heads dancing on top. "What have we here?" he asked. The man had a sweet and slippery tone to his voice.

In a cautious voice, John replied, "A cooler is broken." He didn't take his eyes off the man and told me, "Get your bag, love." And to the man he said, "I didn't know you were in London."

I squatted down and reached in the mist to search for my bag, at the same time I felt John's hand lean on the top of my head and hold me down. I nodded so he knew I understood to stay below the fog. It sounded like John knew this man and something wasn't right. I remained low, reaching my hand around the floor for my bag and my boots.

"I just flew in with specific orders," said the man.

"With orders—interesting."

"Yes, and never did I think it would be this easy."

John dived down next to me. First came the whispered ping of a silencer, followed by the dull thud of a bullet penetrating the wall behind us. I located my bag strap as John grabbed my arm and we crawled through the hovering ground mist and tried to escape—without an escape route.

"John, I have the door covered. There's no way out for you."

Tell me something we don't already know, I thought as we crept across the damp floor until we reached the wall. From there the only exit was to our right.

"The mist is dispersing and will soon reveal you," said the man.

The mana was still in my hand and I moved slowly and put it in my bag. John slipped the notebook into my hand leaving his hands free. I eased the notebook inside my bag while consciously taking slow breaths. Every breath I took disturbed the remnants of the fog. With the notebook in the bottom of my bag, my hand touched my hairbrush.

"You'll need to be a slithering snake to keep hidden. Just another moment or two," he said, toying with us in his syrupy tone.

We didn't have long. I wrapped my fingers around my brush, and without making any noise, I removed it from the bag and set it in John's hand. I hoped he would understand what I wanted him to do. He reassured me with a squeeze of my hand and then his finger tapped the top of my hand, once, twice, and on the third he slid the brush across the slippery floor to our left and we half scooted, half ran to the right.

The pings of the man's gun resonated three times as he tried to shoot the moving brush. The fog thinned. Above it I saw the shooter's profile, a middle-aged man with a sharp chin. He noticed me in his peripheral vision and turned his head. Our eyes locked— his eyes cold and calculating. His arm holding the weapon swung my way. He walked forwards as I stared at the barrel of the gun with the silencer pointed at my forehead. Beside me, John aimed his gun, but before he had the gun in position he slipped on the damp floor. He scuffled and attempted to right himself. That slow-motion sensation people talk about experiencing? That was my experience at that moment. I stared at the gun barrel as the man took another step towards me. The tip of the man's finger tightened on the trigger. The instant the shooter's finger met that trigger was the exact moment his feet tripped over what must have been my boots that I left on the floor. The gun barrel swung upwards and shot holes in the ceiling as the man slipped into the fog.

John righted himself, grabbed onto my arm, and tugged me through the doorway. We ran down the narrow hallway, took the second turn, and bumped into a security guard. I remembered the gun in my bag. I couldn't risk being searched. John had his gun hidden behind my back. The cold metal pressed against my spine as he stood close to keep it concealed. I looked into the guard's face, conjured up instant tears and told him, "We were saying our goodbyes to Mum when we heard gunshots down that hall." I pointed towards the morgue, sniffed, and buried my head in John's shoulder.

The guard pushed us towards the exit and said, "Get out of the building." He doled out orders on his hand-held radio as we ran for the exit. Within minutes we were safe inside the car and headed in the direction of home.

"That man, he knew you," I said.

"He did."

"And you recognized him?"

He gave me a silent glance before looking back to the road. I shook my head. Fine, what was one more mystery? I reached in my bag and removed the notebook and a torch. I opened the notebook and shined the light on it—scribbles, all unreadable except a few words: *Owen's family will be avenged.*

"What is this?" I shook the notebook at him.

"You're on a need to know basis."

Irate, I thought again about what Shaw had asked me. Could I trust John? Being alone in the car with him along a dark country road was not the time for me to test my theory. My mouth opened to ask him a direct question when we passed a sign that read "Wales 78 km." I clamped my mouth shut. We were headed in the opposite direction of home.

Chapter 9
HELENA LINK

John's talk with Owen had put him in a mixture of moods. They had known each other most of their lives. They had remained friends even after discovering they were dating the same woman. John had backed off and Owen married her.

What Owen told him in the morgue could not be written. Much of the conversation had been for Owen's wife and boys. He would take the message to them later and in person. The rest of the conversation, along with information on the gunman, had proved one thing—many of the people he worked with had gone rogue. A faction had surfaced with a plan that worked in direct opposition to the plan he and his superiors set up years ago. This group had generated mistrust in John's unit. The lone gunman at the morgue was proof. The gunman was Calvin Booker, John's mentor and leader. He had orchestrated John's mission and now he wanted him eliminated? It didn't make sense. Instead of setting up a hit on him, Booker was doing the job himself. John couldn't fathom why. Possibly the evil faction had convinced Booker that John had gone rogue, or perhaps Booker wanted to take John down and eliminate his competition for a new plan. Whatever the case, he had to move with extreme caution, especially since he had Zoe with him. Zoe was the weak link, zero training and too trusting, but also the one thing they wanted most. He needed to keep her close.

"Where are you taking me, John?" I asked.

"We're running out of petrol and there's a station ahead."

"We passed a station turnoff ten kilometers back."

He squinted his eyes at me before he again concentrated on the road. It was too dark for me to read his face. The indirect lights of the passing cars cast eerie shadows that drew out his eyebrows and sharpened his chin. I shivered.

"Are you cold?" he asked. Without waiting for my response he reached his arm behind my seat and grabbed a wool blanket. He shook the blanket over me and tucked it around my shoulder.

The man confused me, one minute kind and informative, the next aloof and tightlipped. "John, please tell me what's going on."

"I don't know."

"You made a promise to me. I don't want to be involved in this anymore."

"I'll keep my promise."

"Then tell me what happened in the morgue."

"I'm being truthful with you. I honestly don't know what's happening." His voice sounded resolute and perplexed. I believed him.

"But you do know the man that shot at us," I said, more as a statement, not a question.

"Yes. His shooting at us doesn't make sense." He stared at the road, slowed down, and signaled into the petrol station. He turned off the Bentley's engine and faced me. "I thought he and I were friends."

I took his hand in mine.

"Owen mentioned a name. I'm taking you to help me interview her," he said.

"Phrased like that, I'm guessing she's dead?"

"Yes. She is."

"Did you know her?"

"Very well." He paused and a smile lit up his face. "She's my mother."

With a bombshell like that, I was speechless.

North Wales

The cemetery was a family plot on his family's land in Wales and it spread out over the countryside and disappeared into the night. The plot held what appeared to be more than a hundred various sized grave markers. We walked passed various obelisk, square, and rectangular markers. A beautiful stone Celtic cross expanded towards the sky. The grass was choppy and had intertwined tree roots that made it difficult to walk without tripping. The cemetery had a boundary of stacked rocks interlaced between strips of hedges along the sloping hills. The stars and the moon turned the foliage to a sea foam colour. I couldn't wait to see it during the day.

After the ten-minute walk from the car, we stood at Helena's tomb, which was no small feat. The marble monument was the size of a small house and had epitaphs inscribed on two sides. John noticed me reading them. "These were favorite quotes of hers. She wrote them down with a note to carve them on her marker."

I recognized several of the passages. From Voltaire: "One owes respect to the living. To the dead one owes only truth." From

Dickens: "Let us be moral. Let us contemplate existence." From Aeschylus: "What is there more kindly than the feeling between host and guest?" And quotes from Mother Teresa, Abraham Lincoln and Mahatma Gandhi. I immediately understood the duel meaning of every quote and admired the way she meant for them to clarify her life.

Impressed, I said, "She was well versed."

"Yes, and she was the most capable and inspiring mother with her love of family, books, and learning," John said.

I shined my torch to see the dates she had lived. Listed were the dates 1950 to 2002.

"She died young, and the same year as my father," I said.

"Her heart gave out, but she was both a runner and a swimmer. Very fit. I always thought the investigation should have been more thorough."

"And you never asked her about her last days?"

An owl hooted nearby. What was it with owls setting up their residence in cemeteries?

"I plan to. Are you ready?" John asked.

I retrieved the mana and scratched a small "X" on the monument next to her name and said, "Helena Link, I give you permission to use my body as Host."

I held John's eyes with my own and waited. The fog danced from under the stone like dry ice. It reached for the trees and sky and covered us making it difficult to see. Then it flowed and settled on the ground.

"Hello, dear."

Startled, I looked at John. John's voice spoke to me in a soft and wispy tone—very unusual.

His voice said, "I'm guessing you must be the Writer."

My confusion at not being the Host gave way to amazement.

John's mother had taken John's body. Fantastic. Now what, in fact, did I need to ask her?

"Actually, I'm supposed to be the Host," I said.

"Now that can only happen if a family member is present." John's eyes studied his hands and then his hands touched and prodded his face while the last wisps of fog swirled over the ground.

"You are in John's body," I said.

"Oh…and I so much would like to talk to him." She looked at me and asked, "Are you his wife?"

I laughed. "No. We've been working together for just over a month."

"What is your name, dear?"

"Zoe. Zoe Edevane."

John's body walked and circled around me. His eyes studied me. It felt uncanny.

"Zoe Edevane, you are stunning."

With her comment, a bashful me made an appearance and I lost my train of thought. My thought was a train going over a cliff anyway—I had no idea what John needed to ask her.

"What did John want to know?" she asked.

"He didn't tell me."

"Then he's been independent for too long." Not used to having a man's arm, she linked her arm through mine and we walked over to a stone bench and sat down.

"Tell me what led up to this sudden gathering of info from me."

"After we spoke with Owen he said we needed to talk to you." I was basically thinking out loud.

"Owen? You were on the Isle?" she asked.

"No. In London where his body is now."

"Owen is dead then," she said. "Was it an accident?"

"No. He was murdered."

She gasped and grabbed my hand in a firm grip with both of hers, not realizing the strength she now had with John's hands. I winced from the effect.

"Sorry, dear." She loosened her clasp, but continued to hold my hand. "Who killed him?"

"If he told John, I don't know. But Owen did tell him to speak with you. That's all John said."

She stroked my hand and thought for a moment. "Owen must think the same people who killed me are involved in his death."

"You were murdered?"

She nodded. "Before I died, I interviewed a few people who gave me information. What they told me didn't make sense until the day I died."

We sat in silence while I took out my notebook and pen. The hoots and caws of the owls and nocturnal birds hung in the night air as everything went silent. The reason for the quiet grew apparent when the sounds of racing engines echoed through the hills in our direction.

"That's odd," she said, glancing at the hills.

I held my pen and asked her, "Who were the people you interviewed?"

"Edward and Missy Thomas, and Phil and Lily Woods. John will remember them."

I wrote both names in the notebook.

The sound of engines grew louder and I wondered who would be out this late riding through the countryside. The shift of gears and revving of the engines sounded like motorbikes. I put the notebook in my bag and stood up.

"What's wrong dear?" Helena asked.

"It's possible that John and I may have been followed here."

She stood up and looked over the hills. We stood in silence and listened. It sounded like there were at least three of them. We needed John; I needed John.

"Should we get John back? He'd know what to do." I sounded worried.

"No worries, child. The extra strength of John's body as a Host could prove useful—I know some moves of my own to protect you."

My heart raced. We turned off the torches and ducked behind her enormous monument. I peeked around the side with my cheek against the cold surface. Three or four headlamps danced and dodged around trees and bushes and soon would be dodging grave markers. They headed our way.

"How are you going to protect me?" When she didn't answer, I turned around. She, along with John's body, had disappeared.

"Helena?" I called out. She wouldn't be able to hear me. I couldn't hear anything over the noise of the motorcycles. Desperation became my enemy while I searched for her. I crawled between some of the shorter gravestones and tried to keep myself hidden. I peered around corners and through the bushes. I saw nothing except the blinking headlamps that weaved between the grave markers. I crawled through the grass back the way I came, keeping my body low to the ground, until I stood behind Helena's marker again. What would I do if this woman did something crazy and it cost John his life?

I leaned my back against the marker and saw her. Or rather, I saw the torch she carried light up and begin to spotlight the graves. The bright LED torch beamed its light towards the closest bike, blinding the driver before he could maneuver around an oversized cement bench. Blinded, he drove into the immoveable bench. The wheel of his bike wedged beneath the bench, bringing the bike to a sudden stop, which in turn launched the rider's body forwards— headfirst into a justly called headstone. He crumpled at the neck.

When his body settled to the ground, it didn't move.

Two more headlamps searched nearby. One made a sharp turn towards the moving torch and appeared to want to flank Helena while the other bike slowed down and made a straight shot her way. She moved around to the side of a headstone and faced the bike that headed straight towards her. The headlamp spotlighted John's body. Behind her, the other bike sped up and came her way. I stayed low behind her monument and watched in amazement. She gauged the distance of the incoming cyclist and, using John's height and strength, she jumped forwards. Utilizing a wide grave marker to support her weight, she grabbed hold of the marker and lifted and turned John's body so his hands anchored his body from flying too far. Up came John's powerful legs to kick the approaching cyclist off his bike. I heard the crack of bones when her kick made contact with the rider's sternum and another popping crack as the man flipped over a nearby granite marker. I cringed.

Helena was definitely enjoying this confrontation, which must have made her feel alive. Riding motorcycles through the family plot had been a grave mistake for these men. The smile from my pun didn't last long, not when I noticed my shadow cast beside me by a headlamp. I had lost track of the third bike. I launched myself to the side of Helena's monument in time to miss the spinning front wheel of the third bike rocketing towards me.

The biker braked, set his left foot on the grass for support while he spun the bike into a tight turn—spinning rocks and grass clumps into the air. The helmeted rider smiled eerily at me, leaned forwards, twisted the throttle with his right hand, and headed in my direction. Using my skills as a runner, I leaped around a corner of the monument just as the motorcycle passed me again. I turned the opposite way and ran, passing several markers before I skidded to a stop behind the thick Celtic cross, wider and taller than myself. I ducked behind it to give me some protection and concealed myself in the tall grasses that grew around it. The cyclist turned again and reconfigured his approach. The headlamps jumped from bush to marker to grass tips as the bike travelled my way, searching.

I had lost sight of Helena. I screamed her name as loud as possible, hoping she would hear me and get my coordinates.

"Zoe! Over here!" John's voice yelled behind me, near Helena's monument.

I glance towards the voice and saw John's arms waving. Knowing my life depended on speed, I got my legs to move. The rev of the engine felt right behind me and I tried to run faster. It was difficult to run over the rocky turf. My feet slipped sideways on the small boulders that pushed up from the dirt as I stumbled across some wet grass clumps and tree roots. While running, I noticed a fourth motorbike approaching me on a diagonal course just to the side of Helena. With the trajectory of the two bikes and myself, we'd all meet in a pileup.

John's hand held the torch and shone it in the eyes of the rider behind me.

"Keep coming, Zoe." John's voice encouraged me. "We're going inside the vault."

A black hole formed behind John's back. The direction she shone the torch interfered with my sight and almost blinded me as well. As I approached, she switched the torch from the biker behind me to the biker on the diagonal course. She kept the light on until the exact instant I ran beside her and she shut it off. I then saw the open doorway. Helena, or maybe John, I really didn't know at that point, dove with me inside the doorway and slammed the iron door shut behind us. The outside of the door reverberated loudly as one bike and then the other slid and crashed into its non-budging thick iron.

I sat in the dark, taking deep breaths of air that smelled like earth.

Other than our heavy breathing and the sounds of a dying motor, it was still. "John?" I asked.

The torchlight went on. "No, it's me." The light lit up his face and he smiled, a surprisingly feminine smile. Bizarre as he appeared, I saw his mum.

"Thank you. You saved my life."

She took my hand. "Anything for you, lovey. I imagine your life means something to my John." I didn't comment.

We sat on a tile floor in a rectangular stone room. The tight seal of the doorway made it difficult to see the door.

"Can they open this door?" I asked.

"I doubt they'll be doing anything for a while. Even if they do get up, this door takes practice to open. Because there may be more, we can't go out that way."

After looking around the room I saw no obvious exit, only a marble crypt placed in the middle of the room. "This is your tomb? Is there another way out?"

"Yes, this room has a hidden passageway to the house." She continued to sit next to me. "John doesn't know about this tunnel. You can show him later."

There wasn't any passageway that I saw. We stood up and she walked over to the right side of the door. A silver-cast fig leaf clung to the wall next to the door. She twisted it to the left and then walked to the crypt. She knelt down beside it and pulled a lever under the ornamental top. I expected the crypt to move, but instead felt a shudder and heard a scrape behind me. A tile on the floor lowered a hand's width and moved under the tile next to it. This created an opening large enough for a medium-sized man to squeeze into with his shoulders diagonal to the square.

Helena lit the hole with the torch to reveal a ladder hooked to the wall below the opening. "You go first," she said. "Don't step on the bottom rung. Count five steps and jump to the side. The bottom step shuts the doorway."

I counted five steps and jumped down to a dirt floor and shone my torch around me. The tunnel wound into the depths of the earth and was spacious enough for a tall man. My nose absorbed the musky soil scent and the dampness.

She stepped on the bottom rung of the ladder and the tile doorway slid shut. "When coming from the house, you pull up on the bottom step," Helena explained.

"How far is the house?" I asked.

"About a fifteen minute walk."

Feeling like a tunnel rat, I followed John's back through the weaving dirt and stone-lined passageway. We turned right, left, right, right, and left until I lost my sense of direction. I was glad there were no side tunnels or I would have become lost. This would be easy to show John, someday.

"Are you keeping track of the time?" she asked.

"Time for what?"

"How much time I've been in John's body."

Great. Something else no one prepared me for. "What happens if I haven't kept track?"

"After an hour John's brain will start experiencing memory loss."

In my head I screamed, "What the hell?" But because I walked with John's mother I said in a pleasant voice, although slightly high pitched, "I didn't know that. It's probably close to forty-five minutes. But I'm not sure. Maybe you should give him his body back." John must already suffer from memory loss; he missed telling me that vital piece of information.

Helena chuckled, "Is this your first time being a writer?"

"Um, yeah."

"He can't return until you wipe the mana off the grave marker.

You need to remove the 'X' marking the spot."

Another vital piece of information John failed to tell me.

"Those men are there. We can't go back."

"True. But that's our only option." She pointed ahead. "The entrance to the house is around this corner. We can get some help there."

We made another turn and as promised a ladder, hooked to the wall, awaited us. The top of John's foot pushed up on the bottom rung and an opening appeared; this time a segment of hardwood flooring scraped to the side. We climbed up the ladder to the familiar sound of gunfire. It echoed from outside the house. We dropped to the floor. I found myself in a room where several ancient red fox heads stared down at me from the wall. They were mounted next to a painting of foxhounds and horses, the riders wearing red and white. A water buffalo head loomed above a mahogany fireplace built so large that it made the buffalo head appear small above it. We scooted and then rolled to a safe position beside a leather couch. Motorcycles raced over the gravel driveway outside the home. Another single round was fired. I covered my ears, which rang from the close proximity of the noise. A muffled voice said, "Get off my property, you leather devils, before I shoot up your rides." The voice sounded like that of an elderly American woman.

"That would be Nana," Helena said. "She's revealing her Kentucky, or rather Can-tuck-ee, roots out there." John's face smirked. "She's my ma, born and raised across the pond." As we lay prone on the ground, another gun blast echoed and the windowed doors next to the couch shook. The green drapes hanging above the doors billowed into the room from the outside breeze.

"The old lady must be on her porch out those doors," Helena said. "I'm surprised she can still see to shoot, let alone lift one of those double-barreled shotguns."

We covered our ears as several more shots rang out.

"How many bullets does that gun hold?" I asked.

Helena pointed to a gun cabinet on the other side of the room. The glass doors remained open and at least ten slots were empty. "It appears she has more than one," Helena said.

A pair of hands picked at the drapes, parted them, and then tossed a shotgun onto the couch above us. A head appeared, covered in waist length, spindly grey hair tossed this way and that across high cheekbones and down bony shoulders to cover a purple robe. The untied robe flapped open to reveal loose flesh underneath.

"Nana." John's voice got her attention enough to pull her robe across her chest and knot her tie.

"Hi Johnny, love. I'm finding Grandpa's bird guns to be quite useful. Give me a hand running these madmen off our property."

I instantly fell in love with this feisty old woman who got to the point and had the gun sense that I needed in this line of work. She hobbled across the room to grab another "bird gun" from the gun cabinet.

"Hope these are loaded," she said and gave us a toothless grin as she stepped through the curtain and back outside. She was priceless.

"Shouldn't we help her?" I ran over to the cabinet to take a gun for myself. I picked up a brown one and almost dropped it. The weight of it almost changed my mind.

"We need to get back to the grave soon," Helena reminded me.

The gun-toting Nana poked her head back through the curtain and pulled it to the side. She had one shotgun slung over her shoulder and another held in her arms. "I heard that. Now which one of you aren't yourself?"

I pointed to John.

"And who are you?"

Not sure which of us she was inquiring about, I said, "I'm Zoe

Edevane and that's Helena."

Nana turned to Helena. "Hey love, I know you can shoot, now grab that gun from that twig of a girl before her arms stretch below her knees. Zoe Edevane, follow me." And she disappeared behind the curtain.

"I'm alright," I said to Helena when she tried to take my gun.

No sound came from the motorbikes any more. Even so, I cautiously ventured between the curtains and onto the porch, carrying the shotgun, which if Nana could lift I could too. It didn't weigh more than me and I could free climb a mountain. The porch ran the length of the front of the house and had no railings. On it was a man dressed in a suit, complete with black tie. The night stood still next to this fussy looking individual; I assumed from his raised eyebrows and high-held chin that he was the butler. He nodded at Helena and me while he continued to gather into his already loaded down arms the various guns that lay strewn about the porch—all eight of them. His arms laden and his posture perfect—amazing.

A boxy lorry, driven by Nana, skidded to a halt on the pebble-covered driveway alongside the porch. I hadn't even noticed she left. She leaned over and opened the door. With a commanding tone, she said, "Get in the truck, you two."

I handed my gun to the man when Nana yelled, "We may need that." I took it back from the completely composed butler—his eyebrows still raised. Helena and I jumped off the porch and into the cab of the lorry.

"How much time left?" Nana said over the whine of the engine.

"Don't know," said Helena.

My head hit the back window the same time Nana's slipper hit the accelerator.

Chapter 10
NANA NANA

North Wales

"John?"

I patted his hand and then his cheek, trying to get him out of his delirium. I didn't know how long he had been a Host. From the appearance of his rolling eyes and the drool on his chin, I was sure it had been longer than an hour. I leaned against Helena's monument with John's head in my lap. Two entangled motorcycles sent smoke drifts into the night sky. Both riders lay crumpled in the grass; both pairs of eyes stared, unmoving. I wondered if there was a time frame before interviewing the freshly dead.

Nana had driven back to the house to ring the authorities. I told her we could use my mobile phone, but she insisted she needed to use the number at the house that John had put on speed dial, probably John's "clean up" team. Several men lay dead around us, the other riders had left them behind, along with a third motorbike with its front wheel bent and twisted.

John's face was pale. He went in and out of lucidity, his face relaxed and placid one minute then stressed and anguished the next. My face contorted as I watched him—my heart ached with worry.

"Zoe?" John's voice was weak, but he knew me. The time as Host hadn't made him completely daft. His hand covered my hand that caressed his face. He tried to sit up and pointed to the smoke. "What…what's that from?"

I helped him to sit up. "You became the Host."

He shook his head. "Not possible." He winced and grabbed his head.

I knelt in front of him and put a hand on each side of his face. Some colour returned to his cheeks—maybe my hands helped a little. "Yes, possible. I spent the last, ah, bit of time talking with your mum." Why mention the time and give him any doubts about his brain capacity?

"But that's impossible. No Archivist switches from Host to Writer or Writer to Host, unless their partner died and they change partners," he said.

"That may be. But that's not what happened tonight."

He pointed again to the smoking bike. "That still doesn't explain this, but I can guess."

"We must have been followed. These men tried to kill us."

When he noticed the crumpled bodies, his eyes opened wider. "You did this?"

"Of course not. Helena has some moves of her own."

"I'm sure," he said, his voice sounding stronger.

"Nana is ringing the authorities," I said.

"Nana?" John interrupted. "The authorities?"

Before I said yes, he tried to stand, but toppled to the ground. "Why am I so dizzy?"

"We better wait and let you rest, then we can talk to them," I said.

He used his hands to pull himself up and pressed his body against his mum's memorial. "Zoe, we can't trust the authorities, especially the number Nana is using."

He lifted his leg to take a step and I caught him before he lost his balance. "What is wrong with me?" he asked.

Not wanting to tell him everything, I said innocently, "Maybe this can happen your first time as Host."

"Yeah, maybe." He studied my face long enough for me to feel guilty. "Can you help support me so I can see the faces of these men?"

He leaned on me and I helped him over the grassy ground to where he could see the riders' bloodied faces.

"Do you recognize any of them?" I asked.

"No," John said.

I snapped pictures of their faces with my smart phone. Maybe later he'd be able to identify them; right now he might have a sketchy memory.

"How much time since Nana left?"

"Maybe ten minutes," I said.

"We have about five to get away before they show up."

"It took us fifteen minutes to walk here and you can barely stand."

He let go of me and took three unstable steps before he leaned against a tall marker.

"You just proved my point," I said. I walked over to the vault door at Helena's marker. "We'll stay inside until you feel better, then we can go to the house."

"Anyone can open the vault."

"I know, but thanks to your mum, I have the perfect answer to our dilemma." He raised his eyebrows. I held the secret for once and it felt good.

Five minutes later we sat safe underground on some blankets we found stowed in a chest near the ladder. We drank some water and ate some licorice, both stored inside the chest. When John no longer felt dizzy, he rung his nana and told her to have the butler move his car to the garage, out of sight. He also told her not to trust anyone and not mention him or me at all.

"Nana has all her faculties, but loves to act like she doesn't. No one will question her when she turns on her absentminded charm." He stuck a piece of licorice in his mouth.

"What did Owen tell you that you needed to ask Helena?" I asked.

He swallowed before he said, "First tell me what my mother told you."

I wasn't going to play that game with him. "Do you remember what Owen told you?"

He chewed another piece of licorice while he studied my face. "How long was I a Host?"

The man was intuitive; I'd give him that.

"Don't know. But that hour thing, a bit of important information for me to know, wouldn't you say?"

"Quite right."

"And the part about wiping off the mana 'X' to bring someone back from hosting would have been nice to know."

"Quit with the cheekiness and tell me what Mum said."

"She didn't say much because someone didn't let me know what needed to be asked of her."

He narrowed his eyes at me and yanked off another bite of licorice.

A muffled "Over here" sounded from above us and John put his finger to his lips.

We listened to the thumping footsteps above us. It was difficult to understand any of their angry words. John moved closer beside me until our shoulders touched and he whispered, "Talk quietly and tell me what happened."

I nodded. "I told Helena about Owen and she thought their deaths could be related."

"Her death? She was murdered and she knows?" His shock surprised me and I hoped this wasn't a recent memory loss.

"Are you sure you didn't know she was murdered?" I asked.

"Yes. I have no lapses of memory there. Her heart gave out in her sleep. I suppose I've had thoughts that she might have been poisoned." He thought for a minute and then asked, "Did you ask her who killed her?"

"She had been interviewing people who gave her information that the killers didn't want her to piece together. It started to make sense to her the night she died."

He nodded.

"She had interviewed Edward and Missy Thomas, and Phil and Lily Woods. She thought you'd know them."

"Yes, I know them. What info did she discover?"

I shook my head. "She didn't say. She said it mattered more what they could tell us now."

"You should have made her tell you." His voice was too loud and he knew it.

I rolled my eyes at him. "That's funny coming from you. Besides, at that point we were running for our lives—and for yours."

We sat in silence until the faint voices and footsteps faded away. John had recovered from his dizziness and felt strong again. When he helped me to my feet, he kept hold of my hands. "Zoe." In a quiet voice, almost reverent, he said, "It sounds like I owe you my life. I don't want you to think I'm not grateful."

I glanced down at our clasped hands. "I might actually still owe you a life or two."

He chuckled and I stared up into his eyes. My heart beat as fast as it had earlier that night when running for my life. He leaned down and, instead of kissing my lips, he pecked my forehead; like a father would kiss a daughter. A little bothered, I spun and trudged through the tunnel to lead him to his home.

We approached the ladder to the sound of music playing above us. The song sounded familiar and took only a moment for me to recognize it as a Beatles song. John chuckled. "Nana is not trusting, always thinks the house is bugged or wired with listening devices. She plays loud music to cover conversation."

"Whose conversation?" I asked.

"Ours. Sounds like she's expecting us."

I showed him how the bottom rung of the ladder opened the hidden door. When I pushed up on the rung, the music grew louder, along with a scratchy, elderly voice singing the words to the song.

"She also believes they wrote the song for her." John laughed.

It took me a moment before I asked, "Her name is Nana?"

"She's my nana named Nana. And her husband was Jude."

Nana burst into the room, her cheeks a bright pink. She controlled her grey hair with a low, side-ponytail that trailed down to her waist. She immediately reached up and grabbed John's face between her gnarled hands and asked, "Love, do you know who I am?"

"You're my Nana Nana." John embraced her in a bear hug.

She gave a nod of satisfaction. She smiled at me, a big tooth filled smile that displayed her white dentures. She then took my hand and linked her thin, but strong arm through John's arm. "Now come in here, you two. Sit. I made biscuits."

"Thank you, Nana." John kissed her flushed cheek. "Can we turn down the music?" he asked.

"Soon. First I need to let you know that I didn't recognize one official who showed up tonight, man or woman. They soon tired of my moody senility and left." She had a playfully wicked smile on her face.

She took us through her kitchen, which had too many gleaming white cabinets to count. Her kitchen was larger than my flat at Oxford. We entered her pantry. It had open shelves stacked with pots, canned goods, potatoes, and other veggies, along with another fridge. A square table sat in the middle of the pantry with four wooden chairs placed around it. The table and chairs were blackened with age. John and I, both of us exhausted, slumped into a chair. Nana continued talking as she set a plate of biscuits on the table and finished warming some cream in a copper-bottom pan on a two-burner hob. "Before they arrived, I used that one-time use telephone you gave me and rang the Thomases. Edward wants both of you to meet him before first light at their helicopter pad. I told them not to tell me where they're taking you."

"You're a gift, Nana," John said. "These biscuits are wonderful."

Nana put her hand on John's arm. "Be cautious, Johnny. The missing Hosts and Scribes rumor has been verified. Phil and Lily Woods were taken this morning. From the look of their house, they put up quite a fight. I'm sure someone, maybe one of our own, is trying to get access to the history and books of the Althings."

"I think you're right," John said.

I decided to ask about a point that had bothered me. "Why not let people know the history stored in the Althings?" The look on Nana's face told me that I should not have asked, but I was tired of not knowing what I was involved in and continued my speech. "The vast knowledge of the ancient world that must be contained inside could be remarkable in helping our world today. The science of the ancient world; the knowledge from Egypt, Greece, China, Persia, the Incas and Aztecs; the thinking behind the great minds of world leaders and scientists throughout humanity."

Nana grabbed her chest, feigning a heart attack, and John's eyes bulged.

"Why not?" I asked, after deciding to ignore the hint to shut my mouth.

Still holding her chest, Nana said, "Oh child, there are secrets kept in the Althings that the world is not prepared to know. Untold things that would change all of humanity as we know it. Secrets that many gave their lives and lifetimes to protect and I would give my own life before revealing."

Stunned, I sat in silence and wondered if I would ever know these mysteries. Nana continued to shake her head, but didn't say anything. John finished chewing his biscuit and stood up. "We'd better get some sleep." Nana gave us each a hug, mine a little stiff, before John showed me a darkened bedroom and told me to keep the lights off. Feeling shut out, and shut up, I fell asleep.

Chapter 11
DEAD AND DOWN

North Wales

John's home was near where Phil and Lily Woods lived. He grew up calling the parents Uncle Phil and Aunt Lily. In secondary school, he had courses with their daughter and played rugby with their boys, but he had not known about Phil and Lily being Archivists until Nana mentioned it. And now they were missing.

His gut told him he should go dark. Since he had become a target, he couldn't contact his superiors. He had to stay off the grid and convince Zoe to do the same. Before they left his home he had confiscated her phone and computer. That had not gone well. She had been dialing Shaw's number, which was out of the question. He had to rely on the Thomases and hope they had information to help figure out who was calling the shots. He planned to do everything in his power to protect Zoe and keep her safe. He wouldn't allow anyone near her whose integrity was in question—not unless they explained their motives and let him in on their plans. Only by following this new protocol would he be assured that he could keep her safe.

After very little sleep, John drove us to the Thomas's helicopter pad where Edward wanted us to meet. I didn't know the Thomases. I sat in the car with my arms crossed, miffed. Last night, John had taken my phone and computer. Before we left, he had also taken my credit cards and driving license. With me, I carried about twenty-five quid, a bag of Nana's biscuits, one change of clothes, and my gun. I was at his mercy. Upon seeing how sweet he had been to his Nana, I had reconsidered my feelings towards him, until he took my only means of communication with the outside world.

Who knew where we were off to or for how long? They, Nana and John, had stopped talking to me. I thought maybe my question about letting the world in on the secrets had prompted John to seize my phone and to stop talking to me. Whatever the reason, I sat with my arms folded unable to tweet, text, or speak to anyone.

The person who coined the phrase "darkest before the dawn" had described the featureless landscape I stared at outside of the car window: black sky, black hills, black "ness." John turned onto a gravel road and slowed down. Ahead of us, a small beacon of light blinked on and off three times. We drove towards the signal when the beacon went back on and began to swing around and bob in a frantic manner before being tossed to the side. The light rolled once and stopped, casting its light onto a grassy mound.

John braked and the Bentley skidded to a stop, pinning me in the seatbelt. He turned off the headlamps.

"Get in the back and get down low," John said, his tone desperate.

I unhooked my seatbelt, scrambled between the seats and cowered on the floor behind John.

"Here's your gun." John handed me the gun I thought I still had in my bag.

"How did you…?" But he had already opened the door, shut it behind him, and disappeared into the blackness. Mystified, I stayed low. My legs cramped in the tight space. I had become extremely daft to end up in this situation, again.

Gunshots erupted with muzzle flashes outside the windows. I ducked my head and further compressed myself into the floor between the front and back seats. With John as a companion, gunfire and hiding in cramped places were becoming an everyday occurrence. I threw one of my arms over my head and my other arm around my knees as the shots ricocheted with several close pings—a few slugs hit the Bentley. One passed through the side and deposited itself in the linen-coloured leather seat a few inches from my nose. No bullets hit me, but the increase in adrenalin made the carotid artery in my neck feel like it had kernels of corn popping inside. The sounds of heavy boots staggered outside. I supposed it was John running beside the car. I trusted him to get us out of this one; he seemed to have the technique down. After two additional shots fired, silence overtook the predawn air. Not knowing if the gunfire exchange was over, I didn't move.

A shout came, far enough from the car that I raised my head to listen. At least two men spoke. The voices were too faint for me to identify or understand their words. Worried about John and feeling like a target if something had happened to him, I decided to investigate. These people could be part of the same group who killed my parents. I peeked over the front seat and out the window. The red-orange of early sunrise silhouetted the hills, but I saw no one. The voices had stopped and that worried me, mainly because I hadn't heard a car drive away. I thought of two scenarios: either they were all dead and wounded, or they were searching the area. I waited a few more minutes hoping John would open the door and lead me to safety. The silence continued and my concern for John outweighed any danger for myself. After all, I had a gun and had practiced shooting targets all month. A surge of adrenaline coursed through my veins as I thought of killing anyone associated with my parents' deaths.

Holding my gun firmly in one hand, I opened the door, which disturbed the dawn silence like a rooster call. I rolled out of the car, stood up fast, and took a couple steps before tripping over something lying on the ground. As I stumbled and fell, the gun jolted out of my hand and flew into the shadowed grass. I landed with knees and elbows on top of a warm, unmoving body. Through my revulsion, I scrambled off the body, but slipped and collapsed—my face inches from a face I couldn't see. My heart stopped as I felt the chest and moved upwards to the neck and chin—covered in curly facial hair. This was not John. I inhaled, relieved, until I felt a moist warmth creep through my trousers. I pushed away from the still body and rolled sideways in the grass. I ran my hands over my wet trouser legs and looked at them. My fingers and palms were dark and sticky, and the rosy morning light further enhanced the blood-red colour. I wiped and pawed my hands over the damp grass, trying to remove the blood and stickiness, to little avail.

After several tries to clean my hands, voices floated in my direction and I stopped moving. There were at least two male voices. One moaned in pain and agony, the other sounded like John's. In front of the thin orange line that drew the horizon, I saw two black silhouettes on a rise in the dirt road. One knelt down next to the one seated and coughing. The one kneeling was built like John.

Another moan escaped from the hurt man and when he spoke I barely heard the words, "Our code is broken." He coughed. "One of our own is feeding…our secrets to MI6 and…other agencies around the world." He breathed a raspy breath. "You need to leave…get away…while you can."

Relieved that John appeared unhurt, I crawled around in the grass and rocks sweeping the ground with my sticky hands to find my gun.

From behind me, a deep voice said, "Are you searching for this?"

I remained still. Even without seeing the man, I knew what he had in his hand.

"Get up, slow and easy," said the man.

I stood up with my hands out to my sides and my back to the man. John knelt several car lengths away with his back to me. He stooped beside the once seated man who now lay still on the ground. Suddenly John spun up and around. In his hands the silhouette of his gun aimed at the man behind me.

"Stand down, John," said the man. He had a sinister tone that caused me worry. I didn't move.

The rising sun outlined John's body, painting him as a target.

"Oliver, you too?" John's voice sounded disheartened and tired.

"I've handed over enough secrets to begin my life-long holiday in Barbados as soon as I've finished up a few loose ends." Oliver gave a deep-throated laugh.

John asked, "Was Owen a loose end?"

"Bloody hell. You know that didn't have to go down that way," Oliver said.

"Did you ever consider the future of his wife and boys?" John's voice held pain and anguish.

"Like I said, it was unfortunate." Oliver didn't sound grieved at all. "Now this one, she can't possibly be MI6. My guess—she's your lassie. In the wrong place, at the wrong time, kind of deal."

That's the second time MI6 and spying had been mentioned.

"Yeah, I took her home to meet the family." John's voice no

longer held pain, instead it held revulsion. Although I knew it wasn't aimed at me, both his comment and his intensity made me cringe. How could that explanation give my life more meaning than if Oliver thought I was a spy or a Host? The man obviously wasn't upset after causing someone's death.

Oliver's tone was cheeky. "How nice. And to think they'll never see her alive again unless you put down your gun."

"I have a steady hand, Oliver, and I'm an excellent shot. You best put your gun down."

"I have the kill shot, John."

After standing between two raised guns, and being the brunt of their challenge with one another, I felt woozy and shaky—I had had enough. This man was part of the murderous group; if I distracted him, maybe John would kill him. I put on my best American accent and said, "After two hours of sleep, we're exhausted. How about we have a sit down and discuss this." I began to turn around.

The man said, "Stay where you are." I stopped moving and he continued. "CIA? John, would you go to those lengths?"

"Yes. He would," I said, in my most excellent American twang. John's head turned ever so slightly in my direction, but of course the light obscured him so I had no idea what thought went across his face.

"We can't have—" Oliver began. Several shots rang out. I dropped to the ground, more like I collapsed to the ground—a combination of fright and hysteria. Once I fell, I immediately looked John's way. His outline remained standing—neither of us had been hit. My ears rang in the silence. I turned around to see the man who assisted in the extermination of Owen. A large man, with a few wisps of red hair and a snug belt around his overhanging stomach, had fallen to the ground with a hole in his forehead and two in his chest. My heart felt a coldness that mixed with warmth when I looked towards John.

"Zoe," John said.

My eyes blurred, creating a dizzy spell. I shook my head, but it didn't help my dizziness. I saw two Johns running my way, two sunrises and two guns that looked like my mum's. I reached for one of the guns and grabbed blades of grass and dirt, so I snatched at the other image. My fingers touched the gun barrel and wrapped around it. The double-John image knelt next to me, took the gun from my hand, and tucked it in his waistband. "You won't be needing this," he said. His hands prodded and pulled at my clothes around my chest and my trouser legs, inspecting me. Under other circumstances his touch might have sent my heart fluttering a bit, but I didn't have time to think it over.

"It's not my blood. I'm fine. I tripped and fell on that body." I pointed to the bloodied body sprawled next to the car.

He stopped his physical inspection of me and smiled. "You had me worried." His voice was soft; his face bent close to mine. "Are you sure you're not hurt?"

I nodded, feeling tingles of a different sort, glad he finally ended his silent treatment. I guess being shot at can make one re-think things. John gathered me in his arms and stood me up. He steadied me as we walked. "My bag," I said.

John balanced my staggering body as we walked to the car. The bonnet of the Bentley had a couple bullet holes, another hole had shattered one headlamp, and yet another bullet went through the front-passenger door. I remembered that one. John poked his finger in the hole through the door and whistled. It had been close. He opened the door and reached inside, took out my bag, and looped it over my head. He dropped my gun inside it and we walked towards the helicopter. John's jaw was set; his protective hand held my elbow, almost caressing it. We approached the helicopter and my heart had nearly resumed its normal rhythm when several cars, one at a time, began to crest the hill behind us. The roar of the engines raced our way. We glanced long enough to see the windows rolling down and gun barrels pointing out of them.

"I'm not planning to quit this craziness anymore, John, but don't forget your promise to me."

"Run!" John pulled me along beside him.

The ground around us erupted with bullets striking the mounds of dirt and grass.

"Get inside the bird." He pushed me forwards, turned around, and shot at the approaching cars. I heard a window shatter and I moved faster. His steps were close behind me. I ducked under the spinning rotors and climbed into the open doorway. My mouth dropped open. I found myself staring at a man wearing a blood soaked cap, his body tilted to the side of the pilot's seat.

John climbed in behind me.

"The pilot looks dead!" I yelled, mild hysteria kicking my insides. Had I really just told him I wouldn't quit this craziness?

John maneuvered around behind the pilot's seat, looked at the pilot's lifeless eyes, and pushed him out the open door onto the ground. He pulled the door shut.

"Who's going to fly us?" my voice squeaked. The men with guns were almost upon us. I began to shake.

John situated himself in the pilot's seat, pulled the harness around his body, and gave me a grin. "Me."

"Can you fly?" My teeth chattered; nausea overcame me.

"There's one stick. How hard can it be?" He winked at me and took hold of the stick, revved the engine, or whatever pilots do, and up we went. I then realized he enjoyed fascinating me with his endless display of mysterious talents, even as bullets whizzed past us. A ping of a bullet or two hit the bird. I said a silent prayer, buckled myself in, and peered out of the side window. At least four cars chased us from below. One stopped and several men jumped out, aiming their rifles at us just as John flew us over a hill and out of their sights.

"When are you going to tell me who you really are?" I asked. I crossed my arms around myself in an attempt to stop my shaking. I wasn't sure if I shook more due to the cold or the adrenaline. After taking some deep breaths my nausea subsided somewhat. John ignored my question, made some adjustments, and pushed some flashing buttons on the control panel. Soon I felt warmth blow around my face and legs. After a few minutes, my shaking body and chattering teeth stopped. The helicopter was posh, equipped with leather seats, armrests for the four rear seats, and drink holders. The roomy seats in the back were configured in two sets that faced each other. The nose of the craft was tipped in the rich blue-green colour of a lake. Edward Thomas had known how to travel in style, but now he was dead.

"This is too risky. I said I'd only help with Owen and then your mum. Maybe I was right about quitting in the first place. You should take me home. You promised you'd help me talk to my mum and dad. But I want to talk to them when I'm alive, not dead. John, this is nuts. You're nuts."

"I can't take you home."

"Why?"

"Too dangerous."

"Then where are we going?" I asked.

"Dingwall, Scotland. Ever been there?"

"I don't think so."

"This should be an adventure then."

I must have given him an apprehensive look because he began to laugh, and then held his side and grunted, "Ow."

The sun lit up the entire dome of the helicopter and the blood pooling under his hand. "You've been shot," I said with more calm then I felt.

"I'll be fine." He was calm also, too calm.

"Maybe we should land and get you taken care of."

"In the ocean?"

Sure enough, outside my window was an expanse of blue—the Irish Sea.

His face shone bright from the sunlight streaming inside. I noticed the paleness in his cheeks.

"John?" I said quietly.

He stared straight ahead and said, "Find the emergency kit."

Underneath the rear seats I found a metal chest with bandages, gauze, and ointments.

"This is for cuts not gunshot wounds," I said.

John smiled at me, a bit too weak for my comfort. I gave him some water and undid the buttons of his shirt. The side of his shirt was as saturated as my pants—a blood transfusion gone wrong. I had no idea how I was going to wrap it and stop the bleeding while he flew us.

"You're losing too much blood." I pressed a lumpy bunch of gauze against the hole. As soon as I pressed, John's face went white. The helicopter wobbled sideways sending me against the passenger seat. He moaned.

"I'm sorry, John. We can't have you passing out. Can you put this thing on autopilot while I dress your wound?"

John gave me another weak smile. "Not possible for the terrain we'll be encountering."

I stared into his dark-rimmed eyes. "At some point in our time together, can we sit on a quiet, sandy beach, somewhere remote, and relax and read without anyone shooting at us? Is that even possible?"

"How about Turks and Caicos?" he said, his grin revealed in his tired eyes.

"Sounds lovely."

"In about two hours we'll land in Dingwall. Or at least close enough," John said.

"Two hours?" He was bleeding too much.

"Wrap me tight. We'll make it," he said.

Several tilts and dives through the air later, his torso was wrapped with a long bandage, as tight as possible, below his rib cage. I hoped his liver or kidney hadn't been shot. The bullet had entered in that vicinity. I asked him questions about his family and his favorite places to shoot photos, anything to keep him talking and alert. During the first hour he seemed fine, but forty-five minutes later he began to be nonsensical. He rambled about MI6 and how they probably killed our families.

"John." I attempted to get him to focus on our present situation. "John."

"What?" He sounded drunk.

"Where are we headed?" I hoped he knew.

"The Highlands."

"Is that where Dingwall is?" I asked. If only I had my phone, I could search Dingwall.

"Dingwall?"

"John, where is Dingwall located?" My heart had a desperate adrenaline surge.

He pointed weakly at an LCD screen with a lit up terrain map. "Dingwall…" He was too pale. His unfocused eyes glanced at me. "Uhhh…you're so beautiful."

"I hardly believe you since you can't seem to focus." I had no doubt luck flew us—John certainly wasn't. Luck weaved us over the rippled lochs and around the surrounding autumn coloured hills and snow-capped mountain peaks that shadowed us between tributary rivers and streams. We had to be close to our destination; the land looked like the Highlands.

The helicopter gave a precarious jump upwards as John's eyes shut. I pounded on his shoulder to revive him and he gained a bit of control. "John! You need to land this thing." He could not pass out in the air, not at this altitude. I took a quick look around at the dense tree line on either side of the river he'd been following. A grassy valley nestled in the hills opened ahead of us. I prayed the valley was near Dingwall, or close enough to have quick access to a hospital.

His head bobbed and his eyes drooped. The helicopter plunged downwards.

"John!" I grabbed his shoulder, but no response. I then did something that I would forever deny doing—I pushed on his wound. He needed his own adrenaline surge. His eyes opened up as he cried out in pain. It worked. But we flew too low. If we continued our sideways slide, we'd fly into the pine and birch trees whose branches already brushed our underbelly.

"John, we're here. Find a place and land us." I took his chin in my hand and turned his face slightly to the right hoping he would veer right and away from the line of trees below us and to our left. It worked. He nodded and maneuvered the helicopter away from the green, orange, and red line of the trees. We looked more like a bird flying with a hurt wing. Pictures of rotors stabbing the unforgiving ground and spinning off to cut the cabin in two filled my thoughts and I said a prayer—my first prayer in years—that we wouldn't crash and break apart.

Still airborne, we bounced up and down, closer and closer to the ground and the trees. A clearing opened up in front of us, surrounded by large pines and birches with branches reaching out to us. The center contained golden grasses, reddish-brown, tainted bracken, and other ferns—not a bad area for landing.

"The clearing, John." I pointed. "Aim for that clearing."

A slight clarity appeared in his eyes, no doubt brought on by the relief of seeing an open space. He slowed the craft down and we drifted precariously above the clearing. We twisted and jostled back and forth. He gained control and lowered us until we hovered about three meters from our landing. Then we pitched to the left where a group of waving birch limbs waited for us.

"John!"

He nodded and said, "Control is yaw." And we turned right. The diamond-shaped leaves on the trees blew off and swirled around us in a gush of gold and yellow, but the rotors avoided the branches.

Two meters from the ground, we listed to the right. He corrected and we lurched upwards and back down. Barely above the ground, but not yet touching it, he pulled back on the stick and we dropped. The ground met us with a surge that rattled my spine and kinked my neck. John shut off the helicopter and the rotors slowed. His eyes met mine and his lips turned up in a weak and grateful smile before he flopped sideways and passed out.

Chapter 12
THE KEEPERS

Dingwall, Scotland

His eyes opened. He tried to raise his head, but gasped at the pain that surged through his left side near his ribs. Memories flooded back—he'd been shot. He took a deep breath and winced at the pain it inflicted. At that point he kept still, only his eyes moved as he tried to get his bearings. He saw the leather seats, windows, and rotors. He was lying in the back of a helicopter…

"The helicopter? Zoe?" he thought. He ignored the pain and raised his head to look around for her. She wasn't inside the helicopter. She could be lying outside hurt. He tried to roll over and noticed a piece of paper tied to his wrist. He untied the paper and unrolled a note written by Zoe.

> *John,*
> *Went to get help for our hunting accident. I'm*
> *so sorry.*
> *Love, Z* 1020

Hunting accident? His pain made it difficult for him to think, but he soon realized she used a hunting accident as cover for him being shot. He smiled; it might work. He glanced at his watch. She'd been gone an hour. He gripped onto the passenger seat next to him and tried to sit up. It required too much effort. He slipped down, his eyes rolling back as he succumbed to unconsciousness.

The Highlands, a place to enjoy a lunch atop the hills overlooking the lochs and rivers and smell the crisp, blustery air—unless you needed to find a doctor for your dying friend and you're lost next to a river that you're unable to cross. My breathing came in labored spasms from my brisk walk, or rather my hike. I walked parallel to a rather large river, following it upstream. Downstream made more sense, but while John seemed to barely stay alert, he had flown us over a road and some homes minutes before we went down. I wished I'd paid closer attention to what we had flown over instead of hyper-focusing on John's ability to land us safely. I thought the road ran behind us, upstream and on the other side of the river. With another quick glance from the helicopter window, I had noticed a small bridge that crossed the river. This bridge carried hope that it might lead me to a road where I could hail a car. Following the river also gave me a direct route back to John—he'd die if I could not locate him again. Before I began my hike, I had used rocks to create an arrow next to the river to point the path from the river to John.

So far on my hike I had not discovered any roads, or trails, or signs of people, just birches, bracken and pines blocking my way and squirrels collecting seeds. I also saw several deer. Each animal scurried off into the brush when I approached. Rocks were plentiful in this area and so were the crags. The boulders thickened and pressed along the narrow river path. I had to climb around huge sections of lichen-covered hills of rock too large for me to climb over the top. After winding around these sections I had to make my way back alongside the river. I moved around yet another grouping. This one had so many trees it was hard to tell what came first, the flora and fauna or the boulders.

I held onto a branch that gave me support as I climbed up and over a sturdy rock, slippery with moss. Once over the rock, I let go of the branch and let it swing into its place above me. I looked down and stopped. I stood on what appeared to be a marked path. After taking a couple steps closer to the river, I paused in amazement. The river opened up a beautiful gorge with a splatter of sunrays warming spots across the black water down below me. Above the gorge was the bridge—the bridge that held my hope.

I rushed forwards along the marked path and kept the bridge in sight. The sounds of the river grew loud due to the amount of water jetting over a barricade of dark boulders. The boulders created a waterfall and a wall of black rock upstream from the bridge. The scene made the bridge a perfect photo location for the falls. The bridge was of the suspension type—bridges weren't my favorite and this one in particular could easily have the troll that bedtime stories warned about. I had seen spirits, who's to say all the other things didn't exist too? A sign cautioned that only five people at a time should cross this bridge. Maybe the troll, I imagined, could only snatch and eat five people at a time. I focused on the idea of a human-eating troll to control my fear of a frightening, rickety bridge so weak it could only hold up to five people. The sign failed to mention if they were heavy people or skinny people.

The side rails were a combination of metal on top with chain-link metal fencing on the sides to prevent people from slipping off the wood-support panels lining the planks. I gripped onto the rail and stepped lightly onto the wood panels. Even with my light footstep, the bridge began to sway. My next stride made the bridge bounce. I stopped, unable to take another step. As my white knuckles gripped the side and the bridge continued to flow and sway, I pictured John, shot and bleeding to death behind me. An adrenaline rush of courage moved me across that bridge. I looked down between the slats to see the water rush below. Looking down wasn't such a great idea. I brought my eyes up and took another small and bouncy step. I continued to walk across the wood planks and tried not to think about the thin metal cables that suspended the weight of the bridge to the metal posts on either end. Relieved to see no other person attempting to cross from the other side, I continued to step across.

With a final leap from the bouncing, swaying bridge, I landed with a jolt up my spine where the path continued. I took a few breaths to calm my racing heart and noticed that the path split. One path went upstream and the other went downstream. I had to choose wisely; time was short. I chose the path to the left—downstream. Before long, the path veered away from the river. I grew hopeful that I'd soon reach the end of the trail. Another fork in the road dashed my hope. I turned right and continued away from the river. My progress slowed when the path began to climb. In my exhaustion, I hardly noticed the rich reds and yellows of fall before I stumbled over a rock and face-planted into the foliage. I picked myself up, spit out pieces of yellow leaves, pulled out a bracken frond that had tangled in my hair, and labored onwards.

Growing anxious that I had made the wrong choice, I decided to walk another minute before turning back to try the alternate route. I forced myself to pick up speed and plodded along at a weary jog, my feet dragging over random pebbles on the path. One more bend in the road and the tree line ended. The path stopped. An empty car park spread out before me. I caught my breath and took in my surroundings. Situated alongside the car park was a road—I could hail a car for help.

I ran to the road, stood at the edge, and looked both ways. The road was empty, but a distant sound of engines grew louder. Within seconds, a line of three identical black lorries drove my way. Each lorry was laden with stumps and logs. I jumped up and down and waved my arms above my head. The first passed me before it slowed down, pulled to the side of the road, and stopped. The other two pulled behind the first. The doors opened in succession and three muscular men stepped out. They towered over a petite lady with a softly wrinkled face and spiky-black hair with streaks of grey. She approached me; the softness in her blue eyes made me want to curl up on a couch next to her with a book and have her read to me. She wore a cowl-neck sweater that matched her eyes. Two of the men— other than the tattoos on their arms—were mirror images of one another with coffee-coloured hair that curled over their heads. After a second look, I guessed they were about five or six years older than me. The third man, an older version of the other two, had curly-grey hair and a red beard mixed with grey that covered his face. Each of them wore a button-down shirt with the sleeves rolled up. They all wore mud-splattered work boots. The grey-haired man patted the woman's back and I assumed he was her husband, and the young men their sons. She had a smile on her face until she looked down at my crusty-red pants and the smile disappeared.

"Guid mornin. Can A gie ye a haund?" She had a worried look.

"It's my husband. We were hunting and he caught a stray bullet."

"Where is he?" she asked, her speech slower and more English after hearing my accent. She remained surprisingly calm after my announcement.

"On the other side of the river. I walked along the river's edge forty or fifty minutes before finding the bridge."

"Upstream or downstream?" asked the grey-haired man, his Scots accent thick, but understandable.

"I walked upstream."

"Aye, lass. A ken where he is." She gestured for the men to get back in the lorries and gave them some instructions. "Currie up." She then hooked my arm in hers and said, "Come wi's." She rushed me towards the last of the waiting lorries where the bearded man sat in the driver's seat.

"Our home is near where yer man is. The lads will drop off their trucks and get the car and meet us. We can drive him, blues and twos if necessary, to the infirmary."

"Blues and twos?" I asked.

"Lass, this is yer guid day." The man's bushy grey eyebrows raised. "My Ceana is the doctor in these parts. Has her own ambulance."

I looked at her in surprise. Ceana was staring at my trousers. "From the looks of ye, he's lost a lot of bluid," she said.

I nodded, not wanting to tell her I had soaked up more than one man's blood that morning.

"Ceana's a great doctor. She'll have him fixed and ready to attend the bonfire the morn nicht."

"That'd be Conall. He may be biased, but nae problem; we'll do our best for yer man. The other lads are our sons Sean and Eadan. Now whit's yer name, lass?"

"Zoe. My husband is John." I had forgotten about Bonfire Night. It would be a cause for celebrating if John felt better by then. I'd have liked nothing more than to burn effigies of Guy Fawkes, except I wouldn't be thinking about the man who tried to burn down parliament. Not this November 5th.

It hadn't taken us long to drive to where John landed the helicopter. The river was a couple of minutes of bumpy driving from the main road. Conall drove upstream a few more minutes until we saw the clearing with the helicopter. I had walked the complete opposite way to get help. Fortunately, John still had a pulse. After reaching John, his breathing sounded shallow and his saturated bandage had a dark-maroon hue. I gathered his hand in mine and noticed the note was no longer attached to his wrist; it laid crinkled up in a corner. His eyes were shut now, but he had awoken and read the note. I felt some relief knowing that.

Sean and Eadan arrived in a Land Rover that they drove near to the helicopter. The Land Rover had been converted into an ambulance duly suited for the terrain of the Highlands.

Ceana took John's vitals with a smile and patted my arm. "He's a hard lad. We'll leave the bandage on him 'til we git to the infirmary. I kin get some bluid in him on the way." She turned to Conall. "Ye and Sean, get John in the car." She looked at me. "Let us load up yer things. And Eadan, ye drive the lorry home."

The contents of my bag were tossed about on the floor of the helicopter. Ceana picked up my torch, a shampoo bottle and a hairbrush, and put them inside my bag. And, before I realized it, she had picked up the mana. She paused and stared at it. "Does this go too?"

"Ah, yeah," I said, my voice revealing an odd inflection.

She studied the wax, tried compressing it with her hand, and then glanced over at me before she set it in the bag. After that, I grabbed the remaining items—paper, pens, and a pair of trousers— and stuffed them inside my bag.

"We canna leave yer guns here," she said.

"What?" I asked. John's moaning had distracted me while Conall and Sean loaded him on a gurney.

"Yer guns?" Ceana asked.

I nodded and pulled John's revolver and my pistol out of their hidden spot behind the seats. Ceana didn't raise an eyebrow over the fact we didn't have one hunting rifle in our mix. She had been more curious about the mana than our assortment of supposed hunting equipment.

John's bouncy ride over the rough ground and into the ambulance looked miserable and had him mumbling unintelligible words. I grabbed John's bag, shut the doors of the helicopter, and half jogged half ran to the ambulance. The wheel legs folded under the gurney as they pushed it into the back of the Land Rover. Ceana and I climbed in next to the gurney. The space was tight, but Ceana made room for me on her seat. She hooked John up to an IV, cursing Conall for driving like a brute. Once we drove onto a smooth road and John's IV fed into his arm, Ceana took my hand and stared earnestly into my eyes. The depth of her stare scared me. "Zoe, were ye on a hunting trip or did ye come to Dingwall for another reason?"

"Ceana, that's none of our business," Conall yelled from the front seat.

I felt faint and my mouth went dry. She's a doctor, what did I expect except she could see through my cover. We weren't dressed like hunters. She probably thought we were running from the law.

"Never mind that," she yelled back at Conall.

"Please," I said. "Can you please help him? We're not bad people, but there are strange men after us for reasons I can't explain."

Ceana sat quiet for a moment and adjusted John's IV fluid. After the adjustment, she leaned towards Conall and said, "Ring Eadan, have him pick up Neil and go back and hide that helicopter."

"Why?" he asked.

"Because we'll all be in danger if they don't."

"I don't want to cause you danger," I said. "Drop us off at the hospital. I'm sure we'll be fine."

"Conall, take us home. The infirmary is too dangerous," she said.

"Ceana, we've been married a long while and I usually get ye. But the infirmary is what the lad needs," Conall said.

I looked from one to the other, confused. I wasn't the only one confused; Sean had his eyebrows pressed together, too.

"Conall, I will take care of John in our home. We must ring Nurse Gibbons to meet us there." She still held my hand in hers. She squeezed it gently and said, "Zoe, tell me 'bout the mana, or grave wax, in yer bag."

Conall asked, "Did ye say mana?"

"Yes."

Conall gave Sean a quick glance and said, "Ring the boys." But Sean had already pushed a number on his smart phone.

Maybe the lack of sleep had slowed my brain, but the only thing that registered with me was keeping my secret life secret. "I do grave rubbings," I said.

Ceana continued to stare at me with her intense blue eyes. A thought crossed my tired mind but I pushed it away before it fully functioned as a thought, because the chances were too absurd for me to bring it to fruition.

"Is John a writer?" she asked.

"I'm a writer, he's a photographer." Was she inferring what I thought she was inferring?

"Zoe, I am a writer."

I didn't say anything, but continued to allow what she said to unscramble itself in my mind. I waited and stared back into her eyes, not wanting to reveal anything I shouldn't.

She continued, "I write when Conall hosts." It sounded like she was speaking cryptically, too, not saying much. She paused.

Conall took the phone from his son and gave the location of the helicopter. Whoever was on the other end of the phone must have asked why because his next words were unmistakable. "They are Archivists and someone is after them."

"You are Hosts and Writers?" I asked, almost in a statement.

Ceana took a breath of relief and said, "Yes."

Mystified, I looked at her. "What are the chances of this? I mean, you being the ones I flag down on the road."

Ceana nodded her head. "Ye must ken that we're much assisted in our line of work."

"I didn't know. I've only been an Archivist for a couple of months, and John for less than a year." After the close calls these past couple of months, I had to agree that we were much assisted.

"Aye," Ceana said.

While she checked John's IV again, Conall asked, "Do ye know who shot John?"

"I don't know their names, but they might be MI6."

"That can't be guid," he said. His jaw tightened and he shared a look with his son.

"Whit's yer full names?" Ceana asked.

When I told her, she touched my arm and smiled. "Yer and John's parents were guid people."

"You knew my parents?"

"Yer mum and dad worked with us until yer father died. I'm surprised ye don't remember us. Maybe our home will remind ye."

Knowing that Ceana had worked with my parents gave me much needed comfort. The tension in my muscles began to fade as I relaxed. I put my hand on John's arm. I really needed him to be fine.

Conall turned the Land Rover onto a narrow, paved road lined with green pines and assortments of trees drooping with fall colours. We passed a line of Rowans laden with dotted clumps of red berries that hung in sharp contrast to the yellow-orange leaves. The tree line ended to reveal a grass-covered field with rolling hills of shrubs and trees in the background before being closed from view by another section of fall tints that paralleled the road. These trees were thicker than the others, pressing together to provide a wall of privacy with branches covered in dark burgundy and yellow. The branches interwove with the high-reaching pines dotted along the road. A slight break in the trees revealed a slender section of gravel road. Conall slowed and turned onto the gravel lane. The limbs brushed the sides of the ambulance as he drove us down the road.

Seconds later, the path met a driveway where two of the loaded trucks that I had seen earlier were parked in front of a garage. The garage doors were closed, which made me curious to see what automobiles might be hidden inside. Across from the garage rested their home. As soon as I saw the house, I remembered coming here. The home had hints of German in the design. The two-story was covered in amber-tinted wood and white plaster with a high-pitched, slate roof. The windows were plentiful and artfully framed in wood against a white-plastered canvas. Dark shades of amber wood covered two sides of the home along with the balcony on the top level. The balcony overlooked the surrounding green field where patches of brown announced the coming of winter. The home's backdrop of hills and the foreground of trees lining the road gave it complete privacy.

Ceana raised her eyebrows at me. I smiled in return and said, "I remember." She looked pleased.

I remembered running through the fields playing rugby with a group of laughing and smiling boys and their twin sisters, both wee tots. It had been before my father died—a very happy time.

John's surgery went well. Ceana had me assist, along with her nurse who had worked with her for several years and she felt could be trusted not to report the gunshot wound. After the surgery, John continued to sleep until dinnertime. He woke up grumpy and confused. I told him how we'd stumbled upon a household of Archivists with a doctor and that we'd be staying with the Mackenzies in Dingwall until he felt better. This news calmed him down. What I didn't tell him was how, out of worry about Shaw not knowing what happened to me, I had found a telephone and rang home. If I hadn't, Shaw would have notified the authorities to start a search for me. I recalled a time when I went rock climbing in America and in my haste to leave I forgot to notify Mum or Shaw. I didn't want to relive that mistake again while hiding in Dingwall. I told Shaw a story of how John surprised me with an excursion to Dingwall and we had gone on a morning hike along a river where John slipped and hurt his shoulder. This required him to remain still and rest up. I also had Shaw overnight me a package of clothes, a week's worth, enough to last me while we stayed in Dingwall.

After John awoke, Ceana put fresh bandages on his wound and told him he had no organs damaged and should expect a quick recovery. She brought us clean clothes, a blue button-down shirt for John to slip his arms into, a pair of denims for each of us, and a hand-knit purple sweater for me. Everything fit amazingly well. After his wound was re-bandaged, he insisted on walking to the dining room to join us for dinner. The nurse had gone home after the surgery and Ceana and I each gathered one of John's arms to assist his teetering walk to the dining room.

We sat around a log-style, rectangular table next to a wall of high windows filled with the darkness of the night. Below the windows, glass doors opened to a cement patio. Two wooden benches were positioned on one side of the table and six heavy wooden chairs along the other side with an additional chair on each end.

A mix of red-haired and dark-haired young men filed into the dining room. Most were about my age or older. I recognized two of the young men, Sean and Eadan, who had helped with our rescue. Their muscular builds showed beneath their wool sweaters. Two girls, a few years younger than me, followed behind them. Their copper tresses brightened the room. They all said hello. Two of the youngest elbowed each other as they sat on the bench. Conall took his seat at the head of the table with Ceana seated on the corner next to him. John and I sat in the chairs next to Ceana. Our mouths hung open as we counted the number of mouths to be fed—and not just the quantity, but also the size of the lot. I did not recall this many young ones when playing here years ago. The men had wider shoulders than John and like him they were all muscle. Ceana and her daughters were tiny in comparison. The young ladies were identical except for the cut of their hair; one was cut in a short pixie style and the other wore her locks draped down her back. Each had eyes the crisp-blue of Ceana's,

"This is most of our brood," Conall said. He waved his bicep-pumped arm back and forth as he pointed to them one by one, "Sean, Eadan, Neil, Thor, the twins Iseabail and Barabal, and that's Craig." He smiled proudly and continued. "Our two married sons, Carl and John, live in Shetland, each with a couple wee bairns."

"And two more on the way," added Ceana. She took Conall's hand in hers.

"Nine children," I said.

"Ten, Nathan should be here soon," she said. Her eyes glowed bright.

I had no words for that and John's face said it all. He hadn't blinked since he sat down.

"Each of our brood is an Archivist. Our youngest, Nathan, started last year at fourteen," Conall said. He pointed at a dark-haired clone of the others who walked in and took the last seat. He looked older than his fifteen years.

"A think they're beginning younger the day," Ceana said.

"Puberty brings it on?" I asked.

Giggles erupted from the two younger lads.

"Canna ken for sure," Ceana said. "But we are lucky, since all of them are Archivists we can discuss this secret amongst us."

They were lucky. I'd never be able to discuss this with Shaw.

Ceana said, "Each of them has a partner who they enjoy working with. That is rare too."

"A partner?" John asked.

"The Host or Writer that they archive with," Conall said.

"We get together and do our Archive homework several times a month," Barabal said.

Several of them laughed.

"It's our study group," said Iseabail.

More laughter went around the table.

John looked thoughtful before saying, "With the few numbers of Archivists left in the world, I'm guessing you realize the percentage you have just sitting here in this room."

"Aye, John," Ceana said, with a glance at Conall, "that we do."

"Stew won't be guid cold," said Conall. He held Ceana's hand and grabbed his son's on the other side of him and bowed his head. John and I glanced at one another and linked hands along with everyone else. After the blessing, Ceana took a ladle and scooped lamb stew into navy-blue bowls until they overflowed. The bowls steamed from the top and dripped broth down the sides as each person received one.

"This is very good of you to fix me up and take us in," John said.

"And feed us too," I added.

"Don't ye worry about the denner; we have aplenty."

John said little while we ate. He listened to their descriptions of the events of the day—preparing for Bonfire Night and hiding the helicopter with a brown tarp and pine branches. He helped fill in details while we relayed the narrative of our journey to Dingwall.

Ceana shook her head. "It was guid that I saw the mana ye have or we would have taken ye to the infirmary. The shooters might have tracked ye down because of the gunshot wound." She looked at John and smiled. "Ye have more colour in your cheeks."

"I'm feeling stronger. Thanks."

"Ye're welcome. In our work we're practically kin." She smiled.

Conall dismissed the twins and the two younger boys, Craig and Nathan, telling them not to be late. During dinner, the four had quietly talked amongst themselves, in between texting on their smart phones. After being dismissed, they kissed their parents' cheeks, and Conall gave Iseabail a set of keys. They grabbed jackets off of pegs by the side door and all four of them ran into the night laughing. To John and me, Conall mentioned that they were attending a training class with their partner Archivists.

Watching them leave, I suddenly felt old and wished I could go and attend the class with them. How nice it would have been if Mum and Dad had let me know who I was and gave me the opportunity to learn in special Archive classes. I guessed that it had been too difficult to keep things from Shaw. That left the question of why they didn't teach me after Shaw had left home. I glanced around the table, eight of us left, and of the eight I was one of the youngest—why did I feel so old? Maybe it was the look on Conall's face, the look of someone who wanted answers—answers that were best discussed only in the presence of adults, which, for the first time in my life, included me.

Ceana had us stack the dishes in her porcelain sink and said she'd give them a scrub later. "I think we best have a talk now. John looks like he could use some rest so we best keep it quick."

We moved into a comfortable room filled with soft lights and plush aqua-blue pillows tossed about on four leather chairs and two sofas, all in a rich taupe. In the middle of the room, on the wood floor planks, a creamy circular rug hugged the chairs and sofas in a circle. After one of my stocking-covered feet touched the thickness of the rug I immediately wanted to spin around like a puppy and curl up on it, with a cup of tea set within reach on the flagstone hearth of the fireplace. Perhaps I could forget about killers and grave markers and for a minute stop the thoughts about my parents' murders.

I helped John get situated on one of the sofas and sat next to him, close enough to feel his warmth. His unbuttoned shirt revealed his wrapped up abs and stomach. His chest was exposed and for a brief moment I wanted to rest my head against it. Looking at him was as good as sipping hot tea near a warm fire. I caught him studying my face and flushed, the warmth filling my cheeks. He surprised me and took my hand, interlacing my fingers in his.

After everyone was comfortably seated, Conall said, "John, speak freely and let us ken whit's going on."

John inhaled, grimaced, and then nodded. "Yesterday and this morning some of my worst fears were realized. A group of individuals have found out about us. I don't know exactly who are all involved, but I confirmed that they've kidnapped Archivists, possibly to use them in extracting information from the dead. But for what purpose, I don't know."

Several moments of silence passed before Conall asked, "How

did ye git this information?"

"Edward Thomas," John said. "He was shot this morning while he tried to get us away in his helicopter."

Conall bowed his grey head.

"You knew him?" I asked.

"He once saved my life." Conall's voice was filled with emotion and Ceana took his hand in hers.

"Do ye ken the names of those taken?" Ceana asked.

"Edward's wife, Missy, is one of them. Also Phil and Lily Woods. And others in America whose names I don't know."

Ceana hugged her chest and gasped. "Ah, such guid people."

Conall stood up and slammed both his fists on a dark oak sideboard along the wall next to the fireplace. His powerful fists made the table jump, as well as the rest of us in the room. My heart pounded. He said, "We need to warn those of us that are left. All of our lives are in danger. I thought something was amiss, but wasn't positive. I wanted to wait until our annual gatherin' to bring it up. But they need to ken now. Ye have the proof we need to warn them. What do ye think, Sean?" Conall looked at the man who appeared to be their oldest son living at home. He had his mother's kind eyes that displayed a keen sense of understanding.

"We should change the gatherin' place location," Sean said.

"Of course," said Ceana. "How about we gather at the original Althing?"

"Tha's guid. A think those in charge would agree with that. A verra safe location," Conall said.

I couldn't tell if John nodded his head more from agreement or from feeling poorly. He remained quiet. I asked, "Could we help make the arrangements and get the word out?"

"Nae. Ye two enjoy the holiday the morn and have John recuperate. Besides, since we've been Archivists longer, we ken who to notify." Conall paused, glanced around at his sons, and said, "Lads, yer mum and I need to discuss a few more items with these two. Why don't ye check with those in town about our own security?" The room seemed to expand after the four large figures departed.

Conall remained quiet for a few moments after his sons left. His bushy eyebrows pursed together in thought. When John's head nodded sideways, Conall cleared his throat.

"I ken you're tired John so I will be quick. Ceana and I." He glanced at Ceana, who nodded for him to continue, "We are the ones in charge; we *are* the Keepers. Something you haven't been told yet. We normally wait until an Archivist has been archiving for at least a year and is twenty-one years old. As Keepers of the Archivists and guardians of the law, our job is to hold the gatherin's. We will show ye our Dingwall Althing the morn and tell ye more at that time." Conall gave us a teeth-grinding grin.

I didn't know what that job was, but with the surprised look on John's face I grew curious, and more so because I'd be able to see another Althing. After being amazed and mesmerized by the last Althing, I knew I'd have a hard time sleeping tonight with the anticipation of seeing another archive.

Chapter 13
LAW BOOK

John was mystified. After years of searching, interviewing, paying off adversaries, along with the recent killings, the secret that had eluded them for years was announced casually after dinner. The knowledge that Conall and Ceana Mackenzie were the Keepers meant that where he now stayed might be the Alstead location. If what he had been told was true, a single Alstead place existed, but he had to prove it. Traditionally, the Keepers were the only people who knew the Alstead's location and it made sense that it would be located near where the Keepers lived.

He needed to be careful—not push too hard. He didn't want to endanger the confidence the Mackenzies had in him. The next crucial step would be to discover, or to disprove, the existence of the Law Book and the Book of Lineages. Both books were thought to be a myth.

During the Bonfire Night festivities, he would take a chance and search. Keeping Zoe close had been worth the risk. Without realizing it, she had helped make his cover more real, but caution had always been his number one rule and he didn't want her to know about his plans to find the Law Book and Book of Lineages. He would have searched during the night had he not been so tired and weak.

I awoke hours before the sun would show itself, which really wasn't that early this far north. I pulled on the sweater Ceana gave me and pulled my hair back into a ponytail before I met John, Ceana, and Conall in the kitchen. They were each dressed in knitted sweaters, including John, looking very dapper in blue. After eating scones and gravy, we donned coats and headed to the Dingwall Althing. My breath steamed in the icy morning chill of the air.

Conall opened the door of the lorry closest to the house. We packed ourselves into the front seat with me trying to lean away from John and not put pressure on his wound. He seemed all right and didn't complain, but with every bump in the road he drew a sharp intake of breath. I knew he hurt. I imagined if the circumstances weren't so grave he would have stayed in bed.

It was a short ten-minute drive into town. Other than darkness, there wasn't much to see. Dingwall looked old, but not dilapidated. The streets were clean and cheery with planters of fall flowers at many entrances. The white trim on the aged buildings that lined the streets stood out crisp in the night. The storefronts we passed had dark windows, except for a bakery. Other than the baker, we appeared to be the only ones in town at this hour. Conall turned the lorry into a car park where a circular monument stood in the center. He shut the headlamps off and drove to the darkest corner of the car park before he shut off the engine.

We walked to the monument and stood on the pebble path that surrounded the shrine. The monument had the shape of a grassy, tiered cake with a metal candle rising to the sky and a bottom tier made out of rock. Ceana held us back while Conall stamped on the stones with his heavy foot in an exaggerated zigzag and half-circle pattern. Once he stamped his way to the rock portion of the tier, he pushed on several large crags and twisted two rocks. He then dodged his mass of a body to the left to not fall into the opening that groaned and slid into place under where he had stood.

One thing became clear to me, being an Archivist certainly came with plenty of mysterious and hidden rooms, along with creepy nighttime rendezvous. Not a boring job if one lived long enough to learn its secrets.

Conall shone his torch into the gaping hole and one by one we stepped down the three stairs, ducking so our heads didn't hit the jagged rock ceiling where he made sure to shine his torch. The inside smelled like catacombs with the odor of damp and moldy mud. It irritated me that archives had been placed in a humid storage facility. Again, I was fooled when Conall pressed a black switch, randomly placed on the rocky wall. Once the switch was pressed, the exit disappeared behind us. He then opened a breaker panel that had a row of buttons above the fuses and circuits. He pressed the first two simultaneously and pressed the next four with a second's pause in between each push. He walked behind me to a metal vault door that I hadn't noticed. Not a huge leap for me not to notice—magicians got me every time with their slight of hand. I paid attention to Conall as he twisted the wheel to open it and a rush of suctioned air blew through us.

"Come," said Conall.

We walked past the vault door into a room the size of a small lift. Opposite the side we entered was another vault door. Above us, a low-voltage light gave off a yellow hue. Conall pulled the vault door shut behind us and twisted a metal handle. We waited in the soft light for a few seconds, long enough for my ears to pop.

"It's pressurized," John said.

"Aye," said Conall. He took two steps to the other door and

entered a pass code on a digital display before he twisted the wheel handle until it clicked and the door opened. We entered a room filled with a concoction of ancient and modern devices. Advanced technology with computers and hardware was situated alongside runestones with their runic inscriptions. Some of the runestones stood as tall and bulky as decades old computers. The temperature was more moderate. John and I began to remove our coats and hang them on a wooden coat rack placed between two dark oak desks, but Conall said we'd need them later.

The immense space of the Althing was similar to a library with its rows upon rows of glass and metal shelves. But, unlike the local library, this room contained the manuscripts of the ages: journals, biographies, memoirs, and secrets. Once again, I wished for the time and seclusion to browse through them and discover these secrets. I thought of the eerie conversation with John's Nana. What secrets were stored that humanity was so ill prepared to hear? What information could be so shocking that it must be secretly stored away until human beings were ready to learn about it? I hoped it wasn't the cure for cancer, or even the common cold. Surely those secrets the world should know.

I saw John's eyes watching me and came out of my ponderings.

"I can see your mind tick like a fast-forwarding clock," he said. He took my arm and wrapped it through his. "As much as we would like to, we don't know everything that's written everywhere. I'm still learning myself." He grinned at me.

"We hear rumors of experiences from other scribes, but no one has the time to sit and read all the world's history," Ceana said.

"Then why do it at all?" I thought the obvious needed to be said.

"I believe the purpose is divine," Ceana said.

John laughed, surprising us all.

"Nae, really, John," Ceana said, "How else do ye explain the spirits speaking through us as Hosts?"

"I can't," John said. He then stood silent and contemplative.

Conall cleared his throat and said, "We gather once a year to discuss any discoveries that may benefit society and decide which of them should be leaked to the world."

"That's the meeting you mentioned last night?" I asked.

"Aye, the gatherin' we'll have in Iceland," Ceana said. "We'll contact everyone tomorrow through coded email. Conall loves the email. We decided it best to give very little notice."

"This Althing is more hi-tech than the one on the Isle of Man," John said as he glanced around.

"Because it's the Keeper's Althing," said Conall. "This is the place for many of the bigger secrets and the things that need to be kept from the world."

"We also have a portion of the original mana and the Law Book," Ceana stated.

John's eyes developed the look of a child on Christmas morning. "The Law Book?" John began. "Does it have a lineage line?"

"Nae. Only the current Keepers are listed in it."

John asked, "Is there a Book of Lineage?"

"A Book of Lineage?" I asked, grateful to be finally getting information about the history of what we do.

"I've heard stories about a book that records the lineage line descending from the very first Archivists, but I've never seen one," Conall said.

"That would go back thousands of years," I said.

"Aye," Ceana said.

"But you've never seen this book?" John asked.

"Nae," Ceana and Conall spoke as one.

Questions stormed through my mind and I had to ask, "Who were the first?"

Conall and Ceana shared a look before Conall said, "I donna ken. There are those who believe that direct blood descendants exist. If there's proof out there, I haven't seen it or met anyone who said they were blood descendants. I guess one would have to prove it somehow if they were a direct line."

I glanced at John and recognized his deep-in-thought look with his mouth in a half grin and a furrow between his eyebrows. I decided to ask what I thought he might be thinking. "Can we see it—the Law Book?"

To my surprise, Conall agreed.

"We brought ye here to see it," Ceana said with a smile, her eyes studying our faces.

"After a long discussion, we decided to allow ye both to ken how it's hidden and where," Conall said.

"Not even our kin have seen it or know where it is kept. It is a Keeper secret," Ceana said, her tone solemn.

"Why us?" John asked.

"With the recent events, if something happened to us, the new Keepers would need to have access to this book," Conall said.

"Wouldn't that be one of your children?" I asked.

"Nae. Upon the death of one or both Keepers, the responsibility always transfers to a different family, not kin." Conall further explained, "For nye a thousand years, the Keepers have been a couple who has lived near or within a few hundred kilometers or so of Dingwall."

"How would we know who to give it to?" John asked.

"When something like the death of a Keeper or any problem with the Keepers occur, the new Keepers' names will appear on the inside cover of the Law Book," Conall said. "We've stood around here long enough, come wi's."

We followed him past the lighted rows of shelves that housed the extensive titles. This Althing wasn't shadowy like the one on the Isle of Man. It had bright LED lights that extended down each row of glass shelves. The only similarity to the Isle of Man, besides the archives, was the ancient runestones placed at the head of each shelf. Although these runestones didn't have any translated descriptions hanging from them, they were magnificent to behold and seemed to have been raised from the ground in which they stood. There was a distinct contrast between the old stones and the modern glass.

"Don't you worry about the glass breaking?" I asked.

"Nae problem. This glass isn't breakable," Ceana said.

Impressed, I nodded and we continued to walk past twenty or thirty rows of shelving before Conall stopped. He pointed to a number etched in the bulletproof glass—Roman numeral thirty-three.

"Remember this number," Conall said. He then turned and walked down the row numbered thirty-three. As he walked down the aisle, he stopped at every other bookcase and showed us a particular sequence that I wondered how we would ever remember. On the middle shelf he either pulled the first book forwards or pushed it backwards. He proceeded down the entire length of the row and performed an exact routine.

I grabbed John by the arm. "I hope you're getting this sequence down because there's no way I'll remember the order."

Conall laughed a deep, smooth bellow. "Ye'll do fine. As long as ye begin with bookcase number two on row thirty-three, it doesn't matter which way and which book ye rock, so long as ye have the correct shelf." He stopped as he came to the wall at the end of the row.

"Now this needs to be exact." He pointed to the last set of shelves, a shelf at chest level that only held books with red bindings. "Ye count seven books across and then, with a bit of effort, ye press the eighth book down. Any other book and this place will have a completely black lockdown for four days, long enough for ye to see hallucinations from lack a oxygen. It's eerie and gruesome, feels like a lifetime."

"Sounds like you know from experience," John said, with a smile forming on his lips.

"Ye bet I ken. And I would not recommend it."

Ceana laughed. "He says he was chased by Grendel until Beowulf rescued him."

"Aye," Conall said. "How else do ye explain this?" He lifted up the side of his shirt to show us a white line of several jagged scars.

"Don't give him a thought," Ceana said. "He scraped himself on a rake."

Conall's face went red—a striking contrast to his grey hair. "Ye watch yerself. A may hit book six and let ye see for yerself." Without taking his eyes off Ceana's face, he raised his fist up and before he brought it down John reached under Conall's thick arm and pressed down book eight, which had the title "Beowulf." John swept his arm away before Conall's fist hit book six.

Conall gave John a stare. "Yer a quick one, even wounded." He shook his head. "Took away all our fun."

Deep in the floor a rumbling occurred and the wall next to us divided into a conveyor belt of sections creating a staircase that lead down to a dark unknown. While I watched the stairs heave and plunk as they formed, John wrapped his arms around his torso. He might have pulled a stitch with his race to press the right book. He gave me a reassuring grin.

"Come along." Ceana tossed her head at her husband, turned on a torch she'd been carrying, and walked down the stairs. The torch lit up a structure more similar to the Althing on the Isle. The cave entrance was moss covered and murky. The chill of the air hit my legs first and then my body as I walked down the steps. Glad I wore my jacket, I folded my arms to trap my body heat.

"It's a bit chilly, but we won't be here long," Ceana said. "The chests are over here."

Stored in the cave-like room were two bulky chests large enough for me to sit on and relax. Both were black. One had an iron plate hanging from the ceiling above it with etched words written in Gaelic. Next to that chest was a waist-high runestone with a short, runic inscription. It gave the distinct feeling that throughout the ages there had been the need to decode and label older instructions and artifacts. I deciphered the words from the iron plate. It said "Law Book of Secrets." After Ceana undid the latch on the nearest chest, she and John opened the lid and leaned it against the wall. Ceana shined her light on the contents. I stepped closer to John and we peered inside.

The Law Book was half the size of the chest when shut and most certainly took the other half when the book opened. The binding of the book amazed me with its beauty; the cover had pebble-sized chunks of metal, wood, and gemstones fused together like a mosaic. The gleam of untarnished copper, gold, and silver were mixed with sparkling emerald, ruby, and sapphire gems all mounted on a square silver plate set in petrified wood. The edges revealed a thick border of the polished wood. The book had a profound and heavy appearance, as if only Atlas could carry it.

John bent over and reached his hands towards the book but Conall leapt forwards, grabbed his arm, and stopped him. "Nae, lad."

John was visibly stunned for a second before he recovered and asked, "Will lightning strike or something?"

Ceana shrugged her shoulders and looked at Conall, who took a step back from the chest.

"Maybe we should let this Welsh lad touch the book and see whit happens. Maybe he wouldn't mind a week of paralysis and drooling, and let's not forget the lovely bed pan," Conall said, with a smirk on his face. "Be ma guest and touch it."

"We'll have nae such thing," Ceana said. "He's feeling poorly besides."

"Oh, come on, woman," said Conall, laughing. "Ye take the fun out of everything."

Ceana shook her head. "It was ghastly. Conall had even been warned." She gave him a stern look and shut the chest with a thud.

I realized that during the time we'd been in the room, Conall, apart from jumping forwards to warn John, had given a wide birth on the side of the cave containing the chests.

"See, he won't even cross towards the middle of the room." Ceana chuckled again.

"You've never read the Law Book?" I asked.

"Now how would ye read it if ye canna touch it?" Conall said.

"But the annual gathering with the reading of the laws and information passed around. How is that possible?" John asked.

"Keeper secret," said Conall.

"If we can't touch it and need to see who the next Keepers are, how do we do it?" John asked.

"First ye need to understand," Ceana began, looking intently at John and me, "only the current Keepers are allowed to be near the book. Because of the disappearances of Archivists, we felt it necessary to show ye."

Conall stopped smiling. "It seems we Keepers could become a target."

"Let's hope not," John said.

"You will need to be together." She walked over to the other chest situated on the floor beyond the Law Book chest and pointed at it.

"The Keeper in this grave box will let ye ken what to do."

I didn't notice any name on the chest or any marks. The chest had a smooth lid and sides, no indication that it was a crypt, although it was large enough to contain a person.

"Who is it? A ghost?" John asked.

"Canna say," Conall said. "But he's a sly one."

John and I stared at the chest that, from the explanation given, contained a mysterious and sly ghost. I shivered, hoping we never needed to return here. If we did, I prayed this ghost was more clever than devious.

"That's it?" John asked.

"Ye just needed to ken where it was," Conall said. He walked out of the cave area and into the tunnels.

"But what if something happens to us as well?" I asked.

Conall poked his head back inside the room. "Then the sly one will take care of things."

John and I glanced at each other, mystified.

"Let's head to McGrady's and have some hot tea," Ceana said, giving me a shoulder hug. "They should have a pot on by now."

"Aye," Conall said.

I was cold and John looked like he needed a rest. Conall took us on a different route to exit, letting us know that the way in was only an entrance and it had two exits, one underneath the church and the other hidden by trees. Like the entrance, the exit had two doors with a pressurized system, except we exited into a spot of woods hidden from the car park. Behind us, the Althing had disappeared. If someone stumbled upon it, they would see a shallow cave surrounded by bushes and pine trees.

Chapter 14
EMBERS BURNING

John didn't dare think himself lucky, for coming to Dingwall had almost cost him his life, but the fact that he, physically, had confirmed the existence of the Law Book with its secrets made him both relieved and wary.

The ease of Ceana and Conall's trust in them amazed him. Never in his life had he trusted anyone after knowing a person for twenty-four hours, or even weeks, or months. Caution kept him alive in his line of work, a survival instinct nested in his genes. Nana had taught him well. But even those he knew well could not be trusted, not when one of them, possibly his superior, had put a price on his head.

He planned to enjoy Bonfire Night and then stick around Dingwall to get his strength back. In the time it took for him to recuperate, he hoped to discover how the Keepers were able to handle the Law Book without becoming paralyzed. He shook his head. He had come close. He had anticipated difficulty in handling something so essential to humanity, yet in his excitement he had become careless and too eager. He smiled as he thought that their unconditional trust in him might enable him to obtain all kinds of Keeper secrets while he recuperated.

I sat at the dining table sipping a cup of hot tea sweetened with honey as I waited for John. After the walk through the Althing and through town, John's feet had dragged. For the first time since I met him, his head had drooped and his eyes had stared down at the walkway more than keeping watch on what happened around him. By mid-morning the townsfolk, many dressed in kilts, began a contest to see who could create the highest bonfire stack. From the noise of the uproar and the shouts from the bystanders, the contest had sounded like clan against clan.

We had walked by numerous piles of wood. Some were more pieces of random furniture than tree branches, but we had passed three that were viable wins for the contest. The townsfolk arrived in town carrying armloads of rubbish to toss onto the frenzied stacks that were already piled with ripped plaid couches, tables with broken or uneven legs, and old chests. Even a baby crib and three stained mattresses leaned into one mountainous heap. Because the piles wouldn't be lit until dusk, I knew John wouldn't last without a break so we left the noise, and Conall and Ceana drove us back to their home to rest.

I glanced outside. The view from the dining table was soothing. The sun's light dipped behind a hill across from the house. When dusk came, the fires would blaze. An hour ago, Conall and his family had headed to Dingwall with their trucks loaded down with additional bonfire supplies from around the farm. They had loaded more tree trunks, a broken rocking chair, warped wood, and some petrol to add vigor to the flames. I had seen enough bonfire stacks in town to know they would form a thick and smoky haze that would blanket the streets and hills for days.

The thought of joining the celebration created beads of sweat on my forehead. I had always enjoyed Guy Fawkes Day and other celebrations with crowds of people that made the party interesting, but the dangers of late had made me anxious. Our misfortune had not happened around crowds of people, so maybe that was the key—safety in crowds and stay in a group. The thought of killers who wanted me dead had me wanting to bring my own protection. I stared at Mum's gun on the table in front of me and tried to decide whether or not to hide it in my bag. Did that make me crazy? I did have John—an injured John.

John walked into the room. He carried a gun in each hand and I laughed out loud. He shot me a look. "I figure we can't be too cautious." He raised his shirt to reveal a knife in a leather clip on his hip and smiled at me. "You don't think this is too much?"

"It's smaller than a machete, I think it's fine." I actually thought it would be nice if he did carry a machete. I gasped at my thought process. What had I turned into?

With a grunt of pain, John bent over and put a gun in an ankle holster already strapped in place. The other gun he put into a shoulder holster covered by his coat.

"We can go and have a good time now." He grinned.

"I've got mine." I got up from the chair and picked up the gun.

He stepped in front of me. "No you don't. You have me."

He took my revolver, removed the bullets, and set the gun on a high shelf and the bullets in his pocket. I guess that settled my dilemma. He held out his arm for me to link mine through, but as I did so I accidently brushed my hand across his bandaged wound. He jerked to the side. "Yeow!"

"Sorry," I said, feeling really bad. I could be so clumsy. "Are you sure you're okay to go?"

He gave me a half-grin and with his good side, put his arm over my shoulder. He walked me out of the door into a serene orange-canopied evening just as a white, four-door sedan pulled into the lane and drove towards us. John tensed, dropped his arm from around my shoulder, and stood between the oncoming car and me. I thought it might be the nurse; she had driven a similar looking sedan.

John whipped around, his face an angry red. "Bloody hell, Zoe. You contacted Shaw?"

Shocked by his anger, I concentrated on the car and driver whose familiar face was clearly visible. I didn't know what to say. John took several deep breaths before he turned around to face the parked car. Shaw stepped out of the vehicle and called out, "Hello, chap."

John displayed a merciless grin and remained standing while I met Shaw halfway and gave him a hug.

Shaw smiled at me. "I decided to bring you your clothes instead of sending them overnight." He walked back to the car to grab the bags.

I took that moment to glance back at John and was sorry I did. His grin vanished and his eyes narrowed at me. I shrugged my shoulders and went to help Shaw with the bags. Shaw declined my offer, carried three bags, and once near enough to John, he tossed the largest one at him. John caught it with a grimace as it struck his chest. I also winced.

"Oh, sorry chap. Forgot you were injured."

In a cold voice John said, "How good of you to come all this way."

"I've been wanting to revisit Scotland."

"I'm sure you have."

I opened the door of the house and hoped the tension would be left outside. They set the bags down inside the doorway and Shaw looked at me and asked, "Where were you two headed?"

John tipped his head and said flatly, "You didn't notice the signs of the national holiday as you drove through the countryside?"

Shaw remained staring at me and asked, "You want to go to the bonfires?"

I didn't understand the game they played, but I'd had enough. "What is it between you two?"

John and Shaw glanced at one another. Both raised their eyebrows and said, "What do you mean?"

I looked from one to the other and said, "That…this thing that you're both doing."

They both had innocent expressions on their faces, covering up the earlier looks I know I'd seen. I watched both of them in wonder. Maybe they were just being protective of me and it had created a little competition between them. "Never mind," I said. "Let's go get a pint and enjoy our evening." I put my arm through Shaw's and swung him towards the door, and then raising my eyebrows in warning I glanced at John. He shrugged his shoulders and with his eyebrows raised he tilted his head at me.

The countryside had dots of light on the hills, the approach to town lit up by smoking bonfires. After Shaw questioned me about where we stayed and I made up a story about the Mackenzie's relationship to John, we drove the remainder of the way to Dingwall in silence. We arrived to discover the streets littered with flames, some of the blazes taking up the full expanse of an intersection. We soon learned that unless we wanted to blister the red paint on Conall's Volkswagen Bug, we needed to park. We found a narrow space between the front and back of two smart cars and pulled in between them on Church Street, not far from McGrady's Pub.

We walked down Church Street, passing the Althing location and the crowded car park on our left, and followed the street past the church grounds to a cross street where a blazing fire warmed our faces as we walked by. The street narrowed. We passed the long, stone library on our right and what looked like a row of flats on our left. Church Street ended at High Street and we turned right. To me, the street seemed too narrow for fires, but several burned. I was relieved to see they were a bit smaller in size. The street was paved with unburnable red brick and the shops were made with stone, rock, and plaster—less likely to catch fire. Slender shops clustered next to each other on both sides of the street. We passed the bakery and sandwich shop where a lingering smell of fresh bread made my mouth water.

Teenagers carrying effigies of Guy Fawkes, the man who tried to burn down parliament, ran to the fires and threw him in the blaze. Shaw dropped a few pence into the hands of some children repeating, "Penny for the Guy?" Groups of families and friends, all dressed in plaid, gathered around the fires for the warmth and festivities. Raucous singing and laughter echoed off the buildings and down the road. The heat of the fires warmed the street like a furnace and felt cozy on my face and legs. As we walked along looking for Conall and Ceana, someone pushed a friendly pint into our hands. I began to relax and enjoy myself even though Shaw and John did not say one word to each other.

We approached a bonfire larger than any we had yet passed, built where several streets joined together. John pointed his finger for me to look beyond the blaze. I laughed at the scene of Conall and his lads launching a massive tree trunk onto the flames. When it landed, several embers the size of my hand erupted over the street.

"Watch it!" yelled a shopkeeper involved in a friendly foot display to dance out the embers near his shop.

Shaw tapped my arm. "I'm going to check out a shop we just passed."

"Oh, all right. But hurry, I want to introduce you to Conall and his family over there." I pointed.

"I should be along shortly. If not, don't wait, I can meet them later." He smiled and hurried away.

Conall saw us and hailed us, "Guid eenin, cousins. Come feel the heat from our winnin' fire."

John and I circled the fire. John patted Conall on the back and congratulated him.

"Aye, four years in a row." Conall grinned.

The warmth circulated to both sides of the street. Several parents moved their children and teens away after seeing their pink faces warmed from the heat. Any closer to the flames and I would have to worry about John's guns and his pockets carrying my bullets.

"Are we too close? Is your chest and ankle going to burst like popcorn?" I asked.

John leaned his head back and laughed, then held his side. "No, we'll be fine here." John finished off his pint. "So, cousin? I'm guessing that's our cover."

Conall nodded. "Yer not the only strange faces celebrating with us. I see ye had a man with ye?"

"My brother, Shaw. He knows nothing about our work."

Conall nodded in understanding.

"Is it unusual for strangers to be here?" John asked.

"Aye," said Conall.

He took John's glass as a young woman walked by carrying a tray loaded down with both empty and filled pints. He replaced John's glass with a full one and placed it in John's waiting hand.

"If that's the case, maybe I don't need another," John said.

"Keep it in your hand, lad, ye don't need to drink it." Conall smiled as John nodded, and then Conall said, "Stay near us and speak as little as possible."

A group of lads, consisting of Conall's boys and a few I didn't recognize, had strolled over to us.

Surprising me from behind, Ceana linked her arm through mine. "Quite the holiday this eenin."

I heard the worry behind her words. "Should we leave?" I asked.

"Nae, guid to be in a group. Keep with us and we'll stay away from the strangers."

"Maybe they're tourists. One stranger is my brother, Shaw," I said.

She gave a worried smile. "Tourists with guns?"

Either the people behind the shootings knew we were here, or they had sent people because they thought Dingwall was a possible location where we might seek refuge. The thought of those who were after us knowing we stayed here made me more anxious.

"Cheer up and let's eat," said Conall.

When I didn't see Shaw anywhere, I figured he had picked himself up a lady friend. I didn't mind; the tension had eased with him gone and he knew where we planned to eat.

John and I stayed quiet as Conall and Ceana led us into the back corner of the crowded McGrady's where tables were prepared for us. It might have been my paranoia tricking me, but it seemed that the townsfolk were assisting to keep us from view of the entrance. John must have noticed it too; he confirmed my thoughts when he asked, "The town is helping us?"

"Our corner of the world has many loyal Archivists. They don't take well to our secrets getting out, or to people being shot at and taken," Conall answered.

"How many strangers have you seen?" I asked.

"At least ten," said Sean, Conall's eldest son living at home. He sat down next to Ceana.

"Our guess is they, they being whoever is after ye, have sent spies to every Althing location in the North as a hopeful means of finding ye," Conall said.

"We received a bulletin at the infirmary today informing us to keep watch for a man with a gunshot wound. They gave a guid description of ye, but no photos." Ceana picked up a pint and took a sip.

"They're using official lines to track ye," Sean said.

"Interestin'," Conall said.

I remained quiet and ate the bowl of shepherd's pie the server put in front of me. How did we know whom to trust? Or should I be asking myself whom should I trust? John sat across from me chewing a mouthful of bread that he had dipped in his bowl as I pondered over a few puzzling things about him. He had known the man who shot at us at the morgue; he knew how to fly a helicopter and he always seemed to have resources at his disposal. Was he only a photographer and Archivist, or did he have another life that should concern me? What did I really know about him? He had saved my life, several times, but those events could have been planned or set up. It was almost too coincidental for him to show up and rescue me during each of the shootings at the graveyard. Could I trust myself to think straight when around John? I wanted to hate him for taking me away from my home and putting me in danger. John smiled at me from across the table and my heart quickened. And then there's that—that thing that happens to me whenever he smiles or takes my hand. I gave him a half smile in return. Just a half smile—I didn't want to encourage him. Until I found the answers to some of these questions, I needed to temper these feelings between us. The next day I had planned to do some research on my own, but with Shaw's arrival, my sneaking away alone would be more difficult.

Ceana, Conall, and their family had risked everything by letting us stay with them. Residing at their home had allowed me time to watch them. The interaction they had with one another reminded me of my own family, before the loss of my dad. The total focus they had for one another when they spoke, and the fun interplay between them, triggered happy reminders of my family. I did not want any harm to come to the Mackenzies because of John and me.

Ceana's kindness was also a reminder of what I had lost and made me miss my mum terribly. With this void in my life, I wished I had visited home more during holidays at university to spend more time with her. But I had only thought of myself, spending time with friends, working on my writing career, and travelling. That first year as a student, I never came home, not once. Mum didn't complain about the lack of time I spent with her. She spoke of how proud she was of me and encouraged me to pursue my dreams. In a way, she had brought John into my life and now John could bring her back into mine. Without John's promise to help me speak to my parents again, I was without hope. I did harbor a fear that I'd end up as Mum's Host while she spoke with John, similar to Helena and me. The thought made me grimace knowing the stories my mother could tell.

Ceana's hand on mine brought me back to the pub. "Yer a long ways away, lass."

I glanced around the table. Everyone seemed involved in an intense conversation about hunting and hunting dogs. The twins, Iseabail and Barabal, had left the table, their chairs sat empty. I guess I had been deep in thought; I hadn't noticed the twins leave.

"John told me yer mum was unable to tell ye about the Archivists before she died," she said.

I had to give her credit for her intuition.

"I've seen many new Archivists with far away eyes. And ye have that look now."

I nodded, further amazed by her intuitiveness. "I was thinking about how things might have been different if I had stayed close to home. Mum wanted to let me know about our family legacy. I believe she had plans to tell me during lunch the day I left for Oxford, but I never gave her the chance. She received a phone call and had to go, most likely because of Archivist responsibilities. I decided to take an earlier train without even saying goodbye. The pain I must have caused her."

"Lass, that's too much responsibility fer ye to take on. Ye canna pretend to ken what could have been. Live in the now or these lovely locks will go grey before their time." She tugged a motherly pull on my dark hair. "Seems to me, John came into yer life because of yer mum. It's guid ye found one another. There are Archivists who never find the Host or Writer they're coupled with, which leads to a life feeling unfulfilled and inadequate."

An unfulfilled life sounded more fulfilling than being shot dead.

"Ye understand the implications of finding the Archivist yer coupled with don't ye, Zoe?"

"We're to work together," I said. The men at the table were lost in an obviously funny discussion. Their laughter burst out and they picked up their pints and gave a cheer. The noise made it difficult for me to hear Ceana's next words.

"Aye, but it's far more, lass."

"What do you mean?" I put my last spoonful of potato in my mouth and leaned towards her to better hear what she said.

"Ye and John need to get married."

My food went down the wrong pipe and I started to cough. I grabbed a serviette and choked for a full minute. John leaned over and slapped my back. "I'm okay," I said in a tight voice.

"You're sure?" John asked.

I nodded at him. Ceana laughed at me and then waited until the men were busy in conversation. By then I was able to swallow and clear my throat, and John, Conall, and the boys were about to leave.

"Come along, we're missing the party." Conall signaled to Ceana and we walked out of the pub into a blur of people, strangers to me, but also protectors. The townsfolk scattered around, laughing and enjoying themselves, but I noticed their frequent glances our way to be sure we were safe from the true strangers carousing the streets. I looked around for Shaw, but the streets were too crowded to pick him out. Our protectors may not allow him near us anyway.

Ceana took my arm in her endearing way and we walked to a bonfire stack that appeared to be more glowing embers than flames. There were less people here and I wanted Ceana to continue her explanation. The glowing warmth of the dwindling fire seemed alien to me as my mind tried to focus on something—anything.

Ceana bent close to me and said, "It's destined, pre-determined."

That statement cleared my mind. A society of arranged marriages? I hadn't signed up for that. I shook my head and whispered in a harsh voice, "That's archaic nonsense. I doubt John has any intention of marrying me. We've only known one another a short time. We can continue working together as Host and Writer without getting married."

I searched the various faces nearby, hoping John wasn't close enough to hear our conversation. I felt relief after spotting him on the other side of the burning embers. John's arms hugged his abdomen and he looked poorly. He shook his head as Conall talked to him. My relief turned to shock with the realization that they appeared to be having the same conversation as Ceana and I. John's eyes met mine over the embers and he turned away, quick enough to assure me they discussed the same topic.

"Zoe." Ceana grabbed my shoulders, turned me towards her, and stared into my eyes. "Did ye hear what I said?"

I hadn't listened to her last statement and shook my head.

"Ye both will lose yer abilities unless ye are married," she repeated.

"Your son is fifteen, I doubt you're marrying him off."

"He'll be fine until he's twenty—" I started to interrupt her but she went on, "and we don't understand why, except when ye're twenty or older and ye receive yer powers they disappear unless ye marry the one ye're coupled with. Marriage is a catalyst in our work; it strengthens our powers and protects us."

I glanced out of the corner of my eye to see John's face. His face displayed a painful grimace as he stood with his arms crossed.

"Hasn't John discussed this with ye?"

I shook my head again. From the appearance of his face, I doubted he had known. I didn't want him to feel obliged to marry me. Having an arranged marriage could kill any blossoming romance. I shivered from the double meaning behind the words. "How long do we have until our abilities disappear?"

Ceana took my hand. "Nae Zoe, canna think like that. Aye, ye have feelings for him and he for ye."

"Yes, maybe…we're just getting to know each other." I pointed his way. "Right now he looks like he's going to get sick." I decided to call it like I saw it. Conall patted John's back as John leaned over. I couldn't entertain any more thoughts about my feelings for John. My belief that we had any kind of relationship forming disappeared as he puked into the fire. How lovely.

"Oh my," Ceana said, shaking her head, "I thought he was such a strong, fine lad."

"Yeah. So how long, Ceana? How long before we lose our powers?"

"Eh, once ye've met yer partner it's never less than six months, but never more than a year."

At least that should give us enough time to figure out who was kidnapping the Archivists and who was after us. "I think I should get John home," I said.

She nodded and said, "One more thing."

With some apprehension, I waited for her to continue.

"The two of ye won't lose yer abilities at the same time. If ye marry before ye both lose yer gifts then the ability of the one will be restored. But once neither of ye have powers, there's nae hope. Most of us get married when the ability of one disappears."

In her eyes I saw someone who didn't question the rules, someone kind, loving, and trusting. She squeezed my hand and did that intuitive thing again, and said, "I see myself in ye, Zoe." I thought the opposite about myself, I had none of her qualities—not anymore. I now carried a vindictive heart. I wanted to find who had murdered my parents and then I wanted to destroy them.

"You barely know me. What you think you see no longer exists," I told her while the back of my mind cradled the thoughts of my dead parents and their mysterious deaths. She opened her mouth to say something, but we weren't able to continue our conversation. The sound of gunshots ripped through the air. We both jumped before instinct had us drop to the ground. Laughter echoed through the crowds—possibly a prank. Due to recent events, we didn't want to take that chance and we didn't move, but continued to lie on the ground. I saw Conall and John run around the circle of warm coals. Ceana had a clear look of confusion on her face that likely mirrored my own. Conall helped Ceana up, and John took my hand, pulled me up, and we ran, passing others who crawled for cover and those who continued to laugh. John took me to the alley along the side of the pub and we leaned against the cold, plastered wall.

More laughter rang out, and then shouts of "firecrackers!"

Another deep voice yelled, "Only firecrackers."

John grunted, "Bloody kids."

I laughed. People began to pick themselves up off the ground, brushing ashes off their clothes, and smacking each other on their backs, laughing. Another burst of the firecrackers rang out, this time people laughed and covered their ears, but no one dove to the ground.

I turned around expecting Ceana and Conall to be behind me, but the alleyway was clear.

"Where are Ceana and Conall?" I asked.

John and I stepped out of the alleyway and searched the faces near us, but didn't recognize anyone.

"They probably ran inside. Come with me." John held my hand and we walked into the pub. A few of Conall's older sons were at the bar ordering another pint, but Conall and Ceana weren't there.

John asked, "Where's Conall and Ceana?"

The brothers laughed and elbowed each other while Sean said, "They have a favorite spot behind McGrady's."

John nodded in understanding and smiled. "Well, we're going to head home."

Immediately upon hearing his words I felt a tightness form in my chest. I knew it came from the thought of being alone with him after the awkward talks we had just received.

"We'll come with ye then," Sean said.

I sighed in relief. John gave me a look and asked, "What? Would it really be that bad?"

Misunderstanding John's words, Sean said, "Nae problem, we'll just walk ye to the car."

"No. Come along," I said and hooked my arm through Sean's. "I haven't seen my brother and wanted to make sure he'll make it back." When I said that, I received a look of amusement from John.

"We'll make sure he gets home," said Neil, Conall's most slender son.

Sean and I exited the pub first. As soon as we crossed the threshold, a piercing scream came from the direction of an alley across from the one we had taken refuge in during the firecracker storm. The few stragglers near the fire ran towards the alley, two were the youngest of Conall's sons, Craig and Nathan. We followed them into the alleyway. A man lay on the ground surrounded by several people, including Eadan. I recognized the coat-of-arms tattoo on his arm. A woman with shoulder-length brown hair that hid her face, stood bent over. Her hands covered her mouth while tears streamed between her fingers. With trembling hands, another woman patted her back and tried to console her.

"Has anyone rang for help?" yelled a man who carried some towels and pushed his way through the crowd towards the victim. I looked around for the nurse who worked for Ceana. I had seen her in the distance earlier that evening and figured she'd come to help with a medical emergency. She hadn't shown up yet, nor had Ceana or Conall.

The middle-aged man collapsed on the ground had blood pooled over his hands as he held his side, below his ribs. Eadan arose from kneeling next to him and walked over to us. "It's Mr. Stewart. He said some men took my parents. He tried to help them get away when one of the men shot him."

Chapter 15
CONVINCING

It had become clear to John that he stood alone in his convictions. At the beginning, when he had joined the unit at MI6, they never revealed any intention to become mercenaries whose prime directives were to kill and kidnap. He had thought the mission was honorable. Something had changed. His gut told him that the man he thought was his leader had never been the one in command. If that was the case, this was bigger than he ever thought possible— unbelievable in fact.

He gave himself a few points for being clever; he had not informed anyone that he had become an Archivist. No living person knew except for Nana, Zoe, and Conall's family. He had not known about the possibility of losing his ability as an Archivist once he became one. His talk with Conall had put him in a dilemma. He could not lose his abilities and had to stop that from happening. He would risk anything to prevent the loss of his powers because the alternative was unacceptable. His only option was to marry Zoe. He had feelings for her, but to marry her seemed extreme, and although she was young she would have her own opinions on the matter.

Both the alley and the loading area behind McGrady's Pub were searched for non-existent clues. We gave our statements to the police, but the kidnappers trail had stopped when we discovered they escaped in a helicopter. The disappearance of Conall and Ceana grew further complicated because no one had seen the direction the helicopter had flown away. The brightness of the bonfires had obscured the view of any eyewitnesses from seeing the escape, and the noise of the celebration had hindered spectators from hearing their getaway.

By the time we arrived back at the house, it was well after midnight. Shaw drove back with us, but only to collect his bag and his car. With a smile on his face, he told us he planned to stay the night with a lass waiting for him in town. He looked uncomfortable after the disappearances and I told him to go and enjoy his evening. I knew with Shaw gone John would relax and thus make life better for me.

The bobbies set up tracing equipment on the house phones in case the kidnappers rang for a ransom. We knew the kidnappers wouldn't ring. Conall and Ceana weren't taken because of money, but the police didn't know about that and we didn't elaborate. We all remained in the sitting room—no one wanted to be alone. I couldn't sleep; no one could until early morning when, out of exhaustion, a restless slumber overcame everyone whether they sat on couches, lay on the floor, or reclined in a chair.

I dozed for an hour before adrenaline kicked in from a nightmarish dream about investigating the kidnapping only to discover the bodies of Conall and Ceana. Although tired, I got up and slipped on my shoes. I made sure John slept before I left a note telling him I had gone for a bike ride. I nodded to the policeman, whose eyes were half closed, as he sat at the dining table, grabbed a scarf and a red wool coat, and sneaked out the door. The sun hadn't come up yet, but the hint of pre-dawn grey and amber revealed itself on the horizon. The smoky air from the past night's fires filled my nose with sorrow.

I wrapped a neon-coloured scarf around my head, neck, and ears, and walked to the garage. I borrowed a red bike and pedaled towards town looking like a Christmas elf in my red and neon. Yesterday, I had seen a graveyard near town and headed in that direction. I arrived with cold hands and warm ears. I regretted not wearing gloves, but was grateful I had donned the merry scarf.

During the festivities the previous night, I had commented to Ceana about the graveyard and she gave me names of some former Keepers buried there as well as a Convincer, like Captain John Link who had convinced me and answered many of my questions. A Convincer may have information to help me investigate the events of the past couple of months and interviewing one did not require a Host.

I pedaled the bike up and down the cobbled paths until I found headstones with dates that matched up with what Ceana had told me—the mid 1500s. When I found the general area of the Convincer and Keepers, I got off the bike and laid it between some headstones in the grass. The grey headstones were small and pocked with age, some missing chunks the size of my hand. A few had unreadable dates or names. The names Ceana told me were Ethan and Ina for the Keepers, and their daughter Gillian was the Convincer. As I searched for Ethan and Ina, I discovered their names to be redundant. Over generations many couples had the names Ethan and Ina as well as children with the name Gillian. Many of the dates on the children's markers declared they died as infants. To make things easier, I searched for the Convincer first and started with death dates of Gillians who hadn't died as children. I figured the Convincer wouldn't be a child.

I glanced around to make sure I was alone. A haze floated about the hills and dells—mist mixed with bonfire residue. The sun shone through the haze onto a hill with trees and shadows that rose to the top. The hill gave me privacy to the north and west. On the other side, yellow-leafed bracken and assortments of trees, still thick with yellow and brown leaves, shielded me from the quiet road. No one besides me, and the dead.

Being alone assured me of one thing—I was alone. Nothing brilliant or comforting about walking in a cemetery alone, but at least it was daytime.

I walked along the markers and found one with the name Gillian, born in 1546, died in 1575; my heart pounded—I could wake up another spirit with this rubbing. But the chances of me finding the Convincer with my first try were nil. My plan was to continue from marker to marker doing the routine John had showed me when we woke up John Link until the Convincer appeared. Seemed easy enough. Eventually I'd find her.

I took a deep breath to calm myself and opened my bag to get the lump of mana out. It wasn't in my bag. I turned my bag upside down and watched the contents fall into the grass: torch, gum, tissue, lipstick, mace, but no grave wax. "Damn," I said out loud and repeated the curse each time I picked up an item and shoved it back into my purse. This meant coming back later, most likely at night, during the time when my experiences with graveyards weren't so good. I'd press my luck that everyone would still be asleep if I sneaked back into the house this morning. John would want to know about my bike ride and he'd see through even one lie from me. That was it then, I'd have to sneak out at night after everyone was asleep.

I might be able to convince Sean to come with me. The idea made me feel better, along with my next one—while at the cemetery, I'd search out the possibilities, make notes of where I saw the graves with the correct names, and draw a lipstick "X" to mark them. It would make it easier when I came back.

I pulled out my lipstick and drew an "X" on the corner of the marker with the name of the older Gillian on it. The mark didn't show up well in the light and at night would be non-existent. I shook my head and tried getting a mental picture of this marker's location—the third from the right of the obelisk-looking thing…I couldn't do this, it was ridiculous. The dimensions of the whole place would appear different at night anyway; that left coming back tomorrow. I stared at the marker for a few seconds and walked away.

"Art thou going to speaketh to me or walk away?" asked a slightly shrill, female voice.

I froze in shock and slowly turned around. My heart pounded in my throat. In front of me stood a beautiful woman in white, with kind blue eyes and messy flowing strands of red hair. She was a spirit. No human was that beautiful and mesmerizing, nor could any human that I knew float above the ground. She had to be the Convincer. She had appeared without the mana or the fog.

"Lady, what dost thou want?" she asked.

I continued to have a difficult time finding my voice. "Gillian?" I finally asked.

"Aye, me lady," she said.

"You're a Convincer, right?" I asked.

"Nae." She held out her arms as if looking at them for the first time.

"Ye can see me? Me body?" She sounded surprised and began twirling around—almost touching the ground.

"Yes." Lovely, the one person I needed information from and she appeared a bit daft. At least I understood her accent.

"Whit's yer name?" she asked. She continued to dance and twirl between and around the markers and trees, her red locks circling over her shoulders.

"Zoe Edevane."

"Zoe Edevane." She stopped twirling and paused next to a marker with an unreadable name. With graceful arms, she pointed her slender fingers at the marker. "Try this ground for your Convincer."

I walked closer and knelt on the damp grass. "I can't read the name." I touched the shallow grooves of what used to be the name on the marker.

"Not important," she said, and startled me when she laughed in delight.

"Catriona." She ran to hug a ghost of a teenager with chestnut curls who appeared next to me.

I fell backwards and grabbed hold of two markers, one in each hand, to try and steady myself. I continued to watch the two spirits in front of me speak to one another. Their words came so quick I didn't understand most of what they said. I hadn't used the mana or parchment and didn't know how they appeared. They finished their greeting, turned towards me, and then jumped in delight as their eyes looked beyond me. I didn't want to turn around, but followed their gaze anyway.

"The twins," said Catriona.

A young lad and lassie stood holding hands behind me. They were the same size and looked about seven years old. They were younger versions of Catriona.

"See where we have come," Gillian said, and twirled around with her pale arms out.

"We are near home," the young girl said.

"How long?" the boy asked.

"As long as Zoe needs us, me laddie." Her red hair settled down her back in a shiny glow as she stopped twirling and turned towards me.

As long as I needed them? Were they the Convincers? I regained my composure and stood up. I stared at the twins, still holding each other's hand. "Are you the Convincers?" I asked.

They giggled and glanced at Gillian who floated to them and gave them a hug. She then said, "They are wee babes." She pointed to a marker with the name Samuel.

"Our father," said the young girl.

Ceana had told me that the Convincer was a woman, but maybe there were two. I walked across the grass and touched the marker and asked, "This one?" A large muscular man with shoulder-length hair and a fuzzy beard appeared next to me. I hadn't even said his name. I had only touched the marker. By now my nerves were a bit frazzled and I tried to keep my composure as I stood—the only human—amongst a group of spirits. My mind spun, trying to grasp onto a thread of thought that would support the evidence around me. How had they appeared? What had I done? They were a happy group as they hugged one another, speaking in whispers. They gave quick glances my way and laughter echoed across the markers.

While they enjoyed their reunion, my surprise began to clear. I remembered how my parents wouldn't allow me near any graves. Could it be possible that all I had to do to raise the dead was touch their markers? How was that possible? Or was it? I had to be sure. I walked around and touched seven more markers. I reached down to touch an eighth one—small and low to the ground. Gillian's red hair appeared in front of me and her voice came quickly, "Canna touch that one." She shook her head, a smile playing across her lips.

Seven additional spirits, young and old, all watched me and

waited. I read the marker of the one they didn't want me to touch. The name wasn't legible. The dates read "May 1710" and "June 1710"—an infant.

I moved to the center of the pathway, not wanting to be near any marker lest I touch it and awaken more. I stared at my audience and the glow of white fabric moving about in fun and laughter. They continued to whisper, stealing glances my way. Those glances helped me arrive at a conclusion—they had played me. The red-haired Gillian had known what I was capable of before I did. Well, they had had their fun. It was now their turn to give me the information I needed. With a firm and slightly deeper voice, I said, "I allowed your family to be gathered and now I need something from you." I hid my surprise as they nodded, some walking towards me while others stepped through the air and floated. "I need to find the Keepers and the Convincer. I need their help."

"Whit's happened?" asked Gillian, her blue eyes stared earnestly into my face.

"Our Keepers have been taken," I paused. "And I don't know who I can trust."

Since she had appeared, her blue eyes had a hint of cheeriness—until I mentioned our missing Keepers. The humor in her eyes disappeared. She nodded before she turned around and waved her arm. "Come."

Each of the twins grabbed one of her hands and I followed them. The other ghosts surrounded me in a bright escort, each of their faces full of concern as they talked to each other in a medieval dialect I couldn't understand. The distress in their voices expressed surprise—apparently they didn't know everything that occurred on earth.

We walked to a grassy hill and continued up a steep incline. We stepped through yellow grasses and around markers hidden in the tall grass until we crested the top with me being the only one breathing heavily. The twins and their redheaded mother surrounded a gravesite. The other spirits divided into two groups. Each group circled another site until a fence of flowing white fabric surrounded three markers. All three gravestones were buried behind the yellows and greens of the tall grass.

Their bright faces stared at me. Gillian said, "Ye are divine, Zoe, and although but for a moment, it is an honor to meet one of ye."

I guessed she had never met an Archivist before. I thanked her and watched as she and her entourage took steps along a path I couldn't see. They faded down the marker-dotted hill and through the golden birch trees like a sunset. When they disappeared, my eyes adjusted as if dusk had settled in around me. I approached each of the three headstones and touched the markers as I read each name: Ethan, Ina, and the Convincer, Gillian, whose marker established her as their daughter. A moment later, I stared at three individuals. Once again their beauty and refinement made me want to forever gaze their way. They floated above the grass in their elegant dresses of white, except the gentleman who wore a loose white shirt and dark trousers.

I stood in silence and waited as the former Keepers, Ethan and Ina, greeted one another and then encircled their arms about their lovely daughter Gillian. Their happy countenance and warm embrace made my heart ache. The family resemblance between Ina and Gillian was breathtaking; I wanted to ask if they posed as fairies in their other life. Their crystal-white curls extended just below their tiny waists and their faces held genuine smiles from full, red lips, their smile extending into their silvery eyes.

I questioned why we needed Hosts if we could talk to spirits face to face, and so easily too. Maybe the routine with the mana was an unnecessary system passed down through time. They turned towards me and the women curtsied and Ethan bowed.

"Thank you for coming to me," I began.

"Nae, ye must never say that," said Ina.

"Nae, never, because it is always an honor for us to be graced by one of ye," Ethan said.

I thought the same—so much better to see them instead of talking through a Host. I knew what John's mother looked like only after I saw her picture hanging in his home. Such a striking woman she had been with her confident pose and short black hair bringing out the emerald green in her eyes. Even in the photo she displayed an eagerness for life and majesty in her smile. I would much rather have spoken to her as a spirit than her using her son's body. It wouldn't have felt so awkward.

"What can we do fer ye?" Gillian asked.

I thought about the list of things I needed to learn and understand, and wondered how I should begin. "How much time do we have?" I asked.

"How ever much time ye need our help, or until anyone comes," Ethan said, glancing around.

I took a deep breath and began. "Are you aware of what happens here on earth? To us?"

"At times we see and hear things," said Gillian.

"Do you know about the disappearance of our current Keepers?"

Ethan nodded, "Aye."

"Well, great. Thank you." They gave each other a glance after I expressed my appreciation. I waited a brief second to see if they wanted to add anything. After they remained quiet, I asked, "Do you know where Ceana and Conall are?"

No one nodded this time. Instead the women watched Ethan and waited. "Aye," he said.

I waited for him to elaborate. Instead he looked at the ground.

After a moment passed, Ina spoke up. "We are unable to tell ye."

"What?" I glanced from Ina's eyes to Gillian's pale ones. It never occurred to me that they wouldn't tell me where the current Keepers were. But no one moved or said anything. Irritated, I said, "As a Convincer can you convince me why not."

"We canna tell ye," said Gillian, without blinking.

"Why not?" I asked and my heart pounded. They knew. They knew where Ceana and Conall were and wouldn't tell me? What could I do at this point? I had no answers. I couldn't threaten them; they were spirits. I stood on a precipice here and didn't want to overstep my boundaries—for all I knew they had hidden powers they could use on me, such as zapping me speechless. After a few moments, I realized the power they did hold—silence. After waiting and looking from blank face to blank face, the time turned into an awkward silence. "Can you at least tell me if they are alive?" The awkward silence continued so I moved on to another topic before they disappeared and I was left with nothing.

Frustrated, I said, "People have tried to kill John and me, which makes it difficult to know whom I can trust. Now you're telling me you can't help me. I'm only trying to find out if he was involved."

Gillian spoke, "It is essential that ye and John work together." She paused before continuing. "Ye must also be made aware that our kind is not allowed to be spies or officials of any country. This is not permitted, and yet they have begun to exist. It began when—"

Ethan cut in. "Ye canna say more."

Gillian's eyes narrowed and she appeared agitated and angry. "Father, she must understand."

"Nae, we canna tell her," Ethan said. His eyes met mine with a penetrating stare before he looked away. He then spoke to Gillian in a voice loud enough for me to hear as he pronounced each word with emphasis. "If we speak of this, our descendants will die."

"What?" I stammered.

Gillian and Ina nodded, their eyes large, their closest hands clasping the others.

"Archivists are being taken captive to keep you quiet?" That made sense. That's why they wouldn't tell me about Ceana and Conall.

"Our families are held captive to protect their captors and silence us," said Ina.

"Can you tell me who the captors are?"

They shook their heads.

"How about letting me know who revealed our secrets, the secrets about the Archivist Society?"

"They are dead," Ethan said.

"Were they killed?" I asked. The sadness that crossed their faces gave me my answer.

"Their last words destroyed our covenant of silence," Gillian said.

Ina spoke gently and still. "But saved their children's lives."

I softened the tone in my voice and pleaded with them. "Please. Tell me who silenced them."

Gillian stared at the tree line and then at the grass-covered ground. "We canna," she said.

Their three heads turned at once to face downwards at the backside of the hill. Ina pointed. "Someone comes."

"Ye canna reveal to anyone that ye spoke to us," said Ethan. He put his arm around Ina and quickly said, "If ye must, only mention the Convincer."

Gillian nodded her agreement.

"It has been an honor," Ethan said, and bowed.

"Wait…" They had already vanished. Alone on the summit of the hill, I felt like the center of an hourglass—weighted from above and below. Above, the sun poured down on my shoulders and below, the hill spread out dark compared to the light of Ethan, Ina, and Gillian. Time had slipped away with no enlightenment about Ceana and Conall's whereabouts, but the moment had exposed a shocking revelation.

Chapter 16
THE SLY ONE

John had underestimated Zoe's tenacity. He needed to keep her close by him or she'd get herself killed. She put a huge demand on his skill set by exhausting him every time she went to a cemetery. He had located her at the local cemetery and rushed her off a hillside and out of sight seconds before a helicopter flew overhead. Her tenacity had led her to go on her own and talk with a Convincer, but she had missed the obvious fact that the people after them would, of course, be watching the cemeteries. Again the thought occurred to him how unwise her parents had been to not have trained and prepared her for the possibility that if she did become an Archivist certain skills would keep her alive. If it were possible he'd purchase Zoe skills of her own. He laughed at the thought.

He glanced at his watch—after midnight. The two of them were headed to another dangerous place, a place most assuredly being watched—the Dingwall Althing—to attempt the necessary task of speaking with that sly Keeper. With the kidnapping of Conall and Ceana, they had to go and speak with the sly one, whoever he was.

He knew the people after them watched every possible place they, or any Archivist, might show themselves. Included on their watch-list would be the upcoming funeral for Owen. The family planned to have the funeral as soon as Owen's body was released from the morgue. After he crossed "speaking with the sly Keeper" off his list, he wanted to pay his respects to Owen. He had a plan for a very respectable send-off for his friend and had added extra security for the occasion. He studied Zoe as she walked next to him. He hoped she intended to accompany him to Owen's funeral.

John paced and I stood, trying to keep my toes from being stepped on by his agitated feet. The sly one appalled both of us—not the first term that came to my mind to describe the Keeper of the books. I would describe him as more of a drunken sailor, or irritating like a mosquito you need to slap. He chewed and spat after every fifth or sixth word, most likely a habit he had developed as a mortal and couldn't shake off. He was a conundrum of ideals and lacking in demeanor, a bony twig of a man spirit obsessed about not revealing his name and yet he refused to discuss anything else. With the cold temperature of the cave, I felt for sure that hyperthermia would take us both if this sly one didn't give us the answers we needed, and soon.

John's eyes were red, along with his face. After what seemed like hours debating with this bony spirit with no name, we had achieved nothing.

"We don't care what your name is. It doesn't matter to us," John said. He put his hands on his head and smoothed his hair back.

"That's just it! Nobody cares," lamented the spirit.

John spun around and exhaled. His tired, red eyes looked into mine. "Let's go."

I knew John was right. We had done our best to explain to this obsessed spirit about Conall and Ceana and the kidnappings of other

Archivists around the world, but the sly one would not tell us how to work the book to safely open it and see the names of the new interim Keepers.

I faced the bony spirit man who stood floating in front of me with his arms folded across his chest. I folded my arms and stared back at him. "You are paranoid one minute and want us to care the next, which makes me think of plenty of things I would like to call you. So how about I make up a name and call you Mullog." I smiled at the meaning behind the made-up name. "Mullog, are you really not going to help us out? We're in a bad situation right now. If you care about the Keepers and the Archivist, we need your help."

His arms dropped to his sides. He studied my face and smiled. He then looked at John and probably thought better of smiling at him because he removed the smile from his face when their eyes met. He pointed to John and said, "You're not as smart as you think you are."

After already being shocked by his smile, his tone of voice shocked me more. He sounded like a completely different person. His voice had changed to that of a sexy Italian and he didn't spit at all. His irritating habit had seemingly disappeared. With his sentence completed, we watched in astonishment as his appearance changed from skin and bones to a more defined physique with muscular arms and a broad chest.

John didn't take his eyes from Mullog's eyes as he grabbed my arm. He said, "He's bipolar. We'd better go."

Before John pulled me away, the spirit looked back at me and smiled again. "Mullog?" he asked.

Maybe there was some hope yet. I pulled my arm from John's hand and said, "Yes, Mullog. It's reversed letters of a cave dweller you remind me of."

John laughed.

"You can name me Mullog," he said in his calm sexy accent, and continued "It has meaning to you—how wonderful, mia bella."

I nodded. He turned to John and asked, still using his lovely Italian voice, "Will you name me Mullog?"

John raised his eyebrows and smiled. "You are very odd and peculiar. Elgaems one minute, Mullog the next. It certainly suits you."

Mullog floated in front of John and then drifted to me. His spirit light increased from a soft almost nonexistent light to a brightness that was difficult to gaze at. "Grazie. I will be named Mullog Elgaems." With his voice intonation, the name sounded elegant.

John and I stood in amazement as Mullog stepped forwards through the air, his hands and arms outstretched. Without touching the top of the chest that held the Law Book, the heavy lid creaked open. The emerald, ruby, and sapphire gemstones sparkled from the spirit's light as the book floated through the air as if it weighed nothing, and settled across Mullog's muscled arms.

"You are the quickest I have ever dealt with," he said. He opened the metal, petrified wood and gemstone inlaid cover of the book.

"Quickest?" I asked.

"Yes, mia amica, and I am most impressed because I have never heard that name before."

"You *needed* us to name you?" I asked.

"Why didn't you simply ask us for a name?" John asked. He stole a look at me and rolled his eyes.

Mullog smiled. "Si, but this is so much more entertaining." He held the book open and pointed at a blank line underneath a list of names. The last two names on the list were Conall and Ceana Mackenzie.

John and I watched, fascinated, at a spark forming on the blank spot below their names. I blinked as a white light of ink began to hiss and form letters on the line. The light burned and spun until a line of bright and swirly light formed. John grabbed my arm as we watched the letters fade into place. There, forming and fading in front of our eyes, were our names. I realized that we hadn't told Mullog our names, nor had he asked. Mullog pointed elaborately to the names and said, "Those are your Interim Keepers. John Link and Zoe Beryl Edevane."

"But we can't be the Keepers!" John and my voices rang out at the same time, both of us surprised and angry.

Mullog's black eyes stared into John's eyes and then my own. I shivered. His sly and creepy side grew visible again. "This book never lies," he said in a voice that held a bit of sexy Italian and a bit of coarse sailor. He glanced down at our names, burned into the page. "Zoe Beryl Edevane and John Link. I knew both of your parents. It is an honor to have you two as our interim Keepers." He bowed low to the ground. "Definitely an honor."

The sudden kindness in his voice took me off guard, as did his bow. He exhibited all properness and etiquette. Even John looked uneasy and remained silent.

"You knew my mum and dad?" I asked. I glanced around the small room for a chair. I didn't dare sit on either one of the chests.

His eyes squinted at me in thought before he said, "They were some of our best Archivists."

The book shut and floated across the room to lower itself back into the chest. I smiled at the fact that a book flying through the air seemed so uninteresting and normal to me.

"Mullog, we can't be the Keepers. We aren't married." John had finally found his voice. He looked uncomfortable, shifting his eyes and shrugging his shoulders.

He had a point. I stepped forwards. "That's true. This time your book has to be wrong."

"Of course you must be married to be the Keepers," Mullog said.

John and I both smiled and took in deep breaths of relief.

"Except…" Mullog began, he raised his eyebrows and my breath of relief stopped short. "Except with Interim Keepers there is no need."

John and I stood in silence.

Mullog continued. "Becoming Interim Keepers will extend your powers, giving you additional time to plan your wedding."

"But—" John and I began.

Mullog said, "But of course we must get to the important tasks at hand and plan the gathering to occur in three days."

"What?" I asked. "But how do you know?" To which Mullog raised his eyebrows at me in a knowing fashion.

"The gathering? Too dangerous to consider," said John.

"Of course it's too dangerous to plan it through the mortal chain. We will plan it through the spirit chain of command," said Mullog.

"The spirit chain?" I asked.

"We spirits know those of you mortals who are compromised as well as the compromised spirits. We can avoid them and keep them from gaining any knowledge of the gathering. We can keep you safe."

"How have spirits been compromised?" John asked.

I recalled my conversation that morning with John. I had not told him all I learned at the graveyard. Mullog gave me a look of surprise.

John immediately picked up on the glance and turned to me. "Do you know?"

I tilted my head sideways and raised my eyebrows. Did I deliberately not tell him?

Mullog explained. "Our living descendents are threatened if we say anything about the people who kidnap and kill the Archivists.

We cannot have our grandchildren sacrificed, so we do not talk. It is up to you, mio amico, to find who they are and stop them."

John walked into a corner mumbling under his breath and turned around. "This just gets better," he said, loud and angry. "How can we compete with that?" His hands clenched and unclenched. Concerned, I stepped away from him. His entire body turned towards me, annoyed. "You didn't tell me. Were you going to tell me?"

I shrugged. "Maybe. I only learned about it this morning."

"From the Convincer?" John asked. His hands continued to clench as he spun around and walked to the corner, mumbling again. He crouched down and leaned over, his arms on his knees, his hands smoothing back his hair. Mullog and I remained quiet. To give John a moment at that instant was high on my list. A few minutes passed and John stood up, slowly turning around to face us. "Must we have a gathering?"

"The sooner the better. To keep this gathering safe, do not tell anyone. Leave the informing to me. I will let only those we have full trust in know. We will keep it to the bare minimum. Only a few head Archivists from each continent and we will hold it in Iceland," Mullog paused. John didn't say anything, so Mullog continued. "We must remain silent about our missing Keepers."

Before I remembered my promise not to reveal the names of Ethan and Ina, I blurted out, "But I told Ethan and Ina." After my remark, I received a questioning look from John because this was another item I had kept from him.

"No, no. Then let us hope we can keep this from others," Mullog said, waving his hands in the air.

John and I nodded.

"Amici miei, are you going to stand there or go to Iceland?" Mullog teased us.

We thanked him. As we turned to leave, he yelled after us, "I will not be far from you, mia carina."

With the combination of those words and Mullog's sexy voice, I heard a grumble come from John's throat and he said, "He better not get too close." We walked through what felt like miles of tunnels before John spoke to me. "Zoe, please let me know that you missed telling me that vital piece of information because we've been busy."

He was behind me and I stopped and turned around to face him. I couldn't say yes to that, nor did I want to tell him everything I learned at the graveyard. "I learned several things today and I'm still sorting them out in my own head." That sounded good to me.

"But that isn't all, is it?"

I figured he'd recognize a lie, so I tried dodging his question. "Not really."

His face went grave and his eyes searched mine. "We need to trust one another, Zoe."

"So I'm told."

"But you don't trust me?"

His candid question caught me off guard. Why did he have to be so good at reading people? I couldn't lie, I lacked the ability. "I'm not sure." My head began to spin and I felt weak. I hadn't slept in…I couldn't even recall how long I'd been awake.

John took my arm with his calloused fingers. "Let's get back and let you rest. Then we'll talk."

His gentleness had me rethink what I should tell him. "John?"

He nodded and waited.

"There is something I was told today that may help to reveal those who are after us."

He stayed quiet, his eyebrows rising.

"Spies and leaders of countries are not allowed to be Archivists, yet we have spies that are Archivists today."

He surprised me and nodded his head. "I know."

"You do?"

"For years I've worked on acquiring information about a group of spy Archivists."

"So you know who they are?"

"I know some of them. But there are others I'm investigating because I don't think their intentions are good."

"Oh."

"And, Zoe?" His hands gently enclosed mine. "I am one of them."

I looked up at him in shock. His hands tightened on my own. His mouth opened to say more when a brushing noise came from the dark tunnel behind me. John's mouth snapped shut and his eyes averted to the dark in surprise. I felt a crushing pain on the side of my head, and everything went black.

Chapter 17
THE CUSTARD FEST

John woke up with a start; someone had taken Zoe. He found himself prostrate on the ground and unable to see through the darkness surrounding him. He reached his hands into the air and felt angled and sharp rocks piled next to him. When he prodded the ground, he found his crushed phone. He tried to get up, but felt unconsciousness hover over him. He closed his eyes and inhaled a slow and deep breath until the feeling left. He reopened his eyes and took his time sitting up. He remembered the tunnel collapsing in a cascade of rocks. John pulled out a penlight he kept in his belt and switched it on. The light lit up the wall of rock piled to the ceiling. He wouldn't be getting out that way.

He shook his aching head and tried to recollect what else had happened. Two men had snuck up behind them in the tunnel. One man hit Zoe, which caused her to collapse before they advanced towards him. The three of them had fought and triggered a cave-in. One of the men had been crushed in the debris. His penlight lit up the bottom half of that man near the tunnel wall. The man's upper half wasn't visible from the crush of jagged rocks and dirt that covered him. The other man must have taken Zoe to one of the other exits Conall and Ceana had shown them.

John carefully put his hand in the dead man's pockets and pulled out money and a smart phone. The phone wasn't damaged. He pushed a few screens until he located what he hoped was the information that would lead him to Zoe. He stood up and stumbled through the tunnel. He took a left at a crossroad where Conall had pointed out an additional exit. Within minutes, he opened a door that led into a crypt in the basement of the church. A quick glance at his watch told him the kidnappers weren't more than an hour ahead of him. He had known that kidnapping Zoe would be at the top of the list for several people in his organization. He smiled to himself. His backup plan to keep her safe had been warranted and now proven. He needed to return to Captain Link's gravesite and wait for the spirit to arrive and tell him where they had taken her.

A motor purred and a jolt from a bump in the road woke me up. I wanted to open my eyes and peek outside for road signs or other location markers, but my eyes were blindfolded. My head ached, but other than that I felt comfortable in my lying down position. I tried to think of the smartest thing for me to do. For the moment, I kept my mouth shut and listened. Two men spoke, but a man coughed beside me and made it difficult to hear them or what they said.

"She's waking up," said the coughing man, hacking between his words.

"Give her a sedative." As soon as I heard that rough and gritty voice, I breathed in harshly through the gag covering my mouth and my heart pounded. I could never forget that voice, the voice of Jaak, the man who had killed Pierre in the cemetery where all this madness began. I gave a muffled yell into the gag and struggled, but a scratchy rope held my hands clasped tight together and my legs were bound.

The man continued to cough beside me, spurting his words. "Hand me the bag of needles."

"Get a drink before I put you out of the car. Here."

That voice, definitely an Englishman. What I assumed was a plastic water bottle fell down next to me, rolled, was picked up, and then came the sounds of loud guzzling and swallowing between several coughs. After a few seconds of quiet, I jumped in surprise when a needle pricked my arm. Moments later I couldn't fight the sleepiness that overcame me.

I woke up groggy and nauseated with a soapy taste in my mouth. I tried to move, but my hands and feet remained tied. A dirty rag tied over my mouth created the soapy taste. Thankfully, my eyes weren't covered. A light with a pull string hung on the exposed beam ceiling. Cold air blew in from an open window on the wall next to me. Outside, the narrow window near the high ceiling revealed a dark background. Morning hadn't come, hopefully that meant no more than several hours had passed since they kidnapped me. I didn't see a clock anywhere to narrow that time frame down.

Several other people were in the room with me. Three were tied up and lay on twin beds like mine, but they slept. Two Asian women sat in metal chairs looking around with peculiarly dazed eyes, probably drugged. I didn't recognize anyone and felt disappointed I didn't find Conall or Ceana. Two of the people in the beds had their backs to me with a sheet pulled up to their heads. They both had short, dirty hair, which made it difficult to tell if they were male or female. The third one was a bald man. None of them was John.

The door opened and a burly woman entered. She wore her brown hair pulled back into a tight, plaited bun that pulled her thin eyebrows further apart. Her cream button-up shirt was snug around her husky body and left loose over a frumpy, black skirt that covered her knees and left her hairy shins exposed. Her shoes were dark brown trainers. Her cold eyes looked me over as she walked the few steps to my bedside and took my pulse. She asked, "You missed dinner. Do you want a sandwich?" Her voice was uncaring and her accent German. Could I have been flown to Germany? I moved my head up and down and grimaced from a shot of pain in my skull.

"Remain still and your head won't hurt. Those men are brutes, but they get the job done. I will bring something for you to eat."

A few minutes later, she returned carrying a Kaiser roll with sliced beef and a chunky piece of cheese, slightly melted, spilling over a cloth that wrapped the bottom half of the sandwich. In her other hand, she had a steaming cup of tea. She set them on a table next to me and untied my mouth gag and hands. She then cuffed my right wrist to the side rail of the bed. She made a grin that didn't include her eyes. "Can't have you wandering."

"Do you know where John is?" I asked.

"Eat up." She ignored my question and left the room. I pulled myself into a seated position and ate. The crumbly roll tasted old and the tea hadn't steeped long enough for my liking, but I was alive. Food made me feel better and cleared my head. I figured that if Jaak and his group had wanted me dead I wouldn't be sipping tea. Maybe John was in the next room eating a sandwich and drinking weak tea. I could only hope.

When we were in the Althing, before I lost consciousness, I saw John's shocked face. The memory of our last conversation surfaced. The last thing he had said to me—he was one of them. One of "them" being either a leader of a country, or a spy, and I think I would know if he was a leader of any country. He was a spy. That didn't mean he had anything to do with my kidnapping—or any of the kidnappings. He told me he had been investigating other spy Archivists, but hadn't had the chance to tell me what he had found.

A sneeze reminded me of the others in the room. The sneeze came from one of the women sitting in the chairs. She wiped her arm across her nose and looked at me with a blank stare.

"Hello," I said, unsure if she spoke English.

Her chocolate eyes gazed at me as she swiped her arm over her nose again. She had both crusted and gooey snot along her arm. I felt nausea well up. I quickly looked away and took a deep breath. I hoped she came in like that, or was drugged, because the alternative scared me. The woman sitting on the other chair looked like a posed mannequin, if mannequins could drool.

A scream cracked the silence. It erupted from outside of our room and down the hall. The sound of a tray with an assortment of glass and metal landed on a hard floor. Several pairs of running feet clamored past our door, heading towards the sounds. I heard voices yelling unintelligible words. My heart began to pound and my teeth chattered as I recognized one of the voices. The two Asian women sat still and hadn't moved or blinked during the screaming and commotion. For the moment I envied their catatonic nonchalance. The three people in the beds hadn't budged either. I jumped when the door flew open and the woman who brought me the sandwich appeared. Before I said a word, she popped a needle in my arm. I tried to speak, but she shook her head at me. The cold in her eyes went icy. I remained silent.

"Lay down," she whispered harshly and turned off the light with a pull of a string. She left the room, yanking the door shut behind her.

Inside my head I screamed, "Don't leave me in the dark with Jaak down the hall and the unleashed, catatonic twins in the room." I had no idea what Jaak looked like. If he entered the room, I would not know him unless he spoke. I kept my eyes open. I stared into the dark as long as possible. My eyes watered watching the door and the shadows that passed underneath and back to the darkness where the catatonic women sat. My eyes shifted back and forth, the movement caused sleepiness to come. My eyes closed and then blinked open in panic from an adrenaline surge. What if the unrestrained twins moved around in the dark? I stared into the gloomy blackness and saw shadows that crept my way. I raised my unrestrained arm and swung it above me like a pendulum to protect my personal space from any approaching figure. The lumpy mattress sucked my body into it until my arm flopped beside me. Flat and shapeless sensations overcame me and I dreamt of snot-covered women who drooled and pulled at my hair.

I heard a strange sucking sound and opened my eyes. Light came through the window. I had made it through the night. I turned my head towards the sucking sound and gasped. One of the catatonic twins knelt next to my bed with the ends of my hair in her mouth—chewing.

"What the—" I began to cry out. As soon as I spoke her eyes grew large and she opened her mouth wide. She then belted out a long and laborious scream. My right arm remained fastened to the bedrail. With my left hand, I tried to push her head away before I became deaf. Her head was less than an arm's length from mine. With the lungs of an opera singer, she continued her torturous scream—so I punched her in the nose. My tight-fisted punch only made her scream become nasally. I drew my arm back for another swing when the burly woman hustled into the room, grabbed my arm, and pinned me down. I had no hope against her bulky strength.

A skinny, black man with a long face entered the room. He took the screaming woman's hand and gave her a spoon with what appeared to be vanilla custard on it and shoved it into her mouth. She stopped screaming and licked the spoon like a purring cat while the skinny man helped her get up and walk back to her corner seat. The black man hadn't said a word, not that I could have heard him if he had, but it made it impossible for me to know if he was Jaak.

Both of my ears rang, and the right one made everything I heard mushy and distant. Miss Burly Woman asked me why I had struck the woman. I had to read her lips to understand her words.

"She was sucking on my hair." I grabbed the ends of my hair and showed her. The ends were knotted with food particles mixed in the knots.

She nodded and took a tissue out of her pocket and wrapped my tresses in it.

"Can I bathe or wash?" The messy strands smelled bad.

"We can cut it off." She turned towards the thin man who stood inside the doorway. "Get some scissors."

"No!"

She looked back at me with a grin, like this was a game she enjoyed playing. "How about some rubbing alcohol?"

"Sure. That would work."

Instead of sending the black man who, without a word, walked off on his own, she trotted out the door. A moment later, she returned with a dark bottle and a cloth. "All we have is peroxide." She un-cuffed my wrist and stood to watch.

With no other alternative, I grabbed the bottle. How light could my dark locks go if I washed the peroxide off a moment later? I saturated the cloth. As soon as the dripping cloth touched my hair foam appeared. I wiped the clumps of hair and scrubbed the food particles out. I combed my fingers through my hair and discovered another dry and crusty clump around my face. How long had she treated my hair like a buffet? I poured the peroxide onto the ends of my hair and kept the cloth underneath. Foam puffed up as I treated that section also.

Miss Burly enjoyed my consternation. She stayed to watch with her devilish smile and her hands on her wide hips.

"You finished?" she asked.

"Yes. Where can I rinse my hair?"

She smiled. "Rinse? Humph."

Everything about her stance told me I had a problem. In another few minutes, my hair would streak an unnatural and most likely odd colour. "Oh, come on. Can you at least put more water on the cloth so I can wipe the peroxide out of my hair?"

She yanked the cloth out of my hand, re-cuffed my wrist to the bed rail, and asked, "How about breakfast?"

"Thank you, yes."

She left.

The other beds, along with the people in them, were gone. Only the twins and I remained. Both of them licked spoons with the custard dripping down their pointed chins. I looked away, deeply concerned about how they came into such a state.

Miss Burly returned with a plate of toast and mushy peas, but no wet cloth for rinsing. I gathered that she wanted to prove a point; I was a prisoner, and she was not my hired help.

"What happened to those two?" I pointed to the pudding fest going on next to me.

"Obvious, isn't it?" She glanced at me.

I must have succeeded with my mystified look because she decided to explain. "They Hosted too long." She raised her eyebrows and walked out of the room.

What? I looked over at the women, their tongues searched to find the custard that no longer existed on their spoons. I was not going to end up engrossed in a custard rapture, or feasting on some woman's split ends. I had to get out of there. From the corner of my eye, I caught a glimpse of my hair streaked in orange. Fantastic. Maybe when they finished with their spoons they could lick off the peroxide.

My wrist bled as I struggled to release it from the cuffs. On the table next to me sat my breakfast tray with dried-on mushy pea paste and crumbs from the toast. The room smelled like diapers and bedpans that needed to be disposed of or emptied. Heavy footsteps came down the hall and stopped outside my door. I let my hand hang in the cuffs and remained still. The man's rough voice echoed in the hallway, sending shivers through my entire body, "I want you to prep Zoe." He cleared his throat and spit. "We have a new shipment that arrived and is now ready."

I waited for him to walk into the room, but the sound of his footsteps disappeared down the hall. A tear rolled down my cheek as I stared at the twins. Jaak had probably given that same order for the twins, which put them in their catatonic state. Since killing Pierre, he must have obtained the information of what Hosts and Writers did, but what they needed from us that led them to kidnap and turn Hosts into mindless shadows had me concerned, especially now that my turn had come. I filled my mind with thoughts of Shaw, John, and the Mackenzies, me becoming an Archivist, John being a spy. I may forget that I'm an Archivist with the chance to talk to my parents again. If I ever saw John again, I may not remember that he's a spy. I might not even remember that he's John, or that Shaw is Shaw.

"Ow." A sharp prick in my arm aroused me from a restless sleep. The room was badly lit and I had a little trouble focusing on the two faces nearby. One I recognized as the burly woman and the other face had cold, blue eyes rimmed with redness. His slicked-back hair and bearded face gave him a dark and wild look. His body, from his bowed head to his shoulders and shuffling feet, must have been powerful at one time, but now it appeared destined for the grave— and he smelled, worse than my hair. I remained still and wondered what they had injected in my arm.

The burly woman looked at the man and said, "Get Pete. You are in no condition to help me."

The man's cold eyes held mine. He blinked as if nodding his head would exhaust him too much. He turned around and shuffled to the door. He leaned against the doorframe and said, "Pete! Come help Mat." His gruff voice made me stiffen from the memory it invoked. But this man could not be Jaak. I had pictured him to look more deadly than death-like. He stared at the floor and said, "My brother's expecting me." I shivered. I would never forget that voice.

"Have a safe trip," said Mat.

Jaak coughed and spat on the floor before he pushed his haggard bulk from the door jam and slowly walked away. His cold eyes hadn't surprised me. His dark and wild look hadn't surprised me either, but his pale, translucent skin and weak appearance did. I thought of Pierre and hoped this man who had killed him would suffer plenty.

I turned towards the burly woman. "Mat?"

Her eyes flashed at me. "Matilda."

"Hmmm." I nodded, more relaxed because Jaak was visiting his brother and wouldn't be helping Mat with whatever they had planned for me.

The skinny black man, I assumed was Pete, entered and pointed behind him towards Jaak. "He looks worse." His accent placed him from Eastern Europe too.

Mat gave a quick succession of nods that didn't move one hair of the plaited bun on her head.

"What do you think is making him sick?" Pete asked.

"Maybe drugs, cancer. Who knows?" Mat responded.

"Could be anything," he said.

I glanced from Pete to Mat and felt totally at ease and completely calm. My feeling of peace had nothing to do with Jaak's disappearance and everything to do with the injection they gave me. They each stood on a different side of my bed and both had their arms crossed. My lips curved into a huge grin as I stared back at the mismatched pair.

"So she'll be one who turns into an idiot on this medicine," Pete said.

"With this hair it suits her," Mat said, clicking her tongue at my orange locks.

It grew difficult for me to concentrate on what they said while I tried to speak. The pale light made me feel distant and translucent. My arms grew heavy and my thoughts became mushy and contrived. I felt like I had stared them down for several minutes when at last my words formed. "What do you mean by idiot?" I think it took me five minutes to speak those six words. They had put me in a wheelchair and wheeled me out into the fluorescent-lit hall before I made sense of his simple response of "Yes, as I thought."

I thought a spoon full of pudding might be nice, and laughed when moments later I discovered I held a spoon in my hand and how pleased I was to be licking pudding from it—chocolate—how nice.

"Thank you, Pete."

By the time I thanked Pete for the pudding, Mat had pushed me over a threshold and into a warehouse filled with a lot of caskets, which were spotlighted by bright lights dangling from the ceiling. Pete walked alongside us.

"How odd," I said. Mat pushed me up to a rectangular table where several people in wheelchairs gave me wide-mouthed grins and waved spoons in my direction.

"Hap-py," I said and pointed to a blonde lady in a chair across from me. She nodded and then stuck her spoon in her mouth while she tried to speak. "Cosfins." I laughed out loud when I realized what she said. She pointed to a shiny wooden casket in a pearly brown shade. It was the closest one beside us and also was the first in a long line of coffins of various sizes, materials, and age. Many made from wood were similar to the shiny, pearly one; others made of wood were mere splinters held together by ropes. Some resembled a small mausoleum and I wondered how they could have been moved because they looked large and heavy. They were each positioned on top of pallets that held at least two large sized caskets, and up to four if they were small.

At the head of our table sat a woman in front of a computer and keyboard. I hadn't noticed her until she spoke to Mat. I didn't understand any words except "yes" in German. Mat responded in German and wheeled away the blonde lady who said "bye, bye" to me and dropped her spoon. It clamored onto the concrete floor and Mat kicked it out of the way. She placed the woman next to an open coffin made of dark wood that had chunks of dried mud dotted all over it.

My eyes took in the lady pecking at the computer, the open coffin, my arm with the needle mark—these pieces formed a picture in my mind and I knew what Mat and Pete planned to do. I should have been appalled; instead I felt appeased. Although my head tried to say no, my mouth mumbled "Ja," as I watched.

In front of the blonde woman's face, Pete held up a card with word prompts. "Read this," he told her.

She smiled up at him and nodded. Her lips fluttered with no sound.

"Out loud," he said, and shook his head with impatience.

In a slow, sing-song voice she read, "Saint Bernward of Hildesheim I allow you to occupy my body." Her head tilted at Pete.

The command wasn't quite the same as what John had taught me, but the fog appeared and revealed the effect of these words when administered by an archivist Host. The words were close enough. The fog dissipated in the warehouse to reveal the woman's face, which took on a frown. Her eyes darted around the room in fright. She, or rather "he" didn't say anything, but the woman's small frame almost toppled forwards out of the wheelchair. If she hadn't been strapped in, she would have fallen. Even my sluggish brain comprehended the multiple reasons for the muscle relaxer cocktail they injected in us.

Pete wheeled the frightened Saint Bernward to the table next to the woman at the computer. I was the only other person left at the table. I hadn't noticed the others being taken away. The eyes containing the thoughts of Saint Bernward searched my face and the fear in his eyes became momentarily replaced by surprise. He quickly recovered and left me, in my drugged state, to try and understand what brought on his surprised look. While I thought about it, Mat wheeled me away. We rolled behind a wall of pine coffins stacked three high. Mat stopped my chair in front of one of the large mausoleum-looking crypts made of granite.

When Mat held up my cue card I had only a moment of

hesitation before I began to read out loud, "Saint Francis of Acici, I allow you to occupy my body."

The last thing I remembered was smiling and pointing at the accumulating fog.

Chapter 18
SAVED

Near Aberdeen, Scotland

The sun shone bright, shining on the rusty metal and bleached-out wood buildings of the compound below him. John, several of Conall's sons, and a few trusted townsfolk were hidden behind a thick line of trees and shrubs on a rise above the edge of the compound. The compound was a former military base, an old one judging from the depravity and lack of paint. Scraps of bikes and rusted out car parts had been left lying about. Amongst the wreckage of bike tires and handlebars were neon-green generators. One hummed at the end of each bunkhouse and two ran the larger building situated in the center. Two passenger vans, a bus, and a medical transport car were parked along the road that approached and continued alongside the larger building. The vehicles and generators were the only items that looked new.

A delivery truck arrived and backed up to a loading dock. The men on the ridge remained still and watched as four men—three large, muscular white men and a thin, black man—strained to unload the truck's contents. The truck was loaded with coffins. There were bulky cement coffins and scratched-up wooden coffins.

Some of these had been wrapped with plastic and strung with twine because of their condition. The wood crumbled from rot. The crumbling coffins sat on pallets and were moved by a forklift.

John remained seated on the ground as he watched and gathered intelligence. He waited for Captain Link to let him know which location held the hostages, and what type of security they used at the compound. So far he had seen five men with guns. That meant he outnumbered them by two to one.

Captain Link appeared next to him and said, "The hostages are being held in the main building. Zoe is in the southwest corner. Her room is the second one on the right, past the nurses' station. There are no cameras. Other than two guards and a half-dozen attendants and nurses, there is very little security." He paused. "And, John. Some of the Archivists are in pretty bad shape."

John nodded and gave the signal to proceed with the rescue.

After waking up and finding myself back in bed with my wrist cuffed to the post, I had a moment of panic when I couldn't remember anything about playing Host to Saint Francis. Then I recalled that when becoming a Host one doesn't remember anything. I then worried because I had forgotten that Hosts don't remember what happens when they're hosting. By then my head ached because of too much thinking and I wanted to scream. I had to stop thinking and do something. I had to escape. The ache in my wrist brought me back to my present state. The top of my hand stung and bled where the metal dug into my flesh. Instead of another unsuccessful attempt to release my hand, I chose to look around to see if anything in arm's reach could unlock the cuffs, or loosen the bedrail. If I had to, I'd take the bedrail with me; it would come in handy if I needed to hit someone or something. I didn't know how much time I had, but I planned to go out fighting. If I could release myself from the bed and then find John, we'd be all right. I could still remember him—or at least my mind felt like it contained my normal memory of him. But I did not want to Host again and have another chance of memory loss, especially not knowing how long they kept us under. The pudding twins were proof that Jaak didn't care about the time restraints involved when Hosting. When I asked Mat about the duration of time they kept us under, she gave me her customary blank stare and left the room.

I reached for the spoon used to eat the mushy peas. It was past lunchtime yet the breakfast tray still remained on the table next to my bed. The slim and narrow handle might be useful. I pushed the handle into the head of a screw that fastened the bedrail to the bed. The spoon was too wide, but if I pushed hard enough I could get some traction. Soon I felt the screw loosen, slightly. Not much, but a start. It also gave me hope—something I direly needed at that moment. Through the ringing sound in my ears, I listened for Miss Mat's approaching footsteps if she came to collect the tray. I pushed the spoon into the screw and tried to make it budge again. Somewhere down the hall outside my door I heard a crashing noise, similar to the one from yesterday. Good. They'd be tied up cleaning that mess, whatever it was, and give me time to work on my release. The spoon's pressure on the screw had worked. I gained momentum as the screw began to turn.

Just as the tension started to leave me, a man's voice said, "Interesting." Because of my muffled hearing, I had not heard him approach and I froze. Panic forced the blood to pump through my veins. The screw wobbled. Unable to catch it I watched it fall to the floor. It rolled towards the shoes of the man I pictured standing behind me, near my bed. I hid the spoon in my hand to use as a weapon and rolled over.

"Nice hair." John stood there dressed in a mixture of green and tan camouflage combat gear from head to foot. He also wore a dimpled grin on his handsome face. No doubt he had been the cause of the noise down the hall.

"You weren't captured?" I asked. I then tried to smooth down my orange streaked and dirty hair.

He shook his head and navigated around the bed to unlock my bloody wrist. I leapt at him and threw my arms around his neck, tears streaming down my cheeks.

"You're alright," he assured me, his arms holding me tight.

"I'm not going to become a catatonic hair-sucker," I cried.

He pulled away. "What are you talking about?" Worry showed in his green eyes.

I pointed to the twins licking empty spoons. "They've been used as Hosts without a time frame."

He watched them for a moment and shook his head. "We'll have to leave them, but our people will take care of them. We rang Scotland Yard. You and I need to leave before they get here."

"Where are we?" I asked.

John caressed my aching wrist. "Along the coast near Aberdeen."

"Still in Scotland. Did you find Conall and Ceana?"

His downcast eyes told me he hadn't. He walked across the room and opened a door to a small closet. "That doesn't mean we can't still have hope," he said. He walked back and wrapped me up in a duffle coat he found in the closet, where he also found my shoes.

"What about the kidnappers and the hostages?"

"A couple of vans loaded with what we assumed were Archivists and their guards left before we could catch them. I don't think they'll get far. Those guards who remained are indisposed at the moment. We used some of the meds on them that they used to sedate the hostages."

His arms began to scoop me up to carry me. I said, "I'm not sedated anymore; I can walk." With the realization that I might not smell so good, I didn't want him that close to me. I glanced at the twins. They hadn't noticed John and continued to lick their spoons. Maybe they would become more normal when they were reunited with their families.

"We're five minutes from the helicopter," John said.

He grabbed my hand and we hurried down the hall.

"One of the kidnappers is Jaak, the bloke who killed Pierre," I said.

John stopped and looked at me. "Describe to me what he looks like."

"He's dark and greasy and looks unwell."

John shook his head. "Then he might be any one of these."

Several male orderlies and a couple of nurses lay slumped on the floor, seemingly in a deep sleep. We passed by them and took more notice of the guards dressed in black, each of their hands and legs were being tied together and all were unconscious and bleeding from various wounds they earned during the fight. I shook my head in exasperation. "He's not here. He said something about his brother needing him and is probably still with him."

John shook his head. "Too bad."

We passed the burly Mat tied into a seated position in a chair with her eyes shut; her head hung to the side. She had a string of drool dangling from her open mouth and would have a headache when she woke up. On a table next to her was the brown bottle of peroxide. Elated, I opened the bottle and saturated the bun on the back of her head. I smiled at John, who laughed as we walked away.

A familiar-looking lad dressed in camouflage from his ball cap to his boots came around the corner and almost ran into John. He was

Conall's son, Neil. He said, "Sorry. But ye'll want to come take a look at what I found." Neil nodded towards me and then looked taken aback by my hair. "Ugh, that looks bad."

I reached up and grabbed the ball cap from his head and placed it on my own, tucking my hair behind my ears.

Neil smiled. "Ye do us all a favor, that."

"What did you find?" I asked.

"Aye, yeah, come wi's."

We followed Neil to a warehouse-size storage room at the end of the hallway. The room appeared similar to the one in which the kidnappers had taken me. Pallets were stacked in a pile at eye level and there was a row of various sized caskets, some newer with a thin layer of dirt and others older, made from wood, with the layers of caked on dirt holding them together; others were wrapped in plastic. An expanse of open steel doors at the back of the storage room led to a loading dock with a delivery truck containing one more ancient and brittle casket. John didn't seem surprised at the contents of the room, but when Neil took us to an opening in the floor with a ladder that lead below the compound, John shook his head and pointed into the hole. "At least one person escaped this way and left the evidence to prove it."

The shallow tunnel contained enough light to see the body of a man at the bottom of the ladder. His throat bled from a knife wound that had ripped open his neck.

"Sean and Eadan have already gone down to pursue them and see where the tunnel ends."

John didn't look pleased and said, "They better be careful. It may be the leader they're following." He threw his hand into a stop command and pushed me away safely from the opening. John and Neil aimed their guns into the tunnel, one handgun and one fully automatic, machine-gun, and we waited. Deep voices and heavy footsteps drifted up through the hole. Neil lowered his weapon first. "It's the lads."

Sean and Eadan climbed out of the tunnel and gave me both the look of horror and relief that I was growing accustomed to. They found no one in the tunnel and said that it ended at an exit near the shore. In the distance, they had spotted a speedboat heading out to sea.

"We may be able to catch them with the helicopter," Sean said.

Before we exited the compound, I counted three bloodied guards, eyes open, not moving; not everyone could be approached without a fight. We ran out of the compound and met up with Conall's son, Thor, who stood with several familiar villagers from Dingwall.

"No Conall and Ceana?" John asked.

Thor said, "No, but we extracted some info that may lead us to where they're held."

"I'm sorry," I said, and patted Thor's arm.

"We'll find them. Dinna fash yersel," he said.

I had heard that last phrase a few times, but still wasn't sure what it meant, maybe "don't worry" or something of the sort. We crested the rise of the hill and below us were two helicopters situated behind a clump of Scot pines. The sun reflected from the windscreens as we raced towards them. John took my arm and led me to the smaller chopper. I waved goodbye to the lads and climbed inside. The lads waved back before they scooted their guns across the floor and entered the larger helicopter.

"Where are we going?" I asked.

"Iceland. We have the gathering tomorrow." John switched on the helicopter and the rotors began to spin.

"Word got out?"

"As far as I know, Mullog spread the word to those he trusted. I haven't mentioned it to anyone, not even Conall's sons."

I felt his eyes on me and looked across at him. He smiled and reached his hand over and touched my cheek. "You had me worried. I'm glad you're okay." His eyes flicked upwards to my hair. "How did you get that new look?"

I pulled one of my long strands in front of my face to look at the orange ruddiness. "The twin looking ladies, they…you got there before I…." He patted my knee. Assured he had the same mental picture of the twins that I did at that moment, I didn't need to explain any more.

Moments later, he landed the helicopter next to a waiting plane at a nearby airport. The plane was a private twin-engine with a couple groupings of windows along the sides. We climbed the stairs and John pulled the door shut behind us, and then secured it. The cabin seats were padded leather and looked comfortable. When John told me it had an en-suite shower and clean clothes for me, I couldn't wait. He continued to amaze me. But I raised my eyebrows when he sat in the pilot seat and took over the controls.

"Of course you can fly a plane," I said.

He winked at me.

After the plane reached altitude and leveled out, I located the shower room. I let the hot water run over my face and soaped up my hair a couple of times before I felt clean. I dried myself off and had the luxurious Egyptian cotton towel around me when I heard a man clear his throat behind me. I spun around as a squeaky scream left my lungs. The sly one, Mullog, stood facing the corner of the small room. He turned around with the Law Book held in front of his face to conceal his eyes; his upper arm muscles bulged from the effort.

"What are you doing?" I yelled. "Turn back around."

He didn't move. "Mi dispiace, I have been touring this flying machine and walked in here."

I had forgotten how sexy his voice sounded. "Well, go tour the galley or cockpit and leave me alone." I held my towel pressed against my body.

"I wanted to say ciao and let you know I am here."

"You couldn't wait until I was dressed?"

He continued to stand with the book concealing his eyes.

"Leave!"

"Mi scusi, mia bella, if I go backwards, I will be outside the plane."

I moved aside and pushed my body against the shower wall to unblock the doorway and allow enough room. "You can go, now."

"Buena sera, bellissima."

He squeezed by me and left. I thought I noticed a blush in his cheeks; I knew mine were red. He must have been a handsome man. Like all the spirits I'd seen, he glowed, yet he still showed the olive tones in his Italian skin. He wore his thick, black hair pulled into a low ponytail. Loosened, it would fall below his shoulders. His Michelangelo chiseled physique made me wonder what occupation he had when he was alive.

After getting dressed, I walked to the front of the plane. The cockpit door stood open and the drone of voices carried my way. Mullog sat in the co-pilot's chair next to John. His chin dropped down to his neck when I approached the doorway.

John's eyes scrutinized me. "You look like you're feeling better."

"I can't do anything about my hair, or a few other things for that matter." I narrowed my eyes at Mullog.

John laughed. "He's even apologized to me on your behalf."

Mullog looked indignant. "When riding a flying machine, I prefer going through doors, not walls. My first time riding one I went through a wall and into the sky—a very hostile environment for a spirit carrying a precious book. Most uncomfortable."

"Humph." I turned around and walked to one of the cream tinted leather-cushioned chairs next to a window and sat down.

"You have the mark." Mullog called out from the cockpit.

Annoyed, I asked, "My birthmark? You saw my birthmark? If you weren't a spirit, I'd slap you."

John asked, "Where is this birthmark?"

I heard both of them laugh and John said, "Someday I'd like to see that birthmark myself."

I rolled my eyes, stood up, and walked to the galley. I did not want to discuss my birthmark—a light brown circle with darker patches that resembled all seven continents on my left shoulder blade. My mum had one too. She used to say we carried the world on our backs.

In the galley, I found assorted cheeses and meats. I picked out slices of mozzarella and prosciutto, found a box of crackers, tucked a bottle of red wine under my arm, and walked back to my seat. I layered some mozzarella and prosciutto on a cracker and handed it to John while I raised my eyebrows at Mullog. He looked envious. Midway between enjoying the flavors of cheese, prosciutto, and a few olives, Mullog floated away, book in hand, to resume his exploration of the flying machine.

After Mullog left, I sat in the co-pilot's seat. I studied John and asked, "Who do you work for?"

"MI6." He pressed some switches and made some adjustments before he continued. "My cover is a photographer in South Africa."

"Did you know that Archivists aren't allowed to be spies and vice-versa?"

"Not until you mentioned it."

I nodded and yawned. Exhausted, I leaned my head back and closed my eyes.

I woke up with John tapping my shoulder. Frantically, I glanced around before realizing I was safe. He put both hands back on the controls, pushed several buttons, and said, "Put on your seatbelt. We'll be landing in Reykjavik in a few minutes."

"Do you think we'll be safe holding the gathering here?" I asked, stretching my arms into the air before I put on my seatbelt.

John gave me a reassuring smile and said, "Iceland is the most peaceful nation in the world."

Chapter 19
THE CRYSTAL CATHEDRAL

Reykjavik, Iceland

Their guesthouse stood on the outskirts of Reykjavik, which placed them within an hour drive of their meeting place in Þingvellir. The old, thick, and comfortable one-story house even had a stone fireplace in the great-room—more for appearance than for warmth. Fireplaces were rare in Iceland. John had put a log on and lit it during the first few minutes after arriving. Like many houses in Iceland, this one stayed warm by geothermal heating, but he enjoyed the ambiance of the fire. The place had a bedroom on one side and a main room. It had a green and red plaid sofa bed in the main room, with a petite kitchen that had a stocked refrigerator and a one-burner hob, along with a square table wide enough for only two chairs. A wall-to-wall queen bed filled up the narrow bedroom opposite the kitchen. The washroom was tiny but adequate, with plenty of hot water.

John stoked the fire and then stood in the doorway of the bedroom to watch Zoe's even breaths while she slept. He smiled. Leave it to her to end up with orange streaked hair, but otherwise unharmed. She had proved herself strong under the duress of being kidnapped. Strong like her parents. His nana had told him stories of them, stories that had made him prepare more than usual for his undercover job of working with Zoe's mum.

Zoe had accepted his being MI6. It was somewhat of a relief that she knew. Of course, she didn't know everything he had planned. He wondered if she'd sleep as sound if she knew all of his plans, and if she would try to stop him if she discovered them.

The blackness of the late morning turned to grey, the sun about to rise above the horizon. Gentle hills, covered in amber grasses with patches of green revealed in the pre-dawn light, surrounded us as we drove through a graben, a rift valley situated between the North American Tectonic Plate and the Eurasian Plate. Its beauty both intoxicating and lonely. The drive through such a geologically compromised area thrilled me. The valley held a false sense of serenity in its slopes and dips, which from a distance appeared to be lava, smoothed by time with soil and grass, but were actually laden with fissures and cliffs. The surrounding mountains were white with a layer of snow.

We soon drove alongside the depths of Lake Pingvallavatn, which changed from black to a silvery blue, and warmed to a golden yellow as the sun peeked above the ridges along its borders. The land surrounding the lake had signs of past volcanic activity, from the scattered lava beds and walls of lava lobes we passed near the roadway, to the distant Mt. Hengill, one of over a hundred volcanoes on Iceland. Beyond the lake, evidence of geothermal heat elevated itself in foggy spirals and layers scattered here and there over the landscape.

We passed a sign that read "Tingwall, Þingvöllr, (Old Norse:

field of the parliament)." The parliament began meeting here more than eleven hundred years ago, and recently the entire valley became protected as a national monument. When we drove by the tourist site, I grew amazed thinking about the many secrets kept by the Archivists. They knew the real reasons behind the meetings held here for over a millennia of time, including the meeting today. Throughout time, it had remained a secret—until now, the age of zero secrets and no privacy. I guess time really does tell.

John drove the Land Rover off of the roadway and followed a barely visible path. It led us into the black rocks and what appeared to be a narrow canyon with chunky lava walls that rose above us at least ten meters. Without Mullog showing us where to turn, I doubt we would have seen the path at all. The terrain of the uneven trail grew more difficult to maneuver, even with the Land Rover in four-wheel-drive. The shaded twists of the canyon hid us from the main road. When we approached an impassable blockade from a hardened bed of lava flow, Mullog had us park close to the lava wall. To leave the area we'd have to do a thirty-point turn or back out in reverse. We walked for fifteen minutes before Mullog stopped in front of a portion of the canyon wall that appeared impassable and rose to the sky above us.

"This is the doorway," he said.

We touched the rock and tried to locate any signs of an opening before Mullog showed John a sequence of security efforts we needed to decode before the door would open. He told him to push this root and that lava rock and spin a birch tree branch. It seemed some ancient people had created the security measures. After bypassing nature's security system, a portion of the wall about the size of a car door opened inwards and we entered the Althing.

The door shut laboriously behind us and we stood in the dark, even Mullog had his light muted to nothing.

"Did you bring a light?" I asked.

"No need, amica mia," Mullog said. "Take one step forwards, then wait and you will see."

I held my hands out to keep from running into a wall. With John's rapid breathing beside me, we stepped forwards. After one step across the floor, a click echoed from the heights of the ceiling. High above us, an emerging sunrise of rainbows and light began at the center, like stars, and transcended outwards until the cave spread before us, enormous and dazzling bright with a spectrum of colour. The Iceland Althing was more breathtaking than the other two Althings. Mesmerized by the brightness, my hands shielded my eyes from the impressive glare. "Is this Althing made of crystal?"

"It must be Iceland spar or silver-rock," said John. "It's a form of calcite."

Mullog nodded and floated across the room.

"This is heavenly." I whistled and it echoed off the hard surfaces.

Multi-levels of this silver-rock spiked its crystal structures through the walls and ceiling, many as small as the palm of your hand, others taller and larger than a man. The floors were bright from the rows of light that shone through the layers and bounced off the surface edges of the crystalline features. The most remarkable show of rainbows twinkled inside the crystal shapes themselves.

"How do the rainbows appear?" I asked, my fingers attempting to catch the green, blue, and pink displays from a large formation beside me.

"The polarization of light," John said. His eyes changed shades as the different rainbow hues of blue and green caught them.

"Well, it's brilliant."

Mullog hummed above us, just as intoxicated as we were.

"Where are the archives?" John asked.

Mullog pointed to a lighted tunnel that headed deeper into the cave system. Next to it was a large pillared opening. He beckoned us, saying, "We will tour the records later. Our gathering will begin soon." Mullog floated between the pillars and disappeared. We followed him into the crown of an amphitheatre room. Like the rest of the Althing, the amphitheatre consisted of Iceland spar or silver-rock and it glowed. The silver-rock benches sparkled with a multitude of colours; the walls rose up in silvery columns of smooth crystal and cornucopias of stalagmites. Above us, the crystal formations dialed in an array of rainbows interwoven with the hanging stalactites. Below us, in the center of the room, was an altar made from a chunk of the silver-rock.

The Law Book floated in front of the humming Mullog and glided through the imminent space to settle on the altar.

"That is the Lögberg, the Law Rock," said Mullog, pointing to the altar. His voice echoed in the space and seemed to create waves of light ripples as he spoke.

We walked down an aisle of steps between the rows of benches until we stood next to the Law Rock. I counted twenty rows of shimmering benches that circled the entire space. More than a thousand people could comfortably sit inside along the benches. I thought about the centuries and millennia that Archivists had convened here to determine what mysteries to unfold to the mortal race and those that would remain a secret. I couldn't fathom how the Law Book remained a secret. I would certainly love access to it to read the contents.

"This is where you will address your audience." Mullog stood next to the Law Rock.

John walked across the floor and stood next to Mullog. "Do I read from the Law Book?"

"Yes. There are two pages to read."

"Do I turn the page?" John asked in an uncertain voice.

Mullog looked stricken. "No." He recovered and laughed, shaking his head. "Forgive me, amici miei, I forget you are new. Let me explain. You must address the group as if you cannot see the Law Book, as if it is not there."

"Oh?" John said, perplexed.

"No one can see the book except for you two. It is hidden from all eyes except Keepers and…well that is what you need to understand for now. I will turn the page when needed. Never touch the Law Book, ever."

John and I stared at the book like it had fangs. But I now understood how it remained unknown, a mysterious book hidden from view from everyone but the Keepers. Yet, hadn't John and I seen it when we were with Conall and Ceana? They probably had laws that made that okay. I turned back to Mullog as he explained more to John.

"Do not speak to me. At least not in front of anyone except Zoe."

John nodded. I couldn't get over my surprise upon hearing Mullog say my actual name.

Mullog's eyebrows pushed together on his face and he said, "That is most important. You must act like you are telling them what you know and never look at me or the Book."

John grabbed the sides of the altar and received a harsh look from Mullog, which he ignored, and glanced around the room to practice his speech. "I'll tell them about Ceana and Conall and the kidnappings, and read from the book." John winked at me and grinned. "And as long as we are in this *crystal cathedral,* should we have a song and a prayer too?"

"We used to. Yes, good idea, you lead us in prayer too." Mullog looked serious.

John began to stammer. I slugged him playfully in the shoulder and said, "That sounds like something your skill set didn't prepare you for."

Mullog turned towards me with a face that made me shut my irreverent mouth. "And tesoro mio, you can lead us in a hymn."

My chin dropped, "What? I don't have a memorized hymn."

"Sing anything," Mullog said.

"Yeah, bella donna mia, sing anything." John's eyes sparkled.

I turned around to give an imploring glance at Mullog, but he had disappeared.

"We used to sing *An Innis Àigh*, but more recently *Nella Fantasia*," a woman said. She stood at the entrance to the amphitheatre.

John and I stopped talking and stared up at her. For a brief second, I thought the Queen had walked inside. From her sky-blue hat that covered her grey curls, to the serene and dignified way she carried herself, she could be a stand-in for the Queen. A gentleman appeared behind her and took her elbow to go down the aisle steps, but she remained standing at the top. The man had on a Russian hat and a black trench coat with grey fox-fur around the collar that blended into his hair. The trench coat made him appear taller and thinner than he actually was.

"Deary, which song?" She asked.

Assuming she spoke to me and thinking Mullog would enjoy the Italian, I said, "*Nella Fantasia*."

She hummed a few bars to warm up her voice and then began to sing in a clear soprano. The acoustics in the domed chamber made her voice ring out in surround sound. The sound came out surreal and divine. It became more beautiful with the addition of three more voices, and then five others as people entered the hall and stepped in time down the stairs behind her. The song had several verses and continued to grow until the final verse had a choir of almost fifty mixed voices singing in a cappella harmony.

I had never heard anything more angelic. Tears welled up in my eyes and the sound of the words felt like tiny fingers caressing my eardrums with velvet. I hooked John's arm with my own and as the song was about to finish he leaned towards me and whispered in my ear, "Do you know where I can get some petrol and a match? I'd like to set myself on fire."

His words felt like a needle skidding across a record. I pinched his arm and tried to get the velvet back in my ears, but the song ended.

Ignoring John and his rolling eyes, I clapped my hands. "Bravo. That was lovely, simply lovely. Thank you."

The group of fifty or so sat on the lower half of the benches in a half-circle. Although they sang as one with their beautiful voices, they were a vibrant assortment of couples from around the world. Most arrived wearing coats and gloves. A few had animal hides around their shoulders. The biggest show of differences was the head coverings that each couple wore. From a display of scarves and turbans, to fleece hats and ball caps, everyone together exhibited a catalogue of captivating colours. John and I were the only couple from head to foot in complete black and charcoal grey. Other than my cherry chap stick with a hint of pink, I felt drab and out of place. John looked totally at ease, no doubt a token of his training.

I sat down on the front row between an Asian couple untwining a pair of purple, red, and yellow silk scarves from their necks and an elderly couple removing their red and white Canadian caps. Both couples set their items under the bench. The natural thermal heating made it comfortable and warm in the amphitheatre. Most removed their heavy coats.

John stood next to the altar and introduced us. He explained what had happened to Ceana and Conall. Sighs of sadness went through the hall and then John surprised me. He bowed his head—

silence overcame the amphitheatre—and he offered a prayer of protection for all Archivists and asked for guidance to track down and find the kidnapped victims, and to discover the people who wreaked this havoc.

When he finished the prayer, he went right into why we had gathered. "As you know, and can now see, not all Archivists were permitted to attend this gathering. This is for your protection and stems from the belief that not all can be trusted. But we still need to warn those not present about the kidnappings and the murders. We need to make sure they understand the need to watch everything and everyone around them and be cautious, even around other Archivists." He paused. "We've discovered that some of our own are involved with those responsible for the kidnappings and murders."

A buzz of voices echoed through the hall.

"That's impossible," said a man.

Many agreed.

John held up his hand and silence followed. "I'm not telling you this because I suspect it, I'm telling you this because I know. Oliver Mackinaw was one of these people."

Gasps resonated from several rows.

John continued. "You knew him and I'm sure you find it inconceivable that he's a part of this. The man lived two separate lives. I stand in front of you as a witness against him. He killed Edward Thomas in Wales and he tried to kill me."

More whispers and intense words sounded around the room. John let it sink in for a minute before raising his hand again. The frantic talk continued.

"Please!" John said.

They fell silent.

"There is something else important for you to know. But first I must warn you that although what I'm about to tell you is unprecedented, it's become necessary."

The silence continued. The tension in the room made my heart pound.

John took a deep breath. "We now have spies that are Archivists."

It took John a full ten minutes before he calmed them down. Gone was the angelic singing, replaced by a firestorm of words. I sat still, listening to their surprise and anger. Two couples near me stood up in a passionate debate of why no one could be both a spy and Archivist because of the impossible task of finding a middle ground.

"How can an Archivist uphold his covenant of secrecy and also be a spy?" questioned a man behind me.

"Next we'll have politicians, and we know the wars they've caused in history." I heard that point restated more than once.

Several couples argued in languages I couldn't understand, their faces turned red from the effort. John stood in front of the Law Rock and shouted but couldn't get their attention, nor could his voice be heard above the heated conversations spread throughout the hall.

The way he silenced everyone surprised even me. I saw Mullog point to something on the edge of the Law Rock. John reached his hand to the side where Mullog pointed and darkness enveloped the amphitheatre. John had hit the switch for the lights. It became silent immediately.

My ears rang in the quiet stillness.

"When I turn the lights back on, I want each of you to remain completely quiet." John's voice sounded wary.

There wasn't even an intake of breath. John must have flicked the switch, soon we all sat squinting in the brilliance, but no one made a sound.

"Oliver Mackinaw was a spy," John began and was interrupted by a man's voice. John immediately yelled, "Silence please!" The couple next to me took each other's hand. The man quieted after one word and John continued. "So was Edward Thomas."

He hadn't told me that.

Everyone remained quiet and most sat still. The dark-haired lady on the other side of me wrung her hands together and her husband put his arm around her shoulders and gave her a squeeze.

John's eyes scanned the room before he said, "And so is your Interim Keeper."

A man on the front row stood up. He was a heavy-set man with a triple chin and a dark, red face. He pointed a thick finger at John. "How do we know that you didn't kill Ceana and Conall to take their place?"

"And Edward," shouted a woman from the back.

Around the room a couple of heads nodded. A balding man, two rows back, stood up and said, "Charlie, you know as well as I that the spirits would not have supported this gathering unless John and Zoe were legitimate."

The red-faced Charlie looked satisfied and sat down. Another man spoke from above and behind me. I turned around to see an Asian man, his fedora still placed on his head. "I don't agree." He turned back and forth to face both sides of the audience around him. "We know many spirits are compromised. They could have been persuaded to have this gathering."

His comment created another disgruntled combination of people who stood up and pointed to one another, accusing them of this and that until no one could hear what their neighbor said. Irritation clenched my teeth together—we weren't accomplishing anything and wouldn't save anyone if we didn't work together.

Since the meeting began, the Law Book had rested on the Law Rock and I knew that only John and I could see it. Mullog whispered something in John's ear and John nodded his head. I didn't know what they were up to until the Law Book began to glow. Then the glowing Book started to rise and as it rose sparks of mesmerizing light were sent throughout the room. The light cascaded over the points of the stalactites and stalagmites to spill up the walls and across the ceiling. As the light grew, the voices quieted until a solemn hush was thick in the room. Everyone sat down. Each pair of eyes glistened and watched the book in the captivating light. Hanging in mid-air, the glowing pages of the book opened and settled thickly to one side, like a sunset, before the book floated down and positioned itself on the Law Rock in front of John. The light evaporated from the book and it became its normal radiance of inlaid jewels. The faces of the couples next to me were set in bewildered silence.

John cleared his throat. "This is a momentous occasion that everyone here has the opportunity to witness the Law Book. Please withhold any comments. I'm going to read, or rather summarize, from one of its pages. This page was written thousands of years ago during the formation of the Society of Archivists. In essence it says 'It is now necessary for a league of writers to be formed that will represent and portray the written truth of all humanity on earth with precision and legitimacy. Few living persons accurately describe their lives in their journals and chronicles. They embellish or withhold, they lie, deceive, and misrepresent themselves, all to receive gain and promote their lives until little truth remains. So also do their progeny elaborate and make bold declarations of their ancestors. Rewriting a history that did not occur. Many have no language skills at all. Humanity on earth cannot be sustained if this new moral standard continues.'"

John's eyes glanced away from the book and swept the room of people. "One might ask when the honesty of human beings began to decline? I say that it declined when fear began to dictate truth. This fear can be categorized as worry, fright, trepidation, or concern. When it came to filling the pages with their own life story, many people grew concerned with how they'd be perceived or judged by others. Whether this was a fear of not being remembered the way they wanted, or a fear of how others would perceive them if they genuinely revealed their life's accomplishments and acts, is difficult to determine." John grinned. "But it must have made many a squeamish writer to think of their loved ones reading about how they really performed in this life. Others couldn't read or write at all, and still others held classified secrets. They forgot the reason why each of their individual history was important. They failed to remember that no matter how small or seemingly insignificant they thought their life to be, that their thoughts, wisdom, and ideas benefit humanity in their own way and collectively shape the world, and all of this without the need of falsehoods or pretentious details. They abandoned their knowledge that truth will someday be told." His eyes turned back towards the book. "For this reason, which remains true today, the Archivists became a necessity. Thus commenced the time to interview spirits and record and archive all human lives; always taking into account which mysteries and secrets must be concealed and those that needed to be broadcast to all. Archivists and the Law Book came to be. And—" Mullog waved his arms and shook his head as he rushed to John's side. Of course, no one saw this exchange except me. When John resumed, his voice had a slight shake. "And...we don't know...how we came to be. Many believe it to be divine intervention. But suffice it to say that we're here to stay." John had recovered well, but not before I noticed how pale he had become after he paused. He had read something and whatever it was it scared him. His eyes met mine with an impression that he was seeing me for the first time, which concerned me all the more.

John continued, "Never in Archival history have we had to deal with what we have recently experienced. Because of those who broke our covenant, we have spirits that are forced to reveal hidden truths in order to save the lives of their living families. Zoe has interviewed spirits who know who these groups are, but refuse to name them because their living families are being threatened. For this reason alone it's necessary for Archivists that are also secret agents. This unprecedented move is the only way to infiltrate and take down all those who seek to use our skills. These people use our abilities for their own personal gain, or for the gain of those they work for. Some work with people in power who seek to discover secrets that have died with dictators, kings, or presidents, and they don't care whose lives are damaged or lost to access this information. Can anyone blame those Archivists and spirits who have revealed things to protect their family or their country? What would you have done if put in their situation?"

A tall muscular man from the second row stood up and walked to the front. Pointing at John, he said, "Who's to say you Archivists who became spies weren't the ones that initially gave up our secrets and started this mess?" Hearing his accent gave me an involuntary shiver. Hopefully, it was only a coincidence that he had the same eastern European accent as Jaak.

"Actually, I was an agent before I became an Archivist." John got this in before several things happened at once. Half of the people stood up and the room erupted into numerous heated debates, Mullog disappeared from my view, and the Law Book began to rise. Before it moved more than a few inches, the man who stood near John spun to the side and grabbed hold of the large book. With muscles bulging, he slammed it shut and with a triumphant gesture hugged it to his chest. All the while John appeared unconcerned and watched him. Immediately, the blistering conversations died down and the room grew tense as everyone stared in shock at the man clasping the Law Book, everyone except his companion who smiled and clapped her hands together.

The man laughed a quick and simple laugh and said, "That was too easy." But he didn't take a step before his face went white and his eyes squinted in pain. His mouth grimaced and opened up to discharge a dreadful screech. A scream of horrendous proportions that mixed guttural sobs, soprano shrieks, and extreme misery. He screamed so loud that people, including me, covered our ears. The man stood in place, seemingly unable to move, his arms still clutching the enormous book. Smoke began to bulge from his eyes and nose, and any other orifice a human body contained. People gasped and turned away. His companion screamed, but she didn't move towards him. The man's shouts and his smoking torment continued until he burst into flames. At that point, his companion fainted and the Law Book gracefully levitated away from his grip. It had been the Law Book that had kept him standing in place while levitating. Once the book withdrew from the man's grasp, he buckled over in silence and sprawled onto the ground. When the body hit the ground, the book vanished along with the light in the room. The only available light came from the orange glow of the burnt ashes still sizzling next to the Law Rock. Everyone remained stationary, no one stating the obvious fact that it wasn't a good idea to touch the Law Book.

I covered my nose from the smoke and the stench and waited in stunned silence for John to turn the lights back on. But he didn't. I heard some whispers, quiet crying, and sniffing. Then footsteps echoed from the direction of the altar and what sounded like a switch flipped on and off. People coughed, but no one spoke up until a shaking, elderly voice said, "That's enough, John."

A few mobile phones were held up with dots of light that barely covered any expanse in the room.

"It wasn't me who turned the lights off this time," John said.

"Maybe a fuse blew," said the same elderly voice.

"I can't get the lights back on," John said.

A few nervous whispers went through the crowd. Some booted feet stepped along the top part of the stairs and with it several shadows.

"There's been a breech!" a man exclaimed from the back of the room.

"At least five men dressed in military dress are trying to break into the Althing," said a man waving a torch. He stood at the top of the benches. "We need to get out of here."

Several bursts from a semi-automatic weapon resounded from the hall. A chorus of screams rang out, which made my spine prickle. I ducked my head down but remained seated, not daring to move. A few mobile phones fell to the ground and some went dark.

A distant rumble sounded and splinters of rock and pebbles scattered around us, the rocks more heard than seen. The dots of light from the phones lit up dusty particles floating in the air. A second blast shook the hall and sent larger rock debris that fell and rolled around us. The dust became thick enough to shroud the minute light emanating from the phones. Men hugged their wives and grabbed their seats to steady themselves in the blast—and then panic ensued. People brushed past me in the dark, touching my shoulders and head, but I remained seated and hoped John would come for me. But when automatic gunfire sparked through the hall, chipping at the crystal-like walls, I dropped down, crawled under the bench, and covered my ears. Screams and gunfire surrounded me and ricocheted off the benches and walls.

"John!" I yelled, but I didn't move from under my bench cover. My eyes were pinched shut and my hands gripped my ears. I bent my knees to my chest and tried to make myself as small a target as possible. I don't know how many times I screamed John's name, but at some point he found me and folded me in his arms of protection.

The barrage of bullets and screams seemed to go on forever.

When the gunfire stopped, we waited, and because John didn't move, I didn't either. A couple of seconds later, two grenades exploded. My eyes flew open to see light from a third explosion somewhere near the top of the amphitheater. More screams and thuds of bodies and debris could be heard cascading down the benches and stairs. Then a form of quiet-muffled silence filled my ears. John continued to remain still. I knew he was alive because his breath warmed my hair. A few moments later, calls of the wounded and gurgles of the dying echoed around us. Those alive and closer to the blast coughed from the unseen smoke. Before the smoke and dust made me cough and give my position away, I covered my nose and mouth with my shirt collar. A couple popping sounds disturbed the post-blast silence before a glow stick was tossed over the altar and landed on the other side. It rolled under a bench. The green stick cast an eerie ruddiness to the dust settling on the once clear benches and altar. I remained still and waited.

Chapter 20
DEAD AND GONE

Þingvellir, Iceland

"Don't move," John whispered in her ear. "They have night vision goggles."

He kept Zoe under the bench and listened to the coughing, heavy breathing, and the tapping of footsteps. He didn't know if the footsteps came from the victims only or if the perpetrators walked about looking for survivors. His left arm circled around Zoe, his right hand held his .40 caliber Glock 22 cocked and ready. He needed a pair of their night vision goggles. Without them, he would have to react to any sound or footstep that approached in their vicinity by shooting first. He had no other choice.

"John, I know you're in here." A man's voice broke the silence.

John didn't respond.

"We're trapped, John. How about we put our weapons down and figure a way out of here?"

The man waited a few seconds and said, "Your wounded need help. Or should I make it easy on them and put a bullet in their heads? Hmmm, this one we can't have talking."

A woman cried out, "I won't say anything…no!" Two shots were fired.

"Fools. They were told not to touch the book."

John remained under the bench with Zoe, listening. He didn't recognize the man's voice, but knew the man moved around because when he spoke the sound waves bounced off the surfaces in the hall in different directions. The guy was searching for him and from the increase in volume of his last sentence he had moved closer.

John felt helpless without a torch. The light from a torch would have been useful to aim with and blind the man's eyes. He estimated he had less than a minute before the guy found him. If he spoke or shouted, he would have much less. He hoped his plan worked.

John patted Zoe's arm and put his Glock in her hand. He had taught her how to use it the afternoon before they met Mullog. She had shot targets with remarkably good accuracy. With his gun in her hand, he scooted himself out from under the bench and drew his knife from the sheath hooked at his waist. He crouched low to the ground in a position where he could spring up when needed. Then he called out, "Mullog, show yourself."

"John. You are daft, aren't you?" The man chuckled.

John heard boots stepping down the aisle, but Mullog didn't show himself. Had that sly one left? John wondered.

"Mullog!" The tapping sound of the boots was almost to the bottom of the stairs. He felt a moment of panic and in desperation yelled again, "Mullog!"

A sudden burst of white light flooded the hall, penetrating every silvery wall and bench as Mullog unveiled himself as bright as the noonday sun. John leaped from the floor, drew back his hand with the knife, and aimed at the chest of the man taking his last unsteady step to the floor of the amphitheatre. The man blindly removed his goggles, but never saw the knife as it penetrated deep into the front of his neck. The blade continued through, severing his spinal cord.

The man crumbled to the floor as he dropped the goggles held in his hand.

With his peripheral vision, John saw movement near the top of the aisle. A man tossed aside his goggles to position his automatic weapon at John's chest. John threw himself, head first, towards Zoe. He slid over the floor with bullets chipping the ground in his wake. Still in mid-slide, he reached his hand out for his Glock. On cue, Zoe held the grip so his palm would make contact; he wrapped his fingers around the grip and rolled onto his back. He then brought the gun into position in line with the camouflaged person whose ammunition continued to pelt the ground alongside John's moving body. John's one shot, perfect in aim, entered the man's forehead. The camouflaged arm that held the weapon flayed outward and the body fell backwards, his eyes wide open in dead surprise.

Mullog floated overhead, casting his light over the hall, and announced, "You got them."

"Thanks to you, Mullog," John said.

Still lying on the ground, his eyes searched Zoe's face. She smiled at him and reached for his hand. He took her hand and pulled her out from under the bench. She slid across the smooth floor and he rolled over so that his face was above hers. Her sea-blue eyes caught the bright light and sparkled. Her awkwardly striped hair spread around the floor and framed her beautiful face. Her full lips looked very inviting to him and since she didn't push him away he got closer and said, "Great move back there."

She smiled and he pressed his lips against hers. With the coughing of the wounded in the background, it wasn't quite the kiss he had planned, so he made it brief. Reluctantly, he stood up and pulled her up beside him.

Mullog cleared his throat. "Great move right there, amico mio."

When I heard John yell for Mullog, I knew what he had in mind and I thought it brilliant as long as Mullog still remained in the chamber and didn't mind revealing himself. It worked. I felt faint, not only from the intruders and the wounded, but also from John's kiss. An inopportune time—yes, but the memory of it kept me optimistic while I cared for the wounded.

The grenade blasts had turned the exit into a pile of rock and debris that sealed us in. Most of the rocks were taller than John, and the uneven, heavy chunks had sharp triangular edges. The grenades had opened a couple of dangerous cracks in the floor of the cave and revealed the once sealed thermal core. The cracks unleashed assorted billowy clouds. The clouds escaped through the cracked crevasses and poured heat into the hall. If we didn't find an exit soon, the heat would become unbearable.

Mullog helped us locate first aid kits and a supply of battery charged lanterns stored in the Altar. They gave enough light to see the wounded and assist them so Mullog could darken his own brightness that had helped us locate the supplies. We were relieved to find two doctors and a nurse among the Archivists. They said their professions were excellent choices in our line of work, along with morticians, graveyard workers or grounds keepers, and genealogists. I added writer to their list.

Of the sixty-six in attendance, eleven were dead, eighteen seriously injured, eight grazed either by bullets or rock fragments that became shrapnel, and ten were missing. The remainder of us split up the responsibilities of patching up the wounded, getting the lights on, and finding a safe way out. The doctors bound up the bleeding wounds of the seriously injured. The nurse told those unhurt, or at least able-bodied, how to assist with lacerations and sprains. No one mentioned the burning man or the Law book. The panic in their eyes seemed to indicate that even discussing what happened would prove fatal. John and I decided it might be best if we left the area and took the responsibility of finding a safe exit.

We followed Mullog past the rock and debris blocking our exit and into the next tunnel, which led to the records hall. He acted as both our guide and our light. His light cast more of a soft glow than the white light of earlier. This had definitely been a difficult day for all of us. I felt dark myself, especially after seeing some of the Archivist couples who had died together, arm in arm, trying to protect their companion. Similar to how John had protected me. Once we were out of listening range of the others, I asked, "What made you decide to reveal the Law Book?"

Mullog turned around, his dark eyes flashed. "Mia amica, I recognized everyone but that foolish man and his companion. Today is the first time we have ever had intruders at our gathering. I took measures so it will not happen again."

"Let's hope it doesn't," John said.

I touched his arm and had him face me. "John? I know you saw something in that book. The others may not have noticed, but I definitely did."

His eyes sought Mullog's for help and I said, "Oh no you don't. You two are not going to keep me in the dark."

John reached for my hands and held them. "In this case I don't think we have a choice."

"For now, mia amica, we are forbidden to speak of what he saw. But you will know, maybe even soon." With that said, Mullog winked at me, which made no sense at all so I shirked away and continued down the hall. I had thought that becoming an interim Keeper would diminish the secrets held from me, but that didn't seem to be the case.

We walked on in silence. Mullog stopped in front of a wide door made of oak, darkened by age, and surrounded by carved wooden levers. He told us the pass-code, which consisted of pushing levers up, down, or sideways around the door until it swung open. Another sequence I'd never remember. If I had my phone, I would have snapped a picture of the levers before being coded and again after the sequence was displayed.

"We have the most volumes here. Of course, this is because this is the largest Althing and one of the oldest. Archived here are most of the original families as well as the first kings and queens of Britannia. So many—" Mullog stopped his narrative. The lights worked in here and as row upon row of lights flickered on, Mullog froze.

We stood inside the most expansive library system imaginable. It had crystal-like shelves throughout the spacious cavern. Wooden ladders towered above us to the ceiling that rose a dozen meters high. The shelves continued into the distance as far as the eye could see. And, as far as the eye could see, the endless rows and heights of shelves were empty, completely void of contents—the entire collection from the people who lived in the north countries was gone. The only items left were poppy-coloured runestones, their shear size and weight made them impossible to move.

"I don't understand," he said. His voice showed signs of that sly one whom I wanted to avoid. A look of caution crossed John's face and he put his arm around my shoulders.

Mullog flew over the void, bounding like a humming bird from one side of the empty space to the other side. He mumbled unintelligible words in Italian. He touched several shelves, his hands reached with fingers spread out in the air to confirm the nonexistence of the vast array of records. John and I watched him, both of us unable to find words of comfort. Mullog floated down to stand between us, his light diminished to a ruddy glow. Mullog's eyes narrowed and he spat on the ground. His voice grew rough as he spoke. "Whoever took these had an army of helpers. To move this collection would be impossible in such a short time. Impossible."

John spread his arms in front of him for emphasis. In an extremely soft and coaxing voice, he said, "Mullog, we will find them."

Mullog sighed and nodded. He stared at John and me, and then recovered—a bit. A tear flowed down his cheek. "The secrets kept here, they are not for the world to know."

"Why? Why can't the world know?" I asked, removing my black sweater. The heat had culminated in the records hall as well. John gave me a warning look.

"They aren't ready," Mullog answered. He seemed to shrink in size.

"What are these secrets?" I asked.

"Are you from this world?" he responded.

"Don't be ridiculous," I said.

"You aren't ready to know."

John wiped the sweat from his forehead, definitely as annoyed as I was, but also concerned. "Is it the same as what I saw in the Law Book?"

"Si. And so much more."

"We're the Keepers, can't you tell us?" John asked.

"No, you are interim."

"You mean Conall and Ceana knew everything?" John asked, his voice edgy.

"They were ready."

John stamped his feet and swore, his face red from the heat and anger. He appeared not to care if the sly one came back for a visit. "Mullog, you must be reasonable. The records were stolen so, ready or not, the world is going to find out anyway. You must at least tell me what those additional secrets are so we can prepare for whatever crisis this will bring," John said in as soothing a voice as possible, when inside I felt like screaming.

"What? I'm as much a part of this as you. You, both of you, need to tell me what John saw!"

Mullog paced above us in the air. He muttered in Italian and appeared more like his alter ego. He stopped and glanced around, scratched his chin with his pointing finger, and looked down at us. The anger in his eyes diminished and his light seemed to brighten as he floated to stand in front of us.

"No need, la mia donna." The room became luminescent as he spoke. "We will find these people and take the records before they discover the secrets hidden within them."

The room continued to grow brighter and John and I shielded our eyes with our hands. John looked at me with raised eyebrows. I almost needed sunglasses to see Mullog's smile.

"Yes, but how? We're trapped with no way out," John said.

"You are not trapped. We can take the back exit," Mullog said, and moved away.

John watched Mullog leave and then took some quick and scrambled mock karate-chops in the air behind him. I shook my head at John's exasperation. "We're baking in here. You couldn't have told us this earlier?" John yelled at the spirit's retreating back.

Mullog stopped and turned around. "Do not be ridiculous. I am a spirit; I do not feel heat. I had no idea of the heat."

John spun around towards me with his arm flailing in Mullog's direction. "We're supposed to find the people who miraculously stole the records, are probably the same ones who are kidnapping our people, and this is what we're working with?"

He had a point, but I felt too discouraged to care.

The sun's rays had sunk beyond the lava-riddled hills by the time we brought out the dead and wounded far enough from the Althing to not arouse suspicion about the location. We were in a conundrum of how to stage an authentic scenario to explain the mayhem. We didn't have much time because the seriously wounded were loaded in a van and on their way to the nearest infirmary in Reykjavík.

After my experience of touching grave markers to raise spirits, I kept a distance between the dead and myself. I didn't know what would happen if I touched a body and did not want to discover the result of that now. When John asked me to help him position a dead woman's body, she happened to be the one with the angelic voice, I shrank back with tears in my eyes. He positioned her body by himself.

In the end we made it look like a random attack by masked men. They might even assume it was terrorists—a group of masked men that had attacked tourists while sightseeing. The dead were positioned around some geysers and John put shell casings he had found in the hall in areas where the supposed shooters would have been located. It had been decided that John and I would leave to resume the hunt for the missing Archivists and the ancient books. We could not afford to have everyone detained for questioning while the trail went cold for those missing Archivists, who we were certain had been kidnapped. Mullog had already left to keep the Law Book safe and to see what he could discover.

I gave one more look at the carnage before we turned and walked to the car. Couples lay dead that had given their lives for a cause that

I had only begun to understand and for secrets I didn't know if I'd ever be told, gunned down by an enemy we seemed unable to avoid or discover who they were. The couples were arranged near one another, their miscellaneous colours of scarves and hats strewn about the lava beds. The ground was warm and steamed in the cold twilight. The victims' blood seeped into lava crevasses or over the green moss before dripping into hidden trenches and rifts. A wind gust rolled the red and white Canadian hats and the Russian hat across the stark ground and I turned away from the scene—a scene made imperfect in so many ways. I knew the amount of blood and blood patterns wouldn't tally up for the investigators—but it would be a few days before the investigation would become conclusive enough to discover that. Maybe we'd have some answers by then.

We drove along the dark road and when we crested a hill the amber glow of several greenhouses dotted the landscape in front of us like stars. To keep my mind off what lay behind me, I tried finding a constellation in the light of the greenhouses and found Ryan's Belt and Pisces. The road curved. When it straightened back out, a line of car headlamps came up the road in front of us. The cars began to pass by us. Most of the cars were white and several had blue light bars on the top—the Icelandic National Police heading to the scene.

"I hope we can make it to the guesthouse without being noticed," said John.

I nodded. With John's shirt caked in blood and blood spattered across my shirt and trousers, we looked suspicious. I put my arm across the back of John's shoulders and neck, thinking we'd appear more like a tourist couple in the spotlights of the oncoming brigade. The move startled John and he jerked the wheel into the oncoming traffic—a minor almost imperceptible swerve.

"Bloody hell!" he said, the whites of his eyes glancing at me.

"I thought we'd look more normal and couplish," I said. It sounded daft even to me.

"Couplish? They couldn't even see us." He shook his head and looked into his rear view mirror as a blue light flashed into his eyes. "Warn me next time. A car did a turn about and is coming up behind us."

"I'm sorry." My arm was back, dangling in my lap.

We had the guns stashed away, but there were the bloodstains— obvious blood stains. Our coats were in the back seat, void of blood.

John said, "Get our jackets to cover us up." But I had already reached for them.

"Quicker."

I grabbed his leather jacket and my quilted coat and hauled them between the seats. We thrust our arms into the armholes as John slowed the car to a stop and tried not to swerve while he put his arms into the sleeves of the jacket.

"The passports." John kept his eyes focused on the wing mirror and watched the officer as he opened his door and walked towards our car. His light shone into the back window of our 4x4 Range Rover and wobbled at each of the officers steps. I took the passports out of my bag and held them in my lap, on top of my coat. John rolled down the driver's side window. In my side mirror, I saw another officer stand between the police car and the side of the road.

"Gott kvöld," he said. The officer smiled and held up a small torch that lit up our faces. John and I both smiled back. He wore a black jacket with one stripe on each of his epaulette straps. He had a kind face and appeared a little older than John.

John gave a relaxed laugh and said, "Hello. We're British."

The officer nodded. "I see." He added in good English, "You know why I stopped you?"

John nodded. "I'm guessing it's because I swerved back there.

We've been hiking all day and I'm a bit tired."

The officer pointed his light in our back seat where a couple of backpacks were positioned.

"You have a beautiful country," I said, a little high pitched and not sounding as relaxed as John.

The officer nodded again. "May I look at those?" He pointed to the passports I held on my lap.

I handed them over and John took them from my hand. My hand had a slight quiver to it, so I folded my arms to appear cold.

"Did you see the Geyser?" asked the officer as he opened each passport and looked again at our faces.

John shook his head and before I said anything, he said, "No, probably tomorrow. We were in Pingvellir on some trails, looking for wild life, and taking photos."

He handed the passports back to John and ducked his head down to look at me. "You keep him awake."

I smiled and grabbed John's hand entwining his fingers with mine. "I certainly will." John's eyes met mine with a mischievous glance and he squeezed my hand. I almost laughed out loud when I realized what he was thinking.

We waited in the car while both officers walked back to their vehicle and sat inside. The blue lights went off and the white car did a U-turn and headed back the way we had come. John rolled up the window with one hand, but didn't let go of mine with his other. In a serious tone he said, "So you're going to keep me awake tonight?"

"Not a chance." I pulled my hand away from his.

"How about a little chance?" he asked.

"Not even an atom size chance."

"So there's an ion of a chance," he said.

I rolled my eyes at him and he laughed. He stared at me and revved the engine a couple of times before putting the car in gear.

To change the subject, I said, "I guess we know where the parade of officers are headed."

"We need to pack quickly and get to the airport."

I looked at him in surprise. "Aren't we going to find clues to where the hostages have been taken?"

"They're not in Iceland."

"How do you know?"

"Those who attacked us had a quick getaway set up somewhere close. My guess? They're traveling by plane, boat or ship."

I stared out of the window and then at John. "You remember that I didn't want any part of being an Archivist, but now that I am, I want to get these bloody chaps that are kidnapping and killing us. I'm a big part of this now and I care what happens. I don't want the killings and kidnappings to continue. I'm tired of witnessing these gross murders and the waste of what I'm sure were great minds and intellectual thinkers." I went to put my hand on his leg, but thought better of it. We couldn't afford to swerve off the road. "John, I haven't forgotten the promise you made to me. It keeps me rooted in fighting this craziness. What a gift it was to discover my parents' souls continue; their lives continue."

John took my hand. "I won't let you down. I'll keep you safe— so you can talk to them as a human."

I smiled. "That would be my preference."

A sprinkling of lights glistened in the distance. We were near our destination. I remained quiet, John's hand in mine, and watched the lights grow closer.

John turned the car down a narrow street. He let go of my hand and hit a button on his phone and held it to his ear. I listened, hoping for a clue to where we were headed and was surprised yet again by John's abilities. I couldn't understand a word he said until I heard him mention the Isle of Man.

He hit the end button and I asked, "You speak Icelandic?"

"I lived here for a few years."

"You lived here for a few years?" I repeated, holding my hands out to the surrounding landscape.

"And I picked it up."

"And you just picked it up."

He glanced at me with his eyebrows raised. "Are you going to repeat everything I say?"

"Am I going to repeat," I began and paused. "Not if it's in Icelandic."

"Við erum hér og vinsamlegast halda mér vakandi," he said.

I grinned at him and asked, "What did you say?"

"We're here."

"All those words and you said, 'we're here?'"

"Basically." I began to wonder why he hadn't spoken Icelandic to the officer, when he grabbed my arm and his smile disappeared. "Something's not right." He unhooked my seatbelt. "Get down."

I scrambled between the seat and under the dash. I had barely caught sight of the guesthouse in the distance and hadn't noticed anything out of the ordinary. "What is it? What do you see?"

"Someone's in our room. I saw a torch moving about." He stopped the car and shut off the engine. He reached his arm under his seat and pulled out his Glock. He leaned over and grabbed his knife, stashed between my seat and the console. He looped the sheath around his waist.

"Stay here." He pushed my head down and opened his door.

He slammed the door shut, causing me to jump and hit my head on the dash. I guessed he wanted to announce our presence. I felt abandoned; not only could I not see what happened, but with the door shut I couldn't hear either.

Our place had only one door and two windows, all on the front side. If the intruder ran out, John would catch him. Then I had a thought that made me sweat, even in the cold. What if this was a trap and men dressed in camouflage with the advantage of night vision goggles were positioned outside? I hadn't noticed any cars parked nearby. We had stayed on the outskirts of Reykjavik with a garage as the only other structure in the vicinity.

I waited and thought how smart and cautious John entered situations like this. But I didn't hear footsteps or a door open. He should have been at the door, but no sounds of running footsteps, shouting, or gunshots came my direction. He could have used a knife and that wouldn't have alerted anyone. The sound of a gunshot would travel quite a distance in the flat terrain where we stayed. I became worried; it had been too long. I decided to peek out the window. I twisted around in the cramped surroundings and slowly exposed the top of my head above the window until I could see out. My window faced the street. Of course. I turned my head but couldn't see above the front of the dash. I was wedged into my little space, a near impossible space for me to twist my body far enough to see behind me and out of John's window. I twisted my hips and bent my knees to turn the other way. Once I knelt under the dash with my elbows on my seat, I peered above John's window. The door to our little guesthouse stood open. I saw nothing inside because of the darkness—no movements or shadows.

A light flicked on. I waited for a shout or a lunging shadow, anything besides the stillness that had me holding my breath. Nothing happened. The tiny guesthouse looked serene. In three or four steps, John could cross from one end of the place to the other. That would take only seconds. From my line of sight I saw the open bathroom door, but nothing else. Next to the bathroom was the room that I had slept in with a bed that took the entire space and with no closets. Mentally, I counted until at least a minute passed.

With the outside door ajar and the lights on, I should have seen something.

What if John had been tackled and lay on the floor while the intruder searched for whatever he needed? Or maybe he'd already gotten away. What if John was…?

I grabbed the door handle and opened the door, slid out the side, and down to the cold ground. I crawled through the gravel to the front corner of the car until I had an unobstructed view of the guesthouse. I listened, but only heard a distant hum of cars on the motorway. I convinced myself that whomever John had surprised had to be long gone. That meant John lay hurt. I had waited too long. My heart pumped wildly and I felt sick. I crouched low to the ground and crept forwards.

"Where do you think you're headed?" The woman's voice sounded shaky but strong. Because of the last few weeks, I knew the drill and stopped. The gravel pressed into my hands and knees, stinging. I felt trapped. I had been lucky thus far through these escapades with John. I knew that kind of luck couldn't keep me alive forever. I pictured a gun pointed at my head and wondered what John would do if he were me.

Suddenly the silent house erupted in laughter—a man's and a woman's. The woman behind me took a few shuffled steps my way.

"Zoe?" she asked.

The voice sounded familiar to me. I took a deep breath and stood up. Little pebbles fell from the imprints they had left in my palms. I turned around, half expecting a shotgun to be slung over her shoulder. "Nana," I said with complete relief.

Chapter 21
ALSTEAD

Reykjavik, Iceland

John checked the perimeter first. He walked around the guesthouse and found nothing out of the ordinary. No broken glass, no vehicles. He approached the door and his stealth-like entrance gave way to relief as his eyes met the grey eyes of the smiling Phoebe.

"Am I to guess that Nana has your back?" he asked, giving Phoebe a bear hug.

"Of course," she said. "I assume Zoe's in the car?"

He nodded, a smirk pulled at his mouth.

"Then she'll be surprised by your Nana any moment now."

They laughed and sat down on the small yet plush sofa, sinking into its cushions.

"For obvious reasons, I couldn't come to the gathering today."

He patted her arm. "It's good you didn't come. We were attacked. Eleven are dead with more injured. Ten are feared kidnapped. But you did miss the revealing of the Law Book, and what happens if it's touched."

"Really? Then we are truly in difficult times. And someone actually reached out and touched it?"

"Grabbed it and thought he'd take it home."

"Idiot." With a thoughtful look in her deep brown eyes, Phoebe asked, "So the sly one allowed the book to be seen by everyone there?"

"Yes," John paused before he continued. "Phoebe, when you and Jim were Keepers, did you learn all the secrets?"

"Most of them."

"I saw something written in the Law Book and I'm unsure what to do about it."

"Did it scare the bloody hell out of you?" she asked.

John studied Phoebe's face. "Absolutely. More than anything I have ever imagined."

She nodded her head. "There's only one thing written in the book that causes that much alarm, really two, but they go together. It's our curse. And like you, this curse frightens me more than anything in this world." She paused. "Next to this curse there's a time clause written, remind me how much time we have left."

"One year, one year from the betrayal. Unless we get all our Archivists back from their captors and eliminate anyone that knows our secrets and isn't an Archivist, we will lose our powers and be extinguished, wiped out completely, at the end of one year's time."

The two studied each other quietly.

John took Phoebe by the hand. "But how do we know when our year is up if we don't know when it all began?"

"I don't know, John. I'm surprised the heads of your department didn't tell you," Phoebe said. "There's something else that concerns us. Our records are being taken. What can you tell me about the records stored in Iceland?"

"Not even a trace—everything gone."

She shook her head. "That makes four locations of records taken today, including Dingwall, Gulen, and Tinganes. That's why we came to Iceland, but sounds like we're too late to save its records."

"All of the Blue Bloods came?"

"No. Only Nana and me. But we brought a certain kind of reinforcement."

He took a deep breath. "So it's begun."

She nodded and took his hand. "Does Zoe know everything?"

"No."

"She'll need to be told soon. If we had listened to her parents then this could have been avoided."

"She's not ready to hear about her family's involvement yet. And she's definitely not ready to know about this," John said.

He stood up as Zoe and Nana entered the room, Nana's arm was looped through Zoe's. Nana's other hand patted Zoe's arm in a possessive way. At least Nana liked Zoe. That relieved some of his anxiety.

✾❦✾

"We'll go to Zoe's home before heading to the funeral. I have a plane ready," said Phoebe.

I guess I should have been bothered by the fact that they had spoken for over five minutes as if I had left the room. They had made it clear that they weren't going to give me much information. They told me that Phoebe and her husband used to be Keepers. They mentioned that the "Blue Bloods" were an actual group of Archivists and had worked with my parents, but I was still sore about Aunt Phoebe being the only one that came to Mum's funeral. She should have convinced the others to make an appearance. Or maybe they figured they'd catch up with my mum another time, when it more suited their schedule.

They had already packed my bags and told me we had no time

to change so I went to the water closet. While I sat on the loo, Mullog appeared with his usual impeccable timing. When he appeared, I almost screamed due to my position, but being anxious to talk to him I muffled my scream to a moan, which I hoped no one in the other room heard. He held his book tight against his chest and glanced around to make sure we were alone.

I rolled my eyes at him. "Of course we're alone," I whispered. "Turn around."

Mullog faced away from me. I believe his blush had returned.

"Did you find out anything about who attacked us?" I asked.

"No. The spirits will not talk," he said. "Mia carina, I will return with you to the Alstead," he said in a secretive whisper.

"Alstead? Where's that?" I whispered back.

He spun back to face me.

"Mullog!" I hissed, between my teeth.

He turned back towards the wall. "Your home."

"My home?"

"Yes. Do you not know you live at the Alstead?" he asked.

"I've never heard that before, so no." I stood up and washed my hands and arms to get some of the blood from the massacre off of me.

"Mia tesoro, you have much to learn," he said, so quiet that I had to lean towards him. His face looked serious.

I began to open my mouth to speak and he shook his head. "Not here. Never refer to the Alstead around anyone. Mia donna, I must keep you safe."

A knock on the door made me jump. "Zoe, no time to clean up, the car is loaded," said Aunt Phoebe.

"Out in a minute." I listened to her quick footsteps as she walked away before I spoke again.

"Not even to John?" I asked.

"Especially not to John."

I wanted to ask him why, but instead I nodded, picked up my knapsack, and swung it over my shoulder. I intended to someday ask my parents why they kept everything from me. Certainly they could have prepared me a little and told me some things. Before I opened the door, Mullog and his book disappeared. It gave me comfort knowing his spirit continued at my side as a protector, even if I couldn't always see him.

John opened the car door for me. His hand pressed against my back and sent warmth along my spine as I slid into the back seat. I laid my head back and closed my eyes during the drive to the airstrip. He remained a mystery to me—one minute possessive and protective, the next minute distant and vacant, almost calculating with his words and expressions. When he informed me he was a spy, I thought his actions and behaviors were relevant to his profession, but a wary caution shrouded me after speaking with Mullog. I felt inclined to think that John held something back—something vital.

The night Ceana and Conall told us we needed to wed to continue to be Archivists, irritation had unmasked itself on his face. But he recovered and created a new look, another façade—one difficult to decipher. Whenever I received the chance, I studied John's face, but spotting the irritation had been the only time that I had seen through and questioned his façade.

After a bump in the road, I opened my eyes and inhaled a surprised breath—Mullog floated on his back, his face only centimeters from mine, his Law Book clutched to his chest. He winked at me and I tried not to appear alarmed and create alarm in the others. One glance at their faces told me only I could see him. How did he do that? He smiled and I closed my eyes again.

How could I ever go back to a normal life of not seeing spirits? To go back to that life wouldn't seem normal to me. Maybe I should marry John to keep my abilities. If my life continued to be perilous, at least he kept me safe. At times, we did have our pleasant moments. But it was difficult for me to fully trust him when he held information from me. I wanted to understand him, but realized he may be the type of man one never totally understood.

When this madness ended and I talked with my parents again, I wanted the satisfaction of telling them we had caught the people who murdered them. If I lost my ability to see spirits, I'd never get that chance. Would it be that bad if I chose to live a mysterious life with John to keep my abilities and continue to seek for answers? The possibilities in a life as an Archivist and working alongside John would be unnerving and invigorating all at the same time. And to see my mum and dad again might be worth the risk of marrying him. But where did that leave Shaw? He was all the family I had left. Didn't he have a right to our family legacy, or at least to visit with Mum and Dad too?

I opened my eyes. Two inches from my face, Mullog raised his eyebrows at me like he had read my thoughts and knew what my intentions with John were. My cheeks started to burn hot and I slammed my eyes shut.

Once the plane took off, I waited for someone to explain the things they had discussed and kept so secretive. Instead, everyone went to sleep for the two-and-a-half hour flight—everyone except me. I watched John sleep in the seat next to mine. His eyes were shut and his face turned towards mine. At last, I had the chance to study his face. I leaned closer and his eyes flickered open. Since I could not have shut my eyes fast enough, he stared into them. I felt my face flush warmly. He smiled a warm authentic grin, took my hand in his, and clasped it over his chest before he shut his eyes again.

No doubt he wondered about his own future. I dozed off. In my dreams I ran from men with guns and dressed in camouflage, men who had thrown my wedding dress on the top heights of a blazing bonfire. The white silk covered in lace had burst into flames that sent sparks in all directions. They blew in the wind and turned everything they landed on into another blazing bonfire.

Chapter 22
MARRIAGE SECRETS

Somewhere over the Irish Sea

The pleasure John felt when he caught her staring at his sleeping face and the fact he had awoken with her hand still resting in his made him smile and wince at the same time. They would land soon, but for now he had the pleasure of watching her sleep. Her long, thick eyelashes danced during her REM sleep and her perfectly formed lips pulled down at the sides as if perplexed by a dream. When he first met her, he had thought of her as a spoiled aristocrat. Then she surprised him with an undercurrent of toughness, that when mixed with her beauty, both baffled and thrilled him. But as he watched the consternation of her dream play over her face and the distress she experienced by it, it pained him to think that he was likely the cause of this suffering simply because of her acquaintance with him. Her anguish was something he hoped to remedy. He wanted Zoe to be safe and secure and had developed a plan that assured she would be.

Phoebe had plans of her own and wanted them to marry tonight—as soon as they returned to Zoe's home. The Blue Blood even had the Rector on speed dial. It shocked him that Phoebe planned to blindside Zoe. But he knew if they lost their abilities, all would be for naught. As Keepers, interim or not, they were needed, and with his specialty training becoming a Keeper had been an added bonus. But even with his expertise and all his preparation, he sensed weakness in himself—because he was about to undergo a task he had no training that would help him to accomplish.

Her eyes opened and he braced himself as his usually controlled heartbeat pounded inside his chest.

My face turned red. I felt the heat of it when, upon awakening, I found John's face close to mine, and my hand being caressed by his. His eyes appeared misty and my stomach tickled, or maybe the plane had lost some altitude as it prepared to land. His hand let go of mine and his face came closer. He paused with a question in his eyes as his eyebrows raised. I didn't move, at least outwardly, and it seemed to be the response he hoped for. His face came closer and I shut my eyes. His lips pressed on mine at the same time the plane lost a bit more altitude and I enjoyed a double stomach-flutter. His hand cupped my face as his lips parted mine. I knew that at least if we were destined to be together we would have sparks and excitement.

After several moments, he moved away and I opened my eyes.

His eyes seemed to dilate and he asked, "Marry me."

I couldn't speak. I had not expected that, or his face—the absolute model of sincerity. Why not say yes? We could plan a late summer wedding. During the interim, I'd have Shaw help me to investigate him. We may even solve the mysteries playing out around us. Especially finding Ceana and Conall. I nodded and kissed him again. This time his arms wrapped around me. He let a moment pass before he pulled away and smiled a quirky grin. He stared at me without speaking.

"What?" I asked in my shy, singsong voice.

In a whisper, he blurted, "Tonight."

A race of thoughts went through my mind, several of which were not very flattering. Number one, did he only want to marry me to keep his abilities or had he too felt something during our kiss? I guess I couldn't get too wrapped up over that, because I wanted to keep my abilities too. But how could I plan my dream wedding in an hour with the blood of the dead still clinging to me?

"Look at me. I'm more of a corpse than a bride." I could do a hysterical whisper pretty well. "Not tonight. That's not possible."

John's hands took mine and his fingers rubbed over my fingertips. It had the opposite of a calming effect on me. My blood pumped through my ears and adrenaline took over my limbs. I kept inhaling and exhaling to calm myself—nothing worked.

"Let's get you home and then we'll see," John said.

I nodded and thought of aqua waves crashing on a warm, sandy beach and wished a time warp would thrust us someplace where we made nice memories together before plunging into a frantic wedding.

The plane touched ground, adding to my otherworldly demeanor. I felt like I had entered a time warp where my mind grasped at nonexistent memories of John's and my life up to this point. Other than running away from people who attempted to kill us, we had very little experience together. My temples ached as I became very aware that in order to begin to plan this wedding I needed a bottle of Valium.

Upon entering my childhood home, I experienced a moment of shock and awe, a moment that had me amazed by Nana's and Aunt

Phoebe's nonchalance towards me in Iceland. Their behavior had been deceptively packed with a surprise. As I walked through the entrance hall, Phoebe held my hand and led me into the great hall, flowers were displayed on every available table that held space for the arrangements of long-stemmed red and white roses and white daisies. Canopies of ribbon and greenery were entwined between tall, white columns of lattice.

"This is amazing, so beautiful," I said, feeling both rushed and roped into something I had no say in.

Aunt Phoebe stood on one side of me, and Nana on the other. Phoebe looped her arm through mine and said, "I remember you used to tell me how perfect the great hall would look if decorated with lattice, flowing fabric, and white roses and daisies for a wedding."

"Oh Phoebe, thank you for remembering." The sheer fabric draped and swirled upwards through the lattice to bring attention to the paintings on the high ceiling. The fabric fluttered as the door to the house opened and the quiet, night breeze blew through the entrance and into the great hall. It brought to my mind those dreamy summer days, walking along the seaside with Mum and Phoebe. A few of the other Blue Bloods came to the seaside too, but Phoebe paid me the most attention. She listened and dreamed with me while Mum stared across the ocean. The beauty created in the great hall was a perfect rendering of my dreams.

John walked in carrying our bags from the car, one in each hand. He winked at me and said, "What do you think?"

Such a loaded question. I hadn't actually said yes to him, nor did I have a dress!

Phoebe's arm pulled me forwards. "You have one hour to be ready."

My mouth dropped open, my arms, still specked with blood,

moved out from my sides, and I shook my head. "You did so much work and it looks lovely, but I don't know. I haven't a dress."

John took my hand. "So is that a yes?"

I had no chance to respond. Nana's arm looped through mine and she grinned. "Come on Pheebs, let's show her what we have."

I looked helplessly at John. His eyes sparkled and he said, "I'll see you in an hour."

The ladies hustled me up the stairs, down the hall, and into my room where a wedding dress hung in the corner. I thought of the dream I had while on the plane and swallowed. But the dress was nothing like the one in my dream. This dress had beautiful silky lengths of creamy-white satin and no lace. The bodice was form fitting and pleated, and the neckline elegant and not too revealing. The sleeves were cropped short and had a stole that draped loose around the shoulders. There was a sparkling sapphire and silver clasp to fasten the stole together at the center of my chest. I took a step towards it and Nana held tight to my arm and stopped me. "Not until you clean yourself up." She let go of my arm and the two of them pushed me into the washroom. I had no say in it; I would be married that night.

"Scrub your body from head to toe, my dear," Aunt Phoebe said, and pulled the door shut.

"What about my orange hair?" I said.

Behind the door, I heard Phoebe say, "Not much we can do about that in the brief time we have."

True enough. Besides, the orange streaks were the least of my worries.

An hour later, I stood in front of the mirror that revealed a princess on the outside who felt extremely rushed and frazzled on the inside. The dress fit me perfectly. The creamy-white bodice wrapped around my figure before it billowed gracefully to my side and swirled over my slender hips and legs to lightly kiss the creamy tops of my red-soled shoes. My fingers touched the deep blue of the sapphire clasp.

"Unfurl your brow, my dear," Aunt Phoebe said, in a soft voice.

"This is so…sudden," I said.

She pressed her cheek next to mine, the warmth of her coffee complexion stark against the paleness of mine. Her large eyes studied my face in the mirror as she set her hands on my bare shoulders. "I know dear. This is the way it is with our kind. And it literally takes your breath away—I know."

I nodded and held one of her hands in mine and turned from the mirror to face her.

"I know this life has been harshly dropped on you. Kathryn didn't want you to have the life she had and for a time it seemed you wouldn't. She recognized that the Archivist ability had come to you when you came to her deathbed. I'm sure she grew frustrated by her inability to explain to you the way our life should be explained— over time, with care and concern from a parent—but c'est la vie."

She turned me back to face the mirror and we looked at our reflections in silence.

"She would like to be here with you now. I'm sure."

"Maybe she'll be here in spirit."

Phoebe nodded and searched my eyes. "You are stunning, my dear Zoe. The daughter I never had. Thank you for allowing me to be a part of this momentous night."

I hugged her. Sweet Phoebe, she had never had children and always treated me as her family. I adored her.

Nana had puttered around in a corner while we spoke and when we paused she walked over to me, put a white rose in the side of my hair, and said, "This will cover some of those orange streaks." She smiled. "I don't know if John deserves you, but he will definitely treat you good, or he'll have me to deal with."

We laughed and I kissed her cheek.

There was a light tap on my bedroom door.

"Come in," I called.

The door opened and Shaw poked his head around the door with his eyes shut.

"It's okay, Shaw, I'm dressed."

Shaw opened his eyes normal before they opened wide. "Wow, Zoe, you look bonnie!"

"Thank you, Shaw."

"No. I mean you look all grown up."

Shaw wore a tailored black suit with an untied white tie around his neck.

"You look dapper yourself," I said, relieved he hadn't noticed the orange in my hair.

"With such short notice, it's good I already had this suit." He sounded a bit wary. "I gather this is why you two disappeared so suddenly in Dingwall?"

I tried to cover up both the terror I harbored after being kidnapped and the terror I felt about this wedding. "Sorry we didn't let you know where we were." I felt sheepish and deceitful. I wished I could tell him everything.

"I'll leave you two alone, but don't be long." Phoebe patted Shaw's shoulder before she followed Nana out of the door and pulled it shut behind her. Shaw paced across the room, picked up a photo of Mum and me at the beach in Spain, and set it down. He walked to my dressing table where he picked up a lipstick tube and opened it. He spun it up and down, several times.

I watched him, amused by his obvious unease. "What is it, Shaw?"

He set the lipstick down and turned towards me. "Do you really know this John? This seems so sudden, almost secretive."

I opened my mouth to answer, but he stared at the floor and spoke before I said anything. "Are you…are you pregnant?"

I stared back at him for a brief second before laughing. "No. I'm not pregnant."

He took several firm steps towards me and grasped my upper arms, almost shaking me. "Are you mad? Why the urgency? It's the middle of the night."

The rage behind his words shocked me. I expected a response of disbelief from him, but didn't expect such anger. I had wanted to speak with him sooner, but hadn't had a moment to even gather my own thoughts. Nor had I wanted him to see me before I cleaned the blood off me. His eyes displayed malice in their depths, something that I'd never seen in him before. His squeezing hold on my arms began to ache. "Shaw?"

He shook his head and let go of my arms. "Sorry, Zoe."

Blood returned to the opaque marks left by his fingers and left red blotches in their stead. I didn't know what to think of his response. He was my mysterious brother who left for university when I was nine, but he'd never been unkind towards me. I spent time with him when he came home for brief school breaks, Christmases, and our parents' funerals. His work kept him traveling and living all over the world. Maybe this was a simple overreaction to becoming my protective parent figure.

Shaw gathered my hands in his, gentler this time. His eyes were guarded, but kind. "Don't marry him, Zoe."

What a conundrum. I couldn't very well tell him that I didn't want to marry John and I couldn't tell him the truth behind the spontaneous wedding. He'd see through my lie if I began to ramble about my undying love for John. The passion and attraction I felt for John wouldn't amount to enough substance for a midnight "I-

Do." I stated the most truthful thought possible. "Shaw, marrying John means everything to me." And then I smiled and hoped the smile was genuine, in earnest, and would dispel all doubts.

Shaw continued to hold my hands. "There are things about John that you don't know." He used a most gentle voice. His concern made me adore my protective brother. But his statement surprised me. How could Shaw know about any of John's secrets? Did he know about the Archivists? I held my breath and hoped.

"What things?" I said.

Shaw squirmed for a moment and looked uncomfortable. "I really shouldn't tell you any of this."

I squeezed his hands, my hope building. He had to know about the Archivists. Maybe he was one. "Shaw, I can't very well call off my wedding without knowing more." Which sounded funny to me as I said it. I'd like nothing more than to delay the wedding. "Please. Tell me what you know."

"I met John when I lived in South Africa."

Understanding dawned on me—they must have had a disagreement—probably about the Archivists.

"I knew both him and his wife."

I stared at Shaw and repeated his words. "You knew him and his wife?" My head began to spin with the increased beating of my heart. "This is about a wife? You...you probably just made that assumption. I'm sure he's had girlfriends before me."

"No, Zoe. Sarah, his wife, and I had drinks together at a club. I didn't know she was married until one of my partners told me to stay away from her because she and her husband were criminals."

I felt numb. My hopes crushed. What he said made no sense. Shaw helped me over to the bed and we sat down.

"I didn't want any trouble and stayed away. I later saw her and John together and confirmed he was her husband."

Nausea migrated through my stomach as I snatched at one more thought. "Maybe they're divorced?" I shook my head in wonder. "Why didn't you tell me this earlier?"

"I wasn't sure he was still married and didn't know how serious you were. But when Phoebe told me what you and John had planned, I immediately gave my friend in South Africa a ring to confirm if he was still married."

The look on his face told me the rest, but I heard him out anyway. "They are still together, but he'd been gone on business for several months. For business here in England."

"He's married?" I said in a tiny voice. I don't know what hurt more, Shaw wasn't an Archivist or John was married.

"I'm so sorry, Zoe."

How could that be? If John and I have been Host and Writer together he couldn't have a wife, could he?

Shaw studied my face. "There's more. Apparently, John and Sarah have been infiltrating an age-old organization that happens to have a lot of money."

Shaw paused and watched me as the thoughts trickled through my head. When paired with the holes in John's story, everything Shaw said added up. When Shaw mentioned the "age-old organization" I recognized the significance of that immediately. I asked, "What age-old organization?"

"I have no idea. My friend in South Africa only mentioned it because of how it relates to John and Sarah being con artists."

With my hopes about Shaw dashed again, I had to focus on the fact that John might be a con artist, a very good one. Had John found out about the Archivists through Nana? But John had used his Archivist abilities in front of me—hadn't he? And what about Captain Link? John would never threaten the Captain about his own family to get the Captain to do things, or would he? John's only family member living nearby was Nana. I couldn't imagine him ever hurting Nana.

My brain scurried through a barrage of horrifying thoughts. Had John lied to me? What did I really know about my new life that John hadn't told me? Nothing, except what Ceana and Conall had mentioned. Maybe they had been kidnapped by John to keep them silenced. He had made me promise that I wouldn't speak to anyone about becoming an Archivist, and when we befriended Ceana and Conall, they disappeared—and conveniently after John discovered they were the Keepers. How did I know John and his wife weren't the leaders in this plan to kidnap Archivists, and steal the archives? He was the one thing that remained constant during everything. Before I went to the authorities, I needed proof, but should I marry him to find it? Maybe keeping a distance from John would be safer.

I made my decision and hooked my arm through Shaw's. I felt him relax as he escorted me down the stairs to the great hall. Unfortunately, we appeared as a bride being escorted down the aisle and when we stepped into the hall the music began. Several rows of chairs were filled with an unexpected group of about fifteen people, most of them staff, who stood up when I entered. John stood in front next to the parson.

Bloody hell! Now what was I supposed to do? Clear my throat, stop the music, and announce my intentions, or walk down the aisle and quietly tell John?

I chose the latter.

Shaw gave my hand a reassuring squeeze and let me walk alone to John. I felt betrayed by John and hoped Phoebe and Nana didn't know about any of John's schemes. But how could they not? I'd talk to Phoebe later and find out. With each step closer, I grew angrier. A jumble of words swirled in my head and in the few seconds I had before reaching John I hadn't organized the jumble into anything coherent. Once I reached John I didn't stop. I smiled at the parson, took John's hand, and pulled him to a private spot in front of the twenty or so people sitting behind us. John's smile turned to confusion and mild hysteria when the music stopped playing and I said, "I'm not making you a bigamist tonight." I hadn't moderated my voice in time for when the music stopped and it echoed loud and clear in the great hall. John's mouth dropped in surprise.

In order to more quickly expel myself from center stage, I kicked off my red-soled shoes, ran down the aisle, past the open-mouthed audience, through the foyer, down the hall, and into the library. I opened the secret door to the one room in the house I knew I could be alone and no one would find me. I gathered my satin and silk so the uneven wood and rock steps wouldn't cause any ladders to appear, and I entered my domain. The door sealed shut behind me. I breathed in the scent of dirt and wood, and sighed my relief. But I couldn't stop the tears of humiliation and betrayal from streaming down my cheeks.

Chapter 23
PRIMORDIAL

Prestbury, England

John had never been more confounded in his life and being overwhelmingly so had created a huge lapse in his reaction time. After hearing the word bigamist he knew exactly to what she referred. No doubt in his mind—Shaw had instigated the bigamist issue. Now Zoe was missing. They had searched the house and the grounds for hours and had no clue to her whereabouts. Shaw was missing too and that alone caused John great alarm. Both Nana and Phoebe had wanted to tell Zoe everything, but he had insisted she wasn't ready to hear the details about Shaw and her family. After what he'd discovered in the Law Book, he had partially regretted his decision to withhold the information from her. Not anymore. If she'd been kidnapped and knew about the deadline when all Archivists would lose their powers and be executed, the kidnappers could torture her into revealing this information. If the kidnappers discovered there was a deadline, who knew what they would be capable of doing at that point.

He felt a torturous tug at his heart—a loss he never thought he'd feel again, and he only had himself to blame. He would find her, and when he did he hoped she would give him the chance to explain more about his life to her.

Through my tears, I walked around the grotto, picking up mementos from my parents that lay scattered on the shelves. The objects made me cry more. I studied a picture of Mum and Dad taken in a pub with brown walls and realized it had been taken at Owen's bar on the Isle of Man. Tomorrow would be Owen's funeral. More tears rolled down my face. I had to get a hold of myself, but since I couldn't remember the last time I shed a tear I figured this was healthy—let the misery out. The death of Mum, the other deaths, the kidnappings of Ceana and Conall—and myself— the massacre in Iceland, my brother not able to know about my life, the two-hour planned and failed wedding, and the black mascara smeared on my satin dress.

Little by little, the harrowing ordeals became washed away as I discovered interesting maps and books stowed inside cupboards and chests. I read the titles of aged, leather-bound books and poked at some stuff that looked like biscuit dough that I found in assorted clay chests. By the time I stumbled onto a lever, which of course I pushed, and an oak tree trunk carved into a shelf slid sideways, my tears were dry. The sliding tree trunk exposed an area with tunnel hallways, round doorways, and circular rooms supported and detailed by an assortment of dark woods that framed the doorways and supported the ceilings. A flip of a switch turned on stained-glass sconces that illuminated the halls and rooms; I was enthralled by a hidden world carved beneath my family's property.

One of the round rooms had a wardrobe hung with clothes— clothes my parents had worn. I foraged through the shirts and sweaters containing the woody fragrance of dad's aftershave and Mum's lavender soap. I removed the stole and the dress, both smudged with mascara and dirt, and chose a pair of Mum's loose fitting trousers and a red button-up shirt. I put them on, along with a pair of black stockings and comfortable, well-worn running shoes. I then continued my search with reckless abandonment, tempered by lack of sleep and no clue to the time of day or night.

To insulate myself from prying eyes that may enter the outside grotto area, I found a lever on the inside wall next to the tree trunk. I pulled the lever and closed the opening. Feeling safe and secure, I continued my investigation of this cave within a cave.

The room with the wardrobe was a bedchamber. It contained a wrought-iron day bed with a trundle, both covered in quilts of forest green and matching pillows. From there, I walked into a basic kitchen with an icebox, a porcelain sink, one-burner hob, and a red-painted wooden table with two Windsor-style chairs. The table was pushed against the wall and barely large enough for the two dinner plates set on top. A cupboard hung on the wall of stone behind the hob and sink, and contained granola bars and peanuts. Upon spotting the granola bars, my stomach rumbled. I grabbed a couple and ate them. Realizing the convenience of having my own hide-a-way, I made a mental note to resupply the kitchen with essential and long-lasting food items. I took a drink from the sink and discovered the water was refreshing and cold.

Feeling a bit like Goldilocks, I tried out two plump and cushioned leather chairs in the round study. The second chair felt just right. I leaned back and looked around the room. I thought about my parents spending time away here. I wondered if they ever found out the Archivist secrets that the world wasn't ready to know. Other than the chairs and a secretary-style desk positioned between them, the only object in the room was an interesting chest. The chest was large enough for me to climb inside and sleep in a curled up position with soft pillows if I chose.

A study of the chest revealed a petrified wood lid made from a polished Redwood burl, and the sides of the chest I knew to be hardened lava rock, compressed and cooled for the chest walls and base. I had a pen box version of this same chest. My dad gave it to me the week before he died. He had explained the nature of the lava materials and the near impossible way to form the sides and floor as one continuous piece. He had also told me it was as old as time. I had laughed and hugged him, exclaiming my thanks. Inside, it held pens that I used for a week, until his death, but now planned to use and write my dad's biography—when I could interview him. This would have to be soon, before I lost my powers.

Thinking back to my father's explanation of my box being as old as time, I didn't want to touch this chest. For all I knew it was the Ark of the Covenant. Next to the chest, a crowbar leaned against the wall. The only explanation for the crowbar being placed there would be to use it to pry the lid up—an obvious declaration to the heaviness of the lid and the need to open it. I figured the chest was safe. I tried to lift the lid and it didn't move at all. I picked up the crowbar. Before attempting to pry it open, I studied the heavy-duty hinges that supported the lid. The two hinges resembled an Irish boxer's knuckles. I figured it safe for me to open the lid and let it fall against the wall. Because of the noise the lid would create when the petrified wood contacted the wall, I draped a quilt over its edge. With the crow bar angled into the narrow opening on the side, I pried and heaved the lid with all my weight until it fell backwards with a thud I hoped no one upstairs heard.

I set the crowbar down and peered inside. I had recently seen enough old and ancient books to recognize I had stumbled upon a book older than anything man-made contained in the Althings. The chest stood over a meter in height and width and about half a meter in depth. It contained one tablet-paged book, which underneath had mechanics similar to gears in a clock that now clicked and ticked. The gears' clicks and ticks raised the tablets above the chest to position it for reading with the chest as its table.

The clicking stopped. I shut my opened mouth and stared at the exquisite beauty and etched writing on the tablet pages made of…I didn't know. Each page was a few centimeters thick and almost clear like glass. From the fine edges of the words written and inscribed in the glassy material, colours of yellow, red and blue sparkled throughout the room. I squinted. I would need a pair of sunglasses to more easily read the book and study it. Unsure whether I'd be struck by lightning, turned to sand, or sucked away by an otherworldly wind if I touched it, I just stared at its beauty.

"You can touch it, mia signora."

Behind me, Mullog's voice both startled and struck fear in me during the split second it took me to recognize him. My preoccupation of the tablets kept me from screaming.

"You have to stop sneaking up behind me." I smiled at him. "But I am glad to see you, my friend."

"Si, amica mia," he said.

I nodded, and pointed to the stack. "They are beautiful. What are they made from? Crystal?" I asked.

"No, too fragile. They are diamond."

"Diamond? How is that possible? And they're etched?" I noticed a peculiar writing instrument nestled alongside the tablets. It had narrow clamps and round weights about the size of my palm, and the entire object resembled a record player needle from the 1970's. After observing the writing instrument, I answered my own question. "You etch diamond with diamond."

I thought back to a time when my parents played their favorite music and made their proud announcement that a diamond needle in the record grooves created the sound. I thought that was cooler than the compact disc my friends had. After kneeling, I peered into the depths of the chest at the number of tablet pages made from sheets of diamond. I whistled and said, "The cost—"

"With the clarity and colour—billions." Mullog smiled.

I whistled again and examined them closer. "How are such flat and large sheets possible?"

"That is an archived secret."

"Well, I can definitely see why the world isn't ready to know where diamond sheets that big are found. How have they remained safe?" I stood back up.

Mullog's arms and hands, freed from the weight of the Law Book floating above him, waved around as he spoke. "An Archivist named Vlad tried to use the value in the tablets to rule and become powerful. He brought a group of people to see their beauty and worth. When he opened the chest to show the tablets, he cried out in pain—frightening the people." Mullog shuddered and his hands went still, but only for a brief moment before he continued telling his story. "His body began to smolder. The people watched long enough to see his body burst into flame. They ran, but only a young child escaped with his life. After word spread about what had happened to Vlad and the others in the cave, no one came near that place for decades. By then, all signs of the Althing had been erased and the contents relocated, with the Lineage Book kept by the new Keepers. Only certain Archivists are allowed to see them. And of late they're stored here, at the Alstead. You are in the central room of the Alstead."

"My home?" I held my hands out.

"Yes, your home was built above the one and only Alstead. When your parents were the Keepers, yes they were Keepers, your dad had the idea of relocating the Lineage Book here at the Alstead where the Primordial Mana is kept. He also supervised making three copies of the Law Book for safekeeping on different continents. You've seen my original. We have a copy in Asia, Canada, and one in that closet next to the chest."

Mullog floated above the tablets and made his countenance brighter. He laughed as I shut my eyes and covered them with my hands, but not before I saw the sparks of rainbow hues from the tablets pierce the walls and ceiling. He laughed again and subdued himself to a more restrained light.

"Beautiful light display," I said, uncovering my eyes. I walked to the closet and opened the door. Mullog lit up the inside to reveal a weather-beaten, old chest. Surprised, I said, "But this doesn't look like much. It isn't even padlocked."

"An assumption most people would make. Do not touch it, mia bella. The same protection exists on that chest that exists on the Law Book that I protect."

Remembering the man in Iceland, I took a step back from the chest and asked, "My dad wrote three copies?"

"No. He supervised myself and two other spirits in copying it."

I nodded, shut the door, and turned back to Mullog, eager to hear more fascinating facts about my parents and our history.

"Your parents are very special, Zoe."

I waited for him to say more, but he grew quiet and watched me before saying, "Let us examine the tablets, shall we?"

Curious, I walked over to the chest containing the Lineage Book and reached out to caress the diamond tablets. They were cold to the touch and although I couldn't understand the hieroglyphic inscriptions on the top tablet, they were written in a pattern that resembled a pine tree with branches that grew wider down the page. The top had several characters and what appeared to be numbers directly under the inscription. Below that entry were two additional entries. Each resembled the one above. The entries continued below one another and across the page until the entire tablet's space was filled. Once in a while, there were spots with missing branches. It resembled a pedigree sheet.

I turned page after page and the inscriptions began to change from Egyptian characters to wavy Arabic until several tablets later there appeared to be letters representing names and dates. At that point, I realized what this contained. I looked up at Mullog, still floating above me. He nodded his head. I continued turning the pages and what looked like wavy Arabic letters disappeared and became Greek, Italian, and then German written on groups of pages, while still others were filled with Asian characters. I kept turning the diamond tablets and Celtic and English names appeared among the pages. Eventually, the dates neared the first millennia A.D., and soon this century. My amazement made me breathless.

Another apparent pattern seen from tablet to tablet was the various gems used for the different inscriptions. In the beginning most names were red and black, etched and filled with obsidian and ruby. The more pages I turned, the fewer the names appeared written in obsidian and ruby. Nearing the last of the tablets, I recognized one of my own ancestors' names, then several others until my mum's name in red and my dad's name in black leapt out from the page. My name appeared in red below my parent's names. Listed also were our birth dates and locations, and my parent's death dates. Nowhere did I see Shaw's name.

"What does the red and black mean?" I asked.

"La mia donna, it means you are Primordial," said Mullog. "And only you that are Primordial can see the Lineage Book."

"I'm Primordial?"

"The bloodline of both your parents can be traced to the first

Archivist. All names in red are the women Primordials; names in black are the men Primordials. The clear names are Archivists who do not have direct bloodlines to the first."

I turned back some pages and then forwards, searching for others in red.

"You are one of only five remaining young, female Primordials." Mullog's voice was full of sadness.

I continued to carefully turn pages, searching for the other names in my time. Other than my own name, I found four females with red. One was but a babe and lived in Morocco; another was a teenage Yank named Brynn Wheeler, born in Maine; the last two were…I looked at Mullog. "Ceana and Conall's daughters?" I whispered in surprise.

Mullog was silent.

I asked, "Iseabail and Barabal will be protected by their brothers, right? Unless Ceana or Conall know their kids are Primordial and reveal that information to their kidnappers, they should be safe."

"I do not believe they know," he said.

I took a deep breath and let it out slowly. "What does it mean to have only five Primordial females?"

Smiling from ear to ear and in a cheeky voice, Mullog said, "It means you have a responsibility to marry a male Primordial and have many baby girls."

I inhaled in surprise, not from what I heard him say, but from the name written in black obsidian on the top of the page I had turned. Mullog stopped smiling before he waved his hands at me and asked, "Why didn't you marry him?"

"He's already married."

I turned the page and made a point of studying the page, which listed some male names written in black. "Now, this Frenchman here is only twenty years older than I."

Mullog glanced at the name. "He's one of those killed in Iceland yesterday."

"Oh." I pointed to another. "Heinrich here is my age."

"He lives an alternate life style."

"Maybe we should set up a Primordial sperm bank. We could have Conall's unmarried boys volunteer," I said.

My statement caused Mullog to laugh so hard his light aura blinked on and off looking like a lighthouse beacon. "Oh…oh…mia bella. It has been decades since I have laughed like this." Still floating, he rolled over in the air, held on to his belly, and continued to laugh.

I didn't find anything I said funny. I put my hands on my hips and remained quiet.

"Oh…my…you are most obstinate." He began to calm down and asked, "Are you sure about John? You have not talked with him."

I nodded and plopped down in the leather chair closest to me. A woodsy smell whiffed around me after I sat—my dad's cologne. Had he been told he had to marry my mum? Had they grown to love each other before they discovered they were to be partners in the Archival Society? Our picnics as a family, and days spent by the seashore were always filled with love. They had laughed and talked for hours together, maybe because they had a common bond. But their relationship had seemed genuine and deeply loving. I had never felt they put on a front or a façade in front of Shaw and me. When my parents were alive, they were totally devoted to one another—true love.

I asked, "What about Shaw? Why is his name not written in here? Isn't he Primordial?"

Mullog nodded his head. "But he never received the power."

"He never found his mate?"

"No, the Archival power was never developed in him."

"How is that possible?" That was difficult to believe.

"It is most rare, but it does happen."

"Maybe he's just a later bloomer than I was."

He shrugged his shoulders. "Improbable."

"But possible?"

He shrugged his shoulders again and tossed his hands to his side, but remained quiet.

"Well, I guess I better find someone quick before I lose my abilities." I thought about the Primordial men possibilities.

Mullog floated to the other chair and made a pretense of sitting. "No Primordial female ever loses her abilities."

"What?" That meant so many things. I could touch my parent's graves and talk to them anytime I wanted to. I didn't need to marry John. I searched Mullog's glowing face. "Why didn't anyone tell me that?"

"Few—if any—living Archivists know. And because, mia carina, of what you are thinking about right now. You cannot visit the graves of your mama or your papa."

I glanced up at him. "Why not?"

"Their graves are being watched. It is very dangerous until we stop these people."

"Have you found out who is after us?"

"I cannot get the spirits to tell me who the kidnappers or killers are." His light softened.

"I won't visit the graves until it's safe." That would be difficult— but Mullog was right.

"Grazie, mia tesoro. And you must never tell anyone except your husband that you are Primordial."

"I can see the value in that. What about Primordial men? Do they keep their abilities?"

"John will lose his ability, even if he finds another female. He became a Writer because of your mama, and now you. Your bloodlines are connected." He shook his head sullenly. "You do him a disservice."

I rolled my eyes. "I do him a disservice?"

"I know you think you do not need him because you are Primordial. That is a mistake."

Did Mullog know all my thoughts? We sat in silence until I asked, "Does John keep silent about his being Primordial?"

"He does not know. The female Primordial line keeps the Lineage Book. No one knows his or her lineage unless they are told by a Primordial with the Lineage book, or it has been passed down through their bloodline. But word of mouth can create inconsistencies. Thus, the bloodlines have remained a secret for many years. Although some may suspect they are Primordial because of certain enhanced gifts."

Immediately, his statement of "enhanced gifts" resonated with me. "Could these enhanced gifts allow one to see spirits without mana and a Host?"

Mullog gave a knowing smile. "You have experienced this?"

"Yes."

"That is a rare gift, tesoro mia. You are most fortunate."

My eyes felt heavy and my body ached; I needed sleep, but it was time for me to abandon my quiet post and search out the living. I needed to talk with John. I stood up and stretched. Mullog shut the chest. He made it appear as light as paper until the wooden lid met the black sides of the chest and the thump echoed through the tunnels. After the lid closed, he turned towards me and said, "You talk to John. I believe him to be a good man."

"Mullog?"

He floated close to my side. "Yes, mia bella donna?" He had the most amazing and intimate voice. I blushed when his eyes met mine.

"Can you remain at my side?" I asked.

"If that is what you want."

"Unseen?" I asked.

"I will watch over you as long as I can."

"Thank you." I felt relieved, walked to the entrance, and opened and shut the large trunk of a door. I approached the grotto entrance and heard footsteps behind me.

"Zoe?"

Startled, I spun around. Shaw stood there glancing around. "Were you hiding?" he asked.

I pointed to a bench positioned in a shadowed area next to the wall. He didn't look convinced.

"We've searched everywhere for you. I decided it worth checking in here."

"Oh." That wasn't good. He'd figured out how to get inside the grotto.

He looked at my clothing and asked, "Are those Mum's old clothes?"

"I couldn't very well keep my dress on." I realized I had left the wedding dress in the hidden area of the grotto. Before he asked about the dress, I said, "You figured out how to get in."

"It took me a while. I tried to remember where you stood that first time it opened." He took both my hands in his. "Zoe, John's waiting to talk to you, but before he does I want to make sure you understand something."

I nodded.

Shaw spoke quickly, "You mustn't believe anything he says. He may tell you that his wife died, but I've asked about her and she's still alive. They are planning something and until I find some answers you mustn't let any of them, Phoebe included, know that

I've told you she's alive."

I stared at him and he squeezed my hands. Shaw planned to investigate John and his wife—all good by me. It would keep Shaw occupied while I did some searching of my own and continued to work with the Archivists to find Ceana and Conall.

"Zoe," Phoebe's voice called out from a distance away.

With my brain in a fog of exhaustion, I agreed to my brother's demands. He looked relieved and said, "Let's hurry." I followed him up the stairs to the entrance of the grotto. When we exited, the bookshelves shut behind us as Phoebe, Nana, and John entered the study. John took two quick steps towards me before he slowed down and stopped. His tired eyes searched my face while I saw emotions of relief pass over his own and then a flash of anger when he looked at Shaw.

Phoebe got to me first and hugged me. "I thought you'd been kidnapped." She held me at arm's length and said, "I'm sorry we rushed things." I could tell she wanted to say more, but with Shaw in the room she paused.

Nana nodded at me, her long grey hair hung in a side ponytail and she smiled a big tooth-filled grin. She grabbed Phoebe by the arm and tugged on her. "Pheebs, let's leave these two alone. Come along, Shaw."

But Shaw stood his ground and didn't move. His mouth was set in a thin line. He addressed the group, but his eyes bore into John's. "I think I'll stay." The tension in the room was visible. Phoebe and Nana's cheeks lost their colour. John's biceps seemed to pump as his hands turned into fists by his sides. My heart raced and I felt faint.

"Shaw, it's all right. No wedding will happen."

Shaw didn't stop his intense stare at John. Both men were quite intimidating. I was caught between protecting my brother from John, whom I had seen in action, and a desire to be alone with John, unencumbered by Shaw, which meant my brother needed to leave the room.

The edgy look in Shaw's eyes scared me. "Please, Shaw. I've had no sleep and I'm tired," I said.

"I'd like to hear him explain this implausible charade," Shaw said, through gritted teeth.

Nana bravely stepped around the couch and took Shaw's arm. He jerked it free with no thought about hurting the elderly woman. I shot him a look of surprise even though I didn't doubt for a moment that she could hold her own.

"Come with me, Shaw. We'll go down the hallway," Nana said, unfazed by Shaw's movement.

Other than having clenched fists and narrowed eyes, John remained quiet and motionless. A smart decision as he stood across from the aggressive stance that Shaw held. My brother and I had our quarrels, but I'd never seen him this angry and on the edge of control. Shaw's eyes shifted from John's to mine and I nodded to him with a double meaning behind my nod. I hadn't forgotten Shaw's warning. I breathed in a sigh of relief when he allowed Nana to guide him out of the door.

"You gave quite a show. I don't think anyone was disappointed, except me," John said. His voice was quiet, reserved, and full of hurt.

"You were disappointed? What about me?"

He sighed. "Disappointed in myself. I should have told you about her, about my wife."

I winced in surprise and wondered if he was actually going to tell me the truth or a fabrication. I walked to the sofa and sank down in exhaustion. "So you are married," I said, more as a statement than a question.

John's feet dragged over the carpet and he slumped down on the sofa next to me. My anger had dissipated; I felt nothing except weariness and when his hand encircled mine, I allowed it.

"Zoe, I was married for almost four years. She passed away in a car accident, over a year ago."

Coldness spread from his clasp on my hand, up my arm, and into my heart as I listened to the lie that Shaw had warned me would be told. The cold turned to ice as John continued his explanation. "It's hard for me to talk about, but not for the reasons you might think. I wasn't in love with her or her with me. We thought we were, but we were young. We met on the job. She was MI6. After we had worked together for about two years, our superiors had a job that required us to go under deep cover as a couple. The week before they gave us our assignment, we had discussed getting married, but never set a date. With our mission confirmed, we held an official wedding and went undercover as a genuine husband and wife."

"Were you investigating the Archival Society or is your life all just one big con?" I had to ask.

"Con?" He looked confused—genuinely confused. "Shaw must have used that term."

"Alright. What about investigating the Archivists?" I asked.

"Yes. We were," he said. "But that was before I met your mother and became an Archivist myself. Imagine my surprise when I actually became one. I found out when I met your mum. When I discovered I was an Archivist, Kathryn told me to contact Nana. Nana was thrilled and divulged a host of family secrets. My parents had also never told me they were Archivists. During my past years undercover, my superiors only gave me information pertinent to my assignment, on a need-to-know basis. The group of spies I work with, or worked with, most of them are Archivists, or at least I was led to believe they were. After working with your mum, I gained a better understanding of who we are and began to doubt that all of them were actual Archivists."

I stared into his eyes; I had so many questions for him. "I'm curious how MI6 even knew about the secret society of Archivists. And what you did for them, for MI6?"

He blinked and swallowed before he answered. He said, "I was approached by a man named Booker. You'll remember Booker. He was the man shooting at us in the morgue. He told me he had Intel to keep a unique group of people safe. We were to keep our distance from them and what they were involved in, only report where they went, and take pictures of anyone they met or anyone who approached them. I never knew how Booker received his Intel. We, Sarah and I, were a team and watched different people at different times. At first, our assignment was to watch them from a distance. We did this until we married and were assigned to go deep undercover. We continued our assignment until she died."

"You only took notes and photos of Archivists for four years? You never infiltrated them and attended meetings?" There had to be more to his assignment.

"We lived next door to some Archivists and recorded their conversations. But to us they sounded crazy, talking about ghosts and spirits and such."

I had never heard him talk so much, but he stuck to the facts and most of what he said probably had happened. Although I wasn't an expert in lie detection, I did know that sticking close to the truth helped. It had taken all my will to not yell at him, but I kept my promises made to Shaw and Mullog. I agreed with Mullog, John shouldn't know about my being a Primordial or about the Lineage Book. It was dangerous for me if anyone discovered that my abilities were mine forever.

John sat quietly for a moment and looked at our entwined hands. I blushed thinking this could have been our wedding night. I had to stop thinking like that or I'd throw myself at his mercy. I pulled my hand away and stood up. I needed some sleep to make better sense of everything. With my back to him I said, "I've got to think this over." I was almost to the study door when he softly called my name. I stopped and turned to face him.

"I want to marry you, Zoe, and not just to keep our abilities."

My cheeks reddened. "That reason was never my intention." Well, not anymore.

Chapter 24
TRUST

Thanks to Zoe, John sat in the kitchen, drinking tea, unable to sleep. First, she hid in the grotto for a long enough time that he believed she had been taken hostage again. Second, he felt relief when he saw her and discovered how deep his feelings were for her. If he had played out the last forty-eight hours with the understanding he now had, he would have gotten rid of Shaw—shipped him somewhere far away from Zoe. He and Zoe would have been married and thus assured of keeping their powers, and he would have been at her side to protect her. Including protecting her from the one person she trusted and shouldn't—her brother. He didn't know what Shaw had planned, but he had obviously told Zoe something to cover up his shady dealings.

He should have told her that he had known Shaw in South Africa and proved to her that her brother worked for the actual enemy. She needed to understand that Shaw would tell her anything to cover himself, but she wouldn't have believed him. After all, Zoe had never seen her brother's true character. In South Africa, John had witnessed his other side. Last night in the library, after finding Zoe, they had come close to a brawl. John had kept still hoping Shaw would unmask himself, break character and charge, but Nana and

Phoebe had prevented that from happening.

The final reason he couldn't sleep? That last comment Zoe made before going to bed—it infuriated him. What kind of a game did she think he was playing?

He sipped the last drop of tea, set down the cup, and grabbed his leather jacket. Forty-eight hours of no sleep had rendered him incapable of safely flying the helicopter. He pushed a button on his mobile phone. He'd have Larry pilot them to the Isle of Man for the funeral. After a quiet moment of farewell for Owen, he planned to put in action every trustworthy Archivist and available spirit to assist in locating Jaak and those responsible for the kidnappings, murders, and stealing thousands of year's worth of archives.

Isle of Man

The helicopter left after dawn in a cold and sleeting rainstorm that pelted the windows. I had been unable to speak with Shaw and compare notes about John before we left for Owen's funeral. In the helicopter was the pilot, plus seven others, including myself. The smell of soggy clothes permeated around us as we huddled close to one another for warmth. Even with the heat venting around us, we were cold. Besides Nana, Phoebe, John and I, Sean, Conall's son, had come and also two American men in their thirties. No introductions were made and I didn't press for names. The two Yanks had a "Navy Seal" look about them with their tidy, short hair, sharp eyes, and hard muscled physiques. They were the only ones not wearing a jacket or heavy coat.

We flew over Owen's tavern at the edge of town before we landed in a field nearby. My thoughts gathered around Owen's death and all the loss of life during the recent months. I shivered even though the sun peaked out from the low passing clouds and the heat billowed around me. The door opened and the refreshing smell of rain entered the musty-smelling cab. Blue sky peeked along the horizon beyond the dissipating clouds. I preferred sunshine at funerals and was relieved the rain had stopped.

Our legs became damp as we traipsed through the knee-high grass that grew in the field. I wished I had worn my Wellingtons. Instead, I wore my black boots that now had water droplets running between the leather and my shins. We exited the grass and followed a narrow cobblestoned road. We passed a few rock-faced homes before turning right along another cobblestoned road, too narrow for a car. Several scooters and motorcycles were parked in front of the cluster of slender homes all connected in a row. All were two-stories high. John led us to the maroon door of the fifth house. The house had sunshine-yellow paint with white trim. A red tabby Manx sat sunning itself on the front step. Its copper eyes glanced warily at us and then at the door.

When the door swung open, the Manx ran inside. A boy of about eight, with tousled hair and dressed in a suit with a necktie that he pulled loose, stood inside the doorway. He recognized John. He let go of his necktie—the knot drooped near his heart—and threw his arms around John's legs and squeezed tight. John ruffled the already tousled hair and smiled. The boy put his stocking covered feet on top of John's shoes and John walked forwards into the house carrying his load. A small package of a woman walked through the kitchen carrying a comb in one hand and with her free hand grabbed onto another youngster's shirt as he tried to run by her. She glanced at us and waved us in with the comb.

"Hello, John. Come in everyone. I'm just trying to smooth their hair." Her voice was sweet and sad. Her shoulder-length, golden-red hair was fastened with a brown ribbon at the nape of her neck. She wore a navy cardigan and a brown-tweed skirt that stopped at her knees. Dark-brown leather boots with thick heels gave her some height. Even with her heels, she barely came to the top of my shoulder.

After John introduced everyone, I asked Melanie if she had another comb. A tired smile lit up her face and she handed me the wide-toothed comb in her hand.

"I'll gladly let you have a go at it," she said with a laugh. "Charlie, Edwin, Peter, come let Zoe do your hair. A spray bottle is on the table behind you. I'll find their shoes."

The next half hour was a blur as we prepped the rowdy boys—several times—until we gave up.

"At least they all have their shoes on," Nana said, and shut the door behind us. We followed the unruly boys down the lane to the church. The rowdiness stayed with the boys as they entered the church; they fidgeted and punched each other down the aisle, oblivious to the teary-eyed people watching them. Each boy became solemn when they saw their father's casket. They sat on the hard pew, surrounding their mother, one on each side and Peter sat on her lap, their heads down, their arms crossed over their chests. It broke my heart. I wanted their playfulness to continue, as it should. I understood what they felt; they were even younger than I had been when I lost my father. It had just been Mum and me. Shaw already had a job, recruited right after college. Maybe it would be easier with the boys still in their youth, maybe she would re-marry and find happiness again. I knew the loneliness of birthday cake for two. When my mother hung the Christmas stockings that first Christmas, I took them down and hid them under the sofa. Neither Mum nor Shaw ever mentioned the missing stockings.

If I had married John, is this what we would have had ahead of us, the possibility of orphaned children? John took my hand and led me down the row to sit on the pew behind this young, brittle family. My heart beat out of rhythm as sadness gripped my body. John sat in a seat on the edge of the row and before everyone sat down, I excused myself. I needed some air. John narrowed his eyes and didn't let go of my hand. I shook him off before taking the exit row next to him. He frowned, but I didn't care.

At the back of the church, a tall column held up a dark corner of the ceiling. I headed that direction. The column was large enough to stand behind. I leaned against it for support and inhaled a deep breath. I remained there for a few moments, peering around until the stragglers filed in and found their seats. At that time, I sat on a pew in the back. John's eyes found me and he nodded my way.

A line of grey heads fanned out on either side of Phoebe—the Blue Bloods were in attendance. A few, maybe five, of those who had survived the shooting at the Althing in Iceland were present. But most of the attendees were locals. The Yanks from the helicopter had donned black suits and stood on either side of the entrance. They weren't hiding the fact they had earpieces and I knew they weren't listening to a game. I wondered who was on the other end of their listening devices. The black-suited men were the only two that appeared out of place, even with the overall congregation wearing various shades of black.

I sat numb during half of the service before I removed my noisy heeled boots and carried them as I stealthily sneaked out the open church doors. The security bloke whispered into his collar as I left. I slipped my feet back inside my boots and zipped them up before I headed for Owen's tavern and the Althing. I planned to walk through the Althing and talk to Mullog who I knew floated nearby. Behind me, the sound of a clear soprano voice accompanied by a violin floated into the air. With the church doors left open, the music rolled out and over the valley. The notes of the lament sounded familiar, but I couldn't put a name to the song, perhaps something from Burns.

I followed a road that lined the coast and the music changed from soprano to the bass sound of waves coming in with the tide. On my other side a field spotted with dark green and amber grasses blended into the late autumn terrain. The clouds had vanished and the early afternoon sun brightened the entire scene surrounding me; I wished it could be a metaphor for my life.

The flurry of my heartbeats slowed and I relaxed, taking in the songs of nature. Mullog appeared above the road; he had a solemn face and gave me a reassuring smile. I gave him a grateful look in return, glad that someone seemed to understand why I couldn't stay at the memorial service. He shone in the rays of the sun—a striking man spirit who made my heart quicken. His dark eyes and hair hinted at an olive complexion and he would have been a tall man for his time. He towered above me—floating or not. My first impression of Mullog had not been positive. He had scared and frustrated me, but had since become my trusted confidant and rescuer, and I found myself somewhat attracted to him.

"A back entrance to the Althing is hidden beyond that hedge." Mullog pointed to a small rise surrounded with ferns and clumps of grass higher than my head.

"Great," I said. "I really don't know what I would do without you, Mullog."

His brightness increased. "Tesoro mia, if I had a beating heart it would be fluttering."

We approached the bushes and Mullog said, "Push the shrubbery aside and find a rock key on the ground."

The rock key was unmistakable. A flat rock cut in the shape of a padlock key lay on the ground. I picked it up and glanced at Mullog for the next instructions and burst out laughing. Next to me, he floated with bushes protruding in and out of every edifice of his see-through body.

"What is it, mia cara?" he asked, staring at his prickled body.

"It certainly looks like you should feel those additional appendages," I said, suppressing my giggles.

"When I died, I had a moment of shock realizing that the physical laws of the body no longer applied. Most of us go through that and it can be very liberating, especially those who could not walk or see or hear."

I nodded and turned back to figuring out the key I held.

"The keyhole is at the base of the shrubbery," he said.

After peeling back shrub branches, I located the keyhole with my fingers. I inserted the key and twisted it, all the time wondering how the wall would open with no visible signs of a doorway or an entrance.

"Now push," said Mullog, before he disappeared through the wall.

A slight push and the cracks of a rock door appeared. It looked heavy but swung inwards easily. The weight of the entrance was counter-balanced enough for a light hand. I tucked my head down and stepped in to find Mullog waiting. A few minutes later, we walked through the Althing where John and I had been not long ago, but it felt like ages. I turned towards Mullog to ask a question. The seriousness in his eyes silenced me. He put a finger to his mouth and darkened out of sight. I stood in the quiet blackness for only a moment before a light cast a beam down the hall and voices filled the silence. With steps as light as I could make, I rounded the corner and stopped short. A black man holding a semi-automatic weapon at his hip stood with his back to me. Before I became an Archivist, I had only seen guns on the telly. Now they seemed to be an hourly sighting. The man with the gun directed a group of men pushing wagons loaded with pallets containing the records. The shelves in the room behind him stood empty.

Before I had sense enough to stop myself, I asked, "What are you doing?"

The black man turned around with confusion registered on his face. The men pushing the wagons stopped. Each man wore black clothing and a yellow miner's hat. In the sudden silence, the sound of running feet came towards us from the tunnel behind me. Before the man with the gun answered my question, a familiar voice called out, "All right, men." I spun around in surprise when Shaw appeared. He also wore black clothing and a miner's hat. I don't know who registered more surprise, him or me. He breathed hard and held his hand to his side. The surprise disappeared from his face and he smiled. He gave a quick hand-wave to the men and said, "It's fine. She's with me."

He snatched my arm and said, "Let's get out of their way, shall we?"

Confusion kept me quiet as he led me to a cave-like room where he pulled the door shut behind us. There were two folding plastic chairs on either side of a small, narrow table. It looked like an interrogation room. On the wall hung a wooden sign with "ISLE OF MAN CAVE" carved in capital letters.

As soon as the door shut, I turned to Shaw and asked, "What's going on? You're taking the archives?"

He removed his yellow miner's hat and set it on the table. He pulled out a plastic chair for me and he sat in the remaining chair. "I've been keeping an eye on you, for one," he said, and continued. "And yes, we're moving these."

His emphasis on moving wasn't lost on me. "But why? How is it you know about these books?" I didn't think Shaw knew anything about the Althings, or me, or anything about the Society. Why had John made me promise, for Shaw's safety, not to tell him anything? Were they actually working together—maybe with some rivalry between them?

Shaw's mystified face studied me. "And I didn't know you knew. We're moving the books to a new location, to keep them safe."

"I thought they were safe here."

Shaw stood up and began to pace the short distance across the room—three steps, turn around, three steps, turn around, three steps, stop—he faced me. "Zoe, you need to stay away from John, and anything to do with these places. You need to come with me. I'll take you someplace safe." He started to pace again.

I asked, "Are you and John working together?"

He stopped in mid-stride and slammed his hands on the table. "No, Zoe. Don't you see?"

I shook my head trying to understand, concerned and surprised by his intensity.

"John is involved with a group who are kidnapping people." He went quiet, paced the room twice, and then said, "People…people like me."

I studied him in disbelief, allowing what he said to register with me, but I had to be sure. I pressed him for more information and asked, "Kidnapping people with money for ransom?"

He gave me a puzzled stare. "No. People with rare talents. John is kidnapping them and using them, using us."

"What do you mean?" I asked. I wondered if Shaw was probing with caution in an effort to protect me in case he was wrong.

Shaw continued to examine my face. He asked, "John must have told you about these books, because why else would you be here?" He paced across the room again.

Only an Archivist, in an attempt to keep his promise, would be evasive like this. If Shaw was a Host or Writer it made sense that John wouldn't want me to talk to him. Maybe John lived a double life, pretending around me while on the side he kidnapped Hosts and Writers. Yet, Mullog had told me that I should trust John. Confusion pulled me in two directions. I wished I could talk with Mullog, but he wouldn't appear unless I was alone. I would ask the spirit if the lineage book could be wrong, or need updating, because I believed in my heart that Shaw was an Archivist. My brother was like me.

I jumped up and threw my arms around my brother—stopping him from his frantic pacing. "I'm here because I'm an Archivist too." Obviously it would have been difficult for Shaw to talk to me since he didn't know I was an Archivist. And of course, the covenant, which kept the information about us secret and secure. "Oh Shaw! I'm so happy and relieved. Now we can talk about our history and spend time working together."

I let go of him and studied his face. He didn't appear as excited as I thought he'd be. Possibly because of the danger that surrounded us.

He asked, "How long have you been an Archivist?"

"Apparently my whole life. But I only recently found out. Mum and Dad kept it a secret to protect me."

Shaw looked astonished. "Your whole life? Mum and Dad were protecting you?"

"Yes. Especially after Dad's death." Shaw's face darkened and I said, "So you've known Dad's death wasn't an accident?"

He nodded.

"But Shaw? I don't think John is involved in the murders or kidnappings." I thought about what Mullog had said about John being a good man. "Maybe it's a misunderstanding."

Shaw's eyes sparked. "I doubt that very much. I have reason to believe John had something to do with Mum's death."

"I don't believe that." I took his hand. "Someone wants you to believe that about John. Since our secret was discovered, there have been many deceptions. John might be playing both sides in order to keep us safe. Although, you were right about him being married. I think he tried to marry me so he can keep his powers."

"His powers?"

"Yes. He must marry me to keep them."

He glanced at me in surprise and then thought it over for a moment before he shook his head. He paced the room once before stopping in front of me. He raised his hands and rested them gently, one on each of my cheeks. "Zoe, you've been the one deceived. John kidnapped Ceana and Conall. He and his men have been involved in these kidnappings all around the world."

"No. John was with me when Ceana and Conall were taken."

Shaw sighed and his hands dropped from my cheeks. "Don't you see? He's after what you and I know. He's using you."

My mind clouded and I thought back to John's sources, his knowledge, the happenstance of him being there to rescue me numerous times. I wished Mullog could insert the answers into my brain, because I wanted to know what he thought; should I believe John or my brother? Or maybe there was another explanation altogether. After watching John's genuine concern for Owen's boys today, I had a difficult time believing he could lead this deceptive life.

"And Zoe? John murdered Owen."

"What? No! You don't know that for sure."

"But I do."

I sat down hard in the chair almost missing the seat. Shaw caught my arm and steadied me. A tear rolled down my cheek.

"It'll be fine, Zoe. I'll keep you safe. Stay in here. Don't move and I'll be right back."

After he left, I sat in shock. My mind whirled in turmoil. What if it had been John who poisoned my mum? He knew so much about her and she had trusted him. And Nana—was she really his Nana? Or did he deceive her too? What about Owen? After Owen died and John interviewed him, had he actually interrogated him or threatened Owen's family if he didn't give John the answers he needed? That's what had happened to other spirits.

I glanced around. "Mullog. Are you here?"

When Mullog reappeared, he floated down beside me, his light barely there, but his presence a huge comfort for me.

"I don't know what to think. Can you tell me anything?" I asked.

"I do not know all. I have not seen John or Shaw do anything that concerns me. But, like you, amica mia, I would need to see it or hear of it to know if someone is deceptive."

"So John could have lied about his wife and about what he's doing?"

"Si, I suppose either could be lying."

"But you've mentioned that I should trust John," I said. The lights in the room went out. Total darkness would have surrounded me had it not been for Mullog and his soft glow. I stood up and turned around.

"Cara mia, I will go see what the problem is and be back."

He disappeared while I sat in complete darkness—waiting. I had seen a torch hanging from a belt on Shaw's waist and I figured he would rush back to help me. But I wanted Mullog to return first. After a long thirty seconds, I decided not to sit anymore. I stood up, arms out in front of me, and took my first uncertain step towards the door when it opened. A torch lit my face. I tried to block the brightness by covering my eyes and laughed. "Hey, that's bright."

Three large shadows moved around the person holding the torch, but the torch didn't lower. It continued to blind me. The shadowed figures didn't say a word and I didn't recognize any of their shapes.

"Shaw?" I asked, confused.

The silhouettes moved closer to me. A large hand reached out and grabbed my arm. The hold was strong and powerful. "What are you doing? Where is Shaw?" I asked.

A dull pain seared through my arm as I tried to shake the hold he had on me. My legs were still free. I kicked a sidekick to the man that held the torch and felt a snap. The man dropped the torch. He grabbed his sternum and backed away. I got one more kick through the air before a foul smelling rag smothered my nose. Before I passed out, shock must have registered on my face as I realized I was being taken—again.

Somewhere in the North Sea

I woke up with an aching head and extreme nausea, both familiar. In the badly lit room, I kept my eyes half closed from the pain and looked around expecting to see the catatonic, pudding-sucking twins. The ceiling was low, inches above my head. I turned to my side, saw a bed next to me, and realized I lay on the bottom mattress of a bunk bed. Someone lay in the bed across from mine. Turning sideways made my stomach spin and I leaned over the side of the bed to heave. The body across from me leapt up. A slender, teenage girl grabbed a metal dustbin next to the bed and scooted it across the floor. It stopped beneath my mouth in time to catch the spew. She gave me a moist towel to wipe my face.

"Gross," said a young man with an American accent. The voice came from above me.

"Well, it's not like you didn't do it too," said the girl holding the bin. She too sounded American.

"Yeah, but it's grosser listening to someone else puke," he retorted.

"I would rather help someone else than be the one puking," I said, and studied the towel wondering how many people it had cleaned up after.

"Whatever," said the boy. "It stinks."

The girl smiled at me and set the dustbin down. She picked up a plastic lid from the floor and covered the top of the bin. I leaned back and rubbed my stomach.

"It's the combination of chloroform and being on a submarine," she said.

I leaned on my elbow and watched her. The dirt-covered hoodie she wore might have been a soft yellow at one time. Too tall to sit up straight, she hunched over and stared back at me. She was beautiful, one of those teens who could pass as an adult if she wanted to. She had divided the right side of her dark hair into three tresses and plaited it halfway before she looped a band around it and left the wavy bottom tresses unruly.

"What's your name?" She divided and plaited the other half of her hair while keeping her eyes on me.

"Zoe Edevane."

"Humph," said the boy. He continued in a matter-of-fact tone, "I'm Adam Sorensen and she's Brynn Wheeler, and we're not Americans, we're Canadians, from Toronto."

"I see." The name Brynn Wheeler stuck in my head and sounded familiar to me. I couldn't think how, but the grogginess of my mind and the emptiness of my stomach made it difficult for me to think. My stomach growled.

"Whoa. That better not be more puke surfacing," Adam said.

I still hadn't seen his face, but my imagination formed a picture of him in my mind that made me smile.

"How long have I been asleep?" I asked.

"Maybe two hours," said Brynn.

"Where did they pick you up?" I asked.

"You mean where did they kidnap us?" said Adam.

Brynn rolled her amber eyes and said, "We were on our way to the Isle of Man to see the Althing for ourselves. When we got to the pub no one was there."

After her pause, Adam continued, "So we waited until a guy showed up. Before we knew it, here we were. Puking on the sub."

"They brought you in a few hours after us," Brynn said.

"If you know about the Althing, then are you…?" I waited for them to fill in the information.

"I'm a Host; she's the Writer," said Adam, in his matter-of-fact way.

"We've been on the run since my mom was kidnapped," Brynn said.

"I'm sorry to hear that. How long ago?" I asked.

"Couple months," said Adam—his details, so much help.

"It was August twenty-ninth," Brynn stated.

I poked at the rivets that held the bunks up along the metal walls. Maybe the kidnapped victims were put aboard submarines and that was how they disappeared without a trace. "Have you seen any other hostages since you were taken?" I asked. I hoped they would describe Ceana and Conall.

"No. Only guys with big muscles and big guns," Adam said.

"I saw two dressed in black suits. Most of them sound like Americans or Canadians. I have good ears and overheard one on a cell phone with an Englishman on the other end," said Brynn, with a smile that lit up her almond-shaped eyes.

The men dressed in black suits could be the same men John had brought for security during the funeral. I didn't like how the evidence pointed to him. Suddenly, a memory came to me that pieced together the reason for the familiarity of Brynn's name.

I had to know. "Brynn?"

"Yeah?"

"Were you born in Maine?"

She squinted her eyes at me.

"How'd you know that?" asked the suspicious Adam.

She was one of the five Primordial females. Her name had been written in red in the Lineage Book. I glanced at her and tried to cover my shock.

"I've seen your name somewhere." I continued to watch Brynn.

"Yeah. I guess I have dual citizenship. We hid in Maine for a couple months before coming to England," she said.

"Gee Brynn. Why not just tell her everything?"

The bed squeaked and his head appeared upside down over the side. Because of the translucent whiteness of his skin and hair, for a brief moment I thought he was a spirit. The only colour he had was in his piercing, pale-blue eyes and the lime-green bands that covered most of his braces. His thick smiling eyebrows were white and either raised or lowered depending on one's perception of him leaning over the bed. His hair hung perfectly straight below his head in what might have been a bowl cut. His face was thin and gaunt and turned red from the blood flowing into his cheeks. Even though his face pulled in the direction gravity took the skin, I could see the beauty and perfection in his bone structure—not at all the preconceived picture I had of him. Both kids were thin and had not eaten much while on the run. His brown hoodie was ripped at the wrists and the dirt it held blended into the brown tone.

"I can't tell by looking at her if she's one of us for sure," he said.

"You can't tell because you can't even see her." Brynn smiled at me. "He lost his glasses. He's a near-sighted Albino, and losing his glasses—not a good thing."

That explained the spirit-like beauty of his features.

"Oh, I see her. Who could miss the weird orange streaks of hair?" Adam squinted his pale eyes at me. "She could be a plant, trying to get info out of us."

Brynn sighed. "And he's paranoid."

I disregarded his comments about my hair. "I have to agree with him. We should all be a little paranoid right now."

"Huh. See Brynn? I told her even though we were in the UK we needed to be careful, but she didn't listen to me, and of course we can *see* what happened because of not listening to me." He rolled back over and repositioned himself while mumbling under his breath.

"I know people who will look for us. We will be found, don't worry," I said.

"I hope she's right," Adam said, ignoring me.

He had an irritating habit of addressing people as if they weren't in the same room.

What did our captors have planned for us? Did they know they held captive almost half the remaining primordial females? I thought of scenarios that made me tense with horror. I hoped they weren't capturing us younger females for the sake of breeding. John would be an Oscar contender if he had hidden a side of him that was that ruthless. I refused to believe in his involvement. There had to be another explanation to John blaming Shaw and vice versa. They were probably on the same side and didn't even know it. They had to be searching for me—that is if Shaw had himself escaped from getting kidnapped. For all I knew, he could be locked up in the next room.

Chapter 25
BRYNN AND ADAM

London, England

The bench was hard and cold. John glanced at his watch. He'd waited for over an hour and had planned to be gone by dark. He felt the black limo drift down the street before he actually saw it. It stopped across from him. The driver stepped out, opened the back door, glanced towards the bench, and waited. He got off the bench, ran across one lane of the street, and stepped into the car. The door slammed shut, confining him with a man who, until now, he'd only spoken with over the phone. As soon as he sat down, he turned to the man dressed in an expensive silk suit that sat across from him and asked, "Was it us or them who took her?"

"Nice to finally meet you in person too, John," said the spectacled man that faced him, his Northern European accent strong and familiar. He had a shaved head and round metal glasses framed his cold grey eyes. Seated, his head came to John's shoulder.

John stared at the man. "I gather 'Specs' is not your real name."

"That would be correct."

He rephrased his first question. "Was it Shaw, sir?"

"There are those who know. I am told you are too close to this;

it is best you do not know."

John studied Specs' drawn face and cold eyes for a brief second. "That's rubbish and you know it."

"Careful, John."

He felt his frustration rise, but kept his face neutral. "There's a strong possibility another group is involved. That's why I need to know. If it's not Shaw, or us, then my theory can be proven. I don't see Shaw taking her unless he thinks he's protecting her. He's involved because of me." John paused before he continued. "He's been following me."

The man said nothing; he removed his eyeglasses and polished them. Deep bags of wrinkles rimmed his eyes.

John sensed his explanations becoming too long-winded and tried to keep his voice steady as he continued, "I should have eliminated Shaw in Africa when I had the chance. Sarah and Booker talked me out of it, said we should tail him—use Shaw and find the people he's working for. I have no doubt about Shaw's involvement with Sarah to stage her accident. But this? Kidnapping his sister? It doesn't make sense, unless he isn't acting alone."

He sat in the stuffy car and waited, studying the man for clues. The man remained quiet—methodically polishing his glasses. John wanted to snap the spectacles out of his hands. "Is there nothing you can say to help me out here?" John asked.

The man put his glasses back on and looked across at John. "They do not know who has her." The man's voice became facetious. "For all they know it was you, John."

John studied the man and shook his head in disgust. "Bloody hell, you're the rogue agent." He tried the door handle, but the lock was activated and the door wouldn't open. John tapped on the partition glass and told the driver, "Unlock the door."

The driver remained seated and put the car in gear. Specs pulled a Makarov 9mm from his side and pointed it at John. "For obvious reasons I cannot let you go."

John nodded in understanding.

Specs held his hand out. "Hand over your weapon—slowly."

John reached under his arm and took out his Glock. He aimed it at the man's forehead.

The man clicked his tongue and said, "You have no idea the scope of what we have planned, the money—billions of Euros. Although our investment in you is critical, Zoe is the key."

John narrowed his eyes, kept the gun pointed at Specs, and asked, "How exactly is she the key?"

The man gave a slight nod to the driver before he answered. "I think you know a portion of why she is the key, but only a portion; you know she is an Archivist."

John's eyes widened, his gun remained aimed and ready.

Specs laughed. "You did not think we knew that?" He clicked his tongue again. "In fact, we have known that about her much longer than you. Kathryn knew Zoe was an Archivist—she hid it to protect her daughter. Oh John, you are a stupid man to think your secrets were yours alone and safe from me. You are also a lucky man. Lucky I insisted my brother Jaak not come with me. He is most upset by the loss of so many of his best men."

John's neutral expression faltered.

Specs grinned. "So much that you did not know."

"I could kill you right now." John's gun wavered a little, his mind becoming muddled and his arm weak.

"You would not shoot me, for the obvious reason, Zoe would never be released…from her new life." Specs paused in his words. "But just in case…I have…taken precautions." His gun hand weakly rested on top of his legs, but the barrel still pointed at John.

John watched in surprise as his own hand lost the grip on his gun and the Glock fell with a thud onto the floor of the car. Everything in the car blurred and swam in front of him. He realized the man's nod to the driver had been a sign to release some kind of knockout drug through the air system in the back of the car. He had taken several deep breaths of it, inhaled the odorless chemical into his lungs and felt the effects take over. The man gave John a thin-lipped smile before his eyes shut and his naked head rolled to the side. John's head nodded; his tiredness complete, he slumped against the door—anxiety and worry plaguing a distant portion of his mind. How did they know? Who told them? With him exposed and the Keepers captured did this mean the end of all they had worked for? He drifted into a quiet, anesthetized sleep.

The North Sea

"We should probably show her this." Adam's hand drifted over the top-bunk and handed a smart-phone to Brynn.

"You have a phone? Did you ring for help?"

Brynn shook her head. "Adam lifted it from one of the men who brought you in. But there's no service in here."

She set it in my held-out palm. "Did you look at the messages or contacts?" I asked.

"Yeah. The only message said something like 'take her to the sub, we'll be there shortly with the last of the pallets,'" Brynn said.

"Hmmm. That might have been someone talking about me."

In the Althing, Shaw had been removing the Archives by pallet. Was Shaw involved or was he a victim? I immediately opened up the contact list and touched the E in the alphabet on the side. The list pulled up the E's and I stared in shock—Shaw Edevane. But that could just be a coincidence. I scrolled to the L's and found John Link's name. Fantastic. I knew their paths were connected, but I refused to believe that having their names on this contact list proved they worked with the owner of this phone.

"Well, what did you find?" Adam asked.

"Be patient, I'm still looking."

"Sounds like it's not good," he said.

I ignored him and went back to the A's and read each name, hoping to recognize one of them and spark a memory that might help piece together an explanation. I read names through the C's when a loud knock on our door made us all jump. The door opened as I hid the phone between my mattress and the wall. In walked a smiling Shaw. He looked well, still wore his black shirt and trousers, and his sandy hair had an indentation from the mining hat. I stared in silent surprise, not sure what to think. His eyes glanced over Adam and Brynn, but studied mine.

"What a relief we got you safely away," he said.

In confusion, I repeated his last two words. "Safely away?"

He leaned over and gave me a hug. "Yes. You're safe now. And I apologize for some of the men. They are a bit unorthodox in their tactics. We've been fighting this war far too long."

"Safe? Do you think I'm daft? We're being held captive on a sub. I was drugged; we were drugged." I stood up, but a woozy feeling swept through my stomach and I sat back down.

Shaw smiled. "You're free to walk out of this room."

"We're free to leave?" Adam asked.

"Well, you can stretch your legs and walk to the galley for some food, but since we're in the middle of the ocean I wouldn't advise leaving."

"That sounds like his diplomatic way of saying we're trapped," Adam said. He swung his legs over the edge of the bunk and jumped down. His shoulder brushed Shaw in the tight confines of the room. Shaw's lips pinched together.

"Who are you?" Brynn asked.

"He's my brother, Shaw."

"Really?" Brynn asked.

I nodded. "And he's an Archivist." But my voice lacked conviction.

"Then just what did he get us safely away from that required us to be drugged?" Adam asked. His mouth inches from Shaw's ear.

Shaw backed into the doorway and said, "An operation that went bad. Now follow me up to the galley. They're serving pizza and spaghetti."

The mention of food seemed to still Adam's questions while we followed Shaw into the narrow corridor, ducking our heads around various metal piping. My boots resounded along the walkway like tapping hammers behind the thud of Brynn and Adam's trainers and Shaw's rubber-soled shoes. Shaw led us to a set of metal ladders. One set went up and the other went down. The galley was close, the metallic smell of sweat and moisture became mixed with an enticing aroma of fresh bread, pepperoni, and oregano.

Shaw paused next to the ladder. "This floor and the one below have the berth areas where it's best to be quiet while walking around. We only have a few staterooms, like your room, with a door. Beyond the berth areas and the galley are the engine and mechanical areas as well as the control room. These are off limits and you will be kept from them unless accompanied. Understood?"

"So he's giving us what? Ten feet to walk around in?" Adam said.

Shaw gave Adam a harsh look. "This is for your safety. I can always keep the door to your room bolted."

I took Shaw's arm and said, "I don't think we really care about the mechanical rooms." I glanced at Adam. "Do we?" Adam took the point and nodded. I let go of Shaw's arm and said, "I think we'll be fine hanging out in our stateroom and the galley. Now, shall we go eat?"

"You go ahead. I have work to do," Shaw said.

"But I have so much to talk to you about," I said. I took hold of his arm again, but he narrowed his eyes at me.

"There won't be time for that, Zoe." He walked away, leaving me with my mouth hanging open.

I recovered, followed Brynn and Adam to the galley, and inhaled the intoxicating smell of sourdough bread. Other than a few men taking trays of piled high pizza out of the galley, we were alone. A grey-haired cook, who spoke only Italian, gave us a nod before he loaded slices of pizza and mounds of spaghetti on our plates and handed them to us through a small window with a metal counter. The cook was a short man and his head looked attached to a body without neck or shoulders. His arms stayed close to his side as he manipulated the ladle and spatula in the confines of the tiny, mint-green kitchen. With fluid motion, he kept his head from bumping the metal cabinets and shelves as he spun from one side to the other.

We sat down on a table in the corner surrounded by benches on three sides. After watching Adam eat ten slices of pizza and two plates of spaghetti, I said, "Maybe you should sleep on the bottom bunk."

He laughed, seeming relaxed, a lot more relaxed than I felt. I couldn't shake an uneasy feeling. I wanted to believe Shaw, but who were all the people eating the stacks of pizza? After witnessing the pounds of food Adam ate, it was possible that the pizza went to the crew. But why not come to the galley themselves to get their food?

Since I had nothing in the way of submarine experience, I had only Shaw's word about the sub's design. I felt trapped. Other than saying "the middle of the ocean," Shaw hadn't told us our position or where we were headed.

After Adam ate pizza slice number twelve, I asked, "Do you know anything about submarines?"

Brynn shook her head and Adam said, "A little."

He took a drink of chocolate milk and said, "It's either a nuclear sub or an electric propulsion sub."

"And what does that mean?" I asked, after waiting for him to explain more and give additional insight.

"I'll know more if we surface, or go to periscope depth to charge the batteries. We'll be able to hear the noise as they recharge. The batteries of the electric motors need to be recharged, sometimes once a day in the diesel-electric propulsion subs. A nuclear sub can stay under water for weeks or months at a time, depending on supplies."

"I hope it's a battery one because I'd like to get some fresh air," said Brynn.

"That sounds nice," I said.

"They don't necessarily surface. Like I said, usually just at periscope depth. But we should be able to hear it charging," Adam said, chewing a mouthful of spaghetti.

I nodded. "We'll wait until it gets loud and then see if we can get some air on deck."

"It would be nice to see the sun," Brynn said.

"Maybe your brother wouldn't mind if we looked around and explored," said Adam.

"Oh, I think he'd mind," I said.

"But certainly he didn't really mean for us to remain in our cabin?" Brynn asked.

I shrugged my shoulders. "Why not look around. But carefully." I was curious too.

With full stomachs, we walked out of the galley and tramped along the corridor, talking as we dodged the various metal and mechanical edges sticking out from above us and beside us, including cans of food along the floor. Storage must be a huge obstacle.

"This is my first time being on a sub," Brynn said.

"Me too," I said.

"I've been on a couple at nautical museums in Maryland, New Hampshire, and New York. They were American subs," Adam said. Picking his way over some cans of food, he took a misstep and a few cans of beans fell and clamored as they rolled. While we restacked them against the wall, a man stepped out from a doorway. Anger sparked from his eyes and his bald head hung low with two bandages on his forehead. His wide shoulders actually appeared to expand the corridor. He growled at us in a low voice that carried his incomprehensible words with insult and vulgarity. I didn't know what language he spoke, but his meaning was clear as he pointed back the way we had come. We needed to go back to our bunks. It was either late, or we had approached too close to the engine rooms; we couldn't tell. Without another word, we turned around and headed back towards the ladder.

We took a couple steps along a line of curtains when a curtain of one of the berths opened and a man's head appeared. He wiped his red eyes. His teeth pressed beyond his lips as he hissed at us in what sounded like the same language as the bald man. He looked down and pointed at our shoes. Mainly mine. He rolled off his bunk and blocked our way. He turned his head around and hissed at the person in the bunk above his. We remained still until another head shot out from behind a curtain. This man's eyes bulged and he had wild spiked hair. All three of us jumped at the sight of him. He held out a pair of moccasin type slippers for each of us. I looked at my boots and back at him and smiled an apology. They didn't allow us to take another step until we removed our footwear and put on the moccasin shoes. Brynn and I tied the leather laces around our feet to get them to fit. Before we were allowed to tiptoe back to our room, the two men confiscated my leather boots.

I shut our door and wriggled my toes. With these quiet shoes, I'd be able to scout around and search for other hostages, including Ceana and Conall. Something didn't add up with how Shaw was treating us and until I knew for certain they weren't on this sub, I decided not to say anything more to him. I already regretted mentioning that John would lose his ability to be an Archivist if he didn't marry me.

Chapter 26
CHAIN GANG

Saaremaa, Estonia

John wriggled his hands to loosen the grip of the cords that cut into his wrists. Pain seared from the raw wounds and he paused when the moist warmth oozed over his skin. The ankle chains and wrist ties made it difficult for him to adjust his position. His head and body throbbed. The men who had carried him from the car to this room had been anything but gentle. To make matters worse, there wasn't a single ray of light to be seen.

He inhaled a deep and raspy breath that filled his lungs with the aroma of body odor, feces, and the ammonia smell of rancid urine. He had lost track of time, but hadn't been there long enough to lose control of his own bladder, although someone had warmed his leg a few moments ago. His body shivered from the wet and cold. At least the cold kept the acrid smell to an almost tolerable level, making him somewhat grateful for the chill in the air.

An unseen person moaned on his right, another coughed and groaned in front of him. When they had thrown him into the room and chained his ankles to the wall, he had counted seven men and two young lads sprawled out on the filthy cement floor before the door shut and left them in complete darkness. He sensed the misery around him through the stillness of their coughs and moans. A couple blank pairs of eyes had glanced up at him when he entered and two men had scooted over to allow him some space next to a brick wall. Not a word had been spoken.

His eyes tried to pierce the darkness and make out the sleeping forms of the other men. Nothing. Not even a slice of light under the door—but he might be staring in the wrong direction. He stopped his attempts at freeing his hands from the cords; he didn't want to risk infection, and it was impossible to remove his ankles from the thick metal chains that bound him. None of the other prisoners had their hands tied, but all had at least one ankle chained to the wall.

After being drugged in the car, his memory stopped until the point at being dragged down a fluorescent hallway to the windowless cell. He cringed; he had finally given in to the cramping and wet himself. He now belonged to the room. Discouragement plagued him because he saw no way to escape and rescue Zoe—the metal sound of the dead bolt being fastened when the door shut still echoed in his brain. Irrevocably trapped in a dungeon with no light felt like a time warp of impending doom with his knowledge that time rushed towards the unknown deadline when all Archivists would be slaughtered to protect the secrets of their existence. He had a difficult time grasping that knowledge. Who would do the slaughtering had not been written on the page he'd seen, which could mean there was still hope—if he could find a way to escape this dungeon.

He remained quiet a few more minutes before deciding to talk to the other captives and try to discover something helpful, anything that might give them a chance. He opened his dry mouth and said, "My name is John."

His ears rang in the complete silence that answered him. A few more seconds passed before he asked, "How long have you blokes been in here?"

"Humph," snorted someone.

He thought that question sounded lame even as he spoke. He tried a different approach. "What are they doing with us?"

A second later, "Humph."

Out of curiosity, John waited to see if someone would speak. Maybe one of the blokes with the empty eyes would talk. When the two faces had glanced at him, both sets of eyes had held vacant stares. He had entered a room void of hope. He would achieve nothing until he gave them a shred of optimism. From his brief glimpse of them, he couldn't tell whether they were kidnapped Archivists or random hostages. But from all appearances they didn't have any special training. Only two had any muscle definition. They had been held captive for weeks.

"Are any of you CIA or MI6?" He didn't think anyone would be in the affirmative on that question, but the question did what he intended it to do—warrant a response.

"What are you saying? That they think we're spies?" The voice came from the coughing man near him. His hoarse voice had a refined British accent.

"And you're not?" John asked.

"Of course not. My name is Bert; I'm an accountant. Two of these men had their sons with them when they were kidnapped. One father runs a sheep farm and the other owns a tavern in Leeds. We have Reverend Steve from Scotland and a couple seamen from Ireland. The final bloke is from Norway and speaks very little English. None of us have a clue why we've been kidnapped and deposited in this waste hole for an indeterminable amount of time."

John smiled to himself. He had achieved a response. He said, "I'm a photographer."

"Yet another random bit of information that provides no answers," said Bert.

"Have you been allowed outside of this room?" John asked.

"Not once. They bring a couple pitchers of water each day and a tray of food morning and evening," Bert explained.

"You call that food?" a husky voice said.

"I call it sustenance," said a man positioned on John's left, one of the Irish blokes. "And it's barely that."

John pictured each man unkempt, unshaven, and shackled by his ankles to a wall, being kept alive for what purpose? It angered him to think of Zoe housed in these same inhumane conditions. Specs would regret this; John would make sure of that.

An elbow pushed into John's ribs and jarred him awake as a man crawled, or rather scurried over him. He immediately thought the man was leaping for food because the room had light. He opened his eyes and saw the men huddled together against the wall in front of him, the chains on their ankles taut. Their mouths hung open and empty. The whites of their eyes shone as they tried to both shield their eyes from the brightness and point to warn John of the terror that lurked behind him. The reverend crossed himself—several times. In John's weakened state, he was in no condition to take on any threats, especially if the threat brandished a weapon. The guards had cut the cords from his wrists before he slept that first night. How many days ago? He couldn't say. He stood up, a bit unsteady, and held his arms out before he turned around. His feet slipped on the sewage rotting on the floor. He waved his arms to balance himself, but fell and landed on his knees. He then braced himself for the unknown threat.

"I am happy that my nose cannot smell what you rest in, mio amico."

John smiled with relief. The light came from Mullog who floated above the waste with disgust playing across his olive features. The spirit wore a pleated and pressed sailor uniform. "You are a welcome light in this darkness, my friend." The rapid breathing from the men and boys behind John made him add, "But you know these men are not Archivists and your apparition has scared them."

"Si. These men are descendants of spirits I know. They are held captive to control those spirits, to keep them silent, and make them do what the kidnappers want."

John peered at the men. The two fathers had their arms wrapped around their shivering sons. Their shirts and trousers clung to their bodies from the damp and putrid debris that covered them. The reverend's tweed jacket was loosely wrapped over the shoulders of both lads. The other men, with clothes in the same condition, were huddled nearby, their eyes filled with both curiosity and fear, except for Reverend Steve who continued to make the sign of the cross while chanting in Latin. It surprised John to see the reverend still wearing his dog collar. His black, clerical shirt hid most of the dirt that clung to him.

"Let me introduce you to Mullog. Obviously he's a spirit, but there's no need to fear him." John paused to let that sink in. "I guess we now know the reason behind your captivity."

"Not only the reason for their captivity. John, it is why they took you and Zoe."

John narrowed his eyes. "Hmmm, so they can try and control the Blue Bloods. I doubt they'll have much success in that."

"Va bene."

"Is Zoe here also?" John asked.

"I have not found her. La Signora was seen being carried onto a boat at the Isle and this boat is being searched for. It is difficile. This boat disappeared under the water."

John nodded. "Of course, a submarine. That's how they've made people disappear so mysteriously," John said. He then asked, "Who took her?"

"Shaw was with her."

John's chest expanded and detracted as he inhaled and exhaled loudly. "Hopefully he'll keep her safe."

"Maybe. I hope you are right, for the health of la signora." Mullog stared at John and the other prisoners, their grimy, crusted faces lit by his light.

Bert cleared his throat to speak. "Is anyone coming for us?" His voice had a tremor to it.

Mullog nodded. "A rescue is being planned."

"Who?" asked John.

"A couple of Conall's sons, and a few others. Very difficile, mio amico. You are held in Saaremaa, an Estonian island. There are many eyes watching."

"An island," John repeated. "That does make it difficult to approach by boat or airplane and remain unseen."

Bert cleared his throat again. "These Irish blokes, Brian and Dillon, are seamen."

The seamen nodded their heads; they were the largest in the group. Although thin, their muscles were still cut and well formed, and their eyes wary and watchful. They were about the same age as John with thick facial hair the colour of tar. In the darkness of captivity, John and the two Irish men were the only three who didn't just stand, but moved around in the black abyss encouraging one another and helping one another stay clear of the slime in the center of the room as they strained and breathed through press-ups and sit-ups—anything to keep their muscles from atrophying in the stillness of the confined space.

John guessed he'd been held for over a week. About two days ago, he began to feel the effects of food depravation from the small amount given. The men rotated their full share to give more to the two growing lads who were twelve and thirteen years old. If they were held much longer, they wouldn't have the strength to help one another escape—let alone walk. The reverend and the Norwegian had been captive the longest, and since the day after John arrived they had needed assistance to stand. But neither the Irish blokes nor John could get the others to work through their weakness.

"We know the Baltic Sea. If we're near a dock, we can take a boat and sail to Copenhagen and out to the North Sea. The shipping lanes should be congested enough for us to conceal ourselves," said Brian.

John considered this for a moment. "I don't know if a boat would be fast enough to get us away. We don't know if they have air support."

The light surrounding Mullog brightened. "Do not worry, mio amico. Sean and Eadan have prepared all. When ready, we will get you men to the harbor and aboard our ghost ship."

"A ghost ship?" said both of the lads together. It was the third time John had heard them speak.

"Va bene. Figlio mio, we spirits have united together to help fix a most bad situation." Mullog turned towards John and smiled.

John opened his mouth to say something, but Mullog interrupted, "Someone comes." His light vanished and John blinked his eyes in the darkness. The ten of them sat in silence. The door opened and a tray slid across the floor, half of the green and brown contents sloshed over onto the cement floor to mix with the sewage. The carrier of the food didn't look at any of the filth-covered faces and didn't notice the pale glint of hope in the depths of their eyes.

Chapter 27
ON TOP

The North Sea

My hands pushed onto the cold and slimy metal deck to steady myself and observe the ocean that circled around me to the horizon. I breathed in and out, creating foggy wisps in the salty air that covered my face; I tasted the salt on my lips. The moist air dampened the orange life vest I wore. Brynn and Adam sat next to me. Each wore a similar vest of orange; both had their faces turned into the wind, and Adam had his sensitive eyes closed.

The rolling sea churned around us and the sun reflected like luminous horizontal bookends—down from the sapphire sky above, and up from the sparkling waves below. My heart sang in the fresh air, our third time allowed on top. I had been able to have one short conversation with Shaw since he saw us the first day, and talked him into surfacing when they recharged the batteries so we could go on top. Normally, the ship ran at periscope depth to recharge.

"It's cold out here, but it beats the dark-abyss feeling of the sub." Brynn's eyes squinted at me in the bright sunshine.

"I'm with you. I can't imagine how submariners do it. To remain for weeks, or months, at a time under water is something I couldn't do," I said.

"I could go either way," said Adam. He looked very uncomfortable and with his fair skin looked deathlike in the sunshine. He leaned against Brynn and kept his pale eyes closed.

We had always been alone up top and were surprised when one by one a human head popped up like a meerkat through the hatch beside us. They crawled out of the hole and onto the deck where they continued to crawl. The clan of about twenty was very unsure how to locate a safe position to sit; their hands and knees scooted over the surface during their crawl. Several minutes later, they sat on the center of the deck in a line. Each of their eyes squinted in the sunny rays and their breaths created smoky wisps that disappeared above their heads. Their arms folded around their torsos to block the cold breeze that penetrated the shirts and thin pullovers they wore under their life jackets. Nothing stood out about them to indicate where they were from or who they were.

The sound of the diesel engine revved beneath us and startled the silence of the whispering waves and the people talking. Four men, carrying machine guns in their arms, walked in pairs across the hull to stand on each end of the deck. Their eyes shifted back and forth from those on deck to the surrounding horizon. Two more guards were positioned up on the bridge next to the antenna and periscope. This was the first time I had seen the "meerkat clan" or men carrying weapons during the couple of weeks we had been aboard.

Other than the areas off limits, Brynn, Adam, and I had searched the entire submarine. We had not seen anyone but the submariners and assumed we were the only passengers. I wanted to talk to these new people, but the engines were too loud to ask them in a low voice who they were. The guards warranted a response to be still and not ask questions. I'd need to ask Shaw. I had seen him a couple of times when we had passed the control room on our way to and from the sub hatch. Other than the two times I spoke to him, he had never made an effort to seek me out. Strange how Shaw remained so distant; he felt more like my captor than my brother. We had been treated somewhere between guests and hostages—not welcomed, not unwelcomed—feeling the invisible chains that strung us within an unseen boundary. These additional "passengers" had either been outside of our boundary line or put on board during the night, and I doubted Shaw would make himself available for me to ask him about them.

I turned my back on the meerkats crowding the deck and faced the open sea. The tightness of claustrophobia that had clutched my nerves during the past few days relinquished its hungry grip. I closed my eyes and inhaled the fresh air as a cold hand clamped onto my upper arm, surprising me. I spun around to face the person. Her blue eyes held tears that fell when she blinked and her black hair lay flat and had more lengths streaked with grey than when I had last seen her. I threw my arms around her and cried out, "Ceana." Her name was almost inaudible above the noise of the engines. Ceana released me and gently caught one of the orange locks of my hair that blew in the breeze. She raised her eyebrows at me and smiled. I shrugged my shoulders.

A scraggily man crawled next to her, kneeled, and smiled, his lips hidden behind the red and grey hairs of his unkempt beard. Before his massive arms could encircle me, one of the men with a gun took the gunstock and pounded on Conall's shoulder. Conall gave the man a nasty look and sat down holding his arms in his lap, both hands held in tight fists.

To communicate, I used head and eye motions and looked towards Brynn and Adam. Ceana squeezed Brynn's hand. Brynn's eyes showed the affirmative that she understood these were the two people I had hoped to find. Adam came out of his eyes-squeezed-shut-trance long enough to acknowledge them both with a nod before he went back to his trance-like state that protected his eyes.

Since talk was impossible, we held hands and looked out to sea for the few remaining minutes allowed in the open air. Emotions propelled their way down my spine and my heart ached with comprehension. The relief of seeing them again was repelled by the reactions of the guards, which revealed the truth. Shaw had not rescued Ceana and Conall, and I doubted very much he had rescued Brynn, Adam, and myself. My brother was not the person I thought. I shivered. My stomach tossed and turned at the realization that for a couple of days I had tried to speak with Shaw and tell him the details of my last few months. I had decided to reveal everything to him and watch his reaction. Tears trickled down my face. Could I accept this bittersweet truth? If accepted, I needed to acknowledge that unless they were working together, John was not my enemy—Shaw was. I didn't know if I was ready to give up on Shaw. For all I knew, he was the one who broke our covenant of secrecy, but he was still my brother and I loved him.

The guards began to usher the meerkat clan inside. With reluctance, I let go of Ceana's hand. Her tired eyes searched my teary-eyed face and told me she too knew the truth. I wished to talk to her longer, unencumbered by guards and distance. I climbed down the hatch and Ceana and Conall were taken the opposite way that Brynn, Adam, and I were taken. The walls and ceiling of the sub bore down on my head, my shoulders, and my back more heavily than before the sunshine had lifted my spirits. The weight gave me little room to breath. But Ceana and Conall were alive and that blessing gave me comfort on our walk back to our room, along with Brynn who draped her arm around my back when we sat on my bunk.

Adam pushed our door shut and said, "Bummer, your brother

must be the man in charge of taking all of us."

"Really, Adam?" Brynn said.

Adam stood and looked down at us. "Well, what if he's not really one of us and she said something to him about us?"

"I haven't." But his words stung. He didn't know how close I'd come.

We fell silent as footsteps, sounding like storm troopers, approached. Our door flew open and Adam lurched out of the way as the door clipped his heel. A muscled man with curly black hair that appeared to have been dipped in olive oil leaned over and grabbed my arm, pulled me up off the bed, and through the door before any of us could say a word. Behind him, a man brandished a knife and told Adam and Brynn to stay. He shut the door and stood outside it as the hairy man pushed me down the hall, and said, "You're needed in the mess hall."

A moment later, I sat alone on a bench in the corner of the galley. An aroma of fish frying clouded the room; instead of making me hungry, I felt nauseous. I took a metal bucket from the other side of the room and set it beside me on the bench. My guard breathed impatiently as he stood outside the galley door. I crossed my arms over the table and rested my forehead on them. A few minutes later, I heard the clicking of high heels.

"Hello, Zoe," said a familiar female voice.

I glanced up. "Nurse Gibbons?" I wiped at the drool on my chin and stared at her in surprise. Instead of her usual expression of medical concern and kindness, her brown eyes were cold and narrowed at me. Her customary Florence Nightingale bun had been released into golden hair that lay straight and smooth to her shoulder blades. The perfect complexion of her pale skin was more vivid with her maroon lips. She moved quick and gracefully to sit in a chair across from me. She crossed her legs and studied my face. She bore no resemblance to Ceana's helpful nurse.

"Around here they call me Sarah." She paused to allow that to sink in. It didn't take long for me to realize what the name Sarah meant. My heart quickened and I re-wiped my chin. So this was John's wife. Embarrassed by my appearance, I tried to smooth down my striped and unruly hair with the hand that just wiped my mouth and chin. When I realized what I was doing, I quickly folded my hands together and set them on the table.

This version of Nurse Gibbons seemed older. But it might have been the sophistication that emulated from her maroon lipstick, perfect hair, the pressed feminine, light-grey suit she wore, along with her perfectly manicured nails polished in a soft pink. She held her chin high and watched me with disdain—totally unrecognizable from the soft-spoken and mousy Nurse Gibbons.

Her eyebrows raised, she studied me from head to foot observing my striped, messy hair, before pausing to take in the man's pullover I wore and my un-manicured nails. With no idea of who previously owned the pullover, I had become used to the cigarette odor it came with. Her opinion didn't matter, the pullover had replaced the skirt and button-down top I had worn to Owen's funeral and its warmth and comfort felt luxurious. "Your brother has so much strength and confidence. And you, you have an awkward and naïve, or should I say, simple way about you. I must say, from what I know of John, I was shocked by his fondness for you. So out of character." She held her nails up and looked them over. "And I can't understand where the aggressive envy that Shaw has for you comes from either. Other than your blue eyes, I would never have considered you his relation." She spoke with a pointed and quick clip to her words.

Looking past the obvious ridicule, I said, "Shaw has no reason to envy me. It's preposterous to think that."

"Maybe. You are more of the bookworm and he more the

adventurer."

Her word choices were deliberate. She assumed I was dim-witted enough to start blabbing and reveal something I shouldn't. An uncomfortable silence ensued when I remained quiet. After a moment she continued. "And yet your parents were obsessed by books and adventures."

"Let's not pretend you knew my parents."

She leaned forwards. "Maybe not, but I know plenty about their line of work and how Shaw was never a part of it."

That remark caught me off guard. I didn't want to discuss anything about the Hosts or Writers, at least not with her. "Now, what line of work would that be?" I asked, in a voice that sounded more controlled than my racing heart made me feel.

"So this is how it's going to be? We're going to play this ridiculous game of cat and mouse?" Sarah's eyes narrowed into slits.

"Possibly." I leaned back against the coolness of the metal wall and tried to look as composed and nonchalant as possible. "But exactly who is the cat and who is the mouse?"

"Honestly, Zoe." She stood up and raised her eyebrows, tilting her head ever so slightly. "Your immaturity and naivety astound me."

My immaturity and naivety astounded me as well, especially after seeing her. I had to marvel at John's conflicting taste in women.

"This story does not have a happily ever after, Zoe, where the protagonist wins and gets the bloke and sails off into the sunset. This is real life, with high-stakes and spies that play both sides, like Jaak. I think you know him. Spies who don't pause a millisecond before they slit someone's throat to avoid treason and get their millions, or in my case, billions of pounds."

"Your case? So you're saying that for money, you wouldn't pause before slitting someone's throat?" I asked. My voice shook after her mention of Jaak's name.

She took a breath in and out as if she were being patient with a child. "I'm saying that in this high stake's game we have vicious people that don't hesitate to kill. The people you care about—at least in this life—with one word from me could be sent into the next life."

I glanced at her in shock.

"Yes, that's right, Zoe. I'm the head of this organization. I used to work with Jaak and his brother. We went our separate ways after I came up with a brilliant idea of how to make billions, and Jaak and Specs grew more interested in the power side of our work. I must say it's a relief not to deal with them anymore."

I sat with what I'm sure was a dumb look on my face. Taken by surprise as I was, I had nothing to say to her.

She paused, and added a smile that didn't include her eyes. "Did you think Shaw ran this operation?" She laughed. Even her laugh sounded sophisticated. "He's all brawn with a lot of heart and very little brains. Nowhere near as smart as your parents." She inserted a fluctuation in her voice with the suggestion about my parents being smart that had me wondering about what else she might know. "You do what I say during your captivity and even Shaw will live through this. He can't wait to have his revenge on John. Imagine that. He actually believes John killed your precious Mum. He also believes that John's family had everything to do with your dad's death. Like I said, little up here and easily persuaded." She tapped her head. "If he reversed what he thought with when it came to me, he might actually figure things out."

Stunned, my mouth dropped open.

Sarah studied my face and said, "You Archivists can sure keep your secrets. I don't know why it took so many years to get one of you to talk. This past summer we put a new plan in place; we kidnapped a few from your elite group. Through torture and threats, we discovered many of your secrets and were able to witness how the Hosts and Writers use your mana to host a spirit. From there, we threatened to kill off the grandchildren of these spirits until they gave up their silence and told us details about your Althings and your records. I must say this plan worked brilliantly. You can't imagine the things we've been able to get these spirits to do in order to save their descendants—remarkable really. You Archivists never had the intelligence to realize the fortune you have in those records and by using your talents in different ways. Unbelievable." While she took a breath, I remained silent, unable to respond to her prowess. She certainly was a calculating and dangerous woman. She went on. "It was your mother who almost uncovered our plans. While training John, she overheard a phone conversation that he had with one of my men." I must have showed my surprise because she paused. "Oh don't worry, Zoe, although John was one of my agents he never knew it. I had him kept in the dark. He didn't know I was alive until your *almost wedding,* and rest assured he had nothing to do with Kathryn's death. The poison killed her before she discovered who was involved and what was happening, which was good, but taking her life cost me the confidence of my best agent—John."

Each of her words welled up more hate within me, hot and full of vengeful wrath. I didn't know if it were possible to contain it. There was still more I wanted to know and since she was in such a talkative mood I contained my anger and asked, "What about Owen?"

Sarah laughed her sophisticated laugh. "What about him? Do you want to know who *ordered* the killing or who *did* the killing?"

The hate surged inside me—palpable and escalating. My hand reached for the handle of the bucket on the bench next to me. I gripped it and held on, hoping she would leave before I lost control.

I bit my cheek and forced myself to remain still.

She turned to leave and stopped. Without turning around to face me, she said, "Oh, and Zoe? Don't plan on me ever divorcing John. The thought of him becoming powerless makes my day. Eventually, your brother will kill him." Her face turned to show her profile. "You can return to your room now."

With those words and that demeaning dismissal, I leaped forwards with bucket in hand. I swung it by the handle, aiming for her head and its perfectly tamed mane. She turned, a moment of panic registered in her features. She dropped down quicker than I could have done in heels. My bucket completely missed her head, and due to momentum and physics, when my arm stopped swinging the force of the metal bucket continued its course until it crashed into the side of my own head.

I woke up two hours later.

Chapter 28
THE ESCAPE

Saaremaa, Estonia

"I wish that spirit had told us when to be ready," said Dillon.

"Yes, but what good would that have done? We can't tell whether it's day or night anyway," Bert said.

John nodded to himself. After Mullog left, no one had moved and the tray of slop remained quietly untouched. "Does anyone want to eat anything? If not, I'm going to empty the tray to not raise questions from the guards."

A few verbal denials were stated and John reached out to empty it. His fingers cautiously probed around, but still touched something moist and squishy, which made him involuntarily shiver. He found the tray, turned it over to discard the contents, and set the tray down in time for the door to re-open.

The guards did their usual routine, each wearing rubber gloves. One held the door open while the other used a long pole with a hook to pull the tray across the floor and back near the door where he picked up the tray and set it on a cart that held a load of similar trays. Only this time, the guard at the door suddenly lurched sideways. He buckled over in a slump with his eyes closed. His massive legs still held the door open as he lay sprawled on the floor. The same instant the first guard slumped over, the pole flew out of the second guard's hand and struck him in the side of his head. He also hit the floor unconscious. A ring of keys floated through the air and dropped in John's lap.

John took this as a sign and unlocked his, Bert's, and Dillon's ankles. Bert continued to release the rest of the swollen ankles from their metal prisons while John and the Irish men scrambled the forlorn group of prisoners together. John grabbed the reverend—who seemed intent on giving last rites—by his shirtsleeve and followed the pole that floated down the fluorescent-lit hallway. The men assisted one another and moved slow and wearily, with their eyes alert.

The reverend kept one hand free and after every few steps he took he made the sign of the cross. They stumbled along, looking and smelling like a chain gang returning from a month-long work duty in the stables.

"Are we following a ghost?" asked one of the lads.

"Looks like it," said Bert, squinting in the well-lit hall as he kept his eyes on the floating pole.

The pole stopped and a deep voice with a French accent said, "You must hurry, the resistance is waiting."

"The what?" Bert asked, and looked at John when there was no response.

Surprised, John said, "I don't know. I was expecting an Italian ghost."

"Oui, but Mullog has gone," said the unseen Frenchman.

John shrugged his shoulders and cocked his head. "We better hurry then." He leaned down and picked up the slower of the two lads.

The two Irish sailors each took an arm of the reverend and they half-ran, half-trotted down the hall behind the others. The pole disappeared around a corner seconds before the sounds of men yelling and being clipped and pounded on. The bludgeoning lasted only a moment. John, closest to the noise, stopped. When the quiet resumed, he peered around the corner before he motioned the others to follow him. They stepped cautiously and saw the pole wave towards a door. The unseen Frenchman said, "The resistance is this way."

When the men's haggard faces saw the exit door, their legs picked up speed. They stepped around guards crumpled up on the floor along the narrow hallway, all with puffy bruises forming on their foreheads and cheekbones. A couple of them bled from gashes on their mouths, and one guard's nose pointed a new direction. Submachine guns and pistols lay on the floor around the unconscious guards. The reverend crossed himself again as John, Bert, and the Irish blokes picked up the weapons and swung the straps over their shoulders and put the pistols in their loose trousers.

The exit brought fresh, cold air that gave added energy to the escapees as they guzzled deep breaths of clean air. An empty white bus with about ten rows of windows and seats sat idling on a parkway between the warehouse building they had exited and a dense forest. They were on a rise of land that overlooked the open sea, towards where the street wound down.

"Into the bus," said the ghost with the French accent.

They climbed into the bus, which faced the sea and the orange sunset. John set the lad down next to his father and sat on the plastic bench behind the driver's seat.

"Who's driving?" Bert asked, as he sat across from John.

A ghostly driver appeared to a synchronized intake of breath from the passengers. With the whites of Bert's eyes showing, he searched John's face. "Ghosts can drive?"

John scratched his chin and said, "Let's hope this one can."

The apparition threw the pole out of the door before he sat in the driver seat and pulled the door latch to shut out the cold. "Oui, I can drive." The Frenchman ground the gears several times before he pushed the gear into first. He let up on the clutch and pressed the accelerator. The bus lurched forwards and stalled.

"You were saying?" John asked.

"It has been a little while." The Frenchman turned his head around and gave a glowing smile.

He was a spry little man wearing modern clothes consisting of a denim jacket, white shirt, and black trousers. His hair and eyebrows were as dark as his trousers. He seemed familiar to John, but John couldn't think why.

"How about you float to the back and let me have a go?" John asked.

"No, no. I know where we are going."

John glanced at the perimeter of the Island and the harbor below. "Alright, but if you stall this thing again I'm sitting in your seat and taking over."

The apparition shivered. The reverend crossed himself, and the lads were eager to watch the ghost drive them to safety.

"Are you by yourself?" John asked.

The spirit gave a half turn of his head and started the engine, found first gear, and with a slight lurch the bus picked up speed, and followed the road that ran alongside the tree line.

"You cannot see the others. But they are near." He put the bus in second gear, smooth and sure. "I am Pierre." John's surprised face glanced at the ghost in the mirror.

Bert nodded and said, "We are grateful to you for getting us out of that place."

Pierre took a left turn and then a right. On the road ahead of them was another white bus. "More like you; four bus loads." He caught John's eyes in the mirror. "Most were not able to walk out. Your group is lucky."

"Any deaths?" John asked, thinking about Zoe, Ceana, Conall, and others he knew.

Pierre kept his voice low. "Ten here. But that does not include the other locations around the world."

John whispered, "Around the world?"

Pierre nodded and kept quiet. John understood. He'd get the information later, in private. He watched the bus in front of them and waited for the lights to shine on the heads of those in the other bus. It was too difficult to recognize anyone he knew, and impossible for him to find a dark-haired beauty with a few awkward orange stripes in her hair, or Conall and Ceana. He grew impatient for the buses to stop in order to conduct a thorough search.

The road flattened out to follow the beach. The high tide rolled in with white-capped waves. In front of them, the harbor appeared. It had a "U" shaped dock with only one fishing boat tied to the side of the pier. The dock was long enough for several yachts and sailboats to be moored. It had no boathouse, only a decrepit wooden shack and a car park with plenty of space for the buses.

"That fishing boat looks a bit small," said John. He stood up, impatiently waiting for Pierre to stop the bus and open the door.

Pierre pulled next to the three already parked buses and turned off the engine. He turned around long enough to tell his passengers about the water and boxes of food in the back of the bus. He gave John a look and pulled the door latch open at the same time John grabbed the latch. John felt a mild shock as his hand passed through the ghost's and yanked his hand back. He gave Pierre a surprised look. The sea air blew in a light breeze that refreshed the stagnant air of the bus.

John jumped out. His leap propelled his body through two ghosts that disintegrated into puffs of fog as John whisked through them. He ran straight to the nearest bus. He entered and searched each person's face for any sign of recognition. They looked dreadful—too weak to mind their rescuers being spirits. Shredded clothes, hanging skin void of colour, sunken eyes and cheeks, lips chapped and bleeding from dehydration, but their lips were turned upwards in a slight, but grateful smile at their angelic rescuers floating above and handing them food. His heart sank as he approached the last bus, and so far no sign of Zoe. He stepped in and his hope grew. In the middle of the bus a dark-haired girl sat alone with her face staring out of the window. He stepped towards her and she turned to face him. Her face hopeful—but the face of a stranger. He studied each of the remaining people with no luck.

John took the ham sandwich and bottle of water that someone handed him when he stepped out of the last bus. He ate the sandwich without tasting it, disappointed he hadn't found Zoe. He frowned and focused on the horizon. The setting sun's backdrop did not silhouette any boat or means of escape. If they didn't leave or find refuge soon, the guards would wake up and come after them. Specs and Jaak wouldn't tolerate an escape such as this. The guards were dead men unless they recaptured the escapees.

John studied the hillside with its road carved, back and forth, into its sides. Located on top of the hill was the dark outline of the warehouse. Several pair of lorry lights turned on and began moving along the road near the warehouse. He had no doubt as to where they were headed. He figured they had just over five minutes before those vehicles and guards arrived at the harbor. They had few weapons to delay the guard's attack and it would take at least thirty minutes to load the passengers aboard a boat or other rescue vehicle that was still unseen. The ghosts had become agitated and were yelling among themselves; they were worried also. He was the only one with the expertise to delay their recapture.

John ran towards the shack. He thought it may have petrol or something, anything to create a diversion. Pierre floated above him as he ran.

"What are you doing?" Pierre asked.

"Trying to create a diversion to prevent the guards from approaching too close."

"What can we do?" Pierre continued to glide above John.

John said, "Get everyone outside of the buses. Then, put two of the buses perpendicular to each other and push them over on their sides. Push them into an arrow formation." While still running, John held his hands up in a teepee position. "With the point aimed towards the road and those lorries. Then, position the other two buses on the seaside of those tipped over. Put everyone without a gun between the buses for protection. That should shield them from most of the gunfire if the guards come out shooting."

When John arrived at the shack, he leaned against its outer wooden wall. Pierre was still beside him. "Pierre, go! Create your ray-sees-taunce," he said in his best French accent and waved him away. Pierre disappeared and John, feeling weak and muscles cramping from the run, kicked the door several times before the wood broke apart. He reached his hand between the broken boards and unlocked the rusty handle to open the door. He entered and found several jugs of petrol, a few lengths of thick rope, a plastic container labeled hydrochloric acid, and a stack of dried wood. Bert and the two Irish men, Dillon and Brian, entered behind him. He put them to work, hauling the jugs, rope, wood, and acid towards the buses.

Nearby, the spirits raised their arms like wizards and collectively gave a pushing motion. The buses groaned and creaked but gently turned over on their sides. After John witnessed the ease of turning over the buses, he asked Pierre if the spirits could also pull apart the walls of the wooden shack and position them in front of the overturned buses. No sooner had Pierre disappeared than the wooden walls of the shack cracked apart and soared menacingly above the arms of the spirits to be positioned diagonally against the front of the buses.

Bert and John uncoiled the rope. They started on one end of the former walls of the shack, which now leaned against the buses, and unrolled the rope around the pointed front where the buses met. They continued to uncoil and knot the rope lengths together until they reached the back bumper of the second bus. The Irish blokes followed behind them. The strong smell of petrol permeated the air as they emptied the jugs over the rope and wooden walls until they reached the back bumper.

When finished, John looked expectantly around and asked if anyone had a lighter. No one had a lighter. While they kept an eye on the approaching vehicles on the road along the beach, they scrambled through the compartments of the overturned buses and discovered two lighters next to a pack of cigarettes. Relieved, John handed a lighter to Bert and had him position himself on one end of the rope, with John and the second lighter on the other end.

The Irish men maneuvered themselves behind the bumpers of the front buses. Each opposite the other, they used the bumpers to steady the aim of their AK-47 machine guns at the approaching guards. The reverend and the lads sat huddled together with both of the lads' fathers armed with a pistol, if needed. They, and all the other weakened hostages, sat clustered close together in the triangle between the buses, fear registering in their pale faces and shaking limbs. Their arms pressed against one another for warmth and reassurance.

The Norwegian had surprised John with his expertise in the way he handled a gun. During their escape the man had removed a rifle from the clutches of a fallen guard. While prepping for the assault, he had checked the safety and the ammo in the magazine. He adjusted the site and then used hand signals to indicate he would hide in the clumps of trees and brush across from the car park and to their right, to not create a crossfire situation. He darted across the road and hid himself behind an old tree seconds before the guards would have spotted him on their approach. John barely made out the Norwegian's pale head in the twilight.

With everyone in position, using the seconds before the guards' arrival, John searched the darkening horizon for any sign of their rescue ship. He saw nothing. He looked up at Pierre who stood next to him.

Pierre shook his head and held his hands out towards John, "Je suis désolé. The ship should have been here."

"Not your fault, Pierre. We will make the best bloody resistance possible."

"Oui."

The screeching sound of tires travelled their way, along with the distant resonance of a powerful engine that hummed through the air. Heads turned towards the sea, hopeful. But John recognized the sound. A black helicopter crested the rise above the hill, the rotors buzzing in their direction. They were trapped. They had a small amount of ammunition and not enough resources to buy time until a ship arrived—a ship that hadn't yet appeared on the horizon. When and if it did show, John wondered how they would load the passengers while they held the guards from advancing.

John feared retaliation would take all of their lives. Jaak and Specs had no reason to keep any hostages alive if they knew that the ghostly ancestors of the descendants could no longer be controlled by their capture. He wondered how widespread that assumption could take the death toll. Possibly to Zoe, Ceana and Conall, and many others he knew. He hoped the guards hadn't seen any of the spirits.

He set his jaw and narrowed his eyes as the lorries' engines whined down. They had slowed their approach and stopped at a safe enough distance, unless the Norwegian had the shooting skills of a sniper. The Mosin-Nagant rifle the Norwegian carried had been used for over a hundred years by snipers, but did not have a scope on it. John had not seen any scopes on the guns at the warehouse and anticipated that he and the prisoners were also safe from sniper bullets.

The sun had set and the sky cast a silver hue to the churning sea and the black forest line of trees. The helicopter flew overhead and made a wide circle of the pier. John had told everyone to keep fingers off the triggers until he shot first. He did not want any bullets discharged because of careless unease. They needed to spare their ammo and hope the guards didn't have extinction orders.

John watched in surprise when the helicopter landed next to the pier. He turned towards Pierre, but the ghost had vanished, hopefully anticipating what John wanted to ask him. The rotors of the helicopter slowed and it grew quiet except for the crashing waves against the beach and pier. Pierre reappeared next to John whose trigger finger almost flinched. He didn't know if he'd ever get used to the disappearances and reappearances of the spirits. It made him edgy.

"What did you find out?" he asked Pierre in a low whisper.

Pierre moved as close as possible to John without going through him and held his mouth near John's ear. "Each truck carries four armed men. Besides the pilot, the helicopter has two men." Pierre couldn't see the frightened escapees, but glanced in their direction when a few made low whimpering noises that carried through the cold air. His voice broke as he continued to whisper, "Jaak, and his brother Specs, they debate over whether to shoot you all or attempt to recapture you and use you in other ways. They said they could make a lot of rubles if they sell you to Sarah."

John removed his finger from the trigger and swallowed. "Sarah? Are you sure they said Sarah?"

"Oui. I am sure."

John's mind whirled and put the events together. The news from Shaw that said he couldn't marry Zoe because his first wife still lived meant that Shaw and Sarah must have been working together all along. How else would Shaw have known that Sarah was alive? She must know more about the Archivists than she had let on. He reeled himself back to his present situation and said to Pierre, "We'll wait and let them make the first move. I feel we have more chance of survival in a fight than more days imprisoned in those inhumane conditions." John paused. No one had stepped out of the helicopter yet and the vehicles remained silent and still. He searched the muted light of Pierre's face and whispered, "I was there, at the cemetery that morning, at dawn when Jaak took your life."

Pierre's eyes opened wide and his image darkened.

"Zoe and I were hiding in the trees. I could have done something. Maybe I could have saved you," John said.

Pierre's eyes focused on John's. "Then I would not be here now, as a reformed man. It is better this way, with the resistance."

"You have a good soul, Pierre. And a lot of faith in that resistance of yours."

The ghost smiled before he faded from view. The helicopter door opened and a man jumped down.

John pictured the cold eyes behind the spectacles of the little bald man, the thin lips with his clicking tongue, and the calloused lack of feeling in his mannerisms and voice. The gentle sound of the waves lapping at the pier couldn't put a genteel touch to the man as he spoke loud enough to be heard over the waves. "Tsk, tsk, tsk, John. What am I to do with you?"

John kept his eye on the man standing next to the chopper and saw a taller man whose silhouette he recognized as Jaak, jump down next to Specs. Other than their depravity, the two brothers held no family resemblance to one another. They walked across the pier, one man tall and hairy and the other short and bald. They went towards the car park where the buses lay on their sides. John said, "You land here in your helicopter, wearing your best suit. What are you thinking? That this is some diplomatic rendezvous?" After speaking, John turned and whispered to the air beside him, "Pierre, I hope you can hear me. Get a few spirits and go light them up."

Laughter billowed from the small man. "John, my dear boy, you have a nowhere plan. Can't you see these spirits have led you into a trap?"

Bursts of light that came from five different directions cascaded over the two deplorable men; they stopped. In the brightness they didn't even have a shadow. Jaak's arm, in a lethargic and haphazard manner, rose to shield his eyes. Although he stood two heads taller than Specs, he looked weak and thin. Specs did not blink or shield his eyes.

Specs said, "Tsk, tsk, John. I have snipers in the trees. The light will help put your head in their sights. Do not make a mistake that will cost you and all those with you their lives."

Jaak coughed and spit. His face dripped with perspiration in the crisp night air. His body shrunk in the brightness of the surrounding light.

"Your brother does not appear well," John said.

The little man shot a quick glance at Jaak and said, "I'd be more concerned about the wellness of your group of castaways." He pointed to the empty pier. "Were you expecting a boat?"

"He's stalling," John whispered, hoping a spirit was nearby.

Pierre's voice spoke nearby. "The guards come this way."

It was time. John gave the signal to light the fuel and flicked on his own lighter's flame, tossing it onto the rope. The fire erupted and spread quickly across the rope to light up the wood and debris used around the fronts of their bus protection. Orange, black, and yellow flames leapt into the air providing the necessary shield from any sniper's sight that tried to get a fix on those beyond its shelter. The heat warmed the chilly air and gave comfort to those cowering between the buses.

Specs' thin lips smiled and he opened his mouth to speak, but before he voiced another word Jaak's tall figure collapsed on the ground next to him. Specs' face twisted with concern, the first sign of humanity that John had seen from him.

"Jaak!" Specs cried out. He knelt down next to his brother, reached out and clasped Jaak's large but thin hand in his own. He gasped when the large hand jerked away and Jaak's body began to convulse and shudder. To avoid getting hit by flaying limbs, Specs moved away from the quivering body. He stared in horror as his brother's back arched upwards from the ground. The upward momentum knocked his brother's skull against the asphalt with a thud.

"John, I will kill everyone unless you stop this." Specs loud voice carried into the night.

"That is not my doing." John looked at Pierre who appeared beside him and shook his head.

Jaak rolled over and yelled in agony. He rolled back, his face white, his teeth barred in pain, foam at his mouth, his red eyes blinking tears from the effort, but stared into nothingness.

"What is happening?" Specs tried to grab his brother and hold him down, but the man's shaking was too severe. He crawled away to avoid being pummeled, his glasses falling from his nose.

Jaak's body continued to quiver and jolt and then his skin enlarged and deflated like a giant pulsating heartbeat. A length of skin from his arms separated and then peeled and pulled apart like skin taffy to form two arms on each side of him. The arms pulled until two sets of hands pushed from the skin of the convulsing man's body.

Screams came from the men and women hidden behind the buses. John glanced through the crack between the buses to see if they were being attacked. Sure enough, in order to reach the former hostages, some guards had sneaked around the front of the barricade in an attempt to dodge past the flames that were extinguishing too quickly. The Irish men hadn't had adequate fuel to saturate the wood enough for a prolonged inferno. Several guards stood in front of the flames and paused in their attempt to attack. A measure of revulsion covered the guard's faces as they watched the horrific condition of Jaak's body, which twisted and separated before their eyes.

Specs looked up at the spirits spotlighting the scene. "Stop! You're killing him." He waved his arms in the air. "Shoot them. Shoot them all."

Most of the guards snapped out of their fright, pulled their triggers, and aimed at the buses. The metal buses tore apart with jagged holes the size of golf balls, but the shots did not penetrate through to the inner domain where the captives huddled. John saw the frightened people back away from the break between the buses where they had watched Jaak's wretched body. Two guards made it past the Norwegian's site and penetrated the barricade. John heard two quick shots from between the buses and hoped those two guards were down. Several pops came from the tree line where the Norwegian held his ground to stop the guards who remained behind.

Jaak's body continued to flex and drift in and out. Specs again crawled over to kneel next to his brother whose screams erupted louder than the collection of screams and gunfire coming from the captives and guards. Jaak's hands and arms pushed until every part of the taffy consistency, of what looked like another entity, snapped with the sound of a leather whip striking flesh. As soon as the bodies separated, the gunfire ceased, which amplified Jaak's last, mournful breath. A wraithlike spirit erupted and merged from Jaak's body. The phantom pushed aside the body, which slumped over on the pavement of the car park, and he crawled a distance away. The five spirits of light that spotlighted the wretched scene vanished into darkness. Except for some moans from the wounded guards, silence magnified the night.

The wraithlike man with a muscular and carnal image drifted above Jaak's motionless body. His phantom glow donned an amber hue that extended to the black robe he wore. At first, John thought it was Jaak's spirit, but he bore little resemblance to the lifeless Jaak. His wavy hair was dark and almost touched his shoulders, unlike Jaak's crew cut. His mouth sneered in mirth and cruelty—similar to Jaak. He drifted towards Specs and he spoke with the same vile and gritty voice of Jaak, but instead of the Estonian accent he had an Italian one. "Relax, my brother; those spirits did not do this. Even they are afraid of me and my power."

Specs face, quivering in fear, looked up at the ghost.

"Yes, my brother, I can teach you this power. The power to seize and abide in another."

Even without his glasses, Specs knew the ghost was not Jaak. "Where is my brother? What have you done?" His tone was not fearful, but weak and confused; he reached a shaky hand towards his brother's body.

"Am I not your brother then?" The ghost moved closer to Specs who cringed. "But you have treated me as your brother. Are you only interested in that body lying there, even though it ceased to be Jaak months ago?" The gritty voice trailed off in a laugh.

Specs gathered his thoughts while his trembling hand swept over the ground searching for his glasses. He found his spectacles. He put them on and with his index finger he pushed them up on his nose. He stood up and backed away from the ghost and the body of his brother.

The ghost said, "My brother, do you not want the power I can give to you? Jaak was weak, but I, Jacob, am strong. Have you not noticed that the other spirits flee in my presence?"

"You killed Jaak." Specs turned and saw some guards emerge from the forest. "You there, shoot him." He pointed towards Jacob.

An onslaught of gunfire erupted, this time aimed at Jacob. Jacob's euphoric grin evaporated and he disappeared, but not before Specs' guards had dispatched enough gunfire to kill the pilot and annihilate the helicopter positioned behind Jacob.

"Idiots." Specs cursed at his men and tried to get them to stop.

The bullets stopped, the ammunition running out. Silence followed, other than the tears and sniffles from the captives who held each other and were unharmed by the gunfire.

Specs' shoulders drooped. He walked back towards Jaak's twisted body. He knelt down, his image large next to his once muscular brother. Specs put his hand on his brother's chest and remained there, his mouth set, his eyes closed.

Bert crept next to John and whispered, "What should we do?"

"Keep still. There may be more men with guns in the trees." John held his gun pointed in that direction. He jumped slightly when the voice of the Frenchman said in his other ear, "We will check the forest and be back." John nodded at the air around him.

Bert whispered, "I hope you plan on giving an explanation of what's happened tonight."

John shook his head. "I'm not sure I know. Maybe some kind of possession by a ghost."

Bert said, "Whatever it was, I hope to never witness anything like that again." He continued, "How about the ghosts? Aren't they supposed to smell like sulfur when they appear?"

After Bert's odd statement, John glanced at him.

"No one in the forest," Pierre said, abruptly in John's ear.

"That was quick," said John, his heart pounding.

Bert turned towards Pierre, whose translucent light reappeared, and asked, "Why do people say spirits smell like sulfur?"

"It is human flatulence caused by fright after seeing a ghost," said Pierre, with a grin.

John looked back towards Jaak and Specs. Jaak's body lay by itself on the ground. Specs had disappeared. John's eyes zoomed across the dark landscape of the pier and pylons. No sign of Specs, and no sign of any ship lights either. He swore under his breath. "Pierre, find Specs," John said.

Pierre disappeared. An unexpected foghorn bellowed across the water and echoed over the pier. The sound caused Pierre and the other ghosts to reveal themselves in a burst of surprise that lit up the surrounding area of forest, rocky beach, and pier to the brightness of mid-day. The sound startled everyone, including a couple of guards who remained with the vehicles, their surprised trigger fingers firing shots into the trees. The light silhouetted the Irish men next to one of the lorries. They drew down on the surprised guards, and then some spirits grabbed the guards and whisked them away to restrain them. The light also silhouetted the Norwegian, whose gun pushed against the spine of Specs as he brought the little man in from his attempted escape.

John, along with everyone else in the vicinity, stared at the frigate that had blown its horn. It loomed against the pier, kissing the wood with its long hull. It looked like something brought up from the depths of the sea. Mollusks and barnacles clung to the sides and seaweed draped freely from the three masts unadorned with rigging.

Bert glanced at the frigate and back at John. "How long has that been there?"

"Maybe three hundred years." John shrugged his shoulders and looked as amazed as Bert. The frigate had ghosts on deck, the entire ship lit by spirits. From the captain at the wheel, to those that sat across the masts, the scene was the epitome of a ghost ship. A plank swung and dropped to the pier with a heavy thud. Six people walked down the plank and more than twenty spirits appeared like lanterns trailing from the deck. They soared skywards through the night to light up the swells of smoke still billowing around the buses near the pier.

"Mio amico. What a relief. You need a bath, but you are alive." Mullog hovered above John.

"What took you so long?" John asked.

"We had trouble getting here. Many ancestors of those taken did not trust multiple rescues around the world unless we orchestrated them at the exact same time. Thus, no alarm could be sent to other ghost camps where they would kill or sacrifice their descendants. But a couple, like you, already had their rescue underway."

"Well, we'll live…," Before John could finish, a familiar voice interrupted him.

"Holy Moses, what is that smell?"

John laughed. "As I was saying, we'll live if we can get food and get cleaned up." He opened his arms and began to walk towards his interrupter. "Come here, Nana."

She pulled a knife, the length of her arm, out of a leather sheaf on her hip and waved it in the air. "We British prefer a hello to a hug."

John smiled. "So tonight you claim to be British." Nana laughed at him as he turned towards the next figure coming his way. "How about you, Aunt Phoebe?"

"After you soak in bleach," Phoebe said, wriggling her nose. "And so sorry about the delay." She narrowed her eyes at Mullog.

Towering above Nana and Phoebe stood four of Conall's dark-haired sons. Neil and Thor raised their hands in greeting, and Sean asked, "Any sign of ma parents?"

"No," John said.

Still looking hopeful, Eadan said, "Weel chat later."

John nodded and watched the four guys walk to help the hostages. Spirits were transporting the weakest to the ship. They held the captives gently in their arms and flew them from the pier to the frigate where others, including some ghostly nurses, helped them below. Some spirits floated over to speak with the reverend; he made the sign of the cross and backed up. The spirits shook their heads and despite the reverend's reluctance they each grabbed one of his arms and flew him aboard the deck of the ship.

"Who's the Captain of the ship?" John asked.

"Who do you think?" Nana said, laughter in her eyes.

Phoebe whistled. "And Captain John Link is one fine specimen of a man spirit. How is it possible that with your namesake you never learned how to sail?"

"You know I prefer the air."

"What happened here? Anyone killed?" Nana asked.

John said, "A few guards and Jaak. I'll explain in more detail later. As you can see we caught Specs, who happens to be Jaak's brother. Apparently, for months Jaak's body has been inhabited by a spirit named Jacob."

Mullog gasped. "Jacob?"

John's eyebrows pinched together. "You know him?"

Mullog quivered, "Si. If it is the Jacob I know, he was...," his voice trailed off.

John asked, "He was who?"

Mullog's light weakened. "He was once my brother."

Phoebe put her hands on her slender hips and said, "You failed to mention you had a brother wreaking havoc."

"I did not know he was back. He is very good at deception, mia carina."

"Don't 'mia carina' me. Tell us what he is capable of doing and if you know where he might be hiding," Phoebe said.

Nana cleared her throat and tilted her head towards Bert and the Irish blokes nearby who had paused to listen. Dillon and Bert supported an elderly man whom they were taking aboard the freighter as Brian carried a thin, teenage lad in his arms. While the sick were moved up the gangplank, John, Mullog, and the Blue Bloods moved a safe distance away from the rescue efforts before continuing their conversation.

Phoebe said, "Please continue."

Mullog looked at his feet, which hovered inches above the ground. "Oh, he has many gifts, deception is only one of them. And he has knowledge of many of our secrets. And...I do not know where he would hide," he said in a hushed voice.

"Was he an Archivist?" Nana asked.

Mullog shook his head.

"Then how could he have discovered our secrets? Spirits don't have that knowledge unless they have been one of us," Phoebe said.

John looked at her in surprise.

"That was another thing I meant to tell you, John," said Nana.

"He is good with deception," Mullog said again, in a miserable tone.

"Get to the point," John said.

Mullog motioned for John to follow him away from Nana and Phoebe. The women shook their heads in disgust and Nana threw her hands in the air and said, "Fine, but hurry." John followed Mullog around the shot-up helicopter and to the other side of the pier.

"I am uncomfortable telling this because I have shown myself to more than just you Keepers. The others think I am only another spirit. Mio amico, they do not know I am the Keeper's Keeper."

John shook his hands impatiently. "Alright. Then say what you need to say as if you were just a normal spirit."

"But what I cannot say, I cannot say to anyone, except maybe a Keeper."

"And what is that, Mullog?"

Mullog came as close as possible to John without touching him. He whispered, "I once wanted a holiday from my duties as the Keeper's Keeper and Jacob visited me after I decided this. I mentioned to him that I wanted a holiday. Of course, he did not know why I never left my crypt room with the chests, but visited me often as a loving brother would. He never pried into my affairs. When I told him I wanted a respite, he felt bad for me and wondered why. He convinced me he would not touch anything if I trusted him to watch the chests, as long as I told him why I could not leave the room. He thought I had done something horrible to have myself captured like a spirit criminal. I laughed at this and said I was not a criminal; I was keeping a watch over this room for a group of special humans. He then figured out that I lived in the location, kept secret from all except the Keepers, and protected the Law Book for the

Archivists."

"It seems simple to me," John said. "We'll move the chests and the Law Book to a new location."

Nana's voice travelled across the pier. "We're going to wait for you all on the ship where it's warm."

Mullog's face fell. "They are angry and hurt."

"No worries, Mullog. You've done the right thing only telling me."

Mullog gave John a smile that didn't include his eyes. "I was selfish. I had a nice respite from my duties. While I was on my holiday, Jacob read everything he could and made a copy of the Law Book. He started to copy the lineage line when I returned and discovered his deception." He paused at John's intake of breath. "Si, John, there is a lineage line of Primordial humans, which someday you may even see."

"I hope I can."

"I had to answer to those above me and pay the penalty. That is why I am not allowed visitors other than the Keepers. Nor am I normally allowed to reveal myself to anyone else."

The foghorn blared as a warning the frigate was leaving.

Mullog mumbled, "During this time, we've had an exception to that rule."

"Thank you for being candid with me. I'll keep your secret, Mullog."

Mullog nodded. "Mio amico, you are kind. Let us hope we catch Jacob before he inhabits another body and recruits new warriors for his cause."

"Yes," said John "but is there a way to tell if a body has been inhabited by him?"

Mullog stared at his feet again. "I do not think so."

Chapter 29
FAMOUS ARCHIVES

The North Sea

I had to hand it to Sarah; she played all her parts like an Oscar winner. She had fooled numerous people. My eyes stared into the dark while I lay on my berth unable to sleep and holding an ice bag to the side of my head. I listened to the soft breathing of Adam and Brynn, and thought about what I could do next. Some relief came to me knowing John had not murdered my parents or had anything to do with the kidnappings. My relief counterbalanced the painful knowledge that Shaw had been deliberately led to believe the opposite—thanks to the bedazzling, sophisticated treachery of Sarah. I wanted to grab her, shake her, and toss her around until her suit wrinkled and her nails broke. I sat up, wincing from the pain, partially caused by the humiliation of knocking myself out in front of her. I needed to find Shaw. I had some questions to ask him. I put on my borrowed slippers and crept out of the door, torch in hand.

Small ceiling lights cast a dull appearance on the walls and doors. The stuffy air and my throbbing head made me breathless. My feet stepped quietly and sure as I stole past closed doors and down the ladder towards the galley. Voices came from the galley as I passed; none of them sounded like Shaw. The next door was the officer's galley where I planned to first check for my brother. I hadn't seen him since that morning when I passed the engine room after being up top. I didn't know where he slept and figured I could ask an officer if I found one in their galley—if not, I'd ask one of the crew I saw in the other galley.

I approached the door and stopped. A woman's voice spoke in a soft whisper. Even whispering, I knew it was Sarah. I crept closer so I could understand her words.

"I'm heading to my room now; you're dismissed."

Startled, I hightailed it back to the main galley. Four crewmen's faces tried to cover their startled surprise when I burst into the room. I leaned against the wall and pretended to look at the food choices of rye bread and cheese that remained on the metal countertop, while I really listened for footsteps to pass by the doorway. But she must have changed her shoes. After ample time, and not hearing anyone walk by, I grabbed a slice of cheese, smiled at the crewmen who had gone back to playing cards, and cautiously stepped into the hall.

She hadn't passed the main galley, which indicated that her room was the other direction. She would be too far ahead for me to dash after her. Most likely I'd end up walking loud enough for her to discover me. Too bad I couldn't see her. If I'd been able to follow her, I could have eliminated the one door not to knock on in the officers' quarters. I sighed and since the officers' galley was silent I poked my head into the doorway; no one was there. I walked back to the main galley and grabbed another slice of cheese. I casually asked the group of card players to point me in the direction of the officers' quarters. They smiled to one another and informed me to go past the officers' galley and up one level. I didn't appreciate what they were thinking. I thanked them and glanced at the clock before I left—zero three hundred. I had maybe an hour before the crew began waking for the next shift.

The area they described was an area that during Brynn's, Adam's, and my explorations we had been unable to get to because of guards and locked doors. But tonight felt different and quieter. Since last night had been a sleepless night loading the additional hostages and supplies, maybe tonight the crew had retired early.

After passing the galleys, I came to a set of stairs. I grabbed the metal railing and began to step up when voices approached from above me. I scurried back down and squeezed behind boxes containing canned vegetables and meats stacked in a corner niche. The men spoke softly on the all-engrossing topic of fishing lures and didn't see me as they stepped down the ladder. After they disappeared inside the galley, I grabbed the railings and hurried up the stairs; my slippers made no sound. I came to a corner and paused to listen. I heard only the slight pulse of the propeller and the creaks of the outer shell, which I now knew were caused by depth changes and water pressure, but the sound still made me uneasy. I entered a hallway with wood siding and more height in the ceiling where the air ducts were installed higher to give more headroom. There were no open doors to give any clues. I shook my head. For a moment I viewed myself from what I had seen in Sarah's eyes. She may have been right; how daft I was to think I might find Shaw at this hour. I couldn't very well knock on each door. As soon as my knock was heard, those behind the other doors would be curious and I would be caught. With my luck, I'd knock on Sarah's door first. I pictured it in my head, "Hi Sarah, I thought we could continue our conversation about how ill-fitted I am for John. I also hoped you'd give me some fashion advice."

I stood in the narrow space unable to decide whether to go back to my bunk and try to sleep or continue to explore this part of the sub that had been off limits until now. The sound of a turning doorknob brought me out of my meanderings and to my current precarious position. I searched the hallway for a hiding place. It was straight and narrow with no cans of food on the floor—clean and pristine, Sarah's obvious touch in every cranny. Since the turning doorknob was behind me, I flew forwards, up a short flight of three metal stairs, and hit the end of the passageway, which went either left or right. Behind me the door had opened. I looked left—another narrow and dark passageway. With my peripheral vision, I saw a man step out of the room and as he pulled the door shut someone grabbed my arm and pulled me to the right. I almost screamed, and would have if a hand hadn't covered my face and mouth and turned my wild eyes towards her own wild eyes, which stopped my scream. After the footsteps receded away from us, Brynn let go of my face and Adam loosened his grip on my arm. Because we were too afraid to speak, the three of us grinned at each other in one of those "thank you, but what are you doing here" looks.

Adam pointed his head sideways, indicating we should follow him. A couple of steps later we turned right and stopped. We put our heads close together and Adam said, "I'm pretty sure we're near the area housing the forward torpedo tubes. Let's check it out."

Brynn and I nodded; I'd have to talk with Shaw another time.

Adam walked to a door and with our hearts pounding he opened it. Thank goodness no groans or squeaks occurred—a well-maintained door. Adam shone his torch into the room. It appeared to be a utility closet holding brooms, mops and buckets. But it also had floor to ceiling shelves laden with books.

I grabbed the torch and lit up the covers of the books. Old leather covers in natural buckskin and colours of red, purple, and blue adorned the collection. I pulled one off the shelf, opened it and read aloud. "Claude Monet." We smiled at each other and pulled the door shut.

Brynn's fingers ran across the titles of others. "They all have names of famous people on them."

"These were taken from the Althing's archives," I said. "Here's Victor Hugo, Francois-Marie Arouet, and Marie Antoinette."

"They're all French," Brynn said.

"How cool to Host for one of them," Adam said.

"Actually, interviewing them and writing their history would be better," said Brynn.

Adam rolled his eyes at her. "Whatever."

"Here's some Italian renaissance artists that I recognize: Sandro Botticelli, Michelangelo, Donatello, and Raphael," I said.

"We need to get out of here," said Adam.

"Yes, they wouldn't want us to know about this," I said.

"Let's sneak back here tomorrow night and spend some time reading," Brynn said, her eyes open with excitement. "We can bring snacks, an additional torch, and with the door shut no one would even know."

"You and Zoe can. I'm fine not," Adam said, his voice sad.

"Zoe and I can take turns reading out loud," said Brynn, her tone soft and understanding of his poor eyesight.

"Are there any crusaders?" Adam asked.

"That would be cool. Maybe we can take some books with us," Brynn said.

"Sure," I said. "That may be better than returning so soon."

"Find me a crusader one," Adam said.

"And we'll exchange them later," Brynn added.

She and I searched until we found one that interested each of us. Brynn said she was fluent in French and chose Francois-Marie Arouet and found a crusader for Adam by the name of Godfrey of Bouillon. I picked one that wasn't so old with the name Abba

Bahrey, which had the English translation on the page opposite Bahrey's native tongue.

"We better keep moving," I said, very concerned that we could get caught.

We waited by the door and listened for a few minutes before we opened it and crept out. We had decided to open at least one more door before returning to our room. We wanted to see if they had more stolen archives hidden. The next door led us into the torpedo room where three torpedo tubes were empty of weapons and full of books. Astonished, we began counting them. After counting more than one hundred in each, we decided to get back to our room before someone caught us. Shift change would be soon and I, for one, didn't want Sarah to find out what we had discovered. If she had wanted me to know, her pride would have told me earlier.

Before we turned down the passageway that led through the officer's quarters, Adam talked us into searching the opposite side, the side with the other three torpedo tubes. I hesitated and then decided tonight might be our only chance, but I went first.

We passed the hallway with the officers' quarters and came to a corner. I stopped, and peered around the edge, and pulled back quickly. My heart pounded in my ears. A guard was stationed outside the door that led into the torpedo room on this side. His head bobbed as he stood with his arms crossed. A knife hung in a black leather sheath at his side. I put my finger to my mouth to keep Adam and Brynn silent and motioned back the way we came. Down the stairs, through the passageways, past the galleys, and into our confined sleeping quarters we went. We didn't see or hear a soul, and once we closed our door and hid away our stolen books, we smiled tiredly to one another, climbed into our bunks, and fell asleep. I figured we had not only found some of the stolen archives, but we had discovered where the other hostages were kept.

Chapter 30
TRANSFERRED

I almost fell off my of bunk when what sounded like a cricket bat pounded on our door several times before moving on to the next door to pound on it. I stood up and opened the door.

"What?" Adam called out in a sleepy mumble. His feet fell over the edge of his bunk as he sat with his hands rubbing his head. His white hair stuck up in every direction.

"Come on you two. Something is going on." I rubbed my eyes.

Brynn sat up and we each pulled on our shoes.

A couple beeps sounded and Shaw's voice came over the intercom. "Everyone to your stations. Those passengers who want to can make their way topside during re-charge."

"It's only the re-charge time," Adam said, and then lay back down. "It feels like I only slept an hour."

"Because you pretty much did." Brynn laughed.

"This feels different than the other times," I said. "Grab your jackets. This will be a good time to talk to Ceana and Conall. I'm sure they'll be expecting us."

"I'm kinda hungry too," Brynn said.

"Let's get something from the galley on our way out." I moved to the hallway as Adam jumped down.

Fifteen minutes later, we sat shivering on the deck with about five other people I didn't recognize. Three crewmen blew the smoke from their cigarettes across the horizon and watched us from the tower where the periscope and antennae were. Adam said the area where they watched us from was called the "sail" and said Europeans called it the "fin." He was full of useless information.

A glistening orange stripe of my hair blew over my eyes as a breeze picked up. The water crashed against the ship, sending a spray across the bow. The sun hid behind some clouds and I tightened my life vest, a move that gave me a sense of security. It was still frightening for me to be up top, having only a couple of cables to grab onto if the seas became rough.

Brynn scooted closer to me and hooked her arm through mine for warmth. Adam wore a pair of aviator style sunglasses that one of the crew gave him to help protect his sensitive eyes. He pulled the hood of his jacket tighter around his face to protect his skin and keep him warm. Across from us, a man with bushy eyebrows surfaced above the open hatch. Conall smiled warmly at the three of us before turning to aid Ceana out of the hatch. Hand in hand, they walked the few steps towards us. Before Ceana sat down, she leaned over and touched my hair and the bruise on the side of my face. "I'm sure these have a story behind them."

The comfort of hearing her voice with its hint of Scots warmed me.

Adam and Brynn laughed, and Adam said, "She knocked herself out."

"Are ye alright?" asked Ceana.

"Other than the humiliation, I'm fine." I patted Brynn and Adam's shoulders. "I couldn't introduce you yesterday. This is Adam and Brynn. I've told them all about you two."

Brynn and Adam each gave them a shy smile.

Ceana leaned across to pull Adam's hood farther down on his head. "Nice to meet ye. Yer smart for protecting yer eyes and skin. I worried seeing ye the streen."

The grin on Adam's face grew as he repeated, "Streen?"

Ceana smiled. "Aye, hmmm, means yesterday." She gave him a hug.

"Oh, okay," said Adam. He obviously didn't mind Ceana's mothering.

They sat close to us and turned their backs to face the fin with their knees near their chins to steady themselves. The guards stationed above us went systematically through a pack of cigarettes. The engine noise from the recharge hadn't started yet, but I knew we didn't have long before we wouldn't be able to talk quietly.

Ceana and Conall looked more rested today. They had both cleaned up as well. Conall's beard was combed through and his curly hair contained in an elastic band. Ceana's black hair was long enough to tuck behind her ears, but tousled around her face in the wind.

"I am so glad to see ye and be able to talk, too," Ceana said.

"Aye, but I wish it were under different circumstances," said Conall.

"I agree."

"Is John here?" asked Ceana.

I replied, "No, I don't know where he is. And my brother, Shaw, is part of this charade."

Ceana gave me a comforting squeeze. "Oh, lass, I'm sorry."

"Me too," I said. "Have you already seen Sarah?"

"Sarah?" Conall asked.

"The former Nurse Gibbons," I said.

"Nae."

"In fact, she's in charge," Brynn said.

Adam grinned. "And the one who should have been knocked out."

"What?" Ceana asked.

I ignored Adam's comment. "Yes. Sarah is John's undead wife, and she's in charge of the whole operation."

"Well, she certainly had access to lots of information at my home," Ceana said, shaking her head in disgust. "I dinna ken."

"What have they—" I couldn't say anymore without raising my voice. The engines had begun the recharge. So we huddled together for warmth and enjoyed being together in the fresh, salty air.

After a few minutes, the clouds extended from above us to the horizon and the wind grew more boisterous. A couple of swells pitched water up and gave us a solid spray. We helped each other up and waited as two men helped a woman down the hatch. I glanced across the horizon and focused on a dot in the distance. I squinted to make sure I wasn't seeing a mirage. I tapped Ceana's shoulder and pointed to what I thought looked like a ship. She nodded and caught Conall's attention. Adam was next in line to enter the hatch but before he stepped inside, the engine noise stopped. Except for the sea lapping at the sides of the submarine, it was silent.

A guard's head appeared above the hatch and he climbed out, pushing Adam roughly aside. He had a cruel look on his face. At the same time he stepped on deck, three of the crewmen near the periscope rushed down the ladder on the side of the fin, tossed their cigarette butts into the churning waves, and surrounded us.

"I believe they saw that ship too," Conall said, a smirk playing across his face.

A siren sounded and we were rushed below. When the hatch was secured, Shaw's voice came over the intercom and said, "We are submersing to periscope depth in ten minus nine seconds." After removing our life vests, we were pushed past the engine room where several voices were arguing.

"There is no excuse for not seeing that frigate at least thirty minutes ago."

A woman's voice. I slowed down as much as I dared while passing the engine room and stole a quick look as I passed. Shaw and Sarah were nose to nose, both had red faces.

"What difference would that have made? We wouldn't have had enough charge to go silent," Shaw said.

"We could have had everyone below deck and hidden from their view." Their voices grew faint as we passed through a bulwark. Only one guard pushed us along. Adam and Brynn were in front of me, Ceana and Conall walked behind me with Conall closest to the guard.

Conall caught my eye and said, "Zoe, I guess you ken this ship better than me."

When he finished his sentence, his massive hand made a fist and he spun around and knocked the guard in the jaw. After a snapping sound, the guard's eyes rolled closed and Conall caught him before he caused any noise as he fell. He laid the unconscious man on the floor.

"A have an idea. Ceana, follow Zoe and the bairns, Zoe take them somewhere and hide." Conall winked at Ceana. "And dinna worry about me." He turned and headed back towards the engine room.

I knew the perfect place and so did Adam and Brynn. "Lead the way, kids," I said.

Our noses led us to the galley first. Antoine, the cook with no neck, had pepperoni pizza hot out of the oven. We each chose a couple pie-shaped slices and ate them on the run. We didn't know how long we'd be hiding and we were hungry. We passed the officers' galley where two men played what looked to be an intense game of chess. Their heads were almost touching and they didn't look up as we passed the doorway. No one questioned us on our rush to the closet. Ceana said that they most likely thought we were headed to her bunk area. We turned the opposite way of her quarters and entered the closet without anyone seeing us. I felt safe and saw the others relax too.

Ceana glanced at us and said, "I guess we wait until Conall does his thing and I'm sure it will be obvious."

Brynn, Adam, and I each had a torch. We only kept one on at a time in order to preserve the batteries. Not only had we grabbed torches, we had also stuck the Archive books we removed the night before in the waistline of our trousers. Ceana smiled as we removed them. "We canna get bored in here." She took a book from a shelf in the closet and put it back. "I canna hardly choose from this assortment."

"Did ye meet the sly one?" Ceana asked.

"We certainly did. John almost lost his patience with him and left." I smiled.

"What did you name him?" Ceana asked.

"Mullog."

Ceana turned towards Brynn and Adam. "Mullog is the Law Book protector." She looked back at me and held my eyes in hers. "Who are the new Keepers?"

The way her eyes held mine gave me the impression that she knew the answer without my telling her. "John and I."

Adam looked shocked and Brynn said, "You didn't tell us that."

Ceana nodded and cleared her throat. "There is something I need to speak with ye about. And I don't want to cause ye to worry." Her eyes focused in such a serious fashion that I remained quiet, only nodding for her to continue.

Ceana asked, "Did ye hold the gatherin'?"

I nodded and said, "In Iceland, like you planned."

"Did John read from the Law Book?" Ceana asked.

"He did. The book also revealed itself to everyone there, just before a man burned up when he tried to take it."

Brynn and Adam had wide eyes. I hadn't told them any of this.

"Aye. That has been a long time comin'." Ceana took my hands in hers and asked, "Did ye and John read about the curse?"

"What curse?" I asked before I remembered that John had seen something in the book. "Ceana, John read something in the book, but never told me about it."

"Aye. It's a hard thing to talk about." Ceana glanced at each of us, her eyes soft with concern. She said, "If an Archivist doesn't keep their covenant and betrays anything about our secret society, and if any of our people are captured because of it, all Archivists become cursed. We have one year from that time to kill anyone who knows our secret, to release any of us that are captured, and to gather all remaining Archivists inside the Iceland Althing," Ceana said.

"Or what?" I asked, thinking it was no wonder John hadn't told me.

A tear rolled over her cheek as she cast her eyes down. "Or we all die."

Brynn touched Ceana's arm. "If we don't know when our secret was first discovered, how do we know when our year is up?"

Ceana shrugged her shoulders.

I gripped Ceana's hand. "When I spoke with Sarah, she told me that last summer they put a new plan in place and finally got an Archivist to betray us."

Ceana's hands tightened on mine. "Aye, then we have at least six months. That's guid." Ceana held a book up. "It appears they've been robbing our archives, too. We also need to get all the archive books back."

A set of heavy footsteps approached and Adam shut the torch off. We remained still, not even taking a breath. The footsteps paused outside our door. Brynn's warm hand grabbed mine.

A stern male voice asked, "Who are you?" He sounded like one of the Americans that had ridden in the helicopter to the Isle of Man with me. "Where'd you go?" asked the same voice, sounding a bit more trepid. "What...?"

The voice faltered, and then came a thud. Brynn let go of my hand and hooked my arm with hers. None of us spoke. We remained huddled together in the blackness, trying to keep our breathing from giving us away. I hoped it was Conall outside, knocking out the kidnappers. He wouldn't know where we hid, but I didn't dare open the door to discover it wasn't him. We kept still, but no one opened the door, nor did we hear any footsteps walk away.

"What do we do?" Adam whispered.

"Shhhh," I said.

I listened for anything, footsteps, voices, movement. The sub had gone silent. So silent that when the explosion detonated, my ears could not hear Ceana and Brynn's screams—nor my own. The force of the explosion bounced us around and jolted us. I flew sideways into Brynn. Adam and Ceana fell onto us. The weight of their bodies pressed us into the buckets and brooms that scattered under the shelves. Books fell from the shelves hitting my legs and arms. I covered my head with my arms for protection. After the first explosion came two smaller explosions, followed by stillness. My pulse echoed loudly in my numb ears. A few seconds later came the horrifying sounds of grinding metal; the sub was being mashed and crushed by weight. The sub groaned and popped until the floor had a tilt. It did not right itself.

Adam switched on his torch. We all noticed the tilted floor, but no one said a word. We gave each other some space and climbed from the piles of archived books that buried us. Our equilibrium was off. It made it difficult for us to balance and move. After we re-situated ourselves on the tilted floor, we silently checked one another for injuries. Ceana had a bleeding gash on her cheekbone next to her eye. The rest of us had scrapes and bruises on our hands and I could feel the unseen bumps covered by clothing. After applying a cloth to Ceana's cut, we sat to let our ears clear and regain our stability. Not more than a minute had passed since the first explosion.

My thoughts began to process like a torpedo through my brain and I found it impossible to raise my chest and breathe. Frantic, I tried to speak, but terror kept my words from forming.

"Zoe. We'll be fine." Ceana's voice tried to soothe me.

My body started to shake, and I almost didn't hear her through the ringing in my ears. "No," was all I said. My mind spun through a nightmare. Since I was very young, I would awaken in the middle of a nightmare of water rushing in on me. Its cold wetness would consume my body and suck the air from my lungs. My teeth would clench and my lips press together unable to part as the water covered my face. The suffocating liquid pressed onto my chest and into my ears and nose, flattening my body and my heartbeat until I awoke. When I did wake up, my mouth would pop open and suck in the air to fill my collapsing lungs with oxygen. I never screamed and gave my parents that adrenaline surge that only a frightened child could bestow. I never told them about the dream. I was afraid that discussing the dream aloud would make it happen.

Ceana's hands pressed on my shoulders and brought me back to the closet, and our predicament. Brynn's and Adam's frightened faces stared at mine, Brynn's face mirroring the paleness of Adam's. I had to hold it together. There were two teenagers who looked more frightened than I. Adam's pale eyes stared at me and he said, "Subs have compartments that close so the water can't enter everywhere."

They must have felt the dampness seep in when I did. All our faces turned down at the same time. Water rushed into our hideaway from under the door. We leapt to our feet.

"We need to get out of here," Brynn said. Her voice sounded amazingly calm.

"Maybe they have an escape hatch?" Adam said.

Both Ceana and I reached for the doorknob as the frigid water lapped at our ankles. We stared into each other's eyes. I'm sure my eyes contained the same knowledge that I saw in Ceana's—we were going to drown in the depths of these frigid waters.

"Can we help?" said a voice above us.

Three startled screams came at once from us lasses, and a croak from Adam, before our necks cranked upwards. After one quick look we laughed—the laugh of the deranged who thought they were going to die, an unhinged laugh that, if you're not mad, catches you off guard and makes you more giddy from the fact you might actually be saved from a horrible death. We stared at the faces of four spirits who appeared ready to change their minds about rescuing us.

I found my voice and asked, "How can you get us out of here? We're under water."

"Oui, oui," said a man spirit. He was dressed in glowing denim, his legs disappearing into the wall. "We are here for the Archives. But we can take you out the same way we remove the books."

"We don't have to die first, do we?" Adam asked.

The spirits glanced at him in shock.

"How is that possible?" Ceana asked.

The icy water reached my knees. "Maybe we should worry more about 'now' than 'how.'"

Two of the spirits had loaded their arms with books from the bottom shelf and disappeared.

"What about—" Adam began. He stopped as two additional spirits appeared. Both were female and wore flowing white dresses.

"Pierre," said one of the female spirits, addressing the spirit dressed in denim. "We were informed you needed help."

"Oui," Pierre said. "Transfer these two to the ship." He pointed to Adam and Brynn. Within a second, the female spirits stood, one behind Adam and the other behind Brynn. Before they encircled their arms around the teenager in front of them, the taller of the two asked, "Are either of you Zoe or Ceana?"

Ceana and I nodded and said yes. With no explanation, they disappeared with Brynn and Adam. The fourth spirit left carrying books and only Pierre remained with us. I studied Pierre. "I think I know you. Did a man named Jaak shoot you?"

"Oui, mademoiselle." He gave me a half smile.

I couldn't believe it. "I am so glad to see you are well. I mean you're not alive, but—" I felt the frown form on my face. "Here you are saving me when I didn't do anything to save you. I was there."

"Oui. I know."

Ceana glanced from Pierre to me and grabbed my arm. Her hand was frozen and I shivered, too. The water came to our waists, and my ears popped. Something I didn't think was a good sign. She asked, "What are ye waiting for?"

Pierre looked at the water and his light softened. I also knew that wasn't a good sign. Whenever a spirit's light muted, something bad had happened. Their human feelings remained strong and powerful, and definitely continued with them after death.

"Ceana, the spirit who will rescue you is being summoned," he said.

"What?" I asked. "Well, we don't have much time."

While we spoke, other spirits continued to come and go taking the remainder of the Archives. Ceana's hand reached for mine. Tears formed in her blue eyes and ran down her cheeks.

"Ceana? We'll be rescued," I said, trying to sound encouraging.

Her other hand reached up and touched my cheek. "I ken the one being summoned," she said.

Surprised, I asked, "You know who it is?"

She nodded. The tears streamed down and dripped from her chin to splash like raindrops in the icy water. "My heart felt the pain when it happened."

"When what happened?" I quickly realized what she meant and put my arm around her. "No. Ceana, I'm sure Conall's fine."

A deep voice filled the small closet with its quiet, Scottish tone. "Ceana, mae love."

Tears bubbled in my eyes. Ceana and I let go of one another and turned around. Conall floated, bright and beautiful, in his tartan kilt. A sad grin played between the red and grey hairs on his face. He appeared God-like. "They allowed me to save ye so I can say farewell."

Ceana nodded. Her eyes filled with the words she couldn't say, a lifetime of love and devotion, as they held the eyes of the man who made that lifetime meaningful. I put my arm over her shoulders, but kept an eye on the water that continued to rise. To fill in the silence, I asked, "Did you cause the explosion?"

"Nae. I sent an SOS to that ship. The crew on the sub had an argument, which made it easy. All a sudden, boom. I'm sorry, Ceana."

"Conall…I canna hug ye." Ceana shook from distress and cold.

I said, "Pierre, we need to leave. We'll get hypothermic in another minute."

"Oui." Pierre floated behind me. "Conall, do what I do. Stand behind your Ceana."

Conall shook his head. "Once I transfer her I'll be gone." He drifted in front of his wife. "Tell our kin I love them all. Enjoy them for me…be happy…"

Ceana wiped her cheeks with the back of her hand. "There's so little time," she said, "to tell ye all that's in my heart." Her eyes met his with gratitude and love. "Thank ye, my love, ye saved us."

Pierre nodded. "His SOS let us know for sure you were on this sub."

"It's time," I said.

Conall drifted behind Ceana. Pierre said, "Encircle your arms around her and keep her body in the center of them."

Conall watched Pierre's arms encircle me, and he did the same around Ceana. "I love ye, my bonnie lass."

Ceana sniffed and nodded.

Pierre continued, "When I count to three, close your eyes and picture the frigate, and you will transfer her there. And Madam and Mademoiselle, you will not need to hold your breath."

"Une…duex…toi."

I held my breath anyway.

Chapter 31
TRUTH

The North Sea

I closed my eyes too. A sensation came over my body that might be explained as what you'd feel if you went through a space wormhole or went from zero to sixty in a fraction of a second. I don't know how I didn't get soaked further or feel the water, and I didn't have time to take a breath. I wouldn't have been surprised if I had shrunken infinitesimally small before transferring through water and space. However they did it, Ceana and I materialized on a flat surface still encircled by Conall and Pierre in what felt like less than a second.

When I felt ground under my feet, I opened my eyes. Pierre unwrapped his glowing arms from around me and disappeared to rescue more survivors. There had been pressure from his arms and his body as he transferred me. I wondered if it had been my imagination until I saw Ceana. She faced Conall and her hands reached up to his face. His eyes were full of brilliance and light. For a brief second, her hands rested on his cheeks. He smiled and said, "Remember that ye filled ma life with life. A love ye, my Ceana."

I stood on the crowded deck of a kelp-covered frigate that

smelled of seaweed and wet wood while I witnessed a departure that filled me with such grief that I couldn't move. Spirits drifted overhead and through the several masts, ropes, and tangled netting. People I didn't recognize wrapped towels and blankets around survivors who stood shivering on deck. I recognized the faces of a few submariners who I'd seen eating in the galley. But none of the other survivors cared or understood what was happening. My heart ached for Ceana and her loss, and that I could do nothing to ease her pain.

Four heads bobbed above the crowd and headed our way. The muscular, young men pushed through the throngs of people until they saw their father's state and their weeping mother. Conall was fading, his appearance becoming less holographic and more faint. His sons ran across the deck to be near their father before he was gone. People moved out of their way as the young men drew near and stood beside their champion dad for the few seconds they had before he disappeared. His hand rose in a goodbye salute to his sons and they reached out for him, memorizing the twinkle in his eyes and the smile behind his beard as he completely vanished. Their heads bowed. Sean, Eadan, Neil, and Thor gathered around their mum and circled her in a family embrace. Sean removed his coat and wrapped it tenderly around her shoulders. He nodded towards me; his red-rimmed eyes met mine for a brief second before he turned back to his mum. Understanding their pain, I turned away.

Brynn and Adam, each covered in an oversized fisherman's coat, ran across the warped wood of the deck. The coats flapped as they ran, and they threw their arms around me in a tight hug. Both of their teeth chattered so much that they couldn't talk. I knew their legs must be as numb as mine. We gave Ceana and her family their space and walked across the deck to an olive-skinned spirit who waved and smiled my way.

"Va bene. I am so happy to find you well."

From behind me, a cloak slung over my shoulders and wrapped me in warmth. To my surprise, John's smiling face stared down at my own. "Not as happy as I am." He let go of the cloak and embraced me. He smelled of woodsy soap and aftershave, and although thinner he appeared strong. For several minutes, his muscled arms held me in a tight grip that warmed me and stopped my shivering. He whispered in my ear, "Zoe, my love, I thought I'd never see you again."

After a few minutes passed, Mullog cleared his throat and said, "Maybe we should take them below."

My thoughts were everywhere. John was a good man and none of this was his fault. Brynn and Adam were safe, but Conall was dead. Ceana was alone. We were on a frigate that floated in the air above the water. Because of the curse, we only had six months to live, but for now we were safe…we were safe. That thought I held onto and pulled Brynn and Adam close to my side. Through chattering teeth, I said, "John, this is Brynn Wheeler and Adam Sorensen. They're from Toronto. This is John Link."

Brynn's face went from shivering to surprise. John smiled and immediately took her by the shoulders and studied her. "Is Sam your mum?"

Brynn nodded. "Uncle John?" She threw her arms around his waist and began to sob.

John held her and asked, "What are you doing so far from home?"

I put my hand on his back. "Her mum was kidnapped. She and Adam have been running for their lives for months."

"Sam's been kidnapped? I didn't know she was an Archivist." He studied his niece. "I suppose you are too?"

Brynn nodded between her sobs and said, "Yes. I can talk to you about everything! I'm so relieved." She shivered.

John said, "Darling lass, many hostages have been rescued from around the world. We will locate Sam. I'm sure she's well." He gave Brynn a reassuring smile. "Mullog is right. We need to get below. I have a warm cabin where all of you can get cleaned up and rest."

I searched the deck. Ceana and her family were gone. They must have gone to their rooms, if indeed this "boat" had rooms. The "boat" looked like something that had rested on the ocean floor for centuries before being salvaged for firewood—if it ever dried out enough. "First I need to find Shaw. He was on the sub. Along with Sarah."

John and Mullog exchanged a glance. I asked, "You both know where he is? Is he safe?"

They didn't answer me. Instead, they guided us to a set of narrow stairs that headed into a dark space below deck. I didn't take another step and tugged on John's arm, my heart beating faster. "John? Is Shaw here?"

John's voice was soft and gentle. "No, he isn't here on this ship."

"Did he get away?" I asked.

"Mia tesoro, we do not know if Shaw got away or not. No one has seen his body or his spirit."

"He's probably with Sarah. Have you seen her?" I asked.

Mullog said, "Follow me and I'll explain. We must get you warm." He floated down the stairs in front of us in order to light up our surroundings and waited for us to get to the bottom before he continued to explain. "Conall saw Sarah leave. He said that Sarah and Shaw had an argument about the escape hatch and when to detonate the bomb. Shaw refused."

Probably because of me, I thought.

John said, "Shaw refused to use the hatch because too many people would die. Sarah didn't wait for him and left in a rush."

"They were discussing the bomb?" I asked.

John nodded. "Yes, that's what we believe. She must have been the one to detonate it."

If no one had seen Shaw leave, and no spirits had seen his spirit, I believed Shaw left with Sarah. If anything had happened to him, wouldn't he have come to me like Conall did to Ceana? We were family and he'd want to know I was safe. I still believed that he would care more for me than his mission.

We followed Mullog across the bottom deck and through an area with dozens of hammocks hanging from oak beams. A few expressive snores came from the inhabited hammocks. The sleeping individuals had tartan blankets pulled up to their foreheads. With raised eyebrows, I glanced at John.

John said, "We have had an around-the-clock-crew of spirits and people. The people needed rest. Our cabins are in the fore of the ship, past the galley."

We passed by barrels pushed next to the hull on both sides of us. Some barrels were rolled on their side and others were stacked.

"Did Conall say where Shaw was before the blast?" I asked. We passed the galley, which didn't appear cooking ready and was filled with spirits and humans cleaning it up. Barnacles had moved into the rusted ovens and stoves. The barnacles filled the sinks and clung to the weathered cabinets. Someone grumbled about non-existent pots and a lack of plates and utensils as we passed the scene. After seeing the appearance of the kitchen, I was grateful for the pizza we ate before we hid inside the closet. I wasn't completely starving yet.

No one answered my question about Shaw. We entered a room that was the shape of the bow of the ship. The room had dividers in the middle that consisted of sheets hanging from the rafters. On one side of the divider were ten hammocks hung in a line. Each hammock held a pillow that resembled those that are handed out to passengers on airplanes. Tartan blankets, in a variety of plaids, were folded over the beds. The other side of the divider had a floor-to-ceiling cabinet, which was as tall as John. Arranged on each side of the cabinet were cheery yellow-vinyl couches, and in the middle stood a potbellied stove bellowing warmth into the room. On each side of the exit door was a closet-sized washroom consisting of a toilet and a shower stall. I had become so used to being in tight spaces this room felt open and airy, and it was warm. The temperature of the room caused my toes and fingers to hurt from the thaw they were experiencing.

Brynn and Adam plopped down on a couch. I again asked John about Shaw. "Did Conall mention where Shaw was? I don't think he's dead or he would have come to see me."

Mullog said, "Mia carina, if they choose, an Archivist can have that opportunity to say goodbye to a loved one, but only an Archivist."

"Yes, so if something had happened to him, he would have come to say goodbye," I said.

"But Shaw wasn't an Archivist," John said.

"He told me he is an Archivist. Wait…wasn't an Archivist? You're talking like he's gone." I fell onto the couch closest to me; the splits in the yellow vinyl poked at my legs.

John held his hand up in the air in Mullog's direction and then came and sat next to me. Mullog floated overhead. I barely registered Nana and Phoebe handing Adam and Brynn some dry clothes. Gently, John lifted my chin so my eyes met his. "Zoe, luv. Shaw was never an Archivist. He's been a spy as long as I have, and has intentionally played for the other team. We don't know if he's alive or dead. No one has seen him, nor have they identified any of the bodies as his."

I grabbed John's hand. "May I see the bodies and make sure

Shaw's isn't among them?"

John shook his head. "They remain with the sunken sub in the depths of the sea. The surviving crew is on a raft near the scene. Mullog checked and Shaw wasn't with them either." He smiled and said, "Those survivors have a story they'll never tell."

Mullog said, "Tesoro mia, just hope for the best for Shaw. We have spirits still searching the waters."

"Let me know as soon as they see anything," I said.

"Si. We will let you know."

I said, "Sarah told me that Shaw works for her. But I don't think he fully understands what she's doing."

John said, "I don't think any of us know the extent of what she's done."

"What about the dead bodies. Do you know who they are?" I asked.

John said, "They were eleven of the submarine crew, all killed in the explosion. But, so far, the only Archivist who lost his life is Conall—a heavy loss."

The look on everyone's face after John mentioned Conall's name established the difficulty we were having in dealing with his death. Hard for all to fathom. Nana and Phoebe stood nearby in silence. Adam and Brynn held their dry clothes and hadn't moved. The several spirits in the room, including Mullog, barely gave off any light. We needed time to grieve, but first we had to deal with the curse, which I still had to discuss with John. We had to capture Sarah, something the curse was very explicit about. "What about Sarah?" I asked.

John said, "Conall saw her escape. The spirits searched the entire sub and the vicinity outside. So far nothing."

Phoebe interrupted our conversation. "We need to get Zoe some dry clothes and find some food." From the cabinet, she removed a sweater and a pair of jeans and handed them to me before she left with John and Nana to locate food. I changed into the dry clothing and instantly felt warmer. After checking on Brynn and Adam, both asleep in their gently swinging bed, I sat on the vinyl couch and waited for John to return. He walked in carrying a tray with bowls of soup and warm bread. My stomach rumbled. I guess I was hungrier than I had thought. He set the tray between us. The soup was a vegetable beef and smelled delicious.

After sipping a couple of spoonfuls, I said, "I have something I need to tell you."

He looked at me in surprise. "You do?"

"Yes and I think it has something to do with what you saw in the Law Book during the gathering."

"I'm impressed that you caught that," he said. He drank the rest of his bowl of soup, set it down, and turned his full attention to me.

"Ceana told me about the curse and the one year timeframe."

He nodded. "Did she also give you a date for that timeframe?"

"No. But Sarah became quite talkative with me when she thought she had her plan under control. She said that this past summer they finally turned an Archivist."

John took a breath of relief. "While getting our food, Mullog informed me that we've recovered all of the stolen archives, except for Iceland's, released all but ten Archivists, and disposed of all except three known assailants, which included Jaak and his brother, Specs. With the information you just told me, we have at least six months to apprehend the final three. We're still hoping to find Sarah and Shaw today."

"Who's the third assailant?" I asked.

"Mullog's brother, Jacob. And he's worse than the sly one," John said. "Mullog has rushed off with a host of spirits to keep searching for his brother and regrets not telling you goodbye."

"That's fine. I hope he catches him," I said. "A bad spirit who is Mullog's brother? How can we compete with that?"

"Exactly."

"Do we have to kill them? I don't want Shaw to die. Besides, in Jacob's case, how can we kill a spirit that's already dead?"

"I don't know." John paused and took my hand. "Did Sarah say she'd divorce me?"

"She said she wouldn't."

"Then I guess I'll have to kill her," he said, with a wicked smile. "Don't worry, Zoe, when Mullog returns we'll look through the Law Book and see how the rules apply. Once we find Shaw, maybe he'll be given a chance." He put the tray on the other side of him and moved closer to me. "How about me? Do I still have a chance?"

I laughed as he encircled me in the warmth of his arms and pressed his lips to mine. For once we weren't interrupted. I even ignored the prickly vinyl of the couch.

❦

John shook my hammock to awaken me. "They found Shaw and Sarah." Morning hadn't arrived and he held a torch in his hand. Brynn and Adam didn't stir, and Nana's and Phoebe's hammocks were empty.

"Is Shaw alright?" I asked, sitting up and putting on my shoes.

"He seems to be. He wants to see you."

I took his hand and he led me through the darkness of the frigate, past the barrels, up the stairs, and onto the starlit deck. We entered a doorway where the warmth of candlelight cast a friendly glow. Inside, the room felt anything but friendly. Captain Link, Pierre, and several other spirits floated about the room. Nana and Phoebe sat at a table; Ceana, Sean and Eadan stood around Sarah and Shaw, who were both handcuffed and sitting on a bench. Sarah's eyes met mine and I gave her a vindictive smile. She looked as ragged as I felt. Her feet were bare, her expensive suit dirty and torn, and her nails needed a manicure, but my favorite part of her new look was the traces of seaweed dangling in her hair. Everyone else was red-faced and angry. The sounds of several people speaking at once had quieted down before we entered and I didn't know what they had been discussing. I was so relieved to see Shaw alive that I almost forgot what dire straights he was in. I wanted to hug him and punch him at the same time. John didn't let go of my hand and kept me next to him by the door, which Ceana shut behind us.

John squeezed my hand and said, "We found them on a fishing boat they had commandeered. We wanted you to be able to see Shaw before we take the two of them to a holding cell." One glance at my face and he added, "And no, you can't speak with him alone."

"Must we have a crowd?" I asked.

John nudged his head towards the door. "Captain and Pierre, take Sarah to her cell. Except for Sean and Eadan, the rest of you can go and get some sleep."

Once the room had cleared, John let go of my hand and I ran to hug Shaw. "I'm so glad you're alive." He couldn't hug me back, but buried his face in my shoulder.

Shaw's clothing was dirty and he had black sandals on his feet. From Sarah's condition, she must have put up more of a struggle. Shaw seemed full of remorse and his eyes looked into mine. "I'm so sorry, Zoe." He paused and glanced at John. "I am a stupid bloke. I should have seen the signs of deception, but I couldn't get past my feelings of shame and frustration that Dad and Mum shut me out of their lives. In hindsight, I know that it was only my pride." He shook his head. "I didn't know that Sarah's use of the Archivists actually killed some and ruined the minds of others. What she showed me and led me to believe was that it was for the greater good."

"Well old chap," John began. He gave Shaw a friendly smack on the back. "We were friends before we became enemies."

"What? You were friends?" I asked.

Both of them nodded, and John said, "Unfortunately, our friendship can't stop what happens when someone outside our society discovers our secrets."

"John, no!" I said, "We need to read through the book and see. I will not allow Shaw to be murdered."

Eadan said, "I'm sorry, Zoe, it's either he lives—for the moment—or we all perish. Either way he dies."

Shaw spoke up and I went quiet. "He's right, Zoe. And it's not murder, it's a sacrifice so others will live, and something I will honorably do. It gives you all the ability to continue your work."

I fell at Shaw's feet. Tears streamed down my cheeks. "No. I won't let you." I wrapped my arms around his waist. "I just got you back—you're all I have left."

"I believe it's up to the spirits to decide," Eadan said.

We remained quiet until Shaw asked, "What happens now?"

John said, "It's not necessary for us to, um, do anything right away."

Sean nodded and said, "Eadan's right. We'll wait for Mullog to return."

"Yes," said John. "Everything could change depending on what Mullog discovers."

Through tear-filled eyes, I studied my brother's face and said a silent prayer.

Chapter 32
LIFE

Prestbury, England

The sunshine felt warm on my face. Even warmer because the day had arrived when I'd see Mum and Dad, see and speak to them. John held my hand and walked beside me, our steps in sync. He wore his leather jacket and I had on my wool duffle coat, buttoned up for the light breeze. As we rounded a corner on the flagstone pathway, we faced my family's grave plot that covered a hill near Brightly Manor. The Celtic cross in the center stood guard for all that entered. We followed the rock wall, stacked hundreds of years ago, which surrounded the plot. The wall extended over our land, but also outlined the Alstead caves and my family heritage in the ground below. In the center of the hill, the shadow of the Celtic cross moved like a sundial across the monument of my parents.

John squeezed my hand. I focused on his strength, on the whisper of the leaves, on the moment I would soon see Mum's smile and Dad's cherished gazes. We walked through the gates and I stopped in surprise. Several figures stepped from behind the monument marker.

"You didn't think we would miss this, did you?" said Aunt

Phoebe.

She stood surrounded by Nana, Adam, Brynn, and Sam, Brynn's beautiful dark-haired Mother who had at last been reunited with her daughter.

Adam grinned behind his sunglasses. "After this, we're having an American Thanksgiving dinner."

"I thought I smelled something pleasant coming from the kitchen," I said. I glanced around.

Nana noticed my glance. "Don't worry, Ceana and the twins and some of the other Mackenzies are right behind you." She knew me well.

By the time John and I gave each of them a hug, Ceana and her clan had arrived.

"I dinna want to miss this, and a turkey feast too," said Ceana.

"I'm so happy that you all came." Tears formed in my eyes when I thought of how truly happy I was. Even though Shaw was being held someplace John wouldn't allow me to have knowledge or access to, my family had grown and I knew I'd never be alone. I felt drawn to each person there, for they had given my life purpose. Today, I refused to think about our impending deadline, which could take it all away.

During the last few weeks, we'd been reorganizing the Althings. I had read and cried through many human stories, archived stories of people who lived thousands of years ago, to more recent times. Stories of real people who lived and died in places all over the world with their diversity of heritage and religious backgrounds. The importance of each person's history is manifested by the necessity to compile and preserve each one for future generations to learn from. I enjoyed my new responsibilities in the Archivist society. John and I continued as the Keepers, which we had been informed would help John keep his abilities longer. Most of the enjoyment I had in my new responsibilities was working side-by-side with John as the "keepers of secrets the world wasn't ready to know." Most of which still remained a mystery to me.

We had not seen Mullog since our rescue. It was unprecedented for Hosts and Writers to receive this kind of assistance from the spirits. But these were unprecedented times.

I wiped my eyes and said, "I love you all, and cherish this moment because you're here with me."

Nana grabbed my hand. "Let's get going. I don't want the turkey to burn and I can't wait to see you raise your mom and pop without mana."

I laughed and sniffed. "All right." I reached my hand out; it had a slight tremor. I found a place on the granite monument between two areas covered in green moss and placed my hand there. I then counted to three before I stepped back.

Several seconds passed and nothing.

"How long does it take for the spirits to appear?" Adam asked.

"Not this long." My voice had a tremor now. I reached out and pressed both of my palms firmly on the marker, but still nothing.

Nana held out some mana for me. "Maybe, because they're your parents, you need to use the mana. I brought some just in case."

"Thanks, Nana." I took the grave wax from Nana and made one "X" above my mum's name and another above my dad's. I reached my hand out and again placed it on the cool stone. Nothing happened.

There were several uneasy sighs. Ceana put her arm around me and looked at everyone. "Maybe this should be a private moment for Zoe and her parents."

John patted my back. "Ceana's right. Let's—"

"Or maybe your parents are waiting for someone else to arrive," said a familiar voice behind us.

We all spun around to see Pierre land on the grass with Shaw beside him.

"Shaw!" I ran forwards to greet Shaw with a gigantic hug. He looked good. Wherever the spirits had him imprisoned, they were taking good care of him.

"My, my," said Nana.

Pierre said, "I figured it couldn't hurt to have him here to witness this moment. I will be back tonight." Pierre disappeared.

"It's okay that I'm here?" Shaw looked at John for approval.

"Of course." John patted him on the back.

I gave Shaw a wary smile. "I hope Mum and Dad have been waiting for you to show up, because so far it hasn't worked. I'm beginning to wonder if I've lost my powers."

"Go ahead and redraw the 'X's," Nana said, reassuring me.

Shaw parted the ivy on the monument and patted his hand where I should redo the "X" for Dad. I held up the mana, redrew Dad's "X" and then one for Mum before placing my hand on the granite next to Shaw's. I held my breath and waited until I couldn't hold my breath any longer. But for some reason Mum and Dad could not be summoned.

Shaw asked, "Is this normal?"

Before I could respond, a frantic Mullog appeared. He dodged to and fro in a random fashion above us. "Amici miei, something terrible has happened and I do not understand it." We stared at him in shock. His eyes were wild, his teeth barred, and his light near nonexistent; he lunged in front of Nana, then Ceana, then me. He passed me and abruptly stopped. With the sudden stop in his movements, the Law Book slipped from his arms and dropped to the earth with a thud. It landed on the tip of its wooden spine, angled back and flipped open to a page near the middle. No one seemed particularly interested in the dropped Law Book, except me.

Nor did Mullog seem concerned about shutting it from my prying eyes. Everyone stood in wary silence and watched the frantic ghost. He opened his mouth and spoke. "They are gone…missing…Convincers, former Keepers, all gone."

"What?" John asked, looking as dazed and confused as me.

"Mullog, calm down and explain," Aunt Phoebe said.

I was torn between the gravity of what Mullog said, and the fact that below me, in plain sight, was an open page of the book. Out of curiosity, I took several steps closer to the book and the page displayed, but continued to watch Mullog. His light almost gone, his normal composure nowhere to be seen, Mullog studied my parents' monument for a few seconds before the recognizable personality of the "sly one" came into complete focus. His eyes narrowed with cruelty in their depths. He spat on the ground and angled his merciless eyes in my direction. "Zoe! Your Mum and Dad are gone too." Even with his agitated tone, I understood his cruelty wasn't aimed at me. I was at a loss of what to do or say. Surely my parents weren't gone.

Shaw asked, "Our parents aren't here?"

After a long pause, everyone began to speak at once. During the brief chaos of everyone trying to figure out what happened, I noticed my brother. He kept an eye on Mullog while at the same time glancing at the book. I thought only Keepers could see it, but it was obvious that Shaw was looking at it. I held onto Shaw's arm and whispered, "Whatever you do, don't touch it."

Shaw's nod affirmed my speculation. He could see the book.

"Mullog," said Ceana, firmly. She calmly waited for everyone to quiet down before she continued. "Ye spirits canna disappear."

Mullog's light grew so faint he almost vanished. His voice snarled quiet and low enough that we gathered closer to hear him—but not too close. "Si, never before. But now they have. All around the world are reports of their disappearances."

John's eyebrows pinched together, Ceana raised hers. Nana's shaking white hand looked ghostlike as she grabbed onto Aunt Phoebe's coffee-coloured hand. The twins held tight to their older brother's arms, and I saw the same shock registered on everyone's face. This had never happened before—spirits do not disappear.

"What can we do?" Ceana asked.

Mullog seemed to calm down, somewhat. He said, "Captain Link and Pierre are searching for answers. But there is nothing you humans can do."

The scene around me barely registered when a word from the open Law Book seemed to pop from the page and grab my attention. The word was Primordial, a word with meaning for me. It was written below a beautiful drawing of a couple holding hands. They were drawn wearing white clothing similar to a toga. I thought they might be Adam and Eve. I read the next few words of the couple's description and was assured that they were not Adam and Eve. In fact, I had to read the description twice because my mind couldn't fathom what I had just read. After my second reading, my knees buckled. Shaw caught my arm and held me up. What I read could not be possible. It had to be an artist's rendering of a story. I stared at the book; the significance of that one page tattooed my soul with a painful and staggering implausibility. "What does that mean?" Shaw asked.

"You could read it too?" I asked, in Shaw's ear.

He nodded.

Mullog came back to his senses. The Law Book closed with a snap, but not before the images on the page were imprinted on my mind. Mullog cried out, "No. No. You were not to see that." I couldn't ignore the sadness in Mullog's eyes. "You are not ready."

A tear rolled down my cheek. No, I most certainly wasn't ready to know that. "What about Shaw?"

Shaw steadied me. "I'm okay, you're the one shaking."

I held on tight to his arm to keep myself from falling over. With concern in his eyes, John walked over and held my other arm. Phoebe pointed her index finger at Mullog and asked, "What have you done?"

Nana stepped towards Mullog, "Have you shown something in that silly book that you shouldn't have?"

I stared at Phoebe and Nana. Did they know this secret?

"It is not my fault," Mullog pleaded.

"Of course. It never is," Nana said.

Phoebe stared at Shaw and asked, "Did you see the book too?"

Again, Shaw nodded.

"No, no." Mullog swirled around in a circle. "Only Keepers can see the book." He stopped, slowly turned around, and floated over to Shaw and me. He hovered in the air and stared at us. "Unless…no, that's impossible."

"Unless what?" Phoebe asked.

Nana picked up on some verbal queue of Phoebe's and said, "We," she indicated Phoebe and Ceana, "are former Keepers. Jude and I were the first out of us three. After Jude died, the Keeper responsibilities fell to Pheebs and Jim, then your parents, Zoe. Now Ceana is one of us. And we have all worked with the sly one."

"You never mentioned the Blue Bloods were all former Keepers." John said.

"Wasn't that important," said Nana. "What's important is that the secrets in that book can only be seen by Keepers and former Keepers. Yet Shaw saw the book."

Together, Adam and Brynn said, "I saw it too."

Everyone nodded.

Mullog looked devastated.

"But I didn't see anything inside it," said Brynn. Others agreed with her.

Apparently, only Shaw and I saw the opened page.

"How is that possible? Sam isn't a Keeper. These kids aren't Keepers. Shaw isn't even an Archivist," Phoebe said.

That was when I figured it out. The names of everyone standing around me were listed in the Lineage Book. All of us, including Shaw, were Primordial.

Mullog looked at me and I asked, "Can I tell them?" After he gave me the okay, I said, "Because everyone here is Primordial. We are all the pure bloodlines, or direct descendants, of the first Archivists."

Their faces were full of shock and smiles.

John gave my arm a slight squeeze and said, "You've seen the Lineage Book."

I smiled at his shocked face.

"Wow," Adam said.

Brynn punched Adam and said, "That's an understatement."

Mullog's light grew bright and glowing again. He floated in front of Shaw and me. "Another thing, amici miei, even if you are Primordial, you cannot see the Law Book unless you are an Archivist."

"Say again," said Shaw.

John punched him lightly in the arm. "You're one of us, chap."

"Mullog, are you sure?" I asked.

"Si."

Shaw said, "Except for the death sentence no longer hanging over me, I don't feel any different."

I threw my arms around Shaw. "I can't wait to train you. What did you read in the book?"

The sly one appeared as Mullog became enraged. "No. You

cannot talk about this secret. That page was shown because of a moment of weakness in me," he whimpered. "No one has ever seen this secret."

John looked stunned. "Are you saying Zoe and Shaw know a secret no one else is privy to?"

Shaw said, "I'm not even sure what I saw."

"You must not speak of it," Mullog said.

"Don't worry, Mullog," I said. "I'm happy to keep it." I smiled at John. The lightness I felt from having a secret that I could keep from John helped me deal with the gravity of what it contained.

Nana put her hands on her hips. "That's a dangerous responsibility to have."

I couldn't agree more. Yet my heart warmed from the comfort that even through the disappointment of not seeing our parents, Shaw and I had no secrets now that he had become an Archivist.

Mullog floated above us. "Amici miei, do not forget that we are all in danger. The most important thing is for us to find Jacob and the Archives still missing from the Pingvellir Althing before we run out of time." Mullog soared in front of me. "Mia carina, you understand, right?"

I nodded. I most certainly did understand. Especially knowing what I knew. John's arm tightened around my shoulders, affirming his support. Having him beside me made it all bearable. But if he thought for one moment that he could coax this secret out of me—he was wrong.

READING GROUP GUIDE

1. What if you could discover any world secret by interviewing the dead, who would you want to interview? What secret would you want to uncover?

2. What did you find unique about the setting and how did it add to the story?

3. Did you think the obligations of being an Archivist limited Zoe's and John's freedom?

4. Which character would you most want to interview?

5. What do you think of the trust issues between Zoe and John?

6. What do you think of the duality of the Sly One's personality?

7. What do you think about the Archivists choosing which secrets the world should know?

8. Do you agree with the Archivists that they should not allow a member of their society to be a political leader?

9. What did you think of the ending?

10. What secret do you think Zoe and Shaw saw?

11. If you keep your own journal are you completely honest in everything you write about your life experiences?

12. Do you think our history books accurately portray the history of the world? How about the descriptions and personality characteristics of historical figures?

Acknowledgments:

Writing a first draft is only the beginning. I would like to acknowledge some talented individuals for their enthusiasm and expertise during the process of editing and publishing *Host Writer*. Thanks go to my editor, Jacque Berrett, who I'm fortunate to have stumbled upon; my beta readers: Raquel Hinz, Micadyn Sanders, Janet Taylor, and Jan Williams, who are all dynamic and busy women yet took the time to give me excellent feedback; my website designer and nephew, Nick Sanders with Simplex Creations; and my cover artist, James T. Egan with Bookfly Design.

Thanks to my family; my husband, Mike, and our children, Bailie, Evie, and Alex—for everything—you've traveled along this writing road with me from exploring artwork in Paris, castles in Germany, to cemeteries, museums, and battlegrounds everywhere, thanks for indulging me and for being my alpha readers. Mike, you are the love of my life and a collaborator of candor to whom I trust most with my first read, and I thank you for your insight and extensive knowledge of Britain, the Isle of Man, and weaponry that helped strengthen my scenes. Many thanks to my brilliant parents, Gary and Carole Farnsworth, who created in all their children a love of books and learning; and thank you, Mom, for the most thorough read and edit that you gave this novel—not the first time that you've read or edited papers for me!

About the author: